## Also by Tate James

**DEVIL'S BACKBONE**
Dear Reader
Watch Your Back
You're Next

**MADISON KATE**
Hate
Liar
Fake
Kate

**HADES**
7th Circle
Anarchy
Club 22
Timber

# Dear Reader

## TATE JAMES

Bloom books

Copyright © 2025 by Tate James
Cover and internal design © 2025 by Sourcebooks
Cover design by Antoaneta Georgieva/Sourcebooks
Cover images © Aimee Marie Lewis/Arcangel, Nikolay Zaiarnyi/Getty Images, mikroman6/Getty Images, Veit Störmer/Getty Images
Printed edge images © Alinakho/Getty Images, Jose A. Bernat Bacete/Getty Images, mizar_21984/Getty Images
Internal images © RusN/Getty Images, sergeichekman/Getty Images

Sourcebooks, Bloom Books, and the colophon are registered trademarks of Sourcebooks.

All rights reserved. No part of this book may be reproduced in any form or by any electronic or mechanical means including information storage and retrieval systems—except in the case of brief quotations embodied in critical articles or reviews—without permission in writing from its publisher, Sourcebooks.

No part of this book may be used or reproduced in any manner for the purpose of training artificial intelligence technologies or systems.

The characters and events portrayed in this book are fictitious or are used fictitiously. Any similarity to real persons, living or dead, is purely coincidental and not intended by the author.

All brand names and product names used in this book are trademarks, registered trademarks, or trade names of their respective holders. Sourcebooks is not associated with any product or vendor in this book.

Published by Bloom Books, an imprint of Sourcebooks
P.O. Box 4410, Naperville, Illinois 60567-4410
(630) 961-3900
sourcebooks.com

Cataloging-in-Publication data is on file with the Library of Congress.

Printed and bound in the United States of America.
LSC 10 9 8 7 6 5 4 3 2 1

This book is dedicated to autocorrect, for always dropping ducks where you least expect them.

Duck you, autocorrelation.

Dear Reader, if you've found this diary, then I must be dead. That's the only way I'd have let anyone find this account of what's been happening to me. What they've put me through. What they're still putting me through.

If you're reading this...then I'm dead and the Devil's Backbone Society is responsible. You, whoever you are, will probably be next.

I should probably start at the beginning, so you have context for what I record next, so you can understand how they fooled me for so long and how I ended up where I am now. Probably dead. Definitely dead, because you, dear reader, have found my journal. I swore that if they let me live, I'd destroy any evidence against them...

Because of where I plan to hide this book, you must be a student at Nevaeh University. I was too. When I got awarded the Mariah Greenberg Scholarship, I thought I'd won the lottery. All my dreams were going to come true at Nevaeh. How utterly wrong I was.

The first time I heard about the Devil's Backbone Society was a month after the school year started. I was at a party with my friends, beside Lake Prosper, and overheard some girls whispering about "initiation" and speculating on who would be chosen. The criteria for selection seemed to be obvious. Wealthy, influential, beautiful—only the best were invited to join. But then apparently, each year a few extras were chosen at random. Cannon-fodder, the girls called them.

Someone died. No one will talk about it, and when I tried to ask my TA what had happened, she shushed me very abruptly. All I know is that a girl named Sarah Black supposedly jumped off Cat's Peak at midnight. But if it was unrelated to the DB Society, why is everyone pretending it never happened? Or worse than that, they're pretending she never existed at all. It's creepy, and knowing now what I know of their initiation...I'm 100 percent convinced she was pushed.

You've probably already guessed by now, the DB Society selected me as one of their supposedly "random" initiates this year. Just a week after Sarah Black's so-called suicide on Cat's Peak, they grabbed me on my way to the dining hall for dinner. Someone put a bag over my head, and I was manhandled into a van. For far too long, I genuinely thought I was going to die. I didn't...obviously. Otherwise, I wouldn't be writing this account now. But that first initiation made me realize I needed to start writing things down...just in case I ended up like Sarah. Like I probably have, if you're reading this now.

Shit. If you're reading this...please don't end up like me. Be smarter than I was and <u>don't trust anyone</u>.

# Chapter One

"Fucking hell, are you serious?" I groaned, rubbing the bridge of my nose. When I opened my eyes again, I was confronted by the ugly sight of my badly keyed car. My gorgeous 1973 Pontiac Firebird that I'd lovingly restored with my dad throughout my childhood. My most prized possession…which was now sporting a deep scar from nose to tail through the flame-red paint on her left side.

"Sorry, kid." My well-weathered mechanic shrugged. "Whoever did this really wanted to do damage. Can you claim it on insurance?"

I swallowed back the tears threatening to fall. "No…I only have collision coverage." It was all I could afford on my part-time job, after paying school fees and living expenses.

My mechanic heaved a sigh. "Shit, kid, I dunno what to say. Best I can do is fifty-eight hundred, and even then, I'd have to assign one of the apprentices to do the work. Cars like this—"

"Have expensive upkeep, I know," I grumbled, repeating what he'd been telling me for years with every little repair she'd needed. "She's not mine to sell, Rex, you know that."

He shot me a grin. "I know, but it can't hurt to ask. Next time your old man visits, send him in to see me, yes?"

I rolled my eyes. "Sure."

"So. What are we doing about this mess?" He gestured to the ugly slash in my car, deep enough to have dented the metal in several places. If it were any other car, I'd just leave it and deal with the damage when I could afford it, but I simply couldn't risk the chance of rust. Not on a car like this.

I groaned again, scrubbing a hand over my face. "Fix it. I'll find the money…somewhere." I glanced at my watch. "Speaking of, I need to get to class."

My mechanic nodded, giving me a pat on the shoulder. "All right, kid. Leave her with me. I'll call you when she's done. Might be a couple of weeks, though, to find time and get the paint in."

Not surprising. Parts for my Firebird always took ages, so getting the exact paint match wouldn't be a quick task. "Thanks, Rex."

With a dejected sigh, I made my way out of the garage on foot, hitching my backpack higher on my shoulder as I headed for the bus stop. It was only a few stops to get to the local community college, and without the need to search for parking, I was early to class for once.

Anxiety gnawed at my mind for the whole day, and it was a struggle to remain focused for my philosophy lecture after lunch. Hopefully my subconscious was soaking the information in, because my notebook was full of stress-doodles by the time I left campus for the day.

How the *fuck* was I coming up with an extra five thousand eight hundred dollars when I was just barely scraping by as it was? If I told my mom, the money would be in my account by the end of the day with a healthy excess on top, but that option made my skin itch. For one thing, it wasn't *her* money. For another, the car was my *dad's* baby…and with Mom about to marry another man, it seemed crazy disrespectful. Besides, I was twenty-one and couldn't go running to my mommy for help every time life handed me lemons.

It was a backup option, though. If I could swallow my pride.

As though summoned by my thoughts, my phone rang with

MOM on caller ID. Her picture was a goofy photo of her trying to do heart hands and it made me smile every time it came up.

"Hi, Mom," I answered, bringing the phone to my ear as I trudged toward the bus stop.

"Hi, honey, how was class?" My mom's warm mellifluous voice on the phone instantly eased some of the money stress knotted up in my chest. I smiled and told her all about the latest project my Classics Literature professor had assigned. She loved knowing what I was doing at school, and I loved telling her about it. In some way, explaining it to her helped me to better comprehend the lessons myself.

We chatted for a while, until my bus arrived and I climbed on board. At the bleep of my bus pass, my mom interrupted what I was saying. "Ashley, are you on a bus?" she asked, confused. "What happened to the Firebird?"

I bit my lip, groaning internally. I hadn't told her about the keying, because I *knew* she'd start the subject of money again. She knew how much I loved my car, but she also knew how much it was worth and was of the opinion that it was *just a car*.

"Nothing," I lied. "Just making more environmentally conscious choices. Fuel emissions and all that." I winced, hating every false word I spoke. My mom and I didn't *lie* to one another, and it didn't sit well now.

The awkward pause on the other end of the phone told me she knew I was lying, but rather than call me out on it she just gave a small sigh. "Okay, honey. Are we still seeing you for dinner tonight?"

I wrinkled my nose, cursing silently. "No, I'm sorry. I totally forgot and accepted an extra shift at work." And now, more than ever, I needed the cash. Evening shifts paid better and *usually* tipped better than daytime too.

"That's okay," Mom replied without any judgment, "but Max and I really want to talk to you about something, so could you come by the house tomorrow?"

Max—my mom's boss and *new fiancé*—technically had his own home in Lake Prosper but Mom said it was lacking in *warmth*, so she'd convinced him to move in with her here in Panner Valley instead. They were all kinds of adorable together, even I had to admit, though it had been a tough pill to swallow when they confessed just recently to a nearly eight-year-long relationship. Logically it made sense why they'd kept it quiet; they'd wanted to avoid gossip and playing into stereotypes since Mom was Max's secretary.

"Yeah, for sure. Sorry about that. Please tell Max I'm sorry too. I bet he's already started cooking." Max *loved* to cook and was very good at it. He treated every meal as a fine dining experience.

My mom laughed. "He has, but that's okay. I think Nate is coming by, and that boy eats like he's starving at every meal."

My brows rose. "You were going to spring the stepbrother on me with no notice? Rude. Will he be there tomorrow?" Despite the fact my mom and Max had been engaged for a month, I had yet to meet Max's son, Nate. He must have been just as in the dark as I had been about the nature of our parents' relationship all these years.

"I'm not sure about tomorrow," Mom replied. "I'll ask. But you'll meet him one of these days, I'm sure. You two are always so busy!"

She was right about that, at least in my case. I assured her again that I'd see her for dinner the following day, then ended the call right as the bus approached my stop. It was a four-block walk to the two-bedroom apartment I shared with five other girls, but rent was steep in Panner Valley and I didn't need the luxury of a private room when I had no love life to speak of.

An hour later I was hauling ass through the staff entrance of Serenity, an upscale day spa where I worked as a masseuse. "You're late!" my manager, Meg, called out when I flew into the locker room to change into my uniform.

"Sorry!" I replied, yanking my T-shirt over my head and diving into the black cap-sleeved shirt with my name embroidered on the breast. "I had to take the bus."

Meg wandered over to me and grimaced. "Trouble with that sexy car of yours?"

I sighed. "Yeah, some asshole keyed it like they had a personal grudge. So any extra shifts that need covering…"

She nodded. "Gotcha. Well, your first client is already here. I'll get him sorted out with the questionnaire for you. He's rocking a Rolex so could be a good tipper."

I laughed, buttoning my shirt as Meg headed out to the lounge where my client would be waiting. I hated arriving to work late and frazzled, but it couldn't be helped. Quick as I could, I changed my jeans for the uniform linen pants and smoothed my wavy, cinnamon brown hair up into a professional bun on top of my head.

A quick glance at the clock as I left the lockers told me I was only six minutes late, but it still ate into the client's allotted appointment time so I'd have to make it up…which in turn would see me running late for the rest of my shift.

Serenity had recently started keeping later hours due to demand, and I was a big fan. Evening rates were a lot better and the shifts worked around my classes way easier, but on the downside, we often had seedy businessmen stumble in after happy hour, asking about *happy endings*.

That was *not* the kind of massage we offered.

"He's *hot*," Meg whispered, handing me the clipboard as I passed her in the hallway outside our waiting lounge.

Biting back a laugh, I gave her a glare of reproach, then smacked her lightly with the clipboard. "Shh. Unprofessional much?"

Meg just rolled her eyes and chuckled as she walked away, leaving me to greet my client and introduce myself.

I quickly scanned the survey form that he'd just filled in, gathering the important information in my head as I rounded the corner.

"Hi, Heath, is it? I'm Ashley, I'll be your therapist this evening. Are you—" I raised my eyes from the clipboard to smile at my client and damn near swallowed my own tongue.

*Fuck.* Meg hadn't been exaggerating. He was *scorching* hot.

"Am I...?" he prompted, dark brows raised and amusement dancing in his hazel eyes as I stared like a fucking deer in headlights. Not only was he handsome, but he was tall—almost a foot taller than me—and built. The stretch of his shoulders had my palms itching to shape them.

I blinked a couple of times, trying to remember what I was saying, and my face heated with embarrassment. "Sorry, uh, sorry. I'm Ashley, your therapist."

"You said that part," he informed me with a mock whisper.

*Christ!* "Yep, I sure did. If you'll follow me?"

In an attempt to cover my fumble, I hurried back into the corridor and carefully avoided looking at him *at all* while leading the way to my room. As I did with all clients, I opened the door, then held it for him to enter first but needed to swallow hard as he brushed far too close in the process.

What the hell was going on? He was like something straight out of a sex dream—tall, broad, gorgeous smile...and I was about to get my hands all over him. I needed to get my shit under control, or this would get me fired.

"Uh, I'll leave you to undress," I told him, praying my face wasn't red. "When you're ready, pop beneath the top sheet with your face in the hole." I folded the top sheet back with practiced movements, then quickly dimmed the lights as I exited the room once more.

Once the door was shut, I leaned against the wall and closed my eyes to try and calm down. It was because I'd arrived in a frazzled chaotic state and he was just a very good-looking man. That was it. I had about three minutes while he got undressed, so I had three minutes to find my inner peace once more.

"You okay, Ash?" one of my colleagues, a huge guy called Dwayne, asked as he exited his own room down the hall.

I glanced his way and gave a firm nod. "Yeah, all good."

It was just a hot client. No big deal. We had them all the time and I'd never acted like an idiot before, so this guy was going to be no different. Strictly professional. Once he was face down, he'd just be another body, same as everyone else I massaged. Focus on the muscles, the knots, the points of tension…ignore the rest.

Easier said than done.

## Chapter Two

After knocking on the door to verify my client was ready, I slipped back into the room as quietly—and *professionally*—as I could. I'd been working at Serenity for two years and had massaged hundreds of people in that time, so my processes were like a ritual at this stage. I placed the clipboard down on my little counter and washed my hands thoroughly, usually while making casual small talk to help my client feel comfortable.

This time, though, I needed to silently bully myself into speaking at all.

"So, uh, did you have any problem areas you wanted me to work on, Mr. Jones?" I switched to his surname in an effort to stop the urge to flirt.

He gave a rumbling laugh from the table. "Call me Heath, Ash. You don't mind if I call you Ash, do you?"

Fuck *me*. His voice was going to haunt my dreams later, I just knew it. I had a thing for deep voices, which played into my audiobook obsession.

"Sure," I murmured. "So…problem areas?" I prepped my oils as I spoke.

"Yeah, my left shoulder," he replied in that sexy low voice. "Old rotator cuff injury that gets really stiff in this cold weather."

I nodded to myself, making mental notes and assessing his muscular back with more critical eyes. "Okay, I can help with that. Anything else?"

"Just the usual. Stress tension mostly."

I gave a short laugh without really meaning to do it out loud, then caught myself. *Unprofessional, Ash.*

"Uh, did you just laugh at me?" Heath asked, lifting his face from the table and squinting at me.

My cheeks instantly flamed. "Sorry. That was rude."

He made a small grunt and dropped his face back into the table hole, allowing me to breathe again. "Let me guess, you're wondering why a guy like me has anything to be stressed about?"

I turned to my oils and selected the lavender-heavy *relax* scent to coat my palms. Rather than responding and putting my foot further down my throat, I went through the motions of starting his treatment.

It always took me a few passes over someone's back muscles to get the lay of the land, so to speak. It was painfully obvious how tense he was from those first strokes.

"Try to relax," I murmured, frowning at how his body tightened further as if in deliberate defiance of my order. I stifled a frustrated sigh and resigned myself to simply trying my best. It *sucked* trying to massage someone who was tense and uncomfortable, but it could be done.

To my relief, though, within a few minutes, the tightness started to melt away and his breathing deepened with that perfect level of almost-sleep. My favorite state for clients to be in while I worked.

For the next hour, I worked in total silence as the soothing music of flutes and rain filled the room, mixing perfectly with Heath's deep, even breathing and occasional groans. He woke up when I worked on his shoulder injury—he hadn't been joking about how tight that was—but then immediately slipped back into relaxed dozing when I shifted to his other side.

At the end of his time, I was almost sad to see him go. Weird, considering we really hadn't interacted more than I did with any client.

"Okay, Heath, our time is up," I said softly, not wanting to wake him too abruptly. "How do you feel?"

He gave a low groan, his shoulders flexing as he raised his face. "Holy shit," he mumbled. "That was really good, Ash."

I smiled, pleased with that reaction. "Okay, well, I'll leave you to dress. Take your time and I'll meet you out front."

"Wait." He reached out, grabbing my wrist before I could move away.

Words fled my brain as I glanced down to where his long fingers circled my wrist, tight but not painful. A spark of fear ignited in my chest, but I quickly reminded myself that we had security within screaming distance.

"There was actually another area I wanted you to pay attention to." Not letting go of my wrist, he twisted on the table to sit up. The sheet draped across his lap like a fucking joke, doing absolutely nothing to hide the enormous erection he'd been lying on.

My mouth went dry. Despite the not uncommon misconception about our evening massage services, it was the first time *I'd* been propositioned. Meg had warned me, of course, but this…this was a first for me.

"I think you're confused, Heath," I suggested as calmly as I could, hating the way my voice trembled. "This isn't that sort of massage. And our time is up. So, if you don't mind…"

He didn't seem deterred in the least, his lush lips tilting in a smile like I was flirting with him. "Come on, Ash…help me out here. After the way you just touched every *other* inch of me…"

I shook my head, panicked and embarrassed as hell. "You're *mistaken*," I said firmly as I jerked my wrist out of his grip. "If you're looking for a happy ending, I recommend checking out Jolly Roger's down the street."

He laughed, a rich sound which told me he knew I was suggesting a seedy male-only strip club with lots of extra services on the menu. "That's not the kind of attention I'm seeking, Ash."

I bit my lip, backing away from his enticing stare. Of course I'd noticed he was naked while massaging him, but again, that wasn't uncommon. Loads of clients took their underwear off and it was nothing sinister. Hell, even I preferred to take my panties off for a massage.

"Six," he said, while my mind whirled. Why was I still in the room? He wasn't holding me there and the door was at my back—I could leave anytime I wanted.

I frowned my confusion. "Six...what?"

That sexy smile curved his lips again and he lazily stood from the table, holding the sheet loosely bunched around his waist—thank fuck—and not discarded completely.

Somehow I found myself frozen to the spot, watching as he crossed to the neat stack of his belongings and pulled out a checkbook. What was he, sixty-five? Who the fuck used checks these days?

"What are you doing?" I asked, bewildered, as he scribbled on a check, then ripped it out.

He tossed the book back on his pile of clothes then crossed the small space to where I stood like a fucking statue near the door.

"Six thousand," he informed me, showing me the check written out to *cash* and signed in an elegant signature.

"What?" I squeaked, too stunned to make more coherent words. Six thousand would cover the repairs for my car and then leave two hundred to put against my student loans. It was also an *insane* amount of money, even if I were a professional sex worker. Wasn't it?

Heath's flirty smile was back, his dark eyes dancing with heat. "Six thousand dollars for an extra ten minutes of your time and... *special attention*. What do you say?"

My lips parted, but I was still too shocked to come up with any snappy comebacks or firm refusals. Was it because he was so fucking sexy that I was struggling to leave the room? Or because of the money? Maybe both.

I needed to snap the hell out of it, because that was *not* the line of work I was in.

"I'm flattered, believe me. But that is not the service we offer here at Serenity, and just engaging in this conversation could see me fired. I need this job, Heath, so if you don't mind—"

"No one needs to know, Ash," he said, cutting me off, tilting his head to the side as he studied my face. "Your boss won't ever know what happens in these rooms, right? Unless you tell her, it's just between you and me."

He was right. And it was *so much money*. If we'd met in a bar, I'd have happily given him a happy ending for free, probably would have begged for it. But we didn't and I couldn't, so I shook my head.

"Regardless of who *knows* what happens in these rooms, it's not happening. Thank you, I'm very flattered. But it's a *no*, Heath. I should go, so you can dress." And yet…I didn't move.

He stared at me for a moment, his brow dipped in a slight frown like he was trying to decide if I was bluffing. I held eye contact firmly, refusing to look down for even the slightest glance. As badly as I wanted that money, I wasn't willing to compromise my morals.

"Are you sure?" he asked, sounding confused. "I thought we had a spark."

*Fucking hell.* "We did. But I'm sure. That's *not* a service I offer."

His lips curled up again, in that sexy smirk that was damn near winning me over. "Huh. I'm a little surprised, to be honest. Should I be offended?"

My brows shot up with outrage. "If anyone should be offended here, it's me. I'm going to leave now, and you can get dressed."

He nodded thoughtfully, then folded the check with his fingers and tucked it into my breast pocket. Somehow he even managed to brush my nipple as he did so, and my thighs clenched.

"What are you doing?" I asked, breathless. *Shit.* My resolve was crumbling like a sandcastle.

His answering smile was pure sex. "Keep it."

I shook my head slowly. "Heath, I'm not—"

"I know. But keep it anyway. Call it a tip for unkinking my bad shoulder." He grinned, leaning back slightly as if silently reassuring me that he wasn't going to force anything more. It was oddly comforting despite the thick haze of confusion.

I wet my lips, still unable to tear my eyes from his dark gaze. "I can't accept that, Heath. It's way too much and my boss will *immediately* think something illegal happened in here."

He chuckled. "So don't show her. I won't tell if you don't, Ash."

*Tempting. So very fucking tempting.* It would solve my car problem, and really…why the hell should I be struggling to make ends meet because some asshole keyed my car? That wasn't my fault, so why was I bearing the cost of repairs? Heath was telling me to keep the money *without* needing to suck his cock for it, so why was I protesting?

Like he said, no one else ever needed to know. The check was written out to cash and chances were it would bounce, so this argument would be null.

With that thought, I sighed. "Fine. I'll keep it."

He laughed again, a more genuine sound that struck a chord within me. "Don't sound so thrilled, Ash. I'm sure you meant to say *thank you, Heath.*"

Christ, where were my manners? My face flamed *again*. "Sorry. Yes, that *is* what I meant. Thank you. You have no idea what a difference this makes."

He gave a small shrug, and the sheet slipped. Shit. I was staring at that lower abdomen V where his cut muscles tapered into—

"If you want, I'd accept a kiss," he suggested playfully.

Somehow, I knew he wouldn't force me to do anything without consent but *shit*, for six grand? As hot as the sparks between us were? Fuck it. I rose up on my toes and grabbed his face, dragging him down to my level and crushing my lips against his.

The grunt of surprise that he released said it all. He did *not* expect that, and it only made me want to kiss him more. A split second later, he was kissing me back with a ferocity that set my panties on fire and nearly made me forget I was at work…kissing a *client*. A naked, very turned-on client who had just pinned me to the door and put his hands on my ass.

Oh god, I needed to stop before things got out of control. *More* out of control.

With mammoth effort, I planted my hands on his broad chest and shoved him back a step.

Heath stared at me, bewildered, gasping, and flushed with arousal. Exactly how I felt too.

"Thank you, Heath," I whispered, licking my lips. Then as quickly as possible, I opened the door at my back and slipped out into the hall before I could do something even more stupid. Like fuck him.

Wracked with guilt, I hurried my ass down the hallway to the staff locker room and immediately splashed cold water on my face. The check in my pocket felt like a block of lead so I stashed it in my purse with shaking hands, knowing there was no way in hell I could show Meg.

I skipped the usual procedure of farewelling my client, knowing full well I wouldn't be able to maintain composure. Not after that kiss…

Ugh, I was being ridiculous. The check would *never* clear. It was just a ploy for a free blow job that he could laugh about with his friends later.

With that in mind, I tidied my hair and returned to my room to prepare for my next client.

## Chapter Three

Between Heath leaving, and the end of my shift, I thoroughly convinced myself the check was a fake. So much so, I didn't even look at it again until after I got out of my full day of classes the next day. Even then, it was only because I was searching my bag for some gum and found it while I was walking past my bank and figured it couldn't hurt to take it in.

To my shock, it cleared even if I couldn't read his signature, and it was a check from a business account. An hour later I was paying my mechanic in full for work that hadn't even been completed yet.

At dinner that night, I was vaguely disappointed not to meet Nate—my new stepbrother—but I was riding the adrenaline high of Heath's generous tip, so I couldn't even be mad when Mom and Max announced they were moving their wedding date up.

Not that I needed to be mad. Max was great, and he clearly loved my mom like crazy. It was just awkward because the new wedding date would overlap with the week my dad was in town to visit, and I really, *really* didn't want to see my dad upset. Mom promised me she would handle it, and I left it in her capable hands. They were *her* marriages, after all.

A month later, as I was speeding across town to the airport just after dawn, my phone rang.

"Dad?" I answered. "Shouldn't you be at thirty-thousand feet right now? Your plane isn't due to land for another hour, right? Or am I late?" I was sure I had written the arrival time down accurately when he'd given me his visiting dates earlier in the year.

His weary sigh on the other end should have tipped me off. "I'm sorry, Ashy... I'm not—" He sighed again. "Something came up over here that needed me to stay. I had to cancel my trip home. I'm sorry, kiddo."

Disappointment struck me like an ice pick, and I swallowed back the tears threatening to fall. It'd been nearly six months since I last saw him, and if he was canceling rather than postponing, then it would be another six before he was back again. No wonder his marriage to Mom had fallen apart.

"Okay, yeah, I get it." Maybe he didn't want to be in town the same weekend his ex-wife remarried. It was understandable, even if it was bitterly disappointing for me. "Maybe I could come over there sometime?"

Another sigh. "Not here, honey. It's too dangerous."

I knew that. "We could meet halfway? Go sightseeing somewhere neither of us have been?"

"Maybe. I'd love that, Ash, you know I would. Let me see what I can work out after you graduate, okay?" He sounded tired. He sounded *sad*, and that gutted me. Despite having finalized the divorce with my mom nearly eight years earlier, he'd never stopped loving her. Of that, I was sure.

"Sure, okay. After graduation." It was only six weeks away. As much as I'd kill to continue for my postgrad degree, I couldn't afford it. Not after spending so much time and money studying sports therapy before changing my mind and swapping degree tracks. Maybe I could use my massage therapy training for a few years to save up before returning to study postgrad.

Some muffled voices in the background of the call seemed to distract my dad for a moment, then in the faint distance I could've sworn I heard gunshots.

"Dad?" I asked, instantly worried. He worked as a conflict mediator in South Sudan, and I was perpetually worried that one day he would be killed. Always trying to save the world, that was my dad.

"I'm here, kiddo, but I need to go. Hey, do me a favor will you?"

I swallowed the lump of emotion in my throat once more. "For you? Anything."

"Tell your mom that I'm happy for her and Max. I really am. She deserves the absolute world, and he's the guy who can give it to her." His voice broke, and tears welled up in my own eyes. "I've got to go. Love you, Ashy baby."

"Love you too, Dad," I replied in a whisper, and then the call ended.

*Fucking hell.* Now I was a sobbing mess on the highway going nowhere.

I found the nearest off-ramp and circled back in the direction of my apartment instead. I'd taken the day off work to hang out with my dad, but I also needed to get over to Prosper for Mom and Max's rehearsal dinner tonight. I'd told them I would be a bit late as Dad and I were spending the day together, and they'd been totally accepting of that. Now I wondered if they'd already known my dad wouldn't show.

It sucked, but I could understand. At least now I had the time to chill out and get ready without a rush.

Rather than try to get ready at my own apartment with my five roommates all home and creating chaos, I drove over to Prosper and checked into the hotel that Max had booked for the weekend.

"Ashley!" my mom called out as I was receiving my key card from the receptionist, and I looked over to find her hurrying across the foyer to me. "You're here early! Where's—?"

"He canceled," I told her with a tight smile and a shrug. "Work comes first, and all that." I couldn't bring myself to pass on his message just yet. Not when I was still stinging from disappointment.

Mom's brow creased and I instantly regretted telling her. It wasn't her fault, the reason they'd needed to change wedding dates was due to the hotel renovating. It was now, or in eighteen months.

"Honey, I'm so sorry, I thought he—"

"It's fine." I quickly cut her off. "I get it. We talked about maybe meeting somewhere for a vacation after I graduate instead."

Her sad expression faded and she forced a smile. "That sounds nice. Actually, since you're here early…could you spare a few minutes to pop up to my room?"

"Of course," I agreed, looping my handbag over my shoulder. "Anything for the bride."

Mom laughed, hooking her arm through mine and leading the way to the elevator block. "Have I ever told you, you're my favorite child?"

I rolled my eyes at the old joke. "I'm your *only* child."

She arched a brow at me, grinning. "For the next twenty-four hours, you are. Then it'll be anyone's game. Nate is a very polite boy, you know? And not to mention—" The elevator doors opening cut off what else she was going to say, and she quickly got distracted talking with some friend of hers from work who stepped into the car with us.

Her and Max were staying in the penthouse suite, which didn't shock me in the least. Max was, among his many other attributes, on the Forbes Richest list. At least he wasn't a dick about being one of the chosen few, though.

"Ashley, sweetheart!" He greeted me with genuine warmth as Mom and I entered the impressive suite. "You're early! Carina said you wouldn't be here until dinner. How's Stew?"

From the corner of my eye, I could see Mom trying to subtly shake her head, but Max just looked confused. I sighed and crossed the distance between us to accept the hug he was offering.

"He had something come up," I mumbled vaguely.

"Max honey, I thought since Ashley was here early, we could talk to her about Mrs. Greenberg's thing? Before everything gets crazy tonight?" my mom interjected before Max could offer any sympathies about my dad canceling, and I was thankful for it.

Max released me from his warm hug, beaming with excitement. "Yes! Good thinking. Come sit with us, Ashley. Do you want anything to drink?"

I shook my head, following them over to the enormous lounge area in the middle of their suite. "No, I'm fine. Just curious now. Who is Mrs. Greenberg?"

"Mariah Greenberg." Max sat on an armchair, perched forward on the seat while Mom sat beside me. "She was the great-aunt of a friend of mine and…irrelevant, really. She died a few years back and awarded her whole estate to a scholarship fund at Nevaeh University."

My brows rose. "Very generous of her." But what that had to do with me, I had no clue. I was about to graduate with my bachelor's degree in Humanities from Valley State College.

Max and Mom exchanged a look, then Max shifted his gaze back to me. "Well, part of the fund is reserved specifically for advanced studies. Doctorates, master's, and postgrad degrees."

"Okay…" I narrowed my eyes. Were they trying to suggest I apply? Max had offered to pay my tuition at Nevaeh when I graduated high school, but I'd firmly declined, not wanting to sponge off my mom's boyfriend for such a significant amount of money. Not when Valley State was still a good school and the fees were astronomically less.

Mom shifted in her seat, her knee pressing against mine. "Honey, we know how you feel about taking money from Max, but this is a *scholarship* so…"

Ah, I was right. "So…it's surely too late to apply now, and I bet there are thousands of hopeful applicants so—"

Another guilty look between them. Oh god, what had they done?

"We applied on your behalf," Max told me with a small wince. "About six months ago."

"And you got it!" Mom added, all smiles. "Master's degree in whatever humanities subject you want to pursue. Here." She hopped up and hurried into another room, leaving me bewildered and speechless as I stared at Max.

"Max...what?"

He had the grace to look a little apologetic. "Last time we had dinner, you seemed so depressed about the job prospects you were looking at, and Carina said you'd always wanted to continue your studies."

"I was," I agreed, nodding as I tried to process. "And I do... This is just a shock, Max. I don't—"

"Here!" Mom announced, returning with a manila folder full of paperwork. "The official offer letter. It outlines everything included in the scholarship, such as housing in the dorms, but if you wanted, we could find you an apartment nearby and—"

"Mom." I cut her off with a smile. "Stop. You're babbling. Let me see?"

She handed over the paperwork, and they both waited silently while I read it through. If I was honest, I was checking to see if anywhere hinted at Max having secretly funded the scholarship himself, but that was far-fetched. He was rich, but that didn't make him a liar. If they said it was a legit scholarship, then I had no real reason to doubt it.

"You still have a few weeks to select your courses, but we need to accept the offer by Monday to secure the scholarship funding," Mom told me softly. "We planned to tell you sooner but things have been so crazy and we kind of wanted to do it as a wedding present."

I chuckled. "That's not how wedding presents work, Mom. I'm supposed to give *you* one, not the other way around."

She took my hand in hers, meeting my eyes with her own imploring gaze. "Exactly. Knowing you're getting an amazing higher education at such a prestigious university is the best gift you could give us both. We want you to have the best opportunities in life, Ash baby, and this school can give it to you."

*Jesus.* How the hell could I say no to that?

Fighting the burn of tears, I nodded my acceptance. "Okay."

Mom gasped, her whole face lighting up. "Yes? Really?"

The relief on Max's face almost made me laugh, and I nodded again. "Yes. Thank you. Both of you. I never would have even thought to apply for something like this…I don't even know what to say."

"No thanks needed," Max assured me with genuine happiness in his eyes. "Like your mom said, we only want the very best for our kids."

*Our kids.* As sad as I was for my dad, I was painfully happy for Mom. Max really was the best thing to happen to her, and he already thought of me as his own child. Apparently Mom felt the same about Nate, and I still hadn't met him. Then again, he had gone to private schools and had friends and various functions. I'd been focused on my stuff. Still, I guess it was weird.

After several tight hugs from Mom, I excused myself to find my room and freshen up. They were all due to attend the ceremony rehearsal any minute now, but I'd been excused so I intended to enjoy the enormous tub in my room.

It wasn't until I was neck deep in bubbles and sipping on the complimentary champagne from my minibar that the news fully set in. I wasn't going to be taking a low-paying position as a primary school teacher in Panner Valley after graduation. I'd be moving into the dorms at Nevaeh University. I didn't have that on my bingo card, but I was actually *crazy* excited.

Grinning to myself, I took a gulp of champagne and sank lower into the bubbles. My future was suddenly very bright.

## Chapter Four

My dress for dinner had been selected by Mom's wedding planner, and I'd been strong-armed into wearing it for the sake of *color scheme balance* or some shit, but I felt like the worst kind of imposter as I strode into the restaurant in a lavender satin dress that cost more than six months of my rent.

"Ashley, is that you?" an elegant silver-haired woman gasped as I approached the private dining room that'd been booked for the dinner.

I smiled in delight, holding out my arms. "Nana Grace, don't act like you don't recognize me."

She gave a chuckle, sweeping me into a hug clouded with Chanel No. 5 perfume. "I was just shocked to see you out of jeans, darling girl. You look phenomenal." My grandmother released me and held me at arm's length to take in my gown. Strapless and corseted, with a draped skirt and high slit up my thigh, it was significantly more sophisticated than I usually dressed. "Goodness, you are a showstopper. You must get your looks from my genes, of course."

I laughed loudly at that, since she was my granddad's second wife—Mom's stepmom—and not blood-related to me at all. "Of course. How was rehearsal?"

Nana Grace shrugged. "Boring, to be fair, but these things always are. Let's get you a drink before you join the table. Some of Max's family are a whole handful without a little liquor to soften the blow."

I had only met a few of them, but I could imagine. So I accompanied my grandmother to the bar and told her all about the trials and tribulations of my cramped living situation while we waited for the bartender to mix us up classic daiquiris—Nana Grace's favorite.

We'd just received our drinks and started back toward the dining room when I caught sight of someone strangely familiar.

*Was that…? No. Surely not.*

"Ashley? Is everything okay?" Nana Grace asked, touching my elbow gently.

I blinked rapidly, the familiar person disappearing from view. "Hmm? Oh, sorry. I thought I saw a client from work but that would be insane. Sorry, I think I'm just stressed and tired."

Nana Grace scoffed. "Of course you are, sweetheart. You share a bedroom with two other girls on opposing schedules. I'm amazed you lasted this long. What date do you move into the dorms at Nevaeh?"

My jaw dropped, the familiar guy forgotten. "You knew about the scholarship?"

She grinned, wicked as hell. "Who do you think found it and pushed your mother into seeing it through?"

A light bell tinkled and one of the servers politely asked us to take our seats, so that conversation would need to wait for later. We made our way into the huge dining room and browsed the extravagantly decorated table to find our place cards. Nana was a few places along from where mine was, right beside Mom.

Just as I was about to pull my chair out, someone reached over and plucked my name card off the plate, switching it for Suzette Marie—Mom's best friend and bridesmaid.

"Uh, excuse me?" I protested, confused and annoyed.

"Sorry, Ash, that wedding planner is making mistakes all over the place. You're down here," the guy responded, turning away before I could get a good look at him. He carried my name card farther down the table and set it back down on the seat that must have been Suzette's, then turned to smile at me.

Or smirk. That smile definitely wasn't a *friendly* one.

"Thanks, I guess," I muttered, already uncomfortable. He was handsome, no question about it, an easy head taller than me even in the high heels I wore, with a rich burnt-toffee brown hair that matched Max's perfectly. "Nate, I presume?"

His smirk widened and his whiskey-brown gaze raked over my body in a decidedly unbrotherly sort of way. "You're not as dumb as you look, that's a relief. Sit down, *Sister*. The happy couple is about to arrive."

I rolled my eyes. I knew it was all too good to be true with how lovely Max was. Of course his son was an entitled brat who couldn't handle sharing his daddy.

"We're both adults, Nate. How about we act like it, hmm?" I placed my cocktail down on the table, then slid into my seat as though he didn't exist. Fuck that petty nonsense. Our parents had been dating for *years* and we'd never met, so I saw no need for us to suddenly play happy family. After the wedding, we could go back to six degrees of separation.

He clearly didn't like being dismissed, because he made an irritated huff as he pulled out the chair right beside me and sat down himself. *Damn it.* Why bother swapping my seat with Suzette if he was just going to be an asshole?

"Nathaniel, darling!" the woman in question trilled, approaching where we sat. "Don't you look just delicious in that suit?"

My brows shot right the fuck up. Was my mom's friend hitting on Max's twenty-two-year-old son? *Wow.* Maybe the seat swap wasn't about me after all.

"Suzette, lovely to see you," Nate replied, not standing to greet her properly. "I believe you're sitting beside Carina." He waved in the direction we'd come from, clearly dismissing her.

I tipped my head to see Suzette's reaction, but Mom's friend had her sultry gaze pinned on Nate instead. Was there…history?

She leaned down and whispered something to Nate that I couldn't hear, but his jaw clenched hard enough I could see it. *Interesting.*

"Not interested in Mrs. Robinson?" I murmured as Suzette sashayed away, unable to curb my curiosity. Nate's sharp gaze snapped to me, and I met his unflinchingly. If he thought I'd turn into a simpering mess at a few hard glances, he was sorely mistaken.

After a tense moment, he blinked and looked away. "Something like that."

A wolf whistle rang out and I rose to my feet along with everyone else to clap as my mom and Max made their way to their seats in the middle of the table, all smiles and looking amazing.

When I went to sit again, Nate pushed my chair in for me and I frowned my confusion his way. He ignored me, though, tucking himself into the table and reaching for his glass of water.

Two seats remained empty opposite us, along with one to my other side, and I leaned over to see what name was on my absent neighbor's plate.

*Carter Bassington Jr.*

I rolled my eyes. Why did wealthy families always give their kids such wanky names?

"Ah, there's my seat," a man said just a moment later, and from the corner of my eye, I caught sight of a deeply tanned hand pulling the chair out from the table. "Oh, this is a nice change to the seating chart, Nate. I thought we were stuck with Cougar-Marie all night?"

I shifted in my seat to look at the newcomer who had a definite British accent and was currently eyeing me up like I was the main course meal. Fucking hell, wanky name or not, he was *hot*. Tanned skin, black hair, twinkling dark blue eyes, and the hint of a tattoo showing at the edge of his collar... I found myself staring until Nate draped his arm over my shoulder.

"Carter, I don't think you've met the newest member of our family? This is *Ashley*." The way he purred my name made my skin prickle. What was his problem? He was too damn old to be jealous of his daddy not paying him enough attention.

Carter plucked my hand up from the table and pressed his lips to my knuckles, making my brain momentarily short-circuit and my pulse quicken. "It's such a pleasure, Ashley. We've been hearing so very much about you."

My eyes widened, and I couldn't seem to withdraw my hand from his warm grip. "You have?" I asked instead, puzzled.

"Oh yes," he replied, those beautiful eyes sparkling. "We know *all* the juicy details."

*Huh?*

"Like mother, like daughter, hmm?" Nate added, his arm still over my shoulders and his fingertips stroking across my bare collarbone. "At least now I know what the going rate is."

*What?*

I tugged my fingers free of Carter's grip and shrugged Nate off my shoulders. "What the hell are you—"

My words broke off as I nearly swallowed my own tongue in shock. Now I wished I'd paid more attention to that *familiar face* I thought I'd seen.

"What time do you call this, boys?" Max called out as the two remaining guests took their seats opposite me.

"Sorry, Max!" the blond one called back, but I was too stunned to blink.

"How rude of us," Nate purred. "Ashley, this is Royce D'Arenberg and Heathcliff Briggs—oh, wait, you already met Heath, didn't you? *Intimately.*"

Oh god. The massage appointment...the proposition...it was all a setup. He'd booked that session knowing *exactly* who I was and used a fake surname for *what?* Then it clicked. Heath had tried to pay me for sexual favors which would, by definition, make me a whore. Exactly what Nate was implying.

Rage filled my chest and I glared death at the man who'd starred in far too many of my dirty dreams over the past month. I should have fucking known it was too good to be true.

"I don't know what you told your little friends, *Heathcliff*, but you and I both know nothing happened." *Apart from that kiss.* My glare narrowed and my lip curled with disgust. "How pathetic of you *all* that you need to try and pay a woman for that sort of attention…and how embarrassing that you got turned down. Try harder next time."

A dark, cold expression crossed his face as he stared back at me, not speaking even a word to address my correction of whatever bullshit he'd sold his friends. He just sat there, slouched in his seat like he was king of the damn world, totally at ease. Except for his eyes. He was staring at me like no one else even existed in the room.

"Ah, so you want us to believe that Heath lied to us, hmm?" Nate drawled the words like I was telling a funny joke.

I shrugged, breaking eye contact with Heath to look at Nate in disdain. "I don't much care what you believe, Nathaniel. You clearly have your panties in a bunch about daddy remarrying, but that's an issue for you and your therapist—nothing to do with me. Now, since I'm not a masochist, I think I'll find somewhere else to sit." I pushed my seat back and stood. "I wish I could say it was lovely to meet you all, but frankly I've had more pleasant experiences stepping in dog shit."

Royce—the blond who'd arrived with Heath—snickered, then quickly covered it with his hand. Not that I stuck around to wait for a response. Instead I picked up my drink and strode away from the silly little rich boys and their childish taunts.

"Ash, is everything okay?" Mom asked as I approached her and Max. "Are the boys being kind?" The edge of worry in her tone said she already knew what an asshole Nate was and had never warned me. Nor had she warned me that Nate came as a package deal.

*Great, more secrets.* As if hiding an eight-year affair with her hot boss wasn't enough.

In fairness, Mom and Max had suggested I bring a friend myself, but for one thing, I'd planned on bringing my dad...and for another, I had no close friends.

"Nothing I can't handle," I reassured her. "I hate to do this when I already skipped the rehearsal itself, but I'm actually feeling a bit headachy. Would you be upset if I left?"

"Of course not, honey, don't be silly! Go to bed, get some rest. You don't want that turning into a migraine. I *will* need you tomorrow." Mom gave me a worried frown, then glanced at the drink in my hand. "Alcohol won't help, Ash."

My face heated. "Oh, I was just taking this to Nana Grace."

The frown melted off Mom's face instantly. "You sweet girl. Go, get some rest. I'll see you in the morning."

She and Max both gave me a quick hug, then I made my speedy exit from the dining room. The second I was out of sight, I drained my cocktail in one gulp, then nearly choked on the acidic drink when someone grabbed my arm.

The glass smashed as it hit the floor, but my attacker whisked me into the cloakroom before anyone could connect me with the breakage.

"Nate, what the hell?" I spluttered, coughing a little from the droplets of daiquiri I'd inhaled. "Did I not make myself clear enough? I have no interest in your schoolyard bullying crap."

In the dimly lit cloakroom, it was hard to make out his expression, but the way he had me boxed in against the wall didn't bode well.

"I'm almost impressed, Ash," he murmured, leaning *way* too close into my personal space. "You must be good at poker with how convincing a liar you are, but you forgot one thing."

I scoffed. "Oh, really? And what's that?"

He leaned in closer, his breath feathering my ear as he replied. "You cashed the check."

My pulse raced and my breath hitched. It sure didn't *look* good, and it was way too much money for a tip without anything extra.

There was no use in denying it, though. For all I knew, the money had come directly from Nate himself.

"Nice car, by the way," he told me, pushing back and opening the door. "That paint must have been a bitch to match."

My jaw dropped, but he was gone before I could reply. That mother*fucker* was the one who'd keyed my car!

# Chapter Five

"Are you sure we can't get you an apartment in Nate's building?" Max asked for what felt like the hundredth time. He and Mom had been helping me move into my dorm room and were all kinds of unimpressed at how small the room was and the fact that the bathroom was communal for the coed floor.

I shook my head. "Thank you, but no. This is absolutely perfect for me and honestly a luxury, considering I've shared a bedroom with two other girls for the last three years. I have my own space"—I gestured around the small room, which barely fit the queen-sized bed Mom bought me and a small study desk—"and I'm only a two-minute walk across campus to the majority of my lectures. It's perfect."

Max frowned but didn't push it again. He'd already told me all about the building where he'd purchased a four-bedroom apartment for Nate and his friends to live, way back at the start of their freshman year. To my annoyance, all four of those childish dicks were returning for master's degrees as well, but as far as I could tell—without being obvious—we didn't have any subject crossovers.

"She'll be fine, Max honey," Mom assured him, looping her arm around his waist. They'd just returned from their extended honeymoon in the Maldives and both sported an impressive tan. It made me wish I'd inherited Mom's tannable skin, instead of Dad's fair complexion with a tendency to burn and freckle far too easily.

Max gave a short sigh. "Strong will must be a genetic trait in the Layne lineage."

Mom laughed and nodded. "It is. Come on, we need to finish unloading Ashley's things before five so we can get to dinner."

They *constantly* had social plans. It made me tired just listening to how many engagements they had in a week, but they seemed to love it. I let them help me with the last few boxes from the moving truck, then waved them off when they offered to help unpack. It was my space, and I wanted to take my time setting things up how I wanted them.

In fairness, I didn't want them to see me rearrange my shit a dozen times before it *felt* right…but Mom knew my process.

Once they were gone, I sank to sit on the edge of my bed. There was a *lot* to do to get my room unpacked and put in order, but for now I just needed to catch my breath. It was all still so overwhelming to be starting my master's at Nevaeh at all, when I'd dismissed the possibility of advanced study *years* ago.

After graduating Valley State, I'd taken a quick vacation with my dad in Portugal and told him all about the scholarship. He couldn't have been more supportive, and it gave me the reassurance I needed that this was the right path.

I had to admit…the only part I was truly apprehensive about was my new stepbrother and his buddies. Nate. Fucking hell, what a *dick*. I'd unfortunately crossed paths with him a handful more times after the wedding but managed to escape all of them with only a few sharp words exchanged. I hated to think what being in the same university would be like, especially since it wasn't a huge campus. They didn't even have a Greek row—no fraternities, no sororities…hopefully that meant no stuck-up mean girls or dumb-ass pool parties.

As for Heathcliff Briggs, he could jump off the top of Mount Prosper for all I cared. What a lying, manipulative piece of *shit*. He knew that giving me that money made me look guilty and was all too happy to bald-faced lie about what had happened between us. He was hot and the chemistry had been amazing. But I could find that with any number of other guys.

"Knock, knock!" someone called out, whilst also knocking on my door.

I wrinkled my nose at the goofy intro, then hopped up to see who it was.

"Hello," I greeted the girl standing in the hallway. She was supermodel stunning. Taller than me by at least half a foot, with her strawberry-blond hair tied up in a high ponytail.

"Hi, I'm Carly," she announced, extending her hand for me to shake, "from three-twelve." She jerked a thumb over her shoulder, indicating the door opposite mine.

"Oh cool," I responded enthusiastically. "Neighbors! Are you postgrad too?" She looked around my age, not like the wide-eyed kids fresh out of high school I'd seen on my way in.

Carly nodded. "Sure am. Linguistics with a specialization in Ancient History."

"That's cool, I'm focusing on social studies but I'm going to do some classical literature electives, so we'll probably have some classes together. Oh shit, I'm Ashley, by the way. Ashley Layne." I gestured to myself, realizing I'd not actually given my name yet.

Carly seemed unfazed, though, peering past me to the pile of boxes on my floor, bed, and desk. "Nice to meet you. Uh, do you want some help unpacking? That will take you forever! Where are you even going to put it all?"

I laughed nervously. "Honestly? No clue. I'll make it work, though. Thanks anyway." *But no thanks, all the same.*

She shrugged. "You know where to find me if you want extra hands. I'll check in before I head out to dinner, so you don't fade away beneath those boxes of...what does that say? Model cars?" She quirked a brow and my cheeks heated with embarrassment. Carly didn't laugh at me, though; she just nodded. "Cool. Catch you later, neighbor."

Carly was true to her word, fishing me out of my jumble of clothes a couple of hours later and inviting me to have dinner with her. I accepted, because a girl had to eat and my neighbor seemed nice.

She chatted with ease as we walked across the grassy lawn to reach the central dining hall, telling me about her summer break interning at a museum in Paris. It sounded incredible and a little unbelievable, but it was just something I needed to wrap my brain around. Graduates—and students—of Nevaeh University had the keys to *all* the doors.

Dinner was surprisingly good for school food, and I ate until my belly hurt. Then I needed to remind myself to slow it the fuck down or I'd be sick. I'd been far from *starving* before arriving at Nevaeh but I'd definitely survived on ramen noodles for one too many meals for too damn long.

"Hey, I was thinking about looking for a part-time job," I told Carly as we slowly strolled back to our dorm after dinner. "Do you know of any coffee shops or something that might be hiring?" I figured that was an easier option than searching for a masseuse position near campus.

Carly wrinkled her nose. "I don't think so, but you could check at the Dancing Goats in the morning? That's the only decent coffee shop on campus and they're always packed. None of the baristas are students, though, so…I don't know."

Probably because none of the other students had to think about their disposable income. Although my tuition, room, and board were all provided under the scholarship, I still needed play money. New clothes, coffees, gas, social engagements—it all cost.

"Oh, you could always check with the tutoring office? They constantly need staff and they pay really well."

My brows rose. "Seriously?"

Carly nodded enthusiastically. "For sure. Because no one wants to do it, but they need tutors so...you know, supply and demand and all that shit."

I filed that information away to look into in the morning, and thanked Carly for her advice. When we got back to our floor, she peered inside my room and snickered.

"You're really making progress, Layne. At this rate you might be done by Thanksgiving? Maybe?"

I groaned, eyeing the even bigger mess I'd created. "Maybe I do need help, after all."

"Say no more, girl, I've got you." She nudged me inside. "I'll just grab my speaker so we can listen to tunes. I focus better when I have background music."

"Same," I admitted, but I just hadn't found where my headphones were packed.

A few minutes later, I understood why Carly had been so eager to help. The girl was an organizing *machine* to the point of scary with how quickly she mapped the space and created a plan. Very admirable, that was for sure. It also gave us a ton of time to get to know each other better.

Carly was apparently a former star of the Nevaeh girls basketball team, and she enthusiastically invited me to come along and watch a game in a couple of weeks as she remained a huge fan. She was also determined as hell and didn't even hint at quitting until my whole room was unpacked and sorted out to pristine standards...at a shocking two in the morning.

"Carly, holy shit, I can't thank you enough. You're a lifesaver!" I stared around at my room—my own *private* space—in awe. She'd worked wonders to make all my shit fit without seeming cluttered.

She just shrugged and yawned. "It's all good. Lucky we don't have classes until Wednesday! Actually there was something I wanted to...uh...disclose? Seeing as I figure we're friends now?"

I arched a brow, my hands on my hips. "You've handled my panties, Carly. We're definitely friends now."

She chuckled. "Fair call. Okay so…fuck it. Uh, I slept with your brother. Once. Just one time."

That was unexpected and confusing. "Huh?"

Her pale face had already flushed pink with embarrassment and her brow creased with worry. "Nate? We used to date. Sort of. Or I thought we did and…ugh, this is mortifying. Turns out he was cheating on his girlfriend with me and it all came out in a really nasty way toward the end of last year and long story short, I'm a little bit of a social pariah in some circles of the school. Also…I'm so sorry."

My jaw had dropped. "What? Why are you apologizing to me? I barely know the guy and what I have seen of him, I don't like. This…kind of just validates what a dickhead he comes across as, so if anything *I'm* sorry that he hurt you. What an asshole!"

Carly barked a startled laugh. "Seriously. It was six months ago, but I'm still so freaking embarrassed, and my old friends basically cut me out of their lives, so like…I totally understand if you have second thoughts about being my friend come Wednesday classes. No hard feelings."

"Oh…I see." I pursed my lips, acting like I was really thinking it over. "Well, my whole plan was to come to Nevaeh and secure a strong marriage to a rich friend of my new stepbrother, so I guess we can't hang out anymore. Thanks for your help with my room, though."

Carly's face fell, her lips parting in a mixture of shock and disappointment, and I instantly regretted fucking with her.

"I'm kidding, you drama queen. If anything, this only makes me want to be your friend *more*. I can't stand Nate and his douchebag friends, so start working on our friendship bracelets because you're stuck with me." I grinned, then tossed a pillow at her from my bed to lighten the mood.

She laughed, throwing it back then grabbed me in a quick hug. "Thanks, Ash. You're pretty cool, you know that?"

"I do now," I replied. "Now go to bed. You're tired and emotional and I really don't need you making me cry with all the feelings."

She hugged me again, then left with the promise of meeting for coffee at the Dancing Goats around midday. I closed my door behind her, locking it securely before getting ready for bed.

I was exhausted but full of warm fuzzies about my new friendship. The oily, anxious feeling her confession about Nate gave me was shoved firmly out of my mind. As far as I was concerned, he didn't exist.

# Chapter Six

Carly hadn't been lying when she said her friends had shunned her after whatever went down with Nate. I blissfully hadn't run into him or his pathetic little friends all week, but I'd had plenty of opportunity to see how Carly's ex-friends treated her.

It was their loss, honestly. She was awesome, and if she hadn't been ostracized, I probably never would have had the opportunity to become her friend.

For the most part, it was snide comments and nasty whispers behind her back that I couldn't help but hear. Which meant Carly heard them too, even if she pretended not to. My initial instinct was to lash out and *correct* the behavior, but after entering into a couple of verbal sparring matches with girls I'd never laid eyes on before, Carly asked me to please ignore the whole situation.

It didn't sit right, but I bit my tongue for the next couple of days…until I couldn't any longer.

The whole mess started on Friday morning when Carly and I shared a Political History seminar together, along with one of her biggest tormentors. Jade was the best friend of Paige—Nate's actual girlfriend—and a raging bitch on the best of days.

Friday morning, though, she was in fine fucking form. Throughout the whole seminar, she found every opportunity to toss insults at Carly, calling her a slut in the same breath as she flirted with the handsome young professor. It blew my mind how she could possibly hope to retain the class content and *learn* when she was so preoccupied with her hatred of another woman, but somehow she was managing.

"Ash," Carly warned when I started gripping my pen as if it were a weapon. "Leave it. She'll get bored eventually."

I rolled my eyes, inclined to disagree, but tried to stop imagining what noise Jade would make if I stabbed her with my pen. In fairness, it'd probably snap in half before actually hurting her, but it always worked in movies…a girl could dream.

"Have you got any plans tonight?" Carly asked after the seminar finished. We were making our way out of the building, on our way to the Dancing Goats for coffee before we each needed to head to different classes. "First Friday night at Nevaeh, gonna hit up the party by Lake Prosper?"

"What party?" I asked, yawning. I'd stayed up late, reading over my notes from the first couple of days and letting the information sink in a bit deeper. At least two professors had hinted at the prospect of quizzes, and I wanted to be ready.

Carly sighed. "It's a Nevaeh tradition. First weekend of the year there's a huge party on the west bank of Lake Prosper. Faculty claim they know nothing about it, and it's *not permitted* since so many students are under twenty-one, but there's no way that students are pulling it off without help."

I shrugged. "Not really my scene." And if it was such a big deal, then there would be no avoiding Nate. Or Heath. *Dickheads.*

"I hope you don't think you're going, *slut*," Jade spat from behind us, making me turn to glare her way. "No one wants you there, and if Paige sees you drooling all over Nate again, she'll probably drown you in the lake."

"Okay, that's enough," I snapped, my patience worn way too thin. "It's one thing to call Carly nasty names in class when you're supposed to be *learning*, but threats of physical harm are a step too far. Mind your business, Jade."

Her lip just curled in a sneer. "Who the fuck are you to talk to me like that? You aren't one of us." She scoffed like she thought she was royalty or some shit.

"And thank fuck I'm not," I retorted, shaking my head. "I thought this kind of bullying was left behind in high school. You're an adult, Jade. Start acting like one."

Silly me for thinking she would do as she was told. I turned my back on her, linking my arm through Carly's to continue on our path toward coffee, but Jade had other ideas. A hard shove in the middle of my back sent me reeling, but I managed to catch my balance before I ate pavement.

Fury and outrage flooded through me and I saw red.

"Ash, don't!" Carly yelped as I spun and launched at Jade. It was too late, though, I'd already committed to my tackle and a split second later I had that smug, cruel-tongued bitch face down on the grass beside the path.

I was no fighter, but neither was she, and I had the element of surprise. She didn't stand a chance as I sat across her back and grabbed a handful of her dark hair. I hadn't *really* hurt her. I'd just shocked her more than anything. Bruised her ego. But the way she hollered made out like I was stabbing her or something.

"Holy shit, *shut up!*" I exclaimed, but before I could climb off her, a pair of huge hands clasped my waist and lifted me clear off the shrieking girl.

Those hands *definitely* didn't belong to Carly.

Nope, there was Carly, pale and staring in shock and not holding me off the ground with big, tanned hands around my waist.

"Shut the fuck up, Jade," a British-accented man barked, and I stiffened. More than I already was, which I hadn't known was possible. "Get off the ground. You're an embarrassment to the DBs, carrying on like that."

Two bright spots of color bloomed in Carly's cheeks and she shot me a pleading look. If only I knew what it was she was asking me to do…or not do? Fuck if I knew.

Jade had shut up *real* quick and scrambled to her feet with wide eyes. "Carter! What, um, how are you?"

Nate's bestie just grunted, placing me down so close that I ended up standing on his shoes, and when I tried to move away, he held me tighter. "I'm irritated, Jade, that's how I am. Get the fuck out of here and stop picking fights with my little Spark."

I couldn't see Carter with my back to his chest, but the derision in his tone left no room for disagreement. Jade pouted but dusted herself off and did as she was told.

"You too, Carly," Carter snapped. "I need a moment alone with the new girl to teach her some manners."

Fear and anxiety flooded through me, and I tried to wrestle out of his grip. All I achieved, though, was somehow ending up with my arms trapped where a moment ago they'd been free. Fucking hell, what was he, part octopus?

"Let me go," I growled, remembering I had a voice.

He chuckled, low and cold. "Not a chance, Spark. I gave you an order, Carly. Are you refusing to comply?"

My new friend winced, her face full of apology and regret. "Ash…" She shook her head. "I, ugh, Carter, I can tell her the rules. Can you just let her go? We have a class and—"

"No, you don't. You just finished Political History together and you've got a thirty-minute break before *you* have Ancient Architecture and Spark here is due at Essex Hall for Philosophy."

His knowledge of our schedule shocked me speechless. How did he know that? Why?

Carly looked scared. Downright *terrified*.

"Go on ahead," I told her, keeping my own voice confident and unbothered. "Order my coffee and I'll meet you there, okay? I'm sure whatever Carson needs to tell me, it will be quick and polite."

He just chuckled at my deliberate mistake on his name. Well... if he couldn't use mine, why should I use his?

Carly bit her lip nervously, her eyes darting from me to my looming captor and back again, torn.

"Go on, Carly," Carter purred. "You really don't want to get on my bad side so early in the year, do you?"

I met her eyes and gave her a nod, reassuring her that I would be just fine if she left. I definitely didn't need to go dragging her into whatever fictional grudge Nate's friends seemed to have against me, not when she was already dealing with her own crap.

She gave a pained sigh, then nodded and reluctantly walked away from us.

"Perfect. Now I have you all alone," Carter murmured in my ear, making me shiver. I wasn't an idiot; I knew perfectly how dangerous this situation could end up since Carter held a definite physical advantage.

And yet, I couldn't stop running my mouth. Call it a defense mechanism.

"Oh yay, does this mean you're gonna make up your own bullshit story about fucking me so your bros don't make fun of you for being rejected?"

He laughed again, and I hated that I liked the sound of his laugh. It was oddly infectious and shockingly flirtatious. With my feet still on top of his sneakers, he took two steps off the path and spun me around until my back was against the side of the building.

Now I could see him and he was just as handsome as I remembered from the wedding. Maybe more, since he wore a black T-shirt that did sinful things for his thick biceps wrapped in tattoo ink.

*Shit.* Why were the pretty ones always so personality-defective?

"That's cute," he commented, keeping one hand on my waist as he leaned the other against the wall. "Six grand is a lot of money for *nothing* to happen, Spark. Maybe you didn't fuck him...but you did something. I bet there was even a *spark* between you two."

My face flamed. Heath had said that…but it was right after I rejected him. I guess his version of events was dramatically different.

"See? Your guilty face says it all. Listen, I'm not judging. Chicks have sucked his dick for a whole lot less money, you know?" His lips curled in a smile, the tip of his tongue running over his teeth.

I shook my head, stubbornly refusing to be seduced by his mere closeness—it may have been a while since I'd gotten any—I would never admit that kiss with his friend was the hottest thing I'd had happen in the last four months—but I wasn't going to cave due to hotness when it was so evil. "No, *Carlos*, I don't know. Now did you have something you wanted to tell me or were you just fishing for dirt?"

His oddly dark blue gaze locked on mine for a moment, thoughtful, then he nodded and eased back a slight distance. His hand remained on my waist, hot and heavy, but at least I could breathe a touch easier.

"You can't pull that shit with Jade again. Not in public, anyway." He pursed his lips like there was something more to add but decided not to.

I narrowed my eyes. "She fucking started it, and who the hell made you hall monitor?"

He blinked a couple of times, then grinned. "You've got a bad attitude for a girl who just got her golden ticket to a brighter future, you know that?"

"Oh no!" I gasped dramatically, pressing my hand to my mouth. "Callum Buckingham the Fourth thinks I have a bad attitude? Whatever will I do? Gosh, this will make me lose sleep, for sure."

That sexy grin spread wider on his lips. Did nothing get under his skin? "Cute. But I'm serious about this. Next time you want to start a bitch fight, make sure no one is around to witness it."

I frowned, hearing the serious undertone. "Or what?"

His brows arched. "Or disciplinary action will have to be taken." He started to push off the wall, then gave me a thoughtful look. "If you really wanted to wrestle Jade, I could line up a pool of Jell-O and some string bikinis. Just say the word, Spark, I'll sort you out." With a cheeky wink, he released me and swaggered away with way too much confidence.

Sleazy fuck, of course he had to suggest *that*.

I rubbed the spot on my waist where he'd had his hand and bit my lip as I watched him disappear around the corner. Something about his warning gave me chills, because I didn't believe for a moment he meant discipline by the university staff.

Why the fuck did that make me so *curious*?

# Chapter Seven

After my run-in with Carter, I found Carly waiting anxiously outside the Dancing Goats with my coffee in hand and worry etched all over her face. When she saw me, her relief was palpable enough that it made me think twice about Carter's ominous warning.

"Oh thank fuck," she exclaimed, handing over my coffee. "You're okay? He didn't…um…hurt you, did he?"

I frowned, squinting at her. "Is that something he would do?" Carter struck me as an entitled rich prick, but I didn't get violent or rapey vibes. Maybe I was a shit judge of character, if Carly was this worried.

She hesitated, chewing her thumbnail, then sighed. "I don't totally know. Things have been really weird lately with, um, with some people here at Nevaeh. And Nate has been talking some shit about you…"

I rolled my eyes. "Shocker. The guy literally doesn't know me from a bar of soap but has formed plenty of fictional opinions. Wait, you're still talking with Nate?"

Carly quickly shook her head. "No, good god, no. Just rumor mill, you know? Which sort of makes it all worse than hearing it at the source. I just worry about you, Ash."

With a smile, I shrugged off her concerns. "I can handle myself. Didn't you see what happened to Jade? Anyway, we better get to class before we're late. Thanks for coffee." I gave her a quick hug and cheek kiss, then hauled ass in the direction of Essex Hall.

It irritated me to no end that half my classes were in a building literally named after Nate's family, but I reminded myself that *Nate* wasn't the benefactor. It was likely Max, or even his parents before him.

Immersing myself in the philosophy lecture, I quickly pushed Carter and his big hands out of my head, focusing on the learning. Carly and I didn't have any more classes together, but we met up for lunch and it was all uneventful. I figured since the guys had their own apartment off campus, they probably never needed to eat with the rest of us commoners. Hell, Nate probably had his own chef on standby so he didn't need to demean himself into preparing his own food. Such a diva.

On my way out of the last lecture of the week, I saw Heath crossing the lawn with the hot blond guy from Mom's wedding. Somehow Heath spotted me too and met my eyes with a determined look on his face.

*Fuck that.* I quickly changed directions and took the scenic route back to my dorm. If everyone was going to this party tonight, it'd be nice and quiet on my floor and a great time to study the day's notes.

"Hey, Ashley, right?" a guy said, passing me on the stairs as I headed up to my room.

I nodded. "Yeah, uh…?" I recognized him as living on my floor but had no clue what his name was.

"Jack," he filled in. "Just a word of warning, pets aren't permitted in dorms. If the faculty find out, you could get kicked out."

I wrinkled my nose. "Um, okay? I don't have a pet, though."

He nodded slowly, like we were sharing a secret. "Sure…got it." He winked. "No pets. Maybe come up with another excuse for the barking, in that case."

Confused, I watched him continue down the stairs for a moment, then hurried up the rest of the way to my floor. Sure enough, as I drew closer to the top, distinctive barking could be heard from down the corridor...toward my room.

"What the fuck?" I muttered, hurrying down the hall and fumbling for my key. The barking was definitely coming from my room, that much was obvious, and the second I got the door open, I was hit with the stench.

I gagged, holding the door closed a moment while I blocked my nose and bolstered some bravery before reopening the door.

There, standing in the middle of my bed, was the ugliest dog I'd ever seen. It was growling and tearing my blanket apart, and on the small patch of previously clear floor beside my bed, there were several stinking piles of shit. I had to assume that the animal had pissed on my desk chair if the puddle beneath it was a hint.

On the window, someone had scrawled the word *Bitch* with what looked like red lipstick.

"Whoa, what the fuck?" Carly exclaimed, startling me somewhat. She peered over my shoulder with ease thanks to her height. "Um, Ash..."

I rolled my eyes. "It's not my dog."

"I should hope not," she retorted with a snort of laughter. "Because holy hell. Ew, does it have fleas?"

The mutt itself was now scratching furiously in the middle of my torn-up bed. *Fantastic.*

"Well, at least that's something," I muttered, getting a full view of the canine's undercarriage as she scratched. "Jade was funny enough to deliver a *bitch* to complete her joke."

"Jade," Carly repeated, sounding ill. "Yeah...that checks out. After you ground her into the dirt, I had a feeling she'd be out for blood. Sorry I dragged you into this, Ash."

I sighed, eyeing the dog warily. "It's not your fault. I would have ended up here with or without your help." I'd already told her all about Nate's less than friendly attitude toward me at our parents wedding, but I'd omitted the crap about Heath. No one needed that info, and truthfully, I didn't trust my own conviction in insisting *nothing* happened. Not after I'd spent a month wishing something more *had*.

"Still..." Carly pinched her nose. "I'll help you clean up, but what are we going to do with the dog?"

I pursed my lips, eyeing the furiously scratching canine. I had no idea where Jade lived, to return the favor, but I did know where Carter lived...

"I can handle the clean-up, if you can deliver the dog somewhere?" I arched a brow at her in question. She'd seemed almost *scared* of Carter earlier, but he'd be an idiot to shoot the messenger.

Carly shrugged. "Sure, I'll grab something to use as a leash. Want me to take her to the pound?"

I smiled wickedly. "Something like that."

She gave me a puzzled look but ducked back to her room to find a temporary leash for the mutt. Not wanting to risk getting bitten, I just stood there watching the canine shed fleas all over my bed until Carly returned, then we spent *way* too long trying to wrestle the feral creature into a diamanté collar-style necklace attached to a silk dress tie.

Once we had her secured, I pulled up Nate's apartment info on my phone—Max had given it to me *just in case*—and wrote it down on a scrap of paper for Carly. Then I scribbled another note for Carter, informing him that his good friend Jade seemed to have misplaced her mutt.

I made sure to sign it with my name, so he would know perfectly well that it was me—not Carly—taking action.

"Here." I handed both notes to Carly. She raised her brows at me in question, then read them and groaned. "Ash...this is a bad idea."

"I'm sure it is, but bullies don't learn from their mistakes if we just roll over and show our bellies. I'm sure Carter will see that the mangy mutt gets sorted out and will drop the dog to the pound too."

Carly scoffed a laugh, then ran a hand through her hair. "Fine. But if this goes pear-shaped—"

"I'll tell them I blackmailed you and you had no choice but to be complicit in my petty affairs," I assured her confidently.

She frowned. "Fuck that, I was going to say if it all goes pear-shaped, we will at least have each other when we get run out of town."

I laughed, not expecting her to become a ride-or-die so quick. I didn't hate it, though. Carly grinned back, then clicked her tongue to the ratty-looking canine, tugging her out of my room with the bedazzled homemade collar and leash.

Once she was gone, I reassessed the mess of my room. It smelled atrocious, so the first thing I did was open the windows for fresh air. Then cleaned up the pile of poo and disposed of it in the trash chute.

With that taken care of, I tackled the rest of the room. Far too much stuff ended up getting tossed into the trash, including my bedding and—to my dismay—two of the model cars I'd built with my dad.

Carly returned an hour later and insisted on helping me clean, so it went fairly quickly, and soon we had the whole room stripped and smelling like lemon disinfectant.

"Thanks for your help," I told her with a yawn as we sat on the now-clean floor. "I have to admit, I thought this kind of prank shit was left behind in high school."

"You didn't have the bitchy mean girls who think they're untouchable at Valley State?" Carly wrinkled her nose with confusion. "I'm jealous. Maybe I should have gone there instead."

I snickered. "As if that was an option for you." She'd already told me about her music industry family and how she'd attended the Grammys with her uncle when she was only sixteen.

"New linen delivery is half an hour away," she informed me, checking her phone. She'd insisted on replacing my destroyed bedding, and I'd accepted because I really didn't want to sleep on a bare mattress tonight and the nearest Walmart had already closed.

"You're the best, Carly," I told her. "But I thought you were planning on attending this party at the lake tonight?"

She nodded. "I am, and I think you should too. The whole reason Jade did this *today* was to stop you going to the party—you know that, right? She is desperate for Carter's attention and after that whole scene this morning, she probably thinks you're a threat."

The snort that I let out was far from elegant, but Jesus fucking Christ, I'd rather sleep with that fleabag stray dog than Carter Bassington Junior.

Okay. That wasn't *totally* true—he was sexy as hell and if he weren't evil and didn't have such a shit personality, I'd go for him in a heartbeat.

"Wouldn't it have already started?" It was after nine already. "Or is it one of those after midnight situations?" Which I was pretty sure didn't actually happen in real life because surely people needed to sleep?

Carly just laughed like I was making a joke. "You're funny. All right, I'm gonna go shower and change. Wear sensible shoes, okay? Too many dumb girls twist their ankle trying to wear heels on sand and grass."

"Fine," I grumbled. "I'll need to shower too and wait for my sheets to arrive. Can I meet you there?"

Carly narrowed her eyes in suspicion. "Nice try. Get ready, I'll let you know when the linen arrives."

She disappeared before I could come up with any more excuses, and I sighed. A cool breeze blew in from the open window and I shivered, remembering that I needed to close it before leaving the room. Just in case.

We'd already dragged my bed away from the window while cleaning, so I wiggled into the gap to reach over and close the heavy old window. Another strong breeze caught it as I started to close it, and the damn thing slammed hard enough to make my teeth clench.

Thankfully, it didn't break, and I flicked the old metal latch to lock it, but as I did so, my toe bumped a loose section of the skirting board.

"Shit," I muttered, leaning down in the tight space to try and push the board back into place. When I couldn't reach, I gave my bed a shove to create more space, then discovered the skirting board wasn't *loose* after all. It was cut. Intentionally.

Someone had created a hiding space. How cool.

Dropping to my knees, excitement and intrigue filled my chest. Would anything be in there? I grasped the cut edges of the board with my fingernails and carefully wiggled it free, then tentatively put my hand inside.

---

> Two weeks after I was initiated into the Devil's Backbone Society, another student went missing. She—like me—was a "randomly" selected initiate. I think she's dead, just like Sarah Black, but there's no evidence. No proof. Everyone is saying she ran off with a boyfriend, but I'm not buying it.
>
> I told one of the other Society members that I wanted out, and he threatened me. That confirmed my fears about the latest disappearance...if I'm not careful, I'll be next. So I decided to start this diary to record all the awful things they're doing. If I'm wrong, I'll destroy it. But if I'm right...

I told one of the other DBs about my plan. About how I was going to keep a record of all the shady shit and piece together the murders that I was sure they were responsible for. I never should have trusted him, but he had a way about him...his eyes were so trustworthy, which sounds weird now that I think about it because they're the oddest shade of dark blue. Or maybe it was his accent that fooled me?

Either way, I told him...and now I regret it. But that won't stop me from writing this diary, not a damn chance. If anything, it's more important now than ever.

---

The last week or so—since telling one of the DB initiates about my diary—has been really weird. Nothing has happened. Nothing sinister, anyway. The weekly meeting on Sunday night was so normal, it has my nerves on edge. Did he tell the leaders I was keeping a record? Were they trying to gaslight me into thinking I'd imagined the danger? I never should have said anything...

---

Someone ransacked my room tonight. The Devil's Backbone had an event that required everyone attend—just a dumb gala thing—but when I got home my whole room was trashed. Even the mattress was ripped open, like whoever had done it was searching for something.

They didn't find this diary, though. Now I know my hiding place is secure and I also know not to trust any of the other DBs.

Something really weird is going on with the DB Society. Everyone acts really chill and calm, pretending like they're doing nothing wrong, but I know what I saw. I know they were responsible for the chapel burning down last night because I saw them do it. Sure, they were in their robes and creepy metal masks so I don't know who exactly lit the match, but it was the DBs for sure.

One of the groundskeepers got badly burned while trying to put out the blaze, yet no one is fessing up. They're all so fake, it makes me sick. I need to report them.

---

I know I should report the DBS. Another student went missing yesterday. They aren't calling it missing though. No, the student withdrew in the middle of the night and moved all their things out without a word. I'm not buying it, but Delaney was different. Delaney had asked me about the DBS. I played dumb but now he's just gone.

I've gone to the administration building three times. My courage always fails. There's always a DB there, one I know. It's someone different each time. Do they know what I want to do? Are they making sure I don't? Break is coming.

Maybe I leave and don't come back.

My induction into the Devil's Backbone Society was utterly terrifying. I was snatched off the street at night, a bag pulled over my head and my hands bound. They threw me into a van and drove us up to Cat's Peak. Then one by one, we had to jump, blindfolded, from the ledge.

Most of us survived. Most...but not all.

---

Devil's Backbone Society like to pretend they're just a bunch of rich kids doing dumb rich kid things...because they're bored. They like to pretend they're not all psychopaths and murderers playing god with the petty mortal lives. Everyone in the Society has enough money to make anything disappear. Anything at all. Even the awful shit that happened at the Founders' Gala. If people knew what they did that night...I wish I had proof that I could share with the world.

# Chapter Eight

A sharp knock on my door startled me, and I nearly dropped the handwritten diary I'd been totally engrossed in, since pulling it out of the loose skirting board. A quick glance at the time told me it'd been more than half an hour and I was still in the same dirty jeans that I'd been wearing when Carly left.

"Come in," I called out, knowing full well she would give me grief for not being party ready but also too excited about the mysterious diary to really care. "Sorry, girl, I think I'm going to stay in tonight. I found this—" I broke off, swallowing my own words as I glanced up and found it was *not* Carly standing in my doorway.

"Hey, Ash," Heath said, leaning one shoulder casually against my door frame. "You've been avoiding me."

I closed the diary with a snap, putting it aside as I rose to my feet. "I'm sorry...have we met?"

A flash of irritation crossed his handsome face before his lips curved in a slight smile. "Cute. Is that what you're wearing?"

"Clothes that are on one's body are generally what that person is wearing, yes," I responded with an eye roll. "Did you need something or are you just darkening my door to announce that your feelings are hurt that I'm not bragging about our imaginary sex life?"

"You're not still upset about that, are you? Come on, Ash, you got paid six grand. What do you care what Nate thinks you did for it?" Heath sighed heavily, like I was boring him.

My eye twitched in anger. "Yes," I drawled with overflowing sarcasm, "how silly of me to be angry that you told your childish buddies that I was a whore…after you only paid me just enough to cover the damage that *your friends* caused to my car. You didn't pay me shit, Heath, you simply covered the costs for your own dumb game."

He shrugged. "Same thing. Come on, get changed into something less…*that*. We're late."

"Late for what?"

"The party at Lake Prosper, of course. I told Carly I'd get you there safely, and you don't want to disappoint your friend, do you?" He tipped his head to the side, watching me far too curiously. This Heath was the one I'd met at Serenity, totally different from the douche at my mom's wedding.

Not interested in his games, I closed the small gap between us and grasped my open door. "Carly's a big girl, she can have fun without me. You can fuck off now, thanks." I pushed the door to close, but Heath just nudged it back with his foot, acting like nothing had happened.

"Come on, Ash. Will it make you feel better if I apologize for lying?" Heath's expression softened with a hint of remorse, and I bit my cheek. Damn him for being so…*ugh*!

"It wouldn't fucking hurt," I muttered, scowling as I folded my arms.

Heath's lips tilted up in a small smile, then he took a large step forward into my personal space, kicking the door shut behind him. "Ash…" he murmured, cupping my face with his hand and tilting my head back so our eyes could meet. *Oh fuck.* "I'm sorry I lied about what happened between us."

*Huh? Oh right. That.* "I appreciate the apology," I responded, frantically trying to calm my racing pulse, "but it'd be better if you told your stupid friends that you lied."

That damn smirk was back on his lips. "Ahhh, but I can't do that. You cashed the check, and no one is going to believe I paid you six grand for nothing. Besides, why do you care what my stupid friends think? You and I know the truth."

Why did I care? Oh yeah, because one of those assholes was now family. "Heath..." His name escaped my lips in a frustrated sigh, and he dipped his head lower, making my breath hitch.

"Ash..." he replied, his thumb stroking over my cheekbone. "Get changed. We're late for the party."

"No." Holy hell, that word was hard to get out with him staring at me like he was about to kiss me. His reaction to my refusal only made it worse as he dragged his lower lip through his teeth.

My whole body heated and my skin tingled. Damn it, why'd he have this effect on me?

"I wasn't asking. You've got five minutes, otherwise we can just go in what you've got on." He released me, stepping back so abruptly I stumbled a little. "I'll wait in the hall."

The door closed softly behind him, and my shoulders sagged dramatically as I exhaled. What in the fuck sort of sorcery was that man working on me? I *badly* didn't want to attend the party now, but equally I was burning with curiosity about why *he* wanted me to go. And since my current clothing smelled of bleach and dog pee, I quickly tore open my closet to find something else to wear.

After the way Carter had manhandled me earlier, I wouldn't put it past Heath to just toss me over his shoulder half-naked so I changed into the first thing I could find—a pair of black cut-off denim shorts and a gray cropped T-shirt that always made me feel cute. Carly had warned against heels, so hopefully that translated into casual dress code. Heath had been in jeans and a tee too, so that gave me some confidence.

Exactly five minutes later as I sat on the edge of my bed to tie my sneaker laces, he let himself back into my room. My gaze locked on his, and for a hot second, we both seemed to freeze...then his appraising eyes took in my clothing before he gave a nod.

"Perfect," he murmured. "Let's go."

Irritation flared in my chest as I rose to my feet. "I don't remember seeking your approval, Heathcliff."

He gave an eye roll, a smirk playing on his lips. "My apologies, I forgot who I was dealing with for a minute there." He held my door open, motioning for me to leave the damn room, and I sighed.

It really wasn't the hardest decision to go with him, considering how curious I was about this insane school. Especially now. Especially after reading the first few diary entries from whoever had previously lived in my room. She—like me—had been at Nevaeh on the Mariah Greenberg scholarship which made me feel weirdly connected to the anonymous writer. I wanted to read more…but I also wanted to see what happened at this party.

Was it the same party that the journal mentioned? The mystery had me hooked, so I didn't protest too hard when Heath led the way across the dark campus with his hand on my lower back.

"Is this the way to the lake?" I asked after we left the university grounds and started down a forest path.

He glanced down at me, his expression hard to make out in the darkness. "No, Ash, I thought I'd take you out to the woods to kill you. Right here behind the Arts Department."

I scowled, not appreciating the sarcasm. "You could try," I muttered, sulking a little because, in fairness, it was a dumb question. "I wouldn't make it quiet or easy."

Heath chuckled, a delicious sound that I really wanted to hate. "I'd expect nothing less. You look like you'd be a screamer."

Oh fucking hell, how the hell did he just manage to make me think about sex *again*? It was a talent, that was for sure. Better to keep my mouth *shut* for the remainder of the walk to the lake which was, thankfully, not much farther. Within minutes, we heard the first sounds of music, and I released a slow breath of relief.

Just as we reached the end of the path, Heath shifted his hand from my back to take my hand in his.

"Heath, what—" I tried to tug my hand free but he had a solid grip, our fingers entwined as he led the way into the crowd of students gathered around the shore of the lake.

"Bro, what the *fuck*...?" someone exclaimed, jerking my attention away from Heath. My gaze zeroed in on the blond hottie who'd arrived at Mom's rehearsal dinner with Heath. What was his name again? It was a car thing...Bentley?

Heath tugged me closer to him, his smile wicked as he shot me a cryptic look. "Ash, babe, I don't know that you met Royce properly at Max and Carina's wedding."

Royce. That was it. He was the one who'd laughed when I insulted them all. Their fourth musketeer with the gorgeous blond hair. After that unpleasant meeting with them, I'd done a little bit of prying and discovered that the three of them—Heath, Carter, and Royce—had all lived with Max and Nate for most of their teenage years.

"You're right, we're nowhere near as well acquainted as you two are," Royce agreed, smirking. "I'm not against it, though. What's the going rate? Six grand?"

I glowered up at Heath, waiting for him to clear the air. He didn't, though, fucking asshole, so I jerked my hand free of his. "I'm *so* flattered, Royce, but I'd rather jump into a pond of starving piranhas while wearing a suit entirely made of bananas. Oh look, there's my friend."

With one last death glare at Heath, I slipped away and went in search of Carly, who I'd just caught the briefest glimpse of near the beer kegs.

"Hey, you made it," she exclaimed when I found her. "Thank *fuck*. I was low-key freaking out that Heath lied about you guys making plans, then equally panicking about whether you thought I was a shit friend for not checking with you first and—"

"You're fine, don't stress," I assured her, cutting off her panic spiral. "He *did* lie, yes. But it's fine. He's very convincing, I get it."

Carly's jaw dropped and her eyes widened in outrage. "That *motherfucker!*"

I shrugged. "No harm done, *this* time. What are you drinking?" I nodded to the plastic cup in her hand.

"Vodka and raspberry lemonade," she informed me. "Want one?"

"Fuck yes," I replied, grinning. It was a party, regardless of how I got there, so I may as well enjoy myself with my friend.

As I waited for Carly to pour my drink, I glanced around and my gaze caught on that of Carter Bassington Junior. He stared back at me, a little smile playing on his lips, then raised his drink to me in a little salute.

A chill ran down my spine. They were up to something—and I wanted no part of whatever it was.

## Chapter Nine

Despite the fact that none of the guys directly approached me for the first few hours of the party, I couldn't shake the feeling that I was being watched the whole damn time. Carly didn't seem to notice, though, so I didn't mention it while we drank and danced together.

Surprisingly, Jade was nowhere to be seen.

"You want another drink?" I asked Carly sometime after midnight when we took a break from dancing, both hot and sweaty even though the air still held a distinct chill.

She shook her head, grinning. "Noooo...but I do want to play beer pong." She pointed in the direction of the full-size outdoor Ping-Pong table someone had set up on the grass near the edge of the woods. The current game looked like it was almost done, with one of the teams vomiting on the grass beside the table.

I winced and shook my head. "Count me out, I value my liver too highly for that. I do need to pee, though..." I cast my gaze around the party, biting the edge of my lip nervously. The feeling of being watched had faded, but maybe that was the alcohol calming me down.

"Ah yeah, there's not really any bathrooms," Carly informed me, assuming I was looking for a toilet. "You need to just pee in the bushes or behind a tree. Want me to stand guard?"

Someone called her name, waving her over to the beer-pong table, and I laughed. "No, I'm fine. You go play. I can pee on my own like a big girl. Especially since my douchebag stepbrother and his friends seem to have disappeared."

Carly wrinkled her nose and nodded. "Yeah, they all left about an hour ago. You sure you don't need me to come with?"

My brows rose with skepticism. "Is there anything in the woods I should be scared of?"

She glanced at her watch, then shook her head. "Nope, you're good. Hurry up, then come back and watch me wipe the floor with these losers." She gestured to the two guys who'd claimed the opposition team spot, and I laughed.

"All right, I'll be back."

Still, I glanced around with caution bordering on paranoia as I left the party and headed into the dark and quiet trees to find a pee spot. I was hardly alone, though, passing several couples engaged in romantic activities which pushed me farther into the woods to avoid ruining their mood.

Once I decided on my spot—far enough away to avoid being a voyeur—I took care of business and squatted for a minute to drip dry. The several vodka raspberry lemonades I'd had while dancing had made my head spin, and when I stood up to fix my pants, the world tilted somewhat.

"Whoa," I murmured, my vision blurring a moment. "That… probably means it's time for bed."

Bracing a hand on a tree, I closed my eyes for a moment and took a deep breath. I'd drunk way too much and already regretted it. My hangovers were never fun, so tomorrow looked grim.

"Okay, Ash, pull it together." I sighed and opened my eyes once more, blinking into the darkness. In the distance, I could hear voices so used them as my guide to find my way back…since apparently I'd gone farther into the trees than I'd initially intended.

As I drew closer to the conversation I hesitated. This close to the party, I should've been able to see the lights and hear music but there was none of that. Just a few voices in the darkness ahead and nothing more.

"...just got the most irritating voice," one of the guys said as I took a few cautious steps closer. "If it weren't for her being in the DB Society, I'd have put her in her place by now."

I froze, huddling behind a tree. DB Society? The same one mentioned in the diary?

Wait...that was Carter who was speaking, his accent unmistakable. Who was he talking about? Jade maybe?

"That and because of how she could suck a golf ball through a garden hose," someone else said, chuckling. Classy guys.

"That too," Carter agreed. "Speaking of which, how's Ashley's head game, Heath? Worth the money?"

Oh fuck, I hadn't returned to the party at all. I'd instead stumbled across some kind of private guy chat further into the forest. Knowing my luck, it would be all four of them ahead, and I'd have yet another uncomfortable encounter with Nate and his bad attitude.

Still...this was Heath's opportunity to set the record straight. Right?

"What do you think?" he replied to his friend, giving a smug laugh, and my heart sank. So much for redeeming himself.

"I think you're a fucking idiot," someone snarled, and it only took me a moment to place Nate's voice. "It was one thing to prove she's a whore like her gold-digging mom but you're taking it too far showing up at the party with her. Do you have any idea what people are saying?"

"Yep," Heath replied, unapologetic, "that she's my girlfriend. Fun, huh?"

*What the fuck? Because he was holding my hand when we arrived? Great, just great.*

"But she's not," Carter corrected, "so what are you hoping to gain out of this game, Heathcliff?"

*My thoughts exactly, Carter.*

"Aren't we supposed to be discussing this year's initiate prospects, not staging an intervention for Heath's poor financial investments?" That was Royce, surprisingly reasonable and spiking my curiosity again.

Listening to them talk shit about my fictional sex work was interesting and all, but I wanted to hear more about this secret society that the diary in my room mentioned. The Devil's Backbone Society. They were all clearly involved somehow.

"Are we inducting Ashley?" Carter asked and I needed to clap a hand over my mouth to keep from gasping. "She's an Essex now, after all, and legacy dictates—"

"She is *not* an Essex," Nate spat with palpable venom. "Neither is Carina, no matter what the marriage certificate says. She doesn't get a free pass into the DBs just because my dad is cuntstruck."

My jaw dropped. What a vile shit, Nate was. Mom and Max always spoke so highly of him and this was the crap he said behind their backs?

"Okay but she's also the only scholarship student in postgrad so…" Carter was pushing the issue for some reason, and it made me anxious.

"I said *no*, Bass," Nate snarled. "End of conversation."

A tense silence followed Nate's proclamation, then someone sighed. "Okay so where does that leave us?"

"Ava Morales, Lukas Hart, Zara Liu, Emma Ramirez, Isla Camden, and Simon Brooks." Heath rattled off six names of people I didn't know.

"It'll do," Nate said in a stubborn-fuck tone. "We can always induct more later if they prove worthy."

Another silence gave me the feeling not all of his friends were in agreement, but they also weren't pushing back.

"What do you want to do with them?" Royce asked. "Glass coffin? Ice plunge?"

"Cat's Peak," Nate replied. "It hasn't been done in a few years, and it always weeds out the sniveling time-wasters."

I bit my lip, thinking of the mysterious diary in my room. The author mentioned Cat's Peak in conjunction with someone's death, hadn't she?

"I'll set it up," Royce agreed.

"Heathcliff, you're on acquisitions," Nate ordered, clearly the one in charge out of this crew. "Bass, you—"

"Need to deal with the dog?" the smoking-hot Brit replied in a sarcastic drawl. "Four-legged one, I mean. Jade has already been put in her place."

Nate scoffed. "Overkill if you ask me. It was a harmless prank on the new girl."

"*After* I'd told her to back off," Carter added, "which means her harmless prank was in direct violation of orders."

"Yeah, well, that part couldn't go unpunished I guess," Nate muttered, sounding sour. What a dick. I almost suspected he was the one who'd put the idea in Jade's head to begin with. Maybe I needed to talk to Max about him...

Someone said something too quietly for me to make out, and the other guys laughed. The whole mood had shifted and they started joking around, sounding a shitload more relaxed. It made me painfully aware how long I'd been hiding there, eavesdropping on them. I needed to get my ass back to the party before I got caught.

Holding my breath, I took a slow, careful step away from the tree I'd been lurking behind. Hopefully in the direction of the party. Instantly, a branch snapped under my foot and I froze.

"What was that?" Heath asked sharply.

Fuck. I was so totally fucked. I really didn't want to investigate what they might do if they caught me spying, especially seeing as they were so clearly involved in a secret society or some shit. As silently as possible I shrank back against the tree once more and prayed to gods I didn't believe in that I was hidden.

"Probably just an animal," Carter drawled, sounding bored and tired, "or a branch falling off a tree. Nature, bro."

"Go check," Nate ordered in a snap. "Last thing we need is someone spoiling initiation night by reporting us."

Someone sighed heavily and the crunch of leaves indicated they were closer. I squeezed my eyes shut tight, holding my breath and wishing myself invisible then right when I thought they spotted me, the steps stopped.

"There's no one here!" Royce yelled back to the other guys. "Just a squirrel, you paranoid fuckers."

He sounded so close, I couldn't help but open my eyes to check. Sure enough, he was about three feet in front of me, looking out into the darkness and his back toward me. Holy shit, maybe I was well concealed after all.

"All right let's get out of here," Nate called back.

"I'll swing back past the party," Royce announced over his shoulder, his head tilted in a way I was sure he might see me. "I'll catch up later."

The other guys exchanged a few words as they exited their meeting place in the woods, their voices quickly fading away…yet Royce didn't move. It wasn't until a car engine started up that he sighed and turned around.

"Hello, little squirrel," he murmured, meeting my eyes with pinpoint accuracy despite the darkness. "How much of that did you hear?"

Words failed me as my racing pulse threatened to choke me out. So I just shook my head and tried to breathe normally.

"Hmm, I see…" He stepped closer, closing the gap between us and forcing me to tilt my head back in order to keep my eyes on him. The full moon cast just enough light that his features weren't entirely in shadow but it was still eerie as fuck. "Cat got your tongue tonight, beautiful?"

He reached out and trailed a finger down the side of my face, sending a deep shiver through my body. Fear or something else, I wasn't altogether sure.

"Just cautious not to incriminate myself," I replied, my voice husky and quivering. Nervous. "I got lost, that's all."

He didn't immediately reply, just tilted his head to the side like he was weighing my honesty. Frustratingly, his expression gave nothing away about what he was thinking, and I fought the urge to fidget nervously.

"Well, we can't have that," he finally said in a quiet voice. "I'll help you find your way, little squirrel."

Not offering me a choice in the matter, he snagged my hand in his and tugged me away from the tree in a move that made me gasp in surprise. I stumbled as I hurried to keep up when he strode confidently into the darkness of the forest like he had an inbuilt GPS system.

"Royce, what the hell? Where are you taking me?" I was already out of breath, which said more about my fitness level than his effect on me. I think.

He didn't slow down but cast an amused glance over his shoulder at me anyway. "I'm not leaving you out in these woods alone, lost, and inebriated, Ashley. Think what you want of my friends, but I'm not an asshole."

Then he paused, stopping so abruptly I collided with his back. "Ow, what—?"

"Okay, that wasn't a true statement," he admitted. "I'm definitely an asshole. But I'm not the kind of asshole who knowingly leaves a damsel in distress, feel me?"

He quirked a brow in question, and I was confused—and drunk—enough to simply nod in response.

That seemed to satisfy him, though, and he continued his brisk march in silence until we popped out of the tree line and I looked around with a puzzled frown.

"This isn't the lake party, Royce."

"Oh good, you're not blind. Can you make it back to your dorm from here or do I need to come up and tuck you in? I should warn you, I'm not as generous as moneybags Briggs so couldn't pay *quite* that much..." He tilted his head to the side, running his gaze over me in a leering way. "Then again, maybe you'd be worth going into debt for..."

I rolled my eyes. "Fuck you, Royce. I think you know Heath is full of shit."

Royce just shrugged. "I take that as a no, then?" He pointed across the dark lawn. "There's your building. Off you go, little squirrel."

Too many vodka-raspberries meant no snappy comebacks sprang to mind, so rather than stand there looking up at him, I shook my head and started toward my dorm.

"Oh, by the way," he called after me. "Whatever you think you heard tonight...forget it. It's in your best interest, Ashley."

I paused, spinning around to confront him about this secret society nonsense, but to my shock, he was gone. Just...disappeared into thin air. What the *fuck*? Maybe he was right. I'd had more than enough to drink for one night.

# Chapter Ten

I woke up Saturday morning with a hangover and a head full of questions. To my palpable relief, I hadn't imagined the diary. It was right where I'd left it before the party, tucked in my desk drawer just waiting to be read.

But first...shower. I smelled of dirt and sweat, and I needed to check on Carly to ensure she'd got home safely. It wasn't like me to abandon someone at a party, but after the weird interaction with Royce, I'd crashed out hard.

"What?" she snarled when I knocked on her door after my lengthy shower.

I smiled, feeling a whole lot fresher and reassured she was alive. "Just me!"

A grunt, then the door swung open to reveal a sleepy Carly, hair sticking up all over the place. "Get in here," she ordered, wincing at the sound of her own voice.

I did as I was told, closing the door behind me as Carly crawled back into her tangled sheets.

"You look good," she mumbled with her cheek in the pillow and one eye cracked. "Why do you look so good? Did we drink different vodka last night?"

"I wish." I chuckled, sitting down on her desk chair and pulling my knees up. "I feel like shit, I just *look* better than you because I showered already. You should think about doing the same."

Carly narrowed her one eye at me. "You saying I smell bad or something?"

"Like a fucking sewer, girlfriend. But also, I came to say sorry for ditching you last night. That was a dick move, and I solemnly swear it will never happen again." I held three fingers up in a pledge and Carly snorted a laugh.

"You're not a fucking Scout, Ash. And don't stress it, I was totally fine. Got my ass handed to me in beer pong, vomited in the lake, then Michelle from six-sixteen helped me stagger home. I heard *you* had an interesting night, though." She pushed up from her pillow, grinning wolfishly at me.

Memories of the private conversation I'd listened in on crossed my mind, but that couldn't be what she meant. Could it?

"Um…did I?" I bit the inside of my cheek, frowning as I tried to remember what else had happened after I left her.

Carly's brows lifted. "So you *weren't* seen making out with Royce beside Essex Hall? Rumor mill says things were pretty hot and heavy. You know he's best friends with Heath, though, right?"

Outrage flushed my face hot and my jaw dropped. "That *motherfucker!*" I barely got the words out, my throat so tight with anger. "I wasn't—"

"Girl, it's cool. I'm not judging. I just want the gossip so I can live vicariously," Carly replied with an easy grin, clearly misinterpreting my anger. "Unless you suddenly have a lapse in sanity and hook up with Nate. That…I don't wanna know."

I gagged. "I'd rather lobotomize myself. But we need to clear the air. I was *not* hooking up with Royce last night. Not even close. It didn't even cross my mind." Okay…maybe once. But that had been the vodka messing with my head.

Carly wrinkled her nose. "I'm confused. Why are people

talking like you were getting dicked down against the side of a building?"

I threw my hands in the air, furious. "I don't know! I got lost in the woods after I peed and then Royce escorted me back to campus. That's it."

She stared at me in confusion for a moment, then blinked slowly. "You peed with Royce? Is that a kink thing?"

"What? No!" But how did I explain the missing information about listening in on their conversation, getting caught, and Royce covering for me? It was a lot. And my head was pounding. "Uh, this is insane. First Heath lies about what happened between us, now Royce? What's wrong with these guys? They all have erectile dysfunction that they're too embarrassed to seek help for so instead just make shit up?"

Carly snickered, collapsing back into her pillow. "I dare you to ask them that. No, wait, forget I said that, you'd totally do it."

I would too.

"Okay, this has made me big mad. I'm going to grab coffee and something to help my stomach. You coming?" I extended my leg and nudged her with my toe, making her moan in dramatic pain. "Or I *suppose* I can bring something back for you."

"You're a fucking saint, Ashley Layne," she informed me with a wide, sleepy grin.

I rolled my eyes. "Sure. Just do us both a favor and shower while I'm gone. It smells like beer and vomit in here."

"Ew."

"Agree. Back soon." Leaving her room, I stopped by mine to grab my purse with my wallet and phone. Then at the last minute, I grabbed the mysterious diary as well. Sometimes Dancing Goats had a pretty long wait for coffee so I could get some more reading in.

As predicted, the line to order was out the door, and I sighed as I joined the end of it. I'd tested out the coffee at the one other campus café, and it tasted worse than dirty bathwater...so I'd grudgingly wait in line, knowing it'd be worth it.

"Good morning, gorgeous," a voice purred behind me, and I paid no notice as I assumed they weren't talking to me. Until a large hand rested on the small of my back and a large body sidled up against me. "You don't mind me cutting the line here, do you, Ash?"

"Actually, I do." I glanced behind us at the half-dozen people who'd joined the queue behind. "This guy is cutting the line!" I told them.

No one responded. Hell, they all looked like they were trying *not* to look our way at all.

"Did you enjoy yourself last night?" Heath asked, as though I hadn't just tried to get him kicked out of line.

I folded my arms and huffed an irritated sound, refusing to look up at him. "If you're talking about the party, yes. If you're talking about the bullshit rumor that I made out with Royce, then you and your smug crap can go jump off a cliff."

Heath's fingers flexed on the small of my back, and he made a small sound of…surprise? "You did *what* with Royce?"

I rolled my eyes. "Absolutely fucking nothing. I don't know if he started the rumor himself or if someone else was drunk and *thought* that's what they saw, but—" I broke off with a frustrated growl. "Why am I explaining this to you? If you hadn't lied in the first place, I wouldn't be in this mess."

"Is it really such a mess, having people you don't know think you're romantically entangled with one or two of Nevaeh's most influential students?" His voice was so neutral that I tilted my head to peer up at him. Still, his gaze gave nothing away. I don't know why I'd expected anything more.

Annoyed, I clicked my tongue and turned my attention back to the slowly moving queue ahead. We were almost inside the shop now, so that was a plus. "Why are you here, Heath? My hangover doesn't have the patience for mind games."

"I want coffee," he replied, sliding that hand on my back around to my waist. Holding me like we were some kind of couple. "And the line looked really long, so I cut in with you."

"How convenient," I muttered.

Heath sighed, his breath ruffling my hair like he was looking down at me. I was steadfastly staring at the counter ahead and trying to ignore him, but fuck, it was hard.

"Look, I didn't know about this Royce rumor. He's still dead asleep and I haven't spoken to him since last night. He's also not the type to make shit up, so my guess is that someone else is responsible. Were you even with him last night?"

I almost admitted *yes* but then I might be treading too close to telling him I'd been eavesdropping on their secret society business. So I deflected, instead.

"Oh, he wouldn't make that shit up, huh? I guess that's more your wheelhouse. Why *are* you lying about us again?"

He shrugged, his shoulder bumping me lightly. "Reasons. You know people stop making up rumors when they have some irrefutable truth to run with."

"People need to stop fucking caring what I'm doing. Is it a scholarship student thing?" I glanced around, and couldn't help but admit more than one set of eyes were on us.

Heath laughed quietly. "Something like that. They'll quit speculating if you have a boyfriend…"

I barked a laugh, unable to help myself. The sound was so loud, I drew a whole lot *more* attention and my cheeks flamed as I clapped a hand over my mouth. Bloody hell.

"Are you offering?" My voice was pure sarcasm, but his lips tilted in a lopsided smile and his magnetic gaze captured mine.

"Absolutely yes. But I get the feeling we got off on the wrong foot, so I won't push the issue." He winked, then shifted his gaze away as we moved forward to the front of the line. "Hi, can I please get a quad shot americano, a white chocolate mocha with dark chocolate drizzle, and a salted caramel latte with an extra shot and cookie crumb?" He glanced at me, thinking, then continued, "And two grilled cheese sandwiches."

Surprise held me immobile as Heath paid for the order, then guided me to the side to wait. "Uh...why do you know my coffee order? And Carly's for that matter?"

Heath just grinned. "I have eyes and ears everywhere, Ash."

That was a splash of ice water in my face. It reminded me that he was somehow involved in a secret society which—according to the diary I'd found—had killed people.

"I see," I murmured.

To my relief, some guy I didn't recognize came up to talk to Heath and I was spared the awkwardness of small talk while we waited for our order. Instead, I wandered away and perched on a stool by the window to read.

Just like when I found it, the diary instantly sucked me in. The author's writing wasn't necessarily the *best*, jumping all over the place and leaving out what felt like key information, but there was enough there to hook me.

*...my name, in case you want to do your research, is Abigail Monstera. I'm twenty-one, and I come from Whispering Willows, California.*

"What are you reading?" Heath asked, making me startle enough that I dropped the diary.

His hands were full of our coffees and food, yet somehow he still managed to put it all down and scoop up the book before I could react.

"Nothing," I snapped, grabbing it out of his hands so quickly he squinted at me with suspicion. *Way to make it weird, Ash.* "It's, um, just personal."

He arched a brow, lips tilted in another grin. "Smutty romance, huh? No judgment here, I'm a fan of them myself, but I'm more of an audiobook kind of guy, you know?"

*What the fuck is happening? Why is he flirting with me?*

"Uh-huh. Well, thanks for the coffee." I stuffed the diary into my bag and picked up the tray with mine and Carly's order, then Heath handed me one of the grilled cheese sandwiches in a paper bag.

"Think about what I said, Ash. You're a new, shiny toy right now but people will let up if you're *claimed*." He dipped low and brushed a kiss over my cheek before I could pull away. "It was nice to see you. Have a great weekend."

I watched him saunter out of the coffee shop with that confident, sexy swagger of his and I was painfully aware that I wasn't the only one watching him leave. The man was sexy as hell, and he damn well knew it. But what the hell was that cozy interaction all about if he was telling me to get a boyfriend?

Grumbling under my breath about his head games, I made my way back to my dorm with the free coffee. It wasn't until after I delivered Carly's to her, then tucked back into bed with the diary that I realized what felt so strange about seeing Heath.

He didn't live on campus. And there were much better, much less crowded coffee shops a lot closer to his apartment building. Had he spent the night with someone in the dorms?

Ugh, why did that thought sour my mood so dramatically? I didn't even like the guy.

# Chapter Eleven

The rest of my Saturday was spent reading, then rereading the mysterious diary. Learning all about the previous tenant of my dorm room, Abigail Monstera, and her experiences with the Devil's Backbone Society. All the horrible things she'd witnessed, and then the things that happened to her...until it cut off abruptly some six months after she started keeping the record.

I fell asleep plagued by curiosity about what'd happened to her, sick with anxiety that this society was very much a real thing at Nevaeh and Heath was a part of it.

It irritated me to no end that Heath was wearing me down. My anger at his lies was already cooling, and he had a good point that I *didn't* care what Nate thought. But knowing he was mixed up in this Devil's Backbone Society had my nerves frayed. How shit was my judge of character?

Waking up Sunday morning, I knew I needed to do my research to find out more about Abigail and the DBS. For all I knew, she'd just gotten bored keeping a diary or she'd gotten expelled from the school or...any number of other innocent reasons why she'd left it the way she did. She'd even written she might leave... Hell, I couldn't be sure she wasn't writing some weird kind of fiction. But I definitely wanted to know more.

As I did most mornings, I grabbed my toiletries basket, a towel, and made my way down the hall to the communal bathroom. I was up early so had the whole place to myself and took advantage of the opportunity to wash my hair while no one was rushing me.

Once done, I roughly dried my hair, then wrapped myself in my towel to head back to my room. I'd tried taking clean clothes into the bathroom with me a couple of times but somehow they *always* got wet and literally everyone else on the floor just did the dash in a towel, so I'd adapted.

Stepping back inside my room, though, I instantly regretted my choice.

"What the fuck are you doing in here?" I demanded, glaring death at my intruder and clutching my towel tighter.

Nate's eyes narrowed in a menacing glare as he rose from my desk chair where he'd apparently made himself right at home. My class notes were open on the desk like he'd been looking through them, and I frantically glanced around to see if I'd left the diary out. I didn't see it, though. Wait, I'd tucked it under bed last night before I fell asleep. *Thank fuck.*

"A guy can't visit his new stepsister?" he sneered, full of hatred for my mere presence in his life. "You've been at my college for a whole week now, Layne, and you've yet to say hello? I'm offended."

I scoffed. "If I were trying to offend you, Essex," I replied, taking his obvious cue in using surnames rather than first. De-personalizing the man in front of me. "Then I'd put in a little more effort than simply ignoring your existence."

His lips tightened in obvious anger. "You're not ignoring my friends, though, are you? First you fuck Heathcliff for six grand, which admittedly was just a business transaction, but then I hear you've been fooling around with both Royce *and* Carter? How hard up for money *are* you, Layne? Doesn't my dad give you enough of an allowance to quit your whoring ways? Stay the *fuck* away from them."

My jaw dropped in shock, but I quickly recovered with a wave of nearly blinding rage at this entitled son of a bitch.

"Jealous, Nate? Is your fragile ego bruised because you're being ignored? Aw...baby...don't be like that," I gave an exaggerated pout as I moved closer to him, tucking my towel tighter around me. His eyes widened with obvious confusion as I batted my lashes in the most sultry way I could manage. "If you wanted me to touch your dick, you just had to ask nicely."

Before he could move away in suspicion at my whiplash change of personality, I dropped my fist low and slammed it into his groin as hard as I could from the short distance. It landed as intended, causing him to give a strangled noise as he doubled over in pain, his face turning purple.

"That one was for free, *brother*, since you could never afford me. Now get the fuck out of my room and don't come back again." I gave his shoulder a condescending pat since he was still doubled over, then gave him a firm shove out into the corridor.

He stumbled, noises like choked curses escaping his enraged face, but I slammed the door and locked it before he could cause a scene. *No, thank you.*

For a moment I stood frozen, one hand against the door and the other holding my towel, but Nate didn't come back. After a short while, I pressed my ear to the door and tried to hear if he was still out there, but it was total silence. Had he accepted defeat and left?

Unable to control my own curiosity, I opened the door a crack to peek out. Sure enough, the hallway was deserted as though I'd imagined the whole toxic interaction.

*Weird.*

Closing the door once more, I drew a deep breath. The sudden rush of adrenaline had my hands shaking, so I needed to get a grip. By the time I finished getting dressed and brushed the tangles from my hair, I was mostly calm...if still irate at Nate's accusations.

Now I was supposedly fooling around with Carter too? Presumably this was an assumption drawn entirely from that short interaction when he peeled me off Jade. Damn, I really did get around in this fictional world everyone seemed to live in.

With a sigh, I dropped to my knees to fish out the diary from under my bed...but it wasn't there.

"What the fuck?" I muttered, frowning as I got low enough to see, then used my phone flashlight to light up the space. The *empty* space.

A chill flashed through me, but I immediately tried to reason with my own logic. Maybe I'd left it in my bed? Or on my desk? Or... somewhere else. Maybe I didn't put it under the bed, after all?

Ten minutes later, I'd ripped my room to shreds and confirmed once and for all...the diary was gone.

With shaking hands, I found my phone and scrolled through my mom's messages to find where she sent me Nate's contact card. I'd never bothered to save it because I never wanted to make nice, but this...this required immediate attention.

He didn't answer, which only pissed me off more. After redialing five times, and being sent to voicemail five times, my phone dinged with a text message.

NATHANIEL ESSEX:

> Who the fuck is this?

My eye twitched. I was so infuriated. I tried calling again, but he declined.

Drawing a deep breath I typed out my reply.

ASHLEY:

> Your conscience, dickwad.

Almost immediately, my phone rang with an incoming call from him.

"I don't *have* a conscience, Layne."

I rubbed my eyes to keep from rolling them so hard, they'd likely fall out of my head. "No shit. I need you to return what you stole, Nate."

A short pause met my request, then he made a thoughtful hum. "As fun as it would be to mess with you, Layne, I don't have the time or patience."

"What the fuck does that mean?" I snapped. "Give the diary back, Essex, or I'll—"

"You'll *what*, Layne? Hmm? You'll punch me in the dick again?" He sounded *big* mad at that, and my lips twitched with satisfaction.

Stifling a laugh, I sat heavily on the edge of my bed. "Once is enough. I'll just tell Max what an entitled, rude, antagonistic piece of shit you are. Maybe I'll tell him all about how you keyed my car then tried to set me up to sleep with Heath? He seems like a reasonable guy, your dad. I bet he'd look into those accusations. Then what, Nate? You don't seem like the sort who has his own stream of income…what happens when Daddy cuts you off, I wonder?"

Another pause. Then a grunt of what seemed like surprise. "You're a real piece of work, Layne."

"The feeling is mutual, Essex. Now give me back the diary you stole."

He exhaled sharply. "I didn't take anything from your room, so don't worry. Your dirty little secrets that you confess to your diary are safe wherever you left the damn thing."

Before I could snap back that I didn't believe him, he ended the call.

"Mother*fucker*!" I screamed, just barely resisting the urge to throw my phone at the wall. I really couldn't afford to buy a new one just to vent my anger.

Chewing the edge of my lip, I looked around my room once

more. Had he taken it? My head said yes, unequivocally yes. But there was something *different* about his voice after I threatened to tattle on him to Max. He wasn't fucking around anymore. Would he call my bluff over something like this?

My gut said no. Which left me with the question of *where* the diary was. I'd upended my room; it was definitely gone. So if Nate hadn't taken it...who had? And when?

With that uncomfortable feeling sitting on my shoulders, I grabbed my bag and headed out to the Nevaeh campus library. Maybe I didn't have the diary itself anymore, but I'd read it more than once. I had enough of the information stored in my brain to do some research, starting with Abigail herself and then I'd dive into the DBS itself.

Thankfully, being early on a Sunday, the library wasn't crowded, and I made myself comfortable at one of the study desks near the yearbooks to pull out my laptop. The internet in the library was a shitload quicker than in the dorms and I was quietly scared of another Nate run-in if I stayed in my room. Besides, I was in the right place if Google let me down.

Biting my lip, I typed in Abigail's name. Then hesitated a moment before hitting enter.

My stomach sank as the search results popped up. First on the list...her obituary.

"Fuck..." I breathed, a strange level of grief washing though me. After reading her diary all weekend, really immersing myself inside her head, I felt like I knew her. And now she was dead.

Sniffing back the tears threatening to fall, I forced myself to read through the paltry handful of local news articles touching on the tragic death of a Nevaeh University student. It'd happened during spring break while most of the school was deserted. One of the cleaning staff had found Abigail's body floating in Lake Placid and her death was ruled as suicide.

*Bullshit.* Abigail was *not* suicidal.

Oh man. She'd gotten killed by the Devil's Backbone Society. I could just sense it in my gut. After everything she wrote, all her fears...

I swallowed hard, my mind whirling. The one shred of hope I clung to was the possibility Abigail's diary was entirely fictional. Maybe she'd been suffering a mental condition and hallucinating? That could explain her death by suicide in the end...

"Are you okay?" someone asked, making me startle and look up from the screen I'd been laser focused on.

"Heath. What...what are you doing here?" I frowned, glancing around. Had I somehow summoned him by researching Abigail's death? He was in the Devil's Backbone Society, after all. That much had been clear in the woods during the lake party.

He placed a coffee down on the table and I gave it a slow blink. Again, it was my order.

"I accidentally ordered one of these and it's way too sweet. How do you drink that shit?" His eyes sparkled with amusement; his lips tilted in an easy smile. It was a sexy look on him, and it only served to remind me of Nate's visit to my room. How he'd warned me to leave his friends alone. "Anyway, I figured you could use some caffeine to get through whatever put that frown on your face. See ya."

Heath started to walk away, his own laptop bag over his shoulder, and I made a snap decision. "Wait," I blurted out. "I worked out how you can make it up to me."

He spun back to face me, one brow arched. "Oh?"

I nodded quickly. "Yep. Congratulations, Heathcliff, you just became my boyfriend." Because not only would it *infuriate* Nate, it would possibly offer me some insight into the Devil's Backbone Society.

Heath's eyes widened. "Um..."

"In name only, of course, I'm not actually interested in dating you." *Liar, liar, pants on fire.*

His lips curled into a grin. "Fake dating? I love that trope. Count me in."

# Chapter Twelve

Heath took our new arrangement seriously. Too seriously. Rather than leaving our fake dating to start on Monday, he dragged over a chair and made himself comfortable opposite me at my study table. When I asked what the fuck he was doing, he just shrugged and told me all about his homework, which almost bored me to tears.

It definitely made me too cautious to continue my Devil's Backbone Society research, though, and I reluctantly swapped to my own classwork, which also needed my attention.

When I was done, Heath insisted on walking me back to my dorm with his arm slung around my shoulders.

"I get the feeling you're enjoying this," I muttered as we approached my building.

He glanced down at me with a smirk. "I am."

I rolled my eyes. "I'm still not going to sleep with you. This is purely to stop the gossip…and piss Nate off."

Heath chuckled. "And I'm totally fine with those reasons. But maybe you'll change your mind when you get to know me. I'll have you know, I'm very good in bed."

That claim made me scoff. "Anyone who needs to announce

they're good in bed…is not. But it's cute that someone clearly cared enough to lie to you."

I hitched my bag higher on my shoulder and started to walk away since we were only a few paces from the main entrance of my dorm, but Heath grabbed my hand and hauled me back with an abrupt move.

"What—"

My startled protest was cut short as his lips met mine and my whole brain turned to static. Holy *fuck*. It was exactly as hot as I'd remembered, kissing Heath. A pathetic little moan escaped me as I melted into his grip, his mouth engulfing me as his hand splayed across my lower back to hold me tight. All sense fled my brain and I kissed him back, letting our tongues dance in the sexiest kind of way.

Eventually—far too slowly—better sense prevailed, and I peeled myself away with my palms against his chest.

"Heath," I gasped, short of breath and more than a little dizzy. "What the fuck was that?"

His lips curved in a sly grin that did unspeakable things to my insides. "Just selling the story, babe. I'll catch you later." He released me, then smacked my ass before swaggering away.

I stood there a moment, blinking stupidly in shock, then pulled my shit together and turned back to my dorm. That was when I spotted Jade peering out of a window on the first floor. So…Heath was just making sure she spread the word about us dating? Maybe?

Ugh, what was I thinking? This was an awful idea.

The damage was done now, though, I had no doubt Jade probably already spread the word. She seemed like the type.

With a sigh, I climbed the three flights of stairs to my room and opted to stay in for the rest of my Sunday. At least in my own room I could Google the *crap* out of everything Abigail had outlined in her diary, without anyone around to interrupt with their sultry, dark-lashed eyes and broad shoulders.

Trouble was, without the diary to refer to I needed to rely on my memory for the finer details and names mentioned. In some cases, my search keywords were so vague it gave me absolutely *nothing* but in other cases—like the death of Sarah Black—it generated actual news articles. Finer details weren't included, they never were, but there was enough fact to support Abigail's version of events. A girl had "jumped" to her death off Cat's Peak, the lookout near the top of Prosper Mountain. Several students had served as eyewitness to the "suicide" and given statements, but their names weren't released.

It gave me chills. It'd only happened three years ago. Was Heath a part of the Devil's Backbone that year? Had he been one of the witnesses?

I desperately wanted to know more, but every part of me screamed that it was a bad idea. That I needed to stay *far, far away* from the whole society. If they were killing students then, what about previous years? Surely it wouldn't be an isolated incident?

What about this year? Wasn't Cat's Peak something that Nate had spoken about in the woods while I eavesdropped? Holy shit, my new stepbrother might be a murderer.

My research took a deep dive into all the Nevaeh University student fatalities in the past ten years and found countless *suspicious* deaths. All of them were either suicide or accidental. It was way too many to be a coincidence.

Once again, my search ventured back onto the society as a whole, but the results were limited. Suspiciously limited.

Eventually I needed to stop and close my laptop because my head was spinning and my stomach ached from anxiety.

Thanks to all the conspiracy theories buzzing through my brain, I found it harder than usual to fall asleep which was probably why I woke so easily when my door clicked open…despite me having locked it.

My eyes opened, adrenaline surging through my chest as a large figure slipped into my room and crossed the floor in two strides.

I gasped, drawing a breath in preparation for a scream but before

I could get it out, the intruder clapped a hand over my mouth. A gloved hand, giving nothing away, and I found myself staring into a full-face, metallic, skull-like mask. Whoever had broken into my room was hooded, the shadows concealing his eye color while the mask concealed everything else.

"Shhhh," he ordered, then a moment later removed his gloved hand only long enough to stuff a wad of fabric into my mouth. Stupid me, I was shocked enough that I didn't think to clench my teeth until it was too late. "That's better," he murmured, and his voice flickered recognition despite how quietly he'd spoken.

Nate?!

I lashed out, trying to fight back as he used a belt to hold the gag in my mouth but I was all tangled up in my sheet and he by far held the upper hand in strength. Unless I wanted to get seriously hurt, he *was* going to win this round.

Moments later he dragged me out of my bed with an unnecessarily firm grip on my upper arm, bound my hands, then deposited a black hood over my head to totally obliterate sight and yanked a cord to tighten it just this side of choking me. Overkill, in my opinion, but all of a sudden the chill of familiarity ran down my spine.

Was this what Abigail had talked about? The initiation she went through? Surely not, Nate had been absolutely adamant that I was a Layne and *not* an Essex, therefore had no place in his dumb shit secret society. So why would he have changed his mind so quickly? That conversation had only been two nights ago.

Unable to speak or see, and with my wrists bound tightly at my back, I stumbled as he pushed me forward and braced for impact with my door. It never came, though, and the change of carpet texture told me when we crossed into the hallway.

Rather than pushing me down the three flights of stairs—like I halfway expected—Nate muttered some curses, then picked me up in a fireman's hold to carry me down to ground level.

If I'd been able to speak, I would be taunting him and tossing insults. But as it was I could do nothing more than silently hope this was all an elaborate hazing ritual rather than the more sinister option of Devil's Backbone initiation.

When he finally let me down, it was less of a gentle set down and more of a sack of potatoes being tossed into the back of a truck. It *hurt* and all my pent-up frustration and rage bubbled out as muffled noises from behind my gag. *What a dick.* I'd known he was capable of bullying, but this was a whole step further.

The rumble of a car starting confirmed my suspicion that he was driving me somewhere, but the cold and wind indicated I was in an open tray. So now I needed to hope and pray he didn't drive like a lunatic en route to wherever we were going and kill me in a car crash.

I passed the time by counting seconds in my head, counting them into minutes. It wasn't the most precise way to keep time, but by the time I reached twenty-three the car slowed to a stop.

A car door slammed, boots crunched on gravel, then the metallic clunk of the tailgate lowering indicated it was time to get out.

I didn't move.

"For fuck's sake," Nate muttered, sounding all kinds of irritated. The audacity of him, as though *he'd* been abducted from his bed? "Layne, don't be a bitch. Get out."

*Eat a dick, Essex.*

Huh. Maybe this was payback for the junk punch?

When my only movement was to shuffle further away from his voice, he gave an angry grunt. The tray beneath me dipped with his weight as he climbed up, then wrapped a gloved hand around my ankle and *yanked*.

I let out a strangled yelp—totally muffled of course—as my head smacked against the metal truck bed and Nate hauled me out by my ankle. Like a hunting prize.

"Fucking get on your feet and walk, Layne, or I swear to god I will drag you up this path by your hair," he growled as I tumbled out of the truck and onto the gravel. I'd been sleeping in just a T-shirt and panties, so there was nothing to prevent the grazes on my legs as I hit hard.

I wanted to tell him to kiss my ass, but the fear had taken root in my chest already. Nate wasn't messing around as payback for a nut punch, he was dead serious. He also gave zero fucks if I got hurt along the way, so for my own safety, I got cautiously to my feet.

"Finally," he snapped. "Nice to see you can be trained, after all."

Ugh. Insufferable *prick*.

He gave me a rough push, and I stumbled to keep from falling again. I could already feel blood dripping down my shin from where my knee had kissed the gravel, and the burn of multiple grazes heated me through.

We walked up what seemed like a steep incline, with sharp stones cutting into my feet on each step, for what seemed like a couple of minutes. Then as we approached more voices, chilling wind whipped at my T-shirt and hood.

"Here he is!" someone said as we approached, Nate still prodding my back to keep me moving. "What took so long?"

"Shut the fuck up," someone else hissed. "You don't talk to him like that."

Nate said nothing, just kept pushing me every time I paused until he abruptly grabbed my arm and jerked me to a stop.

"Why is she bleeding?" Heath demanded in a furious whisper, his gentle hand skimming my leg where the grazes hurt the most. "This isn't—"

"Calm down," Nate drawled, sounding bored. "She tripped getting out of my car, that's all. Stubborn bitch didn't want my help."

*Bullshit.* But of course I was gagged and couldn't correct his lies.

"Ash, are you okay? You'll be okay, I pr—"

"Cut it out," Nate growled, cutting off Heath's apology. "Let's just get on with this shit."

This time when he urged me forward, it was with his fingers

around my upper arm rather than just shoving me. Fake fuck, even to his friends.

"Take this one," Nate said, handing me over to someone else in leather gloves. "Get her in line."

Whoever took over was considerably less rough and gently guided me to wherever the fuck they wanted me, quietly telling me to shuffle forward another inch, then tapping my wrist to indicate that was enough. In bare feet, I could feel my toes on the lip of something.

My guts flipped. I knew where we were. Why the wind was so vicious.

"Can anyone tell me where we are this evening?" Nate called out in a deep, booming voice. "You're all smart people. Surely one of you knows."

*Cat's Peak. We're on Cat's Peak.*

"Cat's Peak," a girl spoke up, making me realize that I was likely the only one gagged.

*Great. Thanks a fucking lot, Nate.*

"Is this our initiation?" The excitement in her voice was undeniable. She wasn't scared of dying at all. Didn't she know what'd happened in previous years?

"That's right," Nate confirmed. "Right now, all eight of you are standing on the very edge of Cat's Peak lookout. Below you is a sheer drop of fifty-three feet onto jagged rocks at the base." His voice grew louder as he spoke, like he was pacing along behind us and had just drawn closer to where I stood. "Your task…is to jump."

"You'll catch us, though," a different voice said, this one a man. "Right?"

"Maybe. Some of you." Nate didn't sound human. Pure ice. "The test is to see how badly you want this. Not everyone will survive… People have died during this task in the past. But one thing is certain—if you don't jump, you'll never be given a second chance."

*Holy shit.* He was just outright *admitting* it? That their society had killed students in the past? How was the university okay with this going on?

"Enough stalling," another familiar voice drawled. Royce. "On the count of three, you jump and join the DBS or you fuck off back to your bed and forget this ever happened."

Terror swept through me so hard my whole body broke out in sweat, but ultimately I knew I had the choice. Simply don't jump.

It was my choice, right? And I didn't want to be in their society, so I would just *not jump*.

"One..." Royce called out, "Two...*Three*."

Screams rang out through the night, and a boot kissed my spine, propelling me forward. Someone—I'd put my money on Nate—had just kicked me off the ledge.

I screamed, despite the gag muffling most of the noise. I didn't care, and I was too terrified of my impending death, except I hit the ground *way* too fast and rolled.

Wait. What?

That was grass. And I didn't fall anywhere near hard enough to be from Cat's Peak. Hell, it'd hurt more getting dragged out of Nate's truck.

Laughter filled the air around me, and someone yanked the hood off my head.

We were on grass. A quick glance up told me we'd barely jumped six feet and the *actual* Cat's Peak ledge was a hundred feet away at least.

"What the fuck?" Carter grunted, grabbing my chin. "Why are you gagged?"

I glared absolute death as best I could and his brows hitched.

"Whoa, Spark, simmer down. Nothing to do with me." He loosened the belt and released the fabric from my mouth, frowning at it before pocketing the evidence. "You okay?"

I was *far* from okay, but a quick look around told me everyone else was riding their adrenaline rush with smiles and laughter, enjoying the ruse. Tears pricked at my eyes, and I bit back all the venom I wanted to spit.

Carter was still staring with a concerned intensity that made my chest hurt, though, so I jerked a nod. "Fine," I muttered.

He frowned, then circled behind me to untie my hands. A low mutter about the knots reached my ears, but a high-pitched ringing had started up and everything else was starting to sound dull.

*Fuck.* Was I about to faint?

# Chapter Thirteen

It became really clear, really quickly, that I was in shock. The intense rush of adrenaline that'd hit me when I got shoved off that ledge, totally convinced I would plummet to my death, had left me speechless and trembling amongst all the jubilant, laughing society members.

When Heath approached, I was at my breaking point. "I want to go back to my dorm," I managed to grit out from my clenched jaw.

He frowned, clearly confused, then shook his head. "Sorry, babe, we have a whole welcome celebration thing at the society headquarters."

"No." I wrapped my arms tighter around myself, knowing I was trembling all over. "I don't want to go to some stupid party. I'm cold, I'm scared, I want to go back to my dorm and pretend this never happened."

Indecision rippled over his face, and for a moment, I thought he would agree. He was so sweet when it was just the two of us, like when he bought me coffee…but before he could say anything, Nate slung an arm over Heath's shoulders and gave me a sneer.

"You shouldn't have jumped, Layne," he informed me. "You

don't belong in the Devil's Backbone, no matter who your mom is fucking."

My jaw dropped in outrage. Who was he fucking kidding with that crap? He was the one who'd pushed me! I didn't jump at all, that motherfucker. Mind games, it was all just dumb mind games with Nate.

"Come on, Squirrel," Royce said, appearing out of nowhere and tugging gently on my arm. "I've got a blanket in my car, and you look fucking cold."

Shaking, and still in shock, I let him lead me down the rocky path toward the parking lot. The second time I stumbled on a sharp stone, though, he stopped and picked me up. Not in the rough fireman's throw that Nate had carried me in, but in a gentle cradle that was quite literally to save my feet and nothing more.

"Thanks," I murmured, awkwardly tense in his hold like my body didn't trust his intentions.

"You're freezing," he replied with a frown. His grip tightened, holding me closer like he wanted to share some body warmth.

I gritted my teeth, trying to stop them from chattering. "Y-yeah, w-well, th-that's what h-happens when I g-get dragged out of b-bed and put on the t-t-top of a mountain."

"Stop talking, Squirrel," he grumbled. "You sound like you've got a stutter."

I scowled, but didn't argue the truth of that statement. Besides, we were almost at the cars so I shut up while Royce maneuvered me into the passenger seat of his Bugatti Chiron. He sat briefly behind the steering wheel to turn the ignition on, then fiddled with some buttons to get the heat on.

From the little space behind my seat, he dragged over a mink blanket and tucked it around my legs.

"Th-thanks," I murmured again, buckling my seatbelt with numb fingers as the other black-robed society members and the pajama-clad initiates flowed down the path and climbed into other cars.

Royce said nothing in reply, just shifted into drive and zoomed us out of the parking space so fast, I thought for sure he was going to run Nate over. To my disappointment, he missed.

It only took a minute before I realized he'd turned the seat warmer on, and my eyelids drooped while the warmth soaked into my bones. I'd never been up to Cat's Peak before, but by my best guess on the way up, it was a twenty-minute drive back to my dorm. So I took a little micro-nap all hunched up on myself and snuggled into the blanket.

I should have taken the opportunity to grill Royce with questions, and my better sense was screaming at me not to be stupid and miss the opening. But he remained silent, and I couldn't seem to force any words past my lips. It was so cozy and warm in the passenger seat of his car, and I needed the time to recover from shock and adrenaline surge.

"This isn't my dorm," I finally said when he pulled into a park outside a vaguely familiar building. We were on campus, but a decent distance from the accommodation blocks.

Royce just arched a brow as if to say *congratulations, you're not brain-dead*, then climbed out of the car. He circled around and opened my door while I unbuckled myself, then offered me a steadying hand as I got out.

"Are you okay to walk?" he asked, frowning down at my bare feet. "We've got a first aid kit inside, so we can clean up those grazes. What happened to you, anyway?"

"Nate happened," I snapped, anger welling up again now that I'd warmed up a bit.

Royce just winced, then led me into the building that, as we drew closer, I recognized as the drama department. He used a swipe card access to unlock the doors, then wedged it open presumably to let the others in when they arrived.

"Um, is this allowed?" I asked, stupidly following him like a lost puppy instead of saying *thanks for the ride, I'll be going home now, bye!*

The smirk he tossed over his shoulder was pure mischief, and it made my stomach flip. Was I actually intrigued about this society? Yes. Yes, I was.

"Through here," he said, flipping on a light switch in the costume closet, then pausing to hang his robe and mask on a clothing rail full of empty hangers. Then he pushed open another door into a dark hallway and continued confidently down to another door.

I hesitated only a second before following, then breathed a short sigh of relief to find we were in a dressing room. Just an ordinary theater dressing room, complete with Hollywood-style mirror surrounded in light bulbs.

"Sit up here," he ordered, patting the vanity counter. "I'll clean those grazes before we join the party."

"I don't want to join the party," I informed him, even as I sat where he'd directed. "I also didn't want to be dragged out of bed by a masked fuckwit, tied up, scared half to death and then kicked off a cliff. And yet, here we are."

Royce just arched a brow, saying nothing as he pulled a huge first aid kit out of a cupboard and deposited it on the countertop beside me. It only took him a moment to find wound-wash spray and some dressings, then he went to work on my knees with a gentle touch.

It stung, but I gritted my teeth, refusing to whine about it. Royce was making it crystal clear he didn't want to chat so I wasn't going to waste my breath. That didn't mean I was going to sit there and act like a damsel, though, so I huffed a sigh and smacked his hand away.

"Thank you, I can do this myself."

Royce shifted away, squinting at me. "Okay, tough girl. Have at it."

I rolled my eyes and hitched my leg up on the counter so I could see what I was doing. Grazes *sucked* but they weren't life-threatening, so I could handle a bit of alcohol sting to clean them up.

Royce just stood there watching me with his arms folded across his chest and an unreadable expression on his face. *Fucking creep.* I couldn't get a handle on him at *all*. His whole vibe screamed total asshole, but then he did things like this? Or when he'd escorted me home instead of ratting me out to Nate? Was Royce actually a nice guy?

"So what's up with you and Heath?" he asked, the sound of his voice breaking the silence so abruptly, I nearly dropped the dressing I was sticking over my shin.

I wet my lips, not looking his way. "Why do you care?"

From under my lashes, I caught his casual shrug. "Just concerned about his trust fund balance, that's all. I can imagine you charge a pretty penny to lock down an exclusive deal."

*Great. Back on that old theme again.* Stupid me for thinking Heath and I were fake *dating*, when apparently his friends assumed it was another business transaction.

"He's a big boy, I'm sure he can make his own choices without your input," I replied in a cool voice, already wanting to be gone before Nate arrived to pull more of his bullshit.

Heavy footsteps and raised voices outside the room clued me in to the fact that I might already be too late, and a moment later, the door to the dressing room burst open dramatically.

"What the hell is going on in here?" Heath demanded, glaring daggers at Royce.

"Calm down, Heathcliff," Nate drawled, following him in. "Royce couldn't afford your pricey little whore even if he wanted to." My hand tightened into a fist, and I narrowed my eyes, debating whether I could get across the room fast enough to punch him in the junk again. He must have read my mind, because he shot a disgusted sneer in my direction. "Thinking about touching my dick again, little sister? You are insatiable."

All three of his friends stared at me in some degree of shock, and my cheeks flamed. Trust him to twist what happened and make it sound sexual.

"If by *touch*, you mean nut punch you so hard you couldn't

breathe, then yes that's exactly what I'm thinking about, *brother*. What is your fucking damage, anyway? Can't you get therapy instead of playing high school bully?"

"Okay, that's…" Carter shot a confused look between Nate and I, then shook his head. "…irrelevant right now. Initiates are all downstairs. We should get down there and celebrate. You're a DB now, Spark, congratulations!"

"Thanks, but no thanks," I snapped, irritated at his nonchalance. "I didn't ask for any of this, and I sure as shit don't want to be in your dumb club."

"Why'd you jump, then?" Heath asked, frowning.

I gritted my teeth, furious. "I *didn't*. Someone *kicked* me." I shot an accusing glare Nate's way, and he arched an eyebrow in return.

"Don't fucking blame me, I didn't want you here either. I was overruled since our parents are married…for now." He folded his arms and gave me a look of absolute disgust, enough that I nearly believed him.

But I'd felt that kick to my back, and there was no way in *hell* I'd jumped of my own volition. "You're actually insane. I didn't jump, Nate, just like I didn't drag myself out of bed or drop my own defenseless ass on gravel. Just admit you pushed me, you pussy."

Confusion and a touch of surprise rippled across his face. "But I *didn't*. Like I said, I'd rather you didn't jump—because I don't *want* you here—so why the fuck would I push you?"

"Because you're an asshole!" It was the only explanation. Initially I'd thought he was trying to kill me, but logically I knew there was actually no danger. The ledge had barely been high enough for a sprained ankle, let alone death.

A quick glance at the other guys told me that *none* of them believed me, and I nearly screamed with frustration and rage.

"While I don't disagree with that logic…" Heath said carefully, giving Nate a wary look before indicating to Royce. "We have proof that he was nowhere near you, so he couldn't have pushed you."

"What?" I blinked, trying to process. It was like whiplash.

Royce produced his phone and drifted closer as he searched for the video in question, then handed it over to me as it started to play.

My fingers still trembled as I held his phone, watching the initiation ritual from his point of view. Watching as the collection of hooded, pajama-clad prospects were led to the dumb little ledge. Some of the robed members still wore their masks—the same as the one Nate had worn—but most had taken them off. It took me a moment of watching to spot Nate…pacing the line behind where we all stood.

I held my breath as I watched him pause behind me, his gaze full of hatred as he looked me over. But then he shook his head and strode away as Royce started speaking in the video, giving the countdown.

When everyone jumped—when I was pushed—Nate was clearly seen standing at least a dozen feet away.

"What the fuck?" I breathed, rewinding it to watch again. And again. And *again*. "There!" I paused it and zoomed in.

Royce peered at the phone when I turned it around to show them. "What are we looking at?"

"There!" I said again. "That person. Whoever the fuck *that* is. Press play."

I waited while he did as I said, then by the quick widening of his eyes I had to guess he'd seen what I was pointing out. A black-robed DB stood behind me right as everyone started to jump, then as my body jerked and fell forward, a boot sole could be seen retracting. Evidence I'd been *kicked* off.

"So…someone did push you," Heath murmured, confused as fuck.

"But it wasn't me. *Sorry, Nate*," the dickhead himself sulked. "Now if we're done pandering to Layne's desperate need for attention, we have a party to host." He stalked out of the room again, and it was instantly easier to breathe.

The remaining guys exchanged a few pointed glances like they were sharing some kind of telepathy, but it was way over my head. I didn't much care about Nate's tantrum, either.

"Listen. You have evidence that I didn't jump, therefore I have no place in the Baby-Sitters Club. Right? It was a test of trust and faith and all that crap, and if I was pushed then I didn't meet requirements. So... can we just leave it at that?"

Carter ran a hand over his hair and shrugged. "She's not wrong."

Royce shook his head. "It's too late, she's already—"

"It's not up to us." Heath cut him off. "This is a problem for the elder council."

Both Royce and Carter nodded at that.

"Who is—" I started to ask, then swallowed the rest of the sentence at Heath's sharp look. "Fine. I don't even care. Can I go now? I've got class in the morning and unlike some, I'm actually here for the education."

"Yes," Carter said at the same time Royce said, "No."

Heath gave them both a frustrated glare, then shot me a tight smile. "Yes, I'll take you."

I let out a heavy breath, sliding off the counter to stand on wobbly legs. All the warmth I'd gotten from Royce's car was gone, and I was shivering once more, but I ignored it in favor of getting the hell away from these crazy bastards.

Royce and Carter disappeared toward the theater, and Heath led me back outside into the night. Once the door closed heavily behind us, he shrugged out of his hoodie and pulled it over my head.

"Thanks," I muttered, accepting the garment still warm from his body. I couldn't help wondering why he'd waited until we were outside to offer it, though. Or until we were alone? "Are you scared what your friends will think if you're nice to me?"

He shot me a sharp look, then sighed. "Something like that. Come on, it's not far across this way."

Our brisk walk across campus was silent, and despite Heath

escorting me right to my room, he was cold and distant the whole time. Weirdly, I was the tiniest bit disappointed when he didn't try to kiss me before he left…and it took me *far* too long to remember we *weren't* actually dating.

It was fake. Just like that dumb initiation test. So how had Abigail's friend died?

More questions, and no answers whatsoever.

## Chapter Fourteen

Sleep eluded me after Heath dropped me home. I lay there staring at the chair I'd wedged under my door handle, just waiting for Nate to burst back in with that creepy fucking mask and robe on.

My first class of the next morning was utter torture. My eyelids felt like sandpaper and my focus was totally fucked. So when Carly asked if I wanted to go for coffee, I jumped at the opportunity.

For more than one reason.

"Can I ask you something?" I asked her as we walked across the lawn toward Dancing Goats.

She shot me a worried look, then quickly covered it with a smile. "Of course. What's up?"

I bit my lip, hesitating a moment before throwing caution to the wind. "Were you there last night? On Cat's Peak, I mean."

The instant panic that flashed across her face gave me the answer I needed, even though I hadn't seen her anywhere in the video. Carly was in the Devil's Backbone Society, but I'd suspected as much even before Nate dragged me up there.

"I'm so sorry," she whispered, pale as a damn ghost as she shook her head. "I had no idea."

"Would you have warned me if you did?" After all, we'd only

been friends for a minute, and she'd probably been in the society for years.

She wrinkled her nose. "I want to think I would have," she replied with sincerity. "But I don't know. There are rules…strict ones. But maybe I could have given you some sort of heads up or…I dunno. Maybe I could have made a strong suggestion to wear pants and a bra to bed?"

That made me snort with unexpected laughter. "That would have been nice."

"But you're in now, right? So…I can tell you shit?" Carly seemed a little uncertain on that subject, and I shook my head.

"No, I'm—"

"Good morning, gorgeous," Heath interrupted, draping an arm over my shoulders and kissing my hair. My whole body stiffened up in fright, and my pulse raced. I hadn't seen him coming at *all*. "We going to Goats?"

Carly's brows were so high, they practically touched her hairline. "So…that rumor about you two was true? Jade was running her mouth but you know how she is…"

"That we're dating?" Heath asked before I could reply. "All true."

"Yeah, about that," I spoke up, recovering from my shock. "I've rethought that arrangement and decided it was an awful idea."

"What? Why?" Carly protested. "You guys make a cute couple and I can vouch for Heath not being anywhere near as bad as Nate."

"Careful," Heath murmured.

Carly's cheeks pinked and she gave a nervous laugh. "It was a compliment, dude. Chill."

"It's too late to change your mind, Ash," Heath told me with a lazy grin as I looked up at him. "Word has already spread, *as intended*, so you may as well roll with it."

"Roll with what?" I snapped, shrugging out from under his arm to create some space. "Your friends don't think we're dating, they think I'm on retainer. Which, by the way, I haven't heard you correcting."

"Does it matter? Either way they have to leave you alone, so it's a win-win. Come on, let's get coffee before your first class starts." He snagged my hand in his, linking our fingers together and practically dragging me into the coffee shop, totally cutting the line.

I tried to pull free, but without causing a scene, he wasn't letting go. And I *did* want coffee, so I gave up when we reached the counter. Heath ordered my usual, and his, but then I needed to elbow him to remember Carly's order.

"Thanks, Heath," she said sweetly when he paid.

"Mm-hmm," he replied, locating some high stools for us to sit while we waited. He offered one to me, and then Carly slid onto the second with a wicked smirk, leaving him to stand. "You're lucky I like you, Carly."

She scoffed. "We're related, dude, you have to like me."

"Not true at all," I disagreed. "Technically I'm related to Nate, but I'd happily watch him burn in an oil fire."

"Mutual feeling," the devil in question snapped from behind me.

*Great, what is this? Sneak up on Ashley day?*

I swiveled on my stool with a glare I was perfecting just for Nate. "Heathcliff, you haven't been answering your phone."

Heath repositioned himself so he leaned on the tabletop behind me, giving the impression we were a lot cozier than we really were. "Yeah, I was giving Ash my full attention. What's up?"

The furious narrowing of Nate's eyes and the prolonged eye contact between the two of them hinted at underlying tension and unresolved arguments, which was interesting. I did *like* that my arrangement with Heath was getting under Nate's skin.

"Elders meeting," he snapped eventually. "To discuss the problem."

I rolled my eyes. "Cute."

Heath gave a frustrated sigh. "Fine. I'll meet you there."

Nate shot me another filthy look, then stormed out of the coffee shop once more without another word.

"Dick," I muttered, swiveling my chair once more to face Carly. Then remembered her history with Nate and gave her a sympathetic look. "Sorry."

She shrugged. "You've got nothing to apologize for, dumbass. I unfortunately can't avoid him, but I *can* pretend he doesn't exist whenever our paths cross. So that's something. You should go, though," she said to Heath. "One Briggs on Nate's shitlist is enough."

Heath chuckled. "He couldn't stay mad at me even if he tried. See you later, Ash?"

"Nope, I have assignments to do." And more research into Abigail's life to be done. Because, fuck, I was hooked on that mystery now more than ever. Except the ever-present fear of ending up like Abigail, not to mention the intense animosity from Nate, had me reluctant to actually get closer to the society.

Heath didn't seem deterred. "Cool, meet you in the library at five then?" The barista called out his name, and he went to collect our drinks and delivered them back to us.

"Umm..." I tried to think of a reason why he couldn't join me in the library but came up blank.

Heath took my chin in his fingers and tilted my head back, smacking a quick kiss on my lips, then swaggered his fine ass out of the coffee shop before my head even stopped spinning.

"Uh...that didn't look fake to me," Carly commented with a giggle. "What is the deal?"

I groaned, my lips still tingling. "I don't know. I think I had a brain malfunction and now I don't know what the hell I've got myself into. It seemed like a good idea at the time." I paused, frowning at myself. "Nope. No, it was never a good idea."

My friend just laughed, sliding off her stool and picking up her bag. "Okay well, I like it. Heath's not like the others...not really. He just pretends."

"Two-faced is not typically an attribute I find attractive," I grumbled, grabbing my own coffee to follow her out the shop. "But I'll happily keep taking the free coffees. You heading over to class now?"

She nodded. "Yep. I'd better run, Professor Johnson is a dick if anyone's late."

I smiled but didn't make the obvious childish joke about Johnson being a dick. We bid a quick farewell and went our separate ways.

My next class was in Bard Hall, but for some reason I found myself autopiloting across campus to the drama department. Was that where Nate and the others were meeting with the elders? Whoever the fuck they were.

"Can I help you, dear?" an older woman asked, startling me as I wandered into the building. She smiled in a polite way as I stared back at her.

"Oh, um, sorry I was just…" How the fuck did I explain that I'd come looking for a secret society meeting that might be discussing my fate? Or that I wanted to see if the robes and masks were still hanging in the costume department as though there was nothing to hide?

"Sorry," I said again, shaking my head. "I was looking for a restroom."

The woman arched a brow but indicated along the hallway. "Second door on the left."

"Thanks," I murmured, following her direction and slipping into the ladies' room.

I waited a minute, staring at myself in the mirror and asking what in the *fuck* I was hoping to achieve being inside the drama department. Did I seriously think I could just stroll into the meeting and demand to know who'd pushed me last night? To what end? I didn't *want* to be in the society so I just needed to let sleeping dogs lie.

Decided, I pushed aside my curiosity and left the drama building once more. I needed to focus on my classes, and nothing more. End the weird fake-but-not-so-fake situationship with Heath, make a truce with Nate, and just ignore everything about the DBS.

I held on to that decision all through the rest of my day. But somehow as I pulled out my laptop in the library that evening, I found myself typing Abigail's name into the search engine once more.

*Damn it.*

By the time Heath arrived, my head was fully immersed into the mystery. It was like a drug I just couldn't quit and knowing he was neck-deep in the society only made me more invested.

"Hey," I greeted him, still distracted from the new evidence I'd just uncovered about one of the other students Abigail had mentioned. The finer details of her diary were becoming really foggy in my memory, now that I no longer had the journal to read, but I'd remembered this student's name.

Apparently Clara Devine had died in a tragic car crash when her car skidded on black ice. Sure, it could have been an accident…but Abigail had thought otherwise, so now I was questioning whether it was a cover-up. I shut down the search window so he couldn't see what I *had* been working on and tabbed back to my homework.

Heath dropped his bag across the table from where I sat, but then circled around and grabbed my face in that already familiar way he liked to hold me. Before I could formulate a protest, his lips were on mine.

*Fuck.*

I gasped as he kissed me hard, and he took advantage of my shock to take it deeper. My whole body flushed with heat as his tongue stroked against mine, his lips caressing me in the perfect balance of sweet and spice until my head spun and my pulse raced.

"What…" My question was a breathy croak as he released me, and I cleared my throat to try again. "Um, what…no one is here to see."

He just grinned and took his seat on the other side of the table, smug as a damn cat. "I know. I just like kissing you. So, what are we working on?"

Shock saw me tripping over my words as my face flamed, and I mumbled a brief explanation of my Early Modern Europe research assignment. Heath, apparently, was all-in on the fake boyfriend role and spent the next several hours shamelessly flirting while I got flustered every damn time.

It wasn't until after he walked me back to my room late at night that it occurred to me. I hadn't even *tried* to ask about his DBS meeting. Was that his intention all along? Shit, I had fallen for it hook, line, and sinker.

# Chapter Fifteen

All week, Heath played his role as my boyfriend like he was trying to win a freaking Oscar, but in his defense, no more sordid rumors swirled about me and literally any guy I spoke to on campus. So… either his idea worked, or I had read too much into those initial gossip threads.

And truthfully…I was having fun. So I didn't read too hard into the flimsy motivation and ignored all the orange flags when he smoothly dodged my questions. It was stupid, and I actively acknowledged that fact, but I'd developed a bit of a crush on Heath.

How could I not? He was funny, charming, thoughtful, and so fucking sexy it should have been illegal. It was all too easy to forget everything I'd read in Abigail's diary and pretend that nasty initiation mess never happened, especially considering the inconsistencies between her experience and mine. No one had actually jumped from the peak itself during my ordeal, nor had anyone died.

"I was thinking," he said as he escorted me to my Language Acquisition and Literacy Development class on Friday morning, "we should go to dinner tomorrow night. Have you even been into Prosper yet?"

I shook my head. "Not since the wedding." Which reminded me of the ambush during the rehearsal dinner, and that memory soured the sweet buzz of the moment.

"Okay, so I'll take you out," he announced. "I have to go to a thing tonight but maybe we can—"

Whatever he was going to say cut off abruptly and I followed his line of sight to see Carter sauntering across the lawn with a sly grin on his lips.

"Good morning, lovebirds," he purred as he approached. "How's the fake relationship treating you today? Bored of it yet?"

Startled, I jerked my gaze up to glare at Heath accusingly. "You told him?"

Heath sighed, and Carter snapped his fingers.

"Gotcha!" Carter crowed. "Royce owes me a hundred bucks."

Heath gave a frustrated groan, looping his arm around my waist and pulling me close. "What do you want, Carter?"

The smug bastard just grinned like the cat who got the cream. "I came to steal your girl, of course. What the fuck else would I be doing awake at this time?"

"Excuse me?" I spluttered, confused as hell.

He turned that dazzling grin my way. "You heard me. We all have to attend a gala tonight"—Heath stiffened noticeably beside me, his fingers digging into my hip—"and you're my date, Spark. Do you have an evening gown to wear? Hmm, probably not. I'll send something to your room."

"She's not coming to the gala," Heath growled, practically vibrating with anger. "We already decided."

That made me pause. "Excuse me?" I was echoing myself like a damn parrot but that was how fried my brain was.

Heath gave a frustrated sound as I stepped away from him, causing his hand to drop away from my hip. "It's a society event," he admitted from between gritted teeth, "and you don't want to be involved with the society."

I narrowed my eyes. "That's a conversation you should have *with me*, not *about* me."

"Uh-oh," Carter sang, "looks like trouble in paradise."

"Shut up, Carter," I snapped, dismissing him to focus my anger on Heath.

Bad move.

Carter's jovial mood vanished faster than a lightning strike, and in the space of a gasp, he had me slammed against the nearest tree with a hand around my throat.

"Do *not* speak to me like that again, Spark," he murmured in my ear, his voice the thunderclap to match his movement.

"Carter!" Heath shouted. "Let her go!"

But Carter just met my eyes, his thumb stroking my jaw in threat…or promise. He didn't blink, and neither did I, until Heath barked his name again.

Smooth as silk, Carter's dark storm clouds faded and his expression softened with a touch of a smile on his lips. "My apologies, Ashley, how very rude of me." And yet, he still didn't release my throat. His grip wasn't tight; it was just *there*. "I'll pick you up at seven, all right?"

Dumbstruck, I just nodded, my heart racing.

"Good," he purred, and I'd swear there was a silent, implied *girl* after that that made parts of me tingle. Jesus Christ, Carter was something else.

"Okay, enough," Heath snapped. "You've scared her into doing what you want, now let her go."

Carter ran his tongue across his lower lip, his dark blue eyes dancing with mischief that I was inexplicably drawn to. "You're not scared, are you Spark? You're *curious*. That's why I picked you as my date for tonight. You should ask your *boyfriend* who his date is." As abruptly as he'd grabbed me, he let go and stepped away. "See you tonight, partner!"

I raised a hand to my throat, watching him walk away with a little bounce in his step. "What the fuck just happened?"

"Carter Bassington just happened," Heath muttered, still fuming. "Are you okay? You're not hurt?"

I hesitated, licking my lips. "Is that something he would do? Hurt me, I mean?"

Heath's arched brow was all the answer I needed. Yes, he would.

I swallowed hard and shook my head. "No, I'm not hurt. But *what* just happened? A gala? What did he mean about asking who your date is?"

Heath winced. "It's not...ugh, fucking Carter is *such* a dick. We all have to bring a date to the gala, another DB. Every pair becomes a team for a game."

"Okay...and who is your date?" I was hurt, and I couldn't put my finger on why. Maybe because I was crushing on him and he was just acting the part I asked him to act?

Heath ran a hand over his face, clearly frustrated and uncomfortable. "Jade."

My lips popped open and my eyes widened. "Oh. I see."

"She's devious," he explained, grimacing.

I nodded slowly. "No shit. I guess everyone must know this thing between us is fake, then?"

"No, it's nothing like that. I just...I want to win." He spread his hands wide, exasperated.

"Right. And Jade is the best option for that? Got it."

"Why are you upset right now? I thought you didn't want anything to do with the DBs?" His brow furrowed as he tried to puzzle his way through my reaction.

Good luck to him when I couldn't even work out why I was upset myself. Come to think of it, no one had even told me the outcome of their elders meeting. Was I still initiated or not? Why all the secrets?

"I don't!" I shot back, folding my arms under my breasts. "But *fuck*, Heath, why did you ask—" I cut myself off, swallowing my words before I could sound like I was *hurt*. "Forget it. I need to get to class."

"Ash, wait!" he called after me but I was already striding away, heading for my class that I was probably late for.

I had a lot of self-reflection that I needed to do, and yelling my thoughts at Heath in the middle of campus was not the place to do it. I'd embarrassed myself enough without admitting I'd caught feelings in the span of one short week. *Damn it all to hell.*

Sliding into my class right as the professor started a PowerPoint presentation, I shoved Heath, Carter, the Devil's Backbone Society, and all my mixed-up emotions from my mind. I'd focus on my classes and deal with that all later.

For the most part, I managed to do just that. Until I realized the pattern I'd doodled in the margins of my textbook echoed the tattoo on the side of Carter's neck.

At the end of my day, I headed straight for Carly's room and let myself in after the briefest knock.

"What happened?" my friend immediately asked, looking up from her study notes spread out on her desk. "What'd he do?"

I glowered. "Which *he?*"

Carly winced. "I meant Heath… Did you have another run-in with Nate?"

"Thankfully, no. Carter. Are you going to this gala thing tonight?" I glanced around and noted the dress bag hanging from her closet door.

She turned right around in her seat, taking off her reading glasses and giving me a long look. "Are *you?*"

I shrugged. "Maybe. What is it?"

A goofy smile touched her lips. "It's a gala. You've never been to a gala?"

I glared. "I think you know I haven't, smarty-pants, and despite that fact I do in fact know *what* a gala is…I want to know what *this* one is and why it's part of your creepy secret society."

"Okay, A, it's not creepy, it's historical, and B, it's still just a gala. The Founding Families Gala Dinner to be exact, where they invite a bunch of rich and influential families and squeeze them for hefty monetary donations to the school." She sat back, tucking one foot up on her chair. "So all the DBs go because we're basically all rich and influential families. It makes it an easy setting for, you know, shenanigans."

I blinked at her a couple of times. "Shenanigans?"

She nodded. "Quite so. So…what are you wearing? It's a white-tie dress code, and not being an asshole but I've seen your wardrobe."

"Seriously? I knew it'd be formal but *white tie*? Fucking hell. Um…can I borrow something?" I looked hopefully at her closet, but Carly laughed.

"Unless you're a secret seamstress or you're in twelve-inch platform heels, none of my evening gowns will fit, girl. No offense but you're short as hell."

I groaned but she was right. "True. Don't worry, I'll sort it out." After all, Carter had said say he'd send something over. "But just tell me, is it a dumb idea for me to come to this thing? Am I going to end up stripped naked and duct-taped to a flagpole?"

Carly wrinkled her nose, shaking her head. "What? No. I think maybe you've got the wrong idea about what the society is all about. You'll see tonight, Ash. It's actually really fun."

She seemed sincere and I was deep in the grip of curiosity once again so I sighed. "Okay, I trust you. I guess…I better shower, huh?" I didn't want to go for a myriad of reasons, the biggest being I couldn't deny I was worried about what could happen to me if the diary was true—but at the same time, I couldn't resist the opportunity to learn more about the society itself.

"Please do, I can smell you from here," she teased, holding her nose.

I laughed and flipped her my middle finger before leaving her room. Knowing Carly would be at the gala did make me feel a shitload better about the whole thing, even if I was going with Carter instead of Heath…*and* that Heath would be there with Jade.

Carly wasn't wrong about my wardrobe, but when I got back from the shower, there was an enormous box sitting outside my door. The card tucked under the ribbon just held my name *Ashley* in fancy cursive and was signed C.

If nothing else, Carter was a man of his word.

I carried the box into my room, closing the door behind me and setting it down on the bed. Inside, not only did I find a stunning red satin gown, but also a pair of black strappy heels and some long black opera gloves.

The whole set was breathtaking, and I wasn't even a little bit surprised to find the dress and shoes fitted me as though they'd been made to measure. Carter was just that sort of creep.

"Holy *shit*," Carly exclaimed with a whistle after letting herself in. "You just had that lying around?"

I grinned, tugging on one of the gloves. "You look pretty amazing yourself."

Carly wore a princess-style taffeta gown of soft greens with dozens of intricate applique flowers all down one side. She too wore opera gloves, but hers were a dusty purple to match some of the flower detailing.

"Thanks," she replied, giving a little twirl. "Is Heath coming here to get you?"

My lips parted, and I realized I hadn't told her about our little argument. Turned out, I didn't need to explain, because Carter chose that exact moment to knock on my open door and my mouth went dry.

He was in a full tuxedo with tails, but his shirt was ink black and his cravat a rich red that matched my dress perfectly. He looked *incredible*. Like every rich bad boy fantasy ever dreamed up.

"Ready to go, Spark?" he asked, giving me a lingering once-over. "You look lovely in that dress."

"Um...?" Carly glanced back and forth between us in panic. "What's happening?"

Carter grinned. "War games, Carly dear." He looked at me. "Shall we go?"

I swallowed hard, then tugged my second glove the rest of the way up over my elbow. "Yeah," I replied in a breathy voice. Then, like an idiot with no sense of self-preservation, I took the hand he offered.

# Chapter Sixteen

Nate's furious face greeted me as I stepped out of Carter's chauffeur-driven car and took the hand he offered me for balance. With the pencil-thin heels of my new stilettos, I needed the hand, and since he'd been a perfect gentleman for the whole drive, I didn't hesitate.

"Is this a fucking joke, Bass?" Nate demanded in a strangled growl, his left eye practically twitching with fury as he gave me a once-over. Then his eyes widened ever so slightly as he did it again. For a scarce moment, his lips parted in surprise, then Carter tugged me forward and slammed the car door shut, breaking the spell.

"Are you laughing?" Carter responded, not seeming to have noticed the shift in Nate's mood. He touched a light, gentlemanly hand to the small of my back and nudged me to walk with him… leaving Nate to follow or fuck off.

Nate let out a furious sound, following. "Clearly fucking not."

Carter gave a small shrug. "Well then, I guess it's not a joke. Doesn't your new sister look just divine in Portia Levigne Couture?"

"Bass, don't fucking walk away when I'm talking to you," Nate barked, reaching out to grab Carter's shoulder.

Even I could have told him that was a bad move, but it was Nate, so I found it hard to care when Carter whirled around and grabbed him by the front of his dress shirt. Unlike when I'd been on the receiving end of Carter's light switch mood change, Nate didn't flinch.

"Watch your fucking tone, Essex," Carter snarled, radiating violence.

Nate just shoved him back, dislodging Carter's grip on his shirt. "Eat a dick, Bass. I kicked your ass when we were twelve and I'll do it again now."

As much as I wanted to see Nate get his face ground into the pavement—because my money was on Carter—we were drawing a lot of attention and a familiar couple had just exited a Rolls-Royce Phantom farther along the drop-off line.

"Unless you want Max to see those true colors of yours, Nate," I spoke up, quickly stepping between the two of them before Carter could retaliate, "I suggest you rein in your toddler tantrum."

He paused, brows pinched as he looked at me with confusion. Then when I tipped my head to the left, his gaze followed. The instant shift in his expression and posture said he'd spotted our parents, and he quickly smoothed a hand over his rumpled shirt.

"Nathaniel, Carter," Max greeted the boys as he approached with my mother on his arm. "I trust we aren't interrupting a physical altercation?"

Nate glared at Carter over my head, then pasted on a tight smile for his father. "Not at all. Carter just lost his balance, is all. I suspect he's been drinking again."

Max gave a heavy sigh. "Carter, son, we talked about this…"

Carter snaked a hand around my waist, his palm flat on my stomach as he pulled me back a step into his embrace. "Max, I wouldn't dare drink while responsible for this lovely creature."

Max's eyes widened and he gave a startled noise. "Ashley? Good lord, sweetheart, I didn't even recognize you."

My mother had, though, and was giving me a sly smirk. "Of course you didn't, darling, but she looks magnificent, doesn't she?"

Max's cheeks flamed with embarrassment and he gave me a sheepish smile. "Sorry, honey. I'm used to the boys bringing rather painful girls to these events. You're here together?" He glanced at Carter's hand on my stomach and then cast a puzzled glance to my mom.

She just shrugged and tugged his arm gently. "Come on, leave the kids. I just saw Henry and Alice arrive." To me she gave a warm, reassuring smile. "Ash, you look just divine."

"She gets it from her mother," Carter purred, and my mom barked a laugh.

"Charmer," she accused, grinning. "Come on, Max."

They continued up the main stairs of the enormous mansion home, and no one spoke for a minute. Then Carter gave me a gentle nudge to walk with him, ignoring Nate entirely as he led me toward the entry foyer where Mom and Max had just disappeared.

"This discussion isn't over," Nate snarled from behind us.

Carter's response was to extend his middle finger and continue walking.

"What was *that* all about?" I asked once we reached the top of the stairs and waited for the people ahead of us to check their names off the guest list. "I had the impression the four of you were thick as thieves. Brothers."

He glanced down at me, one dark brow lifted. "We are."

"Okay…so the fact you nearly came to blows back there was—"

He chuckled. "Nate's all bark, no bite. He wouldn't risk messing up his pretty face again, and he knows I'd leave a mark."

"That…is sort of my point."

The couple ahead of us moved inside, and Carter announced our names to the host to mark off on the guest list. I was surprised to hear he used my name, and not *plus one,* but maybe that was the gala's requirement.

"Nathaniel is very upset that I brought you as my date tonight," he elaborated once we were inside the foyer. "Possibly even more upset than Heathcliff, but for different reasons."

A cold stab of anxiety lanced through my gut at the mention of Heath. He was here somewhere with *Jade* of all fucking people. "And that's a good thing because...?"

"Because my friends don't think straight when they're worked up, which means they aren't putting their full efforts into the Society Challenge." He spoke softly, keeping his volume low enough that it felt like a secret. Like he was telling me things I shouldn't know. It gave me a weird, fluttery feeling. "And that means that *we*, Ashley dear, are going to win."

Okay. I was intrigued. "What do we win?"

Carter's sexy grin spread wide as he met my eyes. "The satisfaction of beating Nate, Spark. Don't tell me that's not enough for you—I can see the desire to take him down a peg written all over your pretty face."

My answering smile no doubt told him everything he needed to know. "What do we need to do?"

"All in good time, beautiful. For now, we attend the gala. Do you dance?" He gestured toward the handful of elaborately dressed couples literally *waltzing* around a ballroom. An actual honest-to-fuck ballroom. I had no idea they even existed in this century, but my mind quickly noted that the mansion itself was likely built in a time when balls were more common.

I shook my head. "I do not." A passing waitress offered her tray, and I reached for a glass of champagne, then hesitated. "Am I okay to drink?"

Carter rolled his eyes, taking two glasses off the tray. "Nate's a dick," he said, handing me a glass. "I had a *very brief* substance abuse problem when we were seventeen. Not alcohol. But Max was my legal guardian at the time and got more than a few calls from our school. He assumed it was booze and I never corrected him."

Surprise held my tongue for a moment and I took a sip of the champagne in my gloved hand. Carter just watched me, waiting for a reaction, so I cleared my throat and said what I was thinking.

"You're being very open and honest tonight, Carter. Why?"

His lips curved. "I don't believe in secrets, Spark. They only serve as ammunition for those who want to hurt you. Better to lay everything out there and give them nothing to work with. Ah look, here comes your *boyfriend*." The pointed twist to that word made me groan.

We'd been wandering while talking and had made it across the ballroom but still had a clear view of the entry foyer. Sure enough, Heath had just arrived, looking stiff and pissed off with Jade pasted to his side. As I watched, she batted her long lashes up at him, saying something as lights danced off the heavy jewels around her throat.

"Want to know how I guessed you were faking it?" Carter murmured in my ear, making me jolt out of the trance I'd slipped into as I stared.

I wet my lips, purposefully turning my back on Heath and Jade. *Out of sight, out of mind. Right?*

"Sure. How?"

"Oh, I asked if you *wanted* to know. I never said I was going to tell you." He held my gaze as he sipped his own drink, smug as all hell.

I rolled my eyes. "What happened to not keeping secrets, hmm?"

"I'm not keeping secrets, I'm strategically withholding information. Big difference." His dark blue eyes flicked away from mine, observing someone behind me. "Just a word of warning, Spark, physical altercations at these events are deeply frowned upon. If you want to bitch slap Jade, you'll need to save it for another day."

I scoffed a laugh. "She'll get more than just a bitch slap from me if she starts anything, and you know it."

His gaze flicked back to me with a heat that made me inhale sharply, but whatever he might have said was rudely interrupted by Jade's nails-on-chalkboard voice.

"What is *she* doing here?" she demanded as I turned to look. "This event isn't for initiates."

Carter's brows lifted, but it was Heath who grabbed Jade's arm in what seemed like a painful grip. "Keep your fucking voice down," he snapped.

She gave a pathetic little whine that made my eyes want to roll right back in my head, but Royce captured my attention as he entered the ballroom looking like he'd stepped right out of a GQ Regency shoot. He didn't seem to have a date with him as he sauntered across to join us and snagged a glass of champagne on the way.

"Well, this is an interesting development," he murmured, eyeing me up and down. Slowly. "How fun. Where's Nate?"

Heath seemed to be trying to stare a hole through my head, but I was deliberately *not* looking back at him and, by default, found myself meeting Royce's unreadable eyes. Was he mad to see me here like everyone else was? His expression gave *nothing* away but somehow I had the feeling he was amused.

"Here he is," Carter commented, nodding toward the foyer. As I shifted my eyes off Royce, Carter's arm went back around my waist, his palm flat over my stomach in the possessive way he'd held me outside. What was *up* with that?

Royce noticed it too, giving Carter's hand a pointed look, then raising an eyebrow in question at his friend. Then his gaze shifted to Heath, and a somewhat-cruel, knowing smile curved his lips. Great. Now I was really starting to feel like a pawn on a chessboard I couldn't even make sense of.

Nate still looked like he was in a foul mood as he crossed the ballroom to join us, a pretty but somewhat dazed-looking, blond girl clinging to his hand all the while. She wore a pale pink taffeta ball gown like some kind of fairytale princess, but the state of her hair and smudged lipstick suggested she wasn't as innocent as her outfit.

"Paigey!" Jade squealed in delight, dropping Heath's arm to embrace the blond girl. "Thank goodness you're here, I was starting to worry I'd be stuck with the trailer trash all night."

Oh good, now I was trailer trash.

Nate's girlfriend gave me a cold, lifeless glance, then tucked her arm through Jade's to walk away from us all. Paige leaned in to say something to her friend, and Jade let out a high-pitched giggle as the two of them sashayed away across the ballroom together.

In their wake, none of the four guys spoke. The silence stretched long enough that it became uncomfortable, and I puffed a short sigh.

"Well. I think that's my cue to leave too," I muttered, peeling Carter's hand off my dress.

"Don't go far," Carter told me in a low murmur. "We have a big night ahead of us."

I didn't reply, but that fucking fluttery feeling started up inside me again. What was *that* all about?

# Chapter Seventeen

"Ash, wait up!" Heath called out when I nearly reached the bar set up near the floor-to-ceiling windows at the side of the room. "Can we talk for a minute?"

His fingers wrapped around my arm but it was a gentle touch, unlike when he'd reprimanded Jade. I sucked a deep breath, because *fuck*, my crush on him hadn't gone anywhere. Stupid fake dating idea had me all messed up.

"Sure," I replied, aiming desperately for casual and unaffected. "What's up?"

His brow dipped in a frown. "You're mad at me."

My jaw tightened, but ultimately I had no right to be pissed off. After all, we were *fake*. So, with that in mind, I shook my head. "Not at all. You did nothing wrong. Although, now that Carter knows we're not *actually* dating, there's probably no point in keeping up the charade anymore. Especially since you're here with another girl."

He ran a frustrated hand through his hair, drawing my attention to how great he looked in his tux. White tie was my new favorite dress code.

"Okay, well, I'm mad at you," he announced, giving me a stubborn glare.

I squinted. "Why?"

He gestured in the direction we'd just come. "You're here with Carter!"

"And...?" I wasn't following his train of thought.

His scowl deepened. "And I'm fucking jealous, Ash. I wanted to—"

"Hey..." Carly cut in, sliding an arm around my shoulders. "I'm not interrupting anything intense and serious here, am I?" As if she was fully aware that she absolutely *was*. "Cool. Good chat, Heathcliff. Your date is looking for you, and I need to talk with Ash. Bye."

She smoothly steered me away from Heath and didn't stop until she'd practically dragged me up the grand staircase and parked us on a chaise lounge overlooking the party.

"What was that all about?" I asked, perplexed.

She shot me a long look. "I could ask the same, Ashley Layne. Since when were you caught in a love triangle between Heath and Carter? You really, *really* need to be careful around Carter, he's—"

"Got a short temper? I'm well aware. What's up with *you*, though? You look...stressed."

Carly grimaced, her gaze tracking over the party below us. "Yeah. I had a run-in with Paige and Jade."

"Ah." I hated that she was still being treated like some kind of homewrecking whore when it was *Nate* who'd cheated, not Carly. He was such a prick. I needed to punch him in the dick again. "Are you okay, though? They didn't hurt you?"

Carly offered a weak smile. "They wouldn't ever hurt me physically. It's against society rules." She gave me a wink and shrugged. "That's why they settle for verbal abuse instead. And probably why Jade has steered clear of you all week."

That was surprising, given the implications of Abigail's experience. "Huh. I don't know if I like that rule..." Then again, the phrasing of Carter's warning about bitch-slapping Jade *somewhere else* made me think it'd be okay if no one was around to tattle. That thought made me smile. Then my traitorous imagination added in Carter watching with glee, and my stomach tightened in excitement and a touch of arousal. *Crap.*

"Are you cool hanging out with me until the gala ends? Or did you want to go back to whatever that messy little love triangle was down there?" Her pursed lips and narrowed eyes were full of questions, and I groaned.

"Truth?"

She nodded, looking vaguely offended. "Always."

"There's no love triangle. I'm not even dating Heath, he just… okay, fucking hell, this sounds *really* dumb now but it made sense at the time. I panicked about people starting rumors about me and Royce, and me and Carter, so I asked Heath to fake-date and contain the drama. Wow, okay, that is even worse out loud." I scrunched up my face, resisting the urge to rub at my eyes and smudge my dark eye makeup. "What is wrong with me? That doesn't even make sense!"

Carly cackled with laughter. "Oh my god, you manipulated yourself because you like Heath."

I winced. "I think I did. But he was the one who suggested it."

She rolled her eyes. "Of course he did. He's also the one who kisses you in public, isn't he? To make it seem real?"

My cheeks flamed with embarrassment. "Not just in public," I muttered, feeling stupid.

Carly cracked up. "You're not fake dating, my friend. You like each other. It's *totally okay*, and actually weird that you don't just admit it."

I blew out a long breath. "Ah well, that would be thanks to carry-over resentment from Nate keying my car, then setting me up to look like a sex worker when Heath propositioned me inappropriately at my massage job."

Her mouth just about hit the floor. "Excuse me?"

"Uh…long story. Sort of."

"I have the time." She rose to her feet and gestured to a waitress to bring us fresh drinks, then settled back into the lounge beside me. "Start at the beginning, you dirty secret-keeper."

And so I did.

By the time I finished telling Carly *all* the details, including how sweet Heath had been with me all damn week, and all the kisses that were surely for more than just appearances, I had to admit she was probably right. Heath wasn't *just* faking it. And neither was I.

Except he was here with Jade and hadn't planned to tell me about it, and that still stung.

"Look. The Jade thing is a non-issue," Carly announced. "Trust me. Picking a date for tonight was never about who you wanted to spend an evening with, but everything about who could help you *win*. That's why I'm here with Martin. He has the personality of a rancid fish, but he's smart."

"Speaking of whom…" I tipped my head to the rather unattractive guy heading up the stairs toward us. His tux was pristine like every other gentleman at the gala, and the watch on his wrist screamed money.

Carly gave a quiet groan under her breath, then pasted on a polite smile. "Hi, Martin."

"Carly, it's nearly time for the challenge and we haven't discussed strategy at all. We need to—" He cut himself off, glaring in my direction. "Can we speak alone?"

My friend rolled her eyes dramatically but pushed to her feet nonetheless. "*Fine*. But only because Ash is technically our competition. Catch you later, girl."

Left alone, I decided to look for a bathroom upstairs before returning to the party. Martin had said it was nearly time, and I still had no fucking idea what the challenge even was, so I really should squeeze Carter for some information.

I finally found a toilet—after browsing through several rooms along the way—and cursed out the formal gown attire for a solid five minutes while trying to pee without ruining the dress. When I was done, I used tissues to blot some shine off my makeup, then headed back toward the party.

Distracted as I was with pulling my long black gloves on while I walked, I didn't see the danger until I was too close to avoid collision.

"Just finished with another client, Layne?" Nate sneered as I stumbled back a step. "Whores like you are such hard workers, never missing the opportunity to make a quick buck."

Rage welled up in my chest, and I ground my teeth together. "Is that jealousy, Essex? Is your ego bruised that I'm so repulsed by you that no amount of money could change my mind?"

His lip curled, and he huffed a cold laugh. "That's cute, but we both know it's not true." His dark gaze shifted past me and his brows lifted. "Seriously, Royce, you too?"

Confused, I turned to find Royce strolling down the hall, his shirt untucked and his bow tie loose around his neck. He looked like he'd just had a quickie, but it sure as hell hadn't been with me.

Royce frowned slightly, glancing between Nate and me, then shrugged. "Sure, why not? She's hot."

My jaw dropped. "What? I did *not*—"

"Hey, have you guys seen Ashley?" Carter asked, arriving at our little hallway party. "Oh, there you are."

"Layne and Royce were having a private party up here," Nate announced, smug as all fuck.

Carter just shrugged. "Okay, cool. Come on, Spark, I need you." He grabbed my hand, linking our fingers and tugging me away as Nate tossed another snide comment about how *in demand* my services were tonight.

"What is his fucking problem?" I demanded, raging about Nate's insulting bullshit just as much as I was mad at my own inability to put him in his place. Why the fuck had Royce lied too?

Carter glanced back at me but continued deeper into the house. "The gala is ending," he informed me, ignoring my question, "which means the challenge is beginning. First thing we need to do is find a hiding spot."

"What for?"

"I'll explain once we find a good spot," he replied, glancing behind us before opening a door and ushering me inside.

"Get out!" a woman yelped, clutching her unzipped dress to her chest.

I gasped, backing up a step before recognizing Paige—Nate's girlfriend. But Nate had only just come upstairs when he accosted me so…

"Oh fuck!" I exclaimed, my eyes wide. Royce had just come from this direction looking freshly fucked and based on Paige's appearance…

Carter's hand on my stomach—apparently his favorite way of handling me—guided me smoothly out of the room again before I could say anything more, and the door slammed in our faces.

"Carter, that was—" I started to say in a strangled voice, shocked by the realization that Nate's girlfriend was fucking one of his best friends. I didn't like Nate but *fucking hell.*

"I'm aware." Carter cut me off. "None of our business, Spark. Come on, clock is ticking."

Somewhere to hide, that's what he'd said, wasn't it? "I have an idea."

Carter let me take the lead, hurrying farther down the hall and following when I slipped into a huge bedroom, then opened the adjoining door to an enormous bathroom.

"Over here," I whispered, pulling open the small door I'd tried earlier when looking for a toilet.

Carter stepped inside with me, and all of a sudden, the small, wood-lined room seemed *a lot* smaller. "Sauna? Nice. No one will come looking in here at this time of night."

I smiled at the praise before catching myself. "Okay so…what are we doing? What's the challenge? Is it…dangerous?" Flashes of

Abigail's warnings filled my head, but more and more I was thinking she'd been paranoid or delusional. None of what I'd experienced was matching up to the dark, scary shit she'd described. She'd mentioned a gala, but in her account she'd been asked to steal an heirloom from the hostess, then was punished with a beating for not doing it.

Carter sat down on the bench seat, giving me a small amount of breathing room. It was *dark* inside the sauna, especially once the door closed, so he pulled out his phone and turned the flashlight on. "Dangerous? No. I mean...depends what you'd call dangerous. And whether you get caught." He propped his phone against the wall so it gave us some light but wasn't enough to betray our location, then he opened the bag he'd been carrying.

Curious, I watched as he pulled out a Polaroid camera and four small rubber ducks. Red ones, I thought, though the color was hard to make out.

"Here's the challenge," he murmured, keeping his voice low. "We each get two ducks, but we work in teams of two, so it's four opportunities. Place a duck, take a picture, don't get caught. You get caught by the homeowner or his security—or any other nonplayer—and your team is disqualified."

I frowned, confused. "That sounds...very easy."

Carter chuckled. "It is, if you don't care about winning. Lots of DBs don't even try, so they'll place their duck somewhere boring and obvious and leave before there's even any risk of getting caught. Pussies."

"Okay...so how do we win?"

"That's the spirit, Spark. *We* win by degree of danger. The higher the risk, the higher the reward." He leaned in, his elbows on his knees and a devilish grin on his face. It filled me with excited flutters all over again.

I licked my lips, my brain whirling. "Okay so—"

Before I could get my next question out, the bathroom door burst open and a woman's giggles echoed through the room. Carter stiffened, and I clamped my lips shut like I was scared I might start yodeling or something.

The sauna door was thick enough that we couldn't make out what the couple was saying—a man's voice had joined her a moment later—but the giggles suggested the woman was decently tipsy.

Then a click sounded, and the sauna stove lit up with a dull glow.

"Shit," Carter breathed, and I echoed that inside my head. We were about to be found before I even fully understood the challenge!

# Chapter Eighteen

For about ten minutes, Carter and I stayed frozen inside the rapidly heating sauna waiting to be caught by whoever was out there. Sweat started to drip down my spine and I became acutely aware of how heavy my gown and gloves were with the rising temperature.

"I don't think they're coming in here," Carter whispered, his ear pressed to the door. "Maybe they hit the switch by accident. Sounds like they're wasted."

"If they could accidentally turn it off, that'd be ideal," I whispered back, peeling my gloves off in an attempt to cool down. "I thought saunas usually take like an hour to heat up?"

Carter gave a slight shrug, the motion barely visible in the weak light of his phone. "Rich people get shit to work better than others."

I rolled my eyes. Of course. "What are they doing out there?"

"Do you really want to know?" He shifted his ear off the door and shrugged out of his jacket. "Because honestly it sounds like we might be in here for a while."

I gave a quiet groan, then tried not to watch as Carter tugged his red silk cravat off and started on his shirt buttons. "What...are you doing?"

"Avoiding heatstroke. You should do the same." He finished unbuttoning his shirt, then took it off entirely.

I inhaled sharply enough that I choked on my own breath and tried to cover it up by coughing as quietly as possible. "Um, I'm good. Feels all too much like a Nate-style setup."

"Suit yourself," he murmured, carefully folding his clothes into a neat pile.

I wet my lips, far too aware of how *fucking hot* I was. I didn't love saunas on the best of days, let alone in full makeup in a floor length satin evening gown with a corset waist. Hopefully we could escape soon...or at least crack the door for airflow.

"Okay, um, what's the plan for the ducks?" Distraction was what I needed. Yeah, that'd help.

Carter slouched back against the bench seat, elbows braced behind him. "You're going to faint, Spark. At least sit down if you're not willing to take the dress off."

My jaw tightened with stubborn defiance...but he had a point. With a short sigh, I sat on the lowest bench as far away from him as I could. Which wasn't particularly far since the sauna was only designed for two.

"Happy?" I muttered.

"Not often," he replied in a quietly serious voice. "Don't worry about the ducks, I've got that handled."

I frowned. "So why am I here? I thought you needed my help to win?"

A breathy laugh escaped him. "I do. You're doing exactly that. My friends are the only real competition in this and right now they're all too absorbed with thinking about *you and me* to put their effort into the challenge. You're a distraction, Spark. A pretty one too."

"Oh." I was somewhat taken back by that. "Is that all?"

"Don't underestimate the power of distraction."

I didn't love that. Heath, sure I could see how he possibly wasn't focusing on the challenge. Nate too. He was *pissed* to see me arrive with Carter. But Royce? Not so much. He was far too busy fucking Nate's girlfriend.

"Okay, but I get two ducks to place, right?"

Carter sighed. "No, I get four ducks, and you get a twenty-thousand-dollar designer dress." Fuck that. I stood up and took a step toward the door before Carter surged to his feet to block me. "What are you doing?"

"Leaving," I replied, matter of fact. "I don't care for designer dresses and if you're not letting me have any ducks, there's no need for me to stay."

A frustrated growl rumbled through his chest. "Fine. You can have a duck."

"*Two* ducks," I corrected, silently noting this was the stupidest argument I'd possibly ever engaged in. "And I will make sure they're winning ducks."

"They'd better be," he muttered, placing a hand on my sweaty shoulder. "Turn around."

"Why?" I asked, even as he pushed me to do as he said.

He sighed, his fingers making quick work of unlacing my corset back. "Stopping you from passing out. Old friend out there told his lady that he wants to make her come three times before she's allowed to go to bed and I don't have a huge amount of faith in his skills so… we could be here awhile."

With the touch of his fingers on my back and the insane amount of sweat building on my skin, I couldn't even protest.

"Thank fuck I wore underwear," I mumbled, sighing with relief as the heavy dress fell to the floor.

Carter hummed, his fingers trailing down my damp spine. "Yes. What a relief."

Pretending I wasn't sitting in a sweltering sauna, in the dark, with a shirtless Carter Bassington, I redirected our whispered conversation to focus on where to place the ducks. Because as offended as I was to be nothing more than a *pretty distraction*, I still wanted to beat Nate. Badly.

It took a good half an hour—by which point I was lying on the floor with my head pounding and Carter had stripped down to his boxer-briefs—but the bathroom door finally slammed and silence followed.

"Are they gone?" I whispered, not moving from my squashed lizard position.

Carter pressed his ear back to the door. He listened for a moment, then ever so carefully peered out of the tiny window. "I think so."

Ever so slowly, he opened the door a crack and I nearly gasped with the cool breeze it allowed inside. Then maybe I moaned a little because shit it felt good on my burning hot face.

"Shhhh," Carter scolded with a touch of amusement as he opened the door wider to let more cool air in. "They're probably in the bedroom."

He had a point, but I was just about ready to quit the challenge if it meant I had to stay in the sauna any longer. "I fucking hate saunas," I grumbled, climbing to my feet and pausing while my head swirled.

Carter reached out to steady me, one hand on my elbow and the other on my waist. "You okay, Spark?"

I licked my lips, my mouth dry. "Yep. Just dizzy."

He nodded, then kept his hand on my waist as we moved out of the sauna and into the much, *much* cooler bathroom. On the floor lay a pile of clothes and several condom wrappers. Had there been more than one dude? Kinky.

I desperately wanted to splash some cold water on my face, but wasn't sure if running water would alert anyone to our hiding place so I settled for trickling cold water directly onto a washcloth then pressing that to my face. It was heavenly.

"Here," Carter whispered, handing me a silver satin robe.

I took it, then gave him a sidelong glance. "Is my underwear too distracting, Bassington?"

He scoffed quietly. "Yes." He tugged his suit pants and shoes back on but didn't bother with his shirt or coat. Talk about distracting now that the cover of darkness had lifted.

We waited in the bathroom for only a few more minutes before Carter decided it was safe to exit. He still moved cautiously, cracking the door and pausing to listen before easing it open further.

From the bedroom, deep snores echoed through and it gave us the confidence to quickly, quietly, not even daring to breathe, tip toe out into the hallway.

Even once we were clear of the bedroom, Carter put a finger to his lips to indicate silence and led the way further along the hallway, opening a door to the right with confidence.

"What are we looking for?" I whispered as he closed the door softly behind us both. We were inside an office, full of rich mahogany and leather-bound books. From what Carly had told me while we were getting ready, this house—mansion—belonged to some old oil tycoon who basically just lived for his much younger trophy wife and throwing huge parties.

Certainly the office looked rarely used, and there wasn't even a computer on the desk. Old-school or staged. One of the two.

"Ashley, sweetheart, I didn't come into this challenge without a plan," Carter muttered. "But since you've taken two ducks, I have to go with my best." He rifled through the desk drawers with a pinched expression, hunting for something.

"Okay...so let me help." I circled around the desk and pulled open the other set of drawers.

Carter huffed a short sigh. "Keys. My informant tells me old man Lintan keeps the key to his safe in one of his desk drawers."

I let out a low, quiet whistle. "Very secure," I muttered, but went to work searching for keys.

After a few minutes of hunting—and finding nothing—I decided to pull the drawers out entirely and crawl under the desk to see if it was stuck to the tabletop.

"Give me a light," I ordered Carter, holding my hand out for his phone. I hadn't brought mine, since it didn't exactly fit with my evening gown. He obliged, and I used the flashlight to search for—"Ah-hah! It's not a key, dumbass. It's a combination."

"What?" he exclaimed, dropping to his knees and attempting to see what I was looking at. Except there was nowhere near enough space for both of us and I shoved him back out again.

"Quit it," I snapped. "I'll read the numbers out."

An angry sound rumbled through him, but his legs moved out of my line of sight nonetheless. A moment later the electronic beep of the safe—I assumed—seemed to shriek through the room.

"Okay, go," he whispered.

I carefully, slowly, read the combination out and a second later the safe gave a happy double beep and its mechanical lock flicked open as I climbed out from under the desk.

Carter, grinning like a maniac, placed a duck on top of the huge stack of cash and snapped a photo.

"How do they know who placed which duck?" I asked, watching. "Could someone else find our awesome duck and claim it as their own?"

Carter shook his head, pocketing the picture then taking another on his phone. Backup, I had to guess, since there was a good chance the sauna had fucked our Polaroid film.

"Ducks are color coded *and* marked." He pointed to the little flame symbol on our duck's chest. "That's us."

I nodded, thinking. "Okay but say Nate found this duck… couldn't he just remove ours and place his in the same spot?"

"For one, it's against the rules. For two, I took a digital photo so it would be time stamped *just in case*. Anyone who doesn't do that deserves to be fucked over. Come on, let's keep going."

Again, Carter held me back while he checked if the coast was clear before ducking out into the hallway. He started down the hall to the right, but I had an idea of where I wanted to place my first duck so I grabbed his hand and pulled him the other way.

"What are you doing?" he asked in a confused whisper.

"Shh," I replied, placing a finger on my lips as we approached the bedroom we'd only so recently escaped. The one with two sleeping occupants.

Carter's eyes widened as I reached for the door handle, and he swiftly grabbed my wrist before I could open the door. "Spark," he hissed. "You're going to get us caught."

I rolled my eyes. "Only if you keep talking. Don't you trust me?"

His lips twitched with a shocked smile. "Not for a fucking second."

Fair. I shrugged. "Well…take a leap, I have a great idea."

In truth I expected him to drag me away, not willing to risk disqualification by getting caught. But he gave a short sigh and released my wrist. "Fine," he muttered. "Don't make me regret it."

Grinning, I carefully pushed the door open a crack and listened for the snoring before slipping back inside the room. Carter followed but waited by the door while I tiptoed across to the bed with my duck in hand.

The woman slept peacefully on her side, silk eye mask firmly in place and sheets pulled up to her shoulders. The man, though, snored like a chainsaw as he slumbered face down with one leg hanging off the bed and his bare ass exposed.

Perfect.

Barely daring to breathe, I crouched down and delicately balanced my duck on one of the man's hairy butt cheeks, then indicated for Carter to hand me the camera.

He shifted closer, handing me the Polaroid camera and taking a quick evidence shot on his phone. I lined up the duck in the viewfinder, making sure it was abundantly clear *where* it was placed, then pressed the shutter button.

The flash popped off, filling the room with light ever so briefly and panic swept through me.

Carter's strong hand grabbed the back of my neck, practically jerking me to my feet in his hurry to escape. I didn't argue, practically tripping over myself in my haste, but we paused outside the bedroom to listen.

Nothing.

Then…

Snoring.

"Holy shit," I breathed, a huge grin curving my lips.

Carter just shook his head, staring at me with an unreadable expression. "You're insane, Spark."

He might be right. But it felt so damn good.

# Chapter Nineteen

After my *cheeky* duck placement, Carter informed me he'd changed his plan for where to place his second duck. Turns out, his new plan was to position the duck inside the cup of Paige's discarded bra on the floor of the spare bedroom.

I pursed my lips as he positioned it, thinking. "Is this a winning duck? I mean, it could be anyone's bra. Right?"

Carter shook his head. "Nope." He snapped the picture then turned his smirk my way. "Nate gave her that one, he'll know."

My brows rose as we left the room. "Isn't that going to cause shit?"

"Yes, but that's not really our problem, is it? Besides, I'm sick to fucking death of Nate ignoring the red flags with Paige. She cheats on him constantly and not just with Royce." Carter gave no real emotion to that statement, but the tightness in his shoulders hinted at his annoyance.

I wet my lips, knowing I was walking thin ice talking about his friends. "Sounds like they're as bad as each other, then. Maybe they deserve what they've got."

Carter stopped dead and whirled to stare at me in bewilderment. "Excuse me? Nate is far from saintly but he's no cheater."

I scoffed. "Okay. So he didn't fuck Carly last year?"

Carter rubbed at the back of his neck, confusion fading away. "Ah, that mess. It's more complicated than it seems."

"Uh-huh, sure it is. Listen, it's gross that Paige is fucking around with other guys but Nate's a grade A dickhead, he deserves every little shred of bad karma he gets." I realized too late that I wasn't keeping my voice down and as though the universe was fucking laughing at me, Nate appeared out of a room down the hall with Paige on his ass.

"The fuck did you just say, Layne?" he snapped, face like a thunderstorm. A split second later, his brows pinched and he took in our state of undress.

I panicked. No way in hell was I getting caught in those crosshairs, so I did the only sane thing I could think to do. I grabbed Carter's wrist and took off running.

Carter's unhinged laughter followed as we ran down the main staircase at a speed that threatened a broken neck, but by some miracle we made it to the bottom without falling and I dragged him behind me into the ballroom.

Just as I was about to speak, he grabbed me swiftly and clamped a hand over my mouth.

"Shh," he breathed directly in my ear, smoothly ducking behind one of the heavy velvet curtains. My whole body erupted with flutters and I didn't fight his grip as his other hand splayed out across my ribs. Fucking hell, I needed to get laid and if Carter was offering…

"…just saw two come down this way…" someone said nearby and I froze. Utterly *froze*.

Carter wasn't trying to fuck me, he was keeping us from being caught.

Oof, how embarrassing. Good thing I hadn't acted on those thoughts.

Heavy footsteps echoed through the vacant ballroom, then the man sighed. "Maybe it was just cleaning crew. False alarm." The crackle of a radio suggested he was alone, speaking to security in another part of the house.

"...*copy that*..." the reply came a moment later "...*I've found a couple making out in the pool house.*"

The guard who'd seen us chuckled, then strolled slowly back out of the ballroom once more.

Carter waited a solid minute *after* the footsteps faded before he released his hold on me and we slipped out from behind the curtains.

"That was close," he murmured. "Let's drop your last duck and get the hell out of here. Where do you want to put it?"

I bit my lip, looking up. "There."

Carter followed my line of sight and his brows hitched when he registered what I meant. "You really are insane. How? Are you a secret acrobat?"

I rolled my eyes—something I was doing a lot on this unusual date night. "You're lucky you're pretty, Bassington, because you're fucking dumb. Chandeliers all require the ability to come down for cleaning and light bulb changes." I pointed to the heavy gold chain running from the enormous chandelier to the side of the room. "Lower it for me, I'll place the duck, then we raise it back up. Easy."

His lips pursed as his eyes tracked it out, then flicked to the wide-open doors of the ballroom. "Before security circles back and spots us," he pointed out. "I like it. Close the doors, Spark, I'll get the chain."

Grinning, I hurried to do as he said—hopefully security would think the cleaning crew had closed up—and he climbed onto a chair to reach the pulley chain and unhook the locking mechanism.

Within a minute, he had the chandelier gently lowered and I needed to wipe my mouth to check I wasn't drooling over the way his muscles flexed with the effort. This was definitely a good idea.

"Quick!" he prompted, "I'll be so pissed if we get caught now."

I nodded, refocusing my attention on the best spot for a duck. There was a flat section right in the center of the chandelier that would be perfect…except the damn thing was *huge* up close. It hadn't seemed that big on the ceiling, but standing beside it was a whole different story.

"Spark, come on. Place your duck," Carter hissed, and I waved a hand at him to say *shut up, I'm thinking*. Then I decided *fuck it* and started climbing onto the enormous gold and crystal structure.

Carter's shocked inhale was audible across the room, then he was storming toward me with alarm etched across his face. "What are you doing?" he demanded, "you're going to break something!"

I shrugged. "Too late now." I planted the red duck where I wanted it, right in the middle of the chandelier. "Perfect."

"Okay, good, now get the fuck out of there," he urged.

I shook my head. "Pictures," I reminded him and he tossed me the Polaroid camera.

Just as I lined up my shot, muffled voices sounded outside the ballroom doors and fear shot through me like a lightning bolt. Carter must have heard it too, because he frantically gestured for me to get the hell out of the chandelier.

Trouble was…I was caught. The hem of my lace panties had snagged on something and I really, *really* didn't want to take them off. "Pull it up!" I whisper-yelled at Carter—yes, it was possible to whisper a yell—and gestured urgently at the pulley chain. "Quick!"

The indecision crossing his face was evident, but the voices were right outside the ballroom doors now so it was do or die. He sprinted back to the chain and hoisted the massive light fixture—plus me—back to the ceiling.

Not a moment too soon, as well. The doors opened just as he locked the chain into place and slipped behind the nearest velvet drape.

Three people strode into the room, and I made myself as small as possible in the center of the chandelier, desperately praying to the universe that they wouldn't notice the slight sway to the fixture.

*Please, please, please don't break!*

I had to hope that the chain was strong enough to carry my extra weight. Surely it was, when the chandelier itself must weigh a figurative ton. Sweating, my pulse racing, I slipped my hand down to where my lace was caught and carefully worked to free it as the three people below spoke in low murmurs. One of them said something about Martin, I thought? It didn't help that their voices were muffled by masks.

Wait, what?

Oh shit. The three below me were in full black robes and masks just like Nate wore when he abducted me!

As they passed underneath my position, I glanced over to where Carter hid and tried to make eye contact. He shifted out enough to gesture something, but *fuck* if I knew what he was trying to say. I screwed up my nose, trying to telepathically convey that I had no idea what to do now.

He gestured again, the same thing. I still had no idea what he meant.

Then the three robed people exited the far side of the room and Carter darted out of his hiding spot. Faster than I could blink, he positioned himself directly under me and held out his arms.

"Now!" he hissed.

*Now what?!* Oh. Fucking hell... he wanted me to jump.

No time to think, no time to argue, I carefully shifted from my crouch and climbed out onto one of the chandelier arms. The whole structure tilted dramatically, and my heart lodged in my throat. It was now or never, so I placed my faith in the arms of Carter Bassington Junior.

For the second time since arriving at Nevaeh University, I freefell and saw my short, uneventful life flash before my eyes. But then Carter caught me and everything blurred as he sprinted us out of the mansion.

"Holy shit!" he whooped as he sprinted down the driveway with me still held firmly in his arms. "Holy fucking shit, Spark, you're *insane!*"

"Me?" I protested, holding onto his neck for dear life and determined not to drop the camera. "You're the one who told me to jump off a fucking chandelier!"

"No I didn't!" he exclaimed, laughing somewhat hysterically but not slowing his pace. "Is that what you thought I meant? I said *now* about taking the photo! I would have used the pulley to get you down but you just...jumped!"

Oh. *Oh.* That made more sense, come to think of it.

Carter cackled, finally stopping and putting me down beside his blacked-out SUV parked by the side of the street just out of sight of the mansion. The door popped open automatically and I realized the driver had been waiting for us this whole time.

Carter gestured for me to get in first, and I pulled the satin robe around myself self-consciously as I slid across the leather seat. To my relief, though, the privacy screen was raised and the driver said nothing before starting the engine and pulling out into the road.

"I didn't take the photo," I said with a groan, handing Carter the camera. "I was so focused on getting out without being seen. I didn't take a picture of the last duck."

He shrugged, grinning. "Don't stress. I took one while I was hiding." He pulled out his phone and showed me the zoomed in shot of me crouching in the center of the chandelier with a little red duck beside me. "If we don't win this challenge, Spark, I'm calling it rigged."

I smiled, because I was as confident as him. No way would anyone beat our ducks.

"This was...fun," I admitted reluctantly. "Thanks for inviting me."

Carter snatched up my hand and pressed a kiss to my knuckles. "The pleasure was entirely mine, Spark. You surprised me...and that doesn't happen often."

Fucking flutters were back. I bit the inside of my lip and gave a smile in response. Better to quit while I was ahead, so I yawned and turned to look out my window at the passing night. Then I shivered and Carter draped an arm around me, pulling me closer to lean against his chest.

"Just to keep you warm," he murmured, and I didn't question that logic.

Not once did I wonder why we didn't simply turn the heating on. Idiot.

# Chapter Twenty

Carter dropped me back at my dorm with the information that we wouldn't know who'd won until the morning. Everyone's duck pics needed to be submitted to…someone…and then a winner chosen after review.

Carly was already fast asleep by the time I'd showered and washed my makeup off, so I couldn't even debrief with her. My phone was full of messages from Heath asking whether I was back yet, and asking to talk in person but I didn't have the energy. So I turned my phone off and went to bed instead.

When I woke up late the next morning, I nearly had a heart attack.

"Get the fuck out of my room," I snarled, dragging a pillow over my head even as my heart raced. It was that, or throw it, and I didn't have faith in my aim while half asleep.

"Trust me," Nate replied, surly as ever, "there are plenty of other places I'd rather be right now. It's a shame you're awake because I was about to throw some cold water in your face."

I risked a peek by lifting the pillow. Liar. He was slouched in my desk chair with no water in sight. "You must *really* love getting kicked in the balls. Is it a kink thing?"

Nate's answering smile was cold and full of judgment. "You'd know all about kinks, being a professional. Carter is walking a thin line messing around with you like he did last night...his mother would cut him off if she found out."

That thought actually worried me. Carter and I had *fun* doing the challenge together, and his snap temper hadn't come out even once. The idea that he could be in shit for choosing me as his date...

Except that wasn't what Nate meant, was it? He assumed we were fucking, and for once I didn't totally blame him for the assumption considering I'd been in underwear and a robe, and Carter was just in his suit pants.

"Shouldn't you be worrying about your own miserable relationship right now, not obsessing over my sex life? I know you heard what I said last night. Paige is cheating on you right under your nose."

His expression hardened. "That is why I'm here in your rather unpleasant company, Layne. Carter is acting like he doesn't know what I'm talking about."

I sighed and sat up with a yawn. Nate scowled as I gave an exaggerated stretch, thinking about what I wanted to say on the whole subject. Thankfully I'd changed into an oversized T-shirt before bed, and my blankets covered me from the waist down, so I wasn't giving him a free show or anything.

"Whose T-shirt is that?" Nate asked, startling me with confusion.

I blinked, peering down at what I was wearing. It was nothing special, just a faded sports tee that I liked because it was so soft and well worn. "Uh, mine?" Or it was *now*. It'd originally belonged to an ex-boyfriend. "Weird question. Anyway, get out of my room. In case I didn't make myself clear the last time you visited, you aren't *welcome*."

"Tell me what you know about my girlfriend, and I'll go," he shot back, leaning forward with his elbows on his knees. "I don't see what the problem is."

I coughed a laugh of disbelief, my eyes wide. "You don't? You broke into my room—the door was locked—and sat there like a creep while I slept because you're too scared to ask your girlfriend if she's cheating on you...but you don't see the problem? Uh huh. I guess you didn't get into your master's program based on academics."

His lip curled with anger. "I'm studying for my doctorate, thanks."

I rolled my eyes. "I don't care. Get out."

"Not until you tell me what you know. Why are you playing coy now? You had *plenty* to say last night."

"I'm not playing *anything*, you dick. I also don't owe you *shit*. Even if I wanted to tell you what I know, you wouldn't believe me and you fucking know it. You just want me to say the bad thing so you can discredit it and move on. Go ask your so-called friends, because trust me...they know."

His eyes narrowed in a hard glare. "What the fuck is that supposed to mean?"

I groaned, rubbing the bridge of my nose. "It's like talking to a block of cheese. Get it through your head, Nate. We aren't friends, you and me. I owe you nothing, and don't particularly fucking care that your girlfriend is fucking around on you considering what you did to Carly last year. But even if I did care, you *won't believe me*. So why even waste my breath?"

"Try me," he snapped, folding his arms across his chest. Stubborn fuck.

"Fine," I replied with a tight smile. "Paige is fucking Royce."

Okay. That was a little bit satisfying. I never claimed to be a good person, and hurting Nate gave me a spark of joy.

But then he had to ruin it by shaking his head. "Point proven, Layne. I should have known you'd hold your secrets just to spite me."

I threw my hands up in frustration and flopped back into my pillows. "Okay, whatever, close the door behind you."

"I would say, *blow me*, but I'm not interested in paying your going rate," Nate sneered, shoving out of my office chair and grabbing the door handle aggressively. "If you have *any* humanity, I'd stay away from Carter though. His mother has big plans and none of them involve a whore from Panner City, so don't ruin his future."

Anger and outrage flooded through me. "Which is it, Nate? Heath or Carter? Who am I corrupting today? Or wasn't I supposedly fucking Royce last night too? Oh wait, that was Paige."

The slam of my door was the only response I got, and I flipped over to scream into my pillow. Nate made me *so fucking mad* but I was even more irate that I'd literally told him the truth and as predicted, he didn't believe me.

Furious and totally awake, I got up and dressed. It was Saturday, and I had a shitload of studying to do if I wanted to keep up with classes. I also wanted to find the campus gym to work off some of the shit food and sugary coffee I'd been consuming lately.

As I waited for my coffee a little while later, I was almost disappointed that Heath didn't mysteriously appear like he had so often in the past two weeks. When I ordered and paid, I went as far as texting him back, agreeing that we should talk.

My message showed as delivered, then immediately *read*. But by the time my coffee was ready, he hadn't replied. I bit my lip, staring at the message thread. There was no *rule* that he had to reply straight away but considering how many messages he'd sent during the night, it just seemed odd.

With a sigh, I tucked my phone into my bag and made my way back to my room to study.

I'd picked up coffee for Carly, so knocked lightly on her door when I got back. There was every chance she was still asleep, but she jerked the door open a moment later with a frazzled look on her face.

"Thank fuck, you're here," she exclaimed, gesturing for me to come in. "I checked your room and you weren't there, I thought—" She cut herself off with a deep inhale, like she was trying to calm herself down. "Is that for me?"

"Of course," I replied, handing her coffee over. "What's going on? Did something happen?"

Her head bobbed in a silent *yes* as she took a big swallow of coffee. "Mm-hmm, yes. Martin is in hospital."

My mouth fell open. "What? Why? What happened?"

Carly sighed heavily, climbing back into her messy bed. "Okay so the duck challenge, right? We had a plan to plant our ducks in Lintan's garage like inside his classic cars on the dashboards."

I nodded thoughtfully. "That's a good idea." Not as good as mine and Carter's placements, but still decent. "So how'd Martin get hurt?"

She shrugged. "I have no clue. Turns out the cars are alarmed and we split up in our panic. I took off one way, he went the other. I thought he'd gotten out but then I woke up like half an hour ago and saw a message from Krystal that he's in Prosper Private, in a coma!"

I blinked a couple of times, trying to put the pieces together. "Did he fall or something?"

Carly bit the edge of her lip, nervous. "I don't know. Krystal said someone told her he was beaten up. But who would do that? The challenge is not super legal and all but Lintan's security are professional. If you're caught, you're just escorted off the property and your name recorded. That's it. They wouldn't…" She trailed off, running a shaking hand through her hair. "I don't get it, Ash. Why would someone beat Martin up?"

I wet my lips, thinking back to Abigail's dairy. She'd detailed something similar happening to herself…that at some fancy party she'd failed a task and had the shit kicked out of her. She hadn't been put in hospital, as far as she'd recorded, but the similarity was chilling.

"Would the society have done it?" I asked quietly, hating that my doubts were all back in force after such a fun night.

Carly seemed taken back by that question. "What? No way. Girl, I feel like you have totally the wrong idea about Devil's Backbone. It's not like…a cult or anything. It's just a bunch of rich kids doing dumb shit because we're entitled, arrogant, and bored. Yes, I put myself into the same category, unfortunately. But no one is getting hurt in the DB, and there's no freaking way anyone gets beaten up for failing a duck challenge. It's supposed to be *fun*."

I swallowed back my concerns because her phrasing rang oddly familiar. I seriously wished I still had Abigail's diary to refer back to because the finer details were way too hazy in my mind and getting distorted by my own lived experiences.

"Okay. Sure, I just wondered if maybe that was a thing…"

Carly shook her head firmly. "Definitely not. This had to have been something that happened after he escaped the mansion. Maybe he was walking home and got mugged for his Rolex or something?"

"Maybe," I murmured. "It's possible. Are you going to visit him in the hospital?"

"No, he's not permitted visitors apparently. Ugh, I feel *so bad* because I took his car when I got out. I should have waited…we were partners, after all. I just figured he'd call an Uber." She screwed up her face, guilt etched all over her features.

Just as I was about to reassure her that it *was not* her fault, a heavy knock on her door interrupted me.

"Who is it?" she called out, not getting up off her bed.

"Carter," the response came through the door. "Have you seen Ashley this morning?"

Carly gave me a long, accusing look and I could feel my face heating with a blush that implied something had actually happened last night. When in reality, it'd only happened in my filthy dreams.

Shooting her a *shut up* glare, I opened the door and tried not to blush any harder as I met Carter's eyes. "Hey, what's up."

His brows hitched, then he gave me a sly smirk. "Pack a bag, Spark. Our flight leaves in two hours."

Confusion had me wrinkling my nose. "Um, what? Flight to where?"

His grin spread wider. "Paris, babe…we won the duck challenge!"

## Chapter Twenty-One

Carter had failed to mention that the duck challenge came with a very real prize in addition to the smug satisfaction of beating Nate. Though that was a sweet feeling, knowing how pissed he'd be to miss out. Apparently he'd been planning a romantic weekend in the City of Love with Paige, but now Carter and I were taking the trip instead.

"Nate was in my room this morning when I woke up," I told Carter as we got settled on the private jet waiting for us. "He wanted to know about Paige…"

Carter raised a brow, mildly curious at best. "What'd you tell him?"

"The truth," I replied, buckling my seat belt in preparation for takeoff. "That she's fucking Royce right under his nose."

Carter's expression hardened. "You did?" He blinked a couple of times, staring at me. "How did he take that?"

I sighed. "He didn't believe me."

The tension seemed to rush out of him, and he relaxed back into his huge leather seat opposite me. "Ah. Well, that's not unexpected. Do you want to know about our itinerary?"

The change of subject was obvious enough that I went with it and listened with barely concealed excitement as Carter ran through the details of our prize trip. I'd been to Paris before, with my dad, but it was definitely different to visit with Carter.

Soon after we reached cruising altitude, he pulled out his laptop and put on headphones, informing me that he had some assignments to submit before he could enjoy our trip.

It was a good reminder, so I decided to do the same since I'd brought my work along as well. For several hours we worked in comfortable silence—both listening to our music on headphones—until the flight attendant served us dinner.

After we ate, Carter continued with his work but since I was finished, I got comfy to watch a movie...then promptly fell asleep. In my defense, the whole duck gala evening hadn't given me a lot of time for rest.

When I woke, we were landing and Carter was...different.

"Did you sleep at all on the flight?" I asked him after his fifth grunt—instead of an answer—while on route to our hotel. "You seem grouchy."

His response was a flat-eyed glare and I raised my hands in surrender. Clearly something had happened while I was passed out snoring because the fun Carter from the duck gala was long gone and in his place was someone I could easily identify as one of Nathaniel Essex's friends. Total dick.

Checking in for our hotel, he made a whole scene in demanding separate rooms rather than the suite that'd been booked. Enough so that I could feel my face heating with embarrassment at the people staring.

"Was that necessary?" I asked in a whisper as we stepped into the elevator.

Carter swiped his access card and stabbed the button for our floor. "Yes, it was," he replied, his voice cold. "We aren't dating, it would be inappropriate to share a room. What would your boyfriend think?"

I scoffed, shaking my head. "Cut the shit, Bassington. Even if

Heath and I were dating—which we're not—you wouldn't give a shit what he thought." Then I remembered something Nate had said when he broke into my bedroom back at the Nevaeh dorm. "Is this about your mom?"

Carter's head swiveled so fast I worried he might have pulled a muscle. "Excuse you?"

I licked my lips, sweating under the sudden intensity of his gaze. "Nate warned me that your mom wouldn't approve…I imagine because he's still painting me as a prostitute."

Anger flashed across Carter's expression and his jaw tightened with a flex in his cheek. "Nate has a big fucking mouth."

I rolled my eyes. Again. "So much for Mister I-don't-believe-in-secrets."

He didn't dignify that with a response, just strode out of the elevator ahead of me when the doors opened. We were on the same floor, but separate rooms—per his diva request at reception.

I sighed and followed more slowly. His door was already swinging shut before I even found my room number and swiped the keycard.

"So much for a fun trip," I murmured to myself, stepping into the hotel room. It was a downgrade on the suite we were meant to share, but it was still a *huge* upgrade on my last trip to Paris.

I moved further inside, my breath catching as I saw the view. Floor-to-ceiling windows looked out directly onto the Eiffel Tower, and I stood there for a long time just…admiring. Surly travel companion or not, this was pretty incredible.

Hotel staff delivered my bag shortly thereafter and I made myself at home, taking a shower and relaxing with a coffee and croissant thanks to room service.

Carly had been blowing up my phone so I answered *all* her questions, then checked if Heath had replied. Disappointment settled on me like a wet cloak to see I'd been left on read, and I swallowed the confusing emotions welling up inside.

Carter had told me we had a private tour booked of the Louvre today, so I pushed Heath out of my mind and got ready for some culture and art. Stupidly, I assumed he would meet me in the lobby but the sharply suited tour-guide only had my name on his placard.

We waited for about ten minutes, then asked reception to call Carter's room. When she apologized and told me there was no answer, I realized I'd be touring alone today.

My tour guide was lovely, very knowledgeable and polite, but I was a little sad that Carter hadn't joined me. Even grumpy Carter was kind of fun, but it was an amazing day nonetheless. My guide dropped me back to the hotel in the evening and advised that my dinner reservation was in an hour at the hotel restaurant.

I thanked him and headed upstairs to change. Passing Carter's door, I paused and debated knocking, but decided against it. If he wanted to join me, he knew where I'd be.

Even so, I startled when he slid into the seat opposite me at dinner later that evening.

"Oh, I'm sorry I think you have the wrong table," I said sweetly, recovering quickly. "I'm actually dining alone. My travel companion seems to have a terrible case of gonorrhea and is bedridden. Poor dear."

A touch of amusement tilted his lips. "Is that the story you're going with? How terribly unglamorous." He shook out his linen napkin and placed it over his lap. "Have you ordered already?"

I sipped my glass of wine before replying. "The menu is all in French," I admitted quietly, "and I don't speak French, so I asked the waiter what he recommended."

Carter gave me a sharp look. "What did he recommend?"

I shrugged. "Beats me, I don't speak French."

A genuine smile flashed across his lips. "You're…" he sighed, shaking his head, then gestured for the waiter to attend our table.

For some moments, Carter spoke with the man in fluent French, gesturing to me, to the menu, and generally talking with his hands. It was mesmerizing, and I crossed my legs under the table in an attempt to refocus.

When the waiter left, Carter turned his deep blue eyes back to me and I squirmed. Damn bad boy crush was back in force.

"How was your day?" he asked politely, linking his fingers on the table in front of himself. "Did you enjoy the Louvre?"

I pursed my lips, reminded of his no-show. "It was lovely, thanks. It was such a pleasant surprise to have a day in Paris all to myself with no high-maintenance diva boys around to ruin the atmosphere."

His brows lifted. "High-maintenance diva boy?"

I shrugged. "If the Louboutin fits…" Because I hadn't failed to notice the red sole of his shiny black loafers when he sat down.

Carter's eyes narrowed and I suspected I'd hit a nerve, but I also didn't much care. He'd been in a pissy mood since we landed for *no good reason* and it was rude.

"Do people not call you on your bad manners very often, Carter? Is it a rich thing? Because I'm thinking you're a little out of touch with human decency." I sipped my wine again, needing the liquid courage to keep my defenses up. It was too easy to let bygones be bygones with him sitting right there across the table looking like a delicious snack.

He blinked slowly. "I'm sorry, did you say *human decency*?"

I licked my lips, doubling down. "Yes."

"Wow…" he drawled, shaking his head. "Here was me thinking you might have appreciated me *not* taking advantage and pretending there was only one bed available. I guess I misjudged you, Ashley, maybe you were hoping to suck my dick and slap me with the bill later? What's the going rate, again? Six grand, right?"

Shock saw me nearly choke on my inhale, because the venom behind his words was undeniable.

Rather than a snappy, cutting comeback, all I could think of was how hurtful he was being. And what the fuck had I done to deserve this from him, when I'd helped him win the stupid duck challenge that he cared so much about?

Silence stretched between us and my eyes burned with mounting tears. Fucking hell, why was I reacting like a smacked puppy all of a sudden?

Carter stared back at me, waiting for me to say something. Then his cold expression softened and he sighed. "Shit, Spark, I didn't mean—"

"You did, though," I choked out. "It was my mistake for thinking Nate was the only asshole in your circle, but apparently you're more similar than I realized." Not wanting to suffer any more of his insults, I pushed my chair out and tossed my napkin on the table.

"Where are you going, Ashley?" he protested as I grabbed my coat and purse. "You haven't eaten anything and—"

"None of your concern, Carter," I snapped back. "I'm sure I can exchange a quick blow job for a meal out on the streets of Paris somewhere."

Not waiting around to continue our argument—since we'd drawn a lot of attention already—I stormed out of the restaurant and left him to deal with the bill. It was the least he could do.

Behind me, I heard the shatter of glass but I didn't stop or turn to look. Carter Bassington Junior clearly did not appreciate having his poor behavior pointed out, and was reacting like a child.

Rather than return to my room, I slipped my coat on and headed out into the night. Thank god I'd grabbed a coat for dinner, despite not having left the hotel. Force of habit, more than anything but I was glad for the warmth as I stepped outside.

I was hungry, and in a city like Paris there were *plenty* of amazing places to eat where I didn't feel like such a fish out of water. I'd passed several places earlier with my tour guide that I'd made a mental note of, so started down the street toward the one I'd liked the most.

Bistro Papillion was a tiny little restaurant advertising raclette fondue, tucked between two much larger buildings and from memory it was just three blocks or so away.

Barely one block into my walk and I heard the quick, heavy footsteps of a man behind me.

I sighed. "Carter, I don't want to talk to you. I'm going—" I whirled around to tell him to *fuck off* then cut off abruptly when I realized it wasn't Carter following me at all.

The man approaching was a similar size and build but wore a hood pulled low over his face, disguising his features. No way in hell would Carter be out in public wearing beat up old sneakers like this guy, though.

I sucked a sharp breath, second guessing myself for a moment. Maybe he was just walking in the same direction and—

Nope. I stood frozen as he rushed at me, grabbing the front of my dress and shouting something in French.

*Fuck.* I'd stormed out into the street alone, at night, in a foreign city and my own safety never even crossed my stupid pea-sized mind. Now apparently I was paying the price of that foolishness.

# Chapter Twenty-Two

A scream ripped from my lungs as the man shoved me, making me stumble, but his brutal backhand across my face cut the sound short by knocking the air clean out of me. Was he trying to rob me? Or... worse?

Whatever he wanted, he was making angry, urgent demands but I didn't understand *anything* and the pain from my cheek made my head spin.

"T-take my p-purse," I stuttered, trying to shove my bag at the man, but he snarled something back at me and started shoving me into an alleyway.

Apparently, he wasn't interested in my money.

I drew another breath to scream, but before the sound could leave my lips I was abruptly released. I staggered backwards, losing my balance and falling on my ass in shock as I tried to process what'd just happened.

Panicked screams of pain clued me in and I found my attacker on the ground of the alleyway with a dark shape looming over him. Hitting *him*. The thud of fist hitting flesh reached my ears between the man's agonized wails and I gasped.

"Carter?" It was instinct supported by absolutely zero evidence but my gut *knew*. I scrambled to my feet, foolishly rushing forward instead of running for my goddamn life. I couldn't just leave him, though, what if the guy had a knife or a gun and Carter got hurt?

"Carter! Stop!" I exclaimed, confirming that it was indeed my handsome travel companion with a bad attitude currently beating the ever-loving shit out of my mugger. "Stop, you're going to kill him!"

Blood already coated the man's face, and he'd stopped wailing, which suggested maybe he was unconscious, so I grabbed at Carter's wrist to stop his next swing.

In a flash, he turned on me. A startled squeak escaped me as his bloody hand circled my throat and my back slammed into the brick wall of the alleyway. Carter's deep blue eyes were practically black in the darkness, and for a moment it was like he had no clue who I even was.

Then he startled, his expression shifting from furious determination to shock and regret in an instant. "Spark? What the—" He cut himself off, swallowing hard and shaking his head in stunned disbelief. "You *stupid woman!* What were you thinking? You could have been hurt!"

My jaw dropped. "Me? You! Don't call me stupid, you arrogant, spoiled shithead! How dare you—" Carter silenced my insults in the only way that could have possibly worked in that moment.

He kissed me.

My brain short-circuited with shock…then before I could fully comprehend what was happening, I realized I was kissing him back. Oh shit, kissing Carter was like licking a live wire and I couldn't stop myself from doing it again, and again, not caring that I'd be burned.

His hand on my throat increased pressure, his thumb and index finger digging into the flesh below my jaw like he was holding me captive. Like I wasn't a totally willing participant as I grabbed his shirt and pulled him closer. My whole body flushed with intense heat as I remembered how delicious he'd looked in the sauna wearing nothing but his boxer-briefs with sweat running down his artfully tattooed chest.

A rogue whimper escaped as he bit my lip, and the sound only seemed to encourage him to kiss me harder. This time his other hand gathered the fabric of my dress, scrunching it up and out of the way until he could grasp my bare thigh and hitch my leg up around his waist.

The moment I tilted my hips forward, I collided with his thick hardness and he let out the most delicious moan that made me desperate for more. I roughly yanked on his shirt, untucking it and sliding my hands beneath, searching for the button of his pants.

"Spark," he groaned, kissing my jaw as I flicked his button through the eyelet and grasped a handful of his straining erection. I could safely say I was no longer thinking straight. My face throbbed from the smack my attacker delivered, but I'd all but forgotten about the pain thanks to the heady arousal flooding through my whole body.

Carter bit my earlobe, and I gasped. Fucking hell, why did *that* feel so good? He immediately followed the bite with sucking, and I nearly combusted as my head rolled to the side. Then I locked eyes on the unmoving man just six feet away, a pool of blood under his head.

Tension snapped through me and I inhaled sharply. "Carter... is he dead?" I could hardly believe I was even asking...but it didn't look good. Then immediately after that thought, my eyes burned with overwhelming emotion. "You saved me."

Carter pulled away just far enough to meet my gaze, his dark eyes serious. "You scared the fucking life out of me, Spark. Never, *ever* do that again."

The intensity of that statement burned me up inside, even if it made my stubborn defiance raise its head. "Don't tell me what to do."

His brows lifted as he drew a deep breath. Then a soft, ice-cold laugh huffed out. "I want to fuck you so badly right now."

"We shouldn't..." I replied with a breathy whisper. It wasn't a *no* though. Damn it, I was one hundred percent going to regret this later but I couldn't seem to make my own better sense prevail. As if my body was mocking my indecision, a delicious shiver ran through me from where his hand grasped my thigh and I moaned.

Carter dipped back in to kiss my mouth, teasing me with light pecks rather than the soul consuming depth of our first kiss. "Shouldn't..." he repeated "...but?"

Smart man, he heard the silent *but* implied. "But I want to."

His response to that admission was his hand shifted from my thigh to my throbbing pussy, his long fingers hooking the crotch of my panties aside and plunging inside. My gasp echoed through the alley and my eyes fluttered shut with the heady pleasure, all my focus centered around his fingers buried in my cunt. So freaking good.

"Carter," I whined, rocking against his hand. My intention was to say *we can't do this* but instead what I said out loud was, "I need more..."

He kept finger-fucking me as I desperately freed his thick cock from his underwear and pumped my fist along his length. Crap on a cracker, he was big. If I wasn't already saturated I'd be worried he would hurt me, but as it was I couldn't think of anything so sensible. I just needed him inside me.

A low groan rolled from him as he released my throat and grabbed my other thigh, hitching me up around his waist so I no longer had feet on the ground at all. It also positioned us perfectly so the transition from his fingers to the tip of his cock was almost magnetic.

"Oh!" I exclaimed as his broad head slipped in. We were forgetting something important, I was sure of it, but every time the thought pricked at my mind, I violently shoved it aside. This was the only important thing I needed to think about.

"Spark..." Carter hissed, his jaw tight as he shifted his position slightly. "Don't scream, we need to be fast." Then he thrust in hard and fast, pinning me to the wall with his dick.

I screamed. Then he chuckled and covered my mouth with his hand.

"I said *don't* scream," he whispered with a laugh. "Otherwise, someone might come to investigate and that would be bad."

Oh shit. Because of the mugger.

My gaze flicked to the man still lying motionless on the ground a short distance away, and the whimper I let out was more panic than arousal. Carter's hand smelled strongly of blood, metallic and earthy, but the way his dick filled me was confusing my emotions. Especially when he started to rock back and forth, exquisite shivers of pure pleasure chasing through my core.

But then...the mugger. *Was* he dead? What would that mean for Carter if he was?

Carter seemed to read my mind, or maybe just followed my gaze and guessed, but his hand shifted from my mouth to cover my eyes instead. "Just don't look," he told me in a rough whisper, his lips chasing kisses over my jaw once more. "Don't look, just feel." He emphasized that point by thrusting harder and making me groan.

Fuck. This was *so wrong*. Not just the fact that his hands were literally stained with blood and his victim lay possibly dead nearby... but also for the fact he was a total dickhead and had been treating me like crap all day. I really, really shouldn't be fucking him but I also couldn't find it in myself to stop...

"Oh my god," I gasped, my fingers clenching against his tight oblique muscles as he fucked me. "Carter, we really shouldn't be—*ah, yes!*" He'd just found my sweet spot, and my whole body started to coil up and shake. "Holy shit, don't stop, I'm so close."

His breath came in rough pants as he did as he was told, repeating the same stroke again and again, his lips brushing my neck, and his hand firmly planted over my eyes. It was bliss and allowed me to forget where we were for just the few minutes I needed to shatter.

"Carter!" I moaned, crashing into orgasm without any attempts to hold it at bay. My pussy clenched tight around his girth, my legs holding him close like I wanted him to climb inside my skin and chills broke out all over my flesh. It was utterly delicious.

He shuddered and groaned, his teeth tugging at my earlobe again. "Perfection," he whispered, hoarse and breathless. "Once won't be enough."

With that confusing statement, he pumped his hips hard a half dozen times then grunted his own release deep within my cunt. There was no attempt to pull out, and I sent up a mental thanks to my past-self for getting an IUD to eliminate pregnancy risk.

For a few moments, we stayed exactly as we were, locked together and breathing heavily. Then Carter slowly raised his hand from my eyes and crushed a kiss to my mouth. It wasn't a quick kiss, taking his time to kiss me thoroughly and adding to the intense head spins I was already suffering before he gently withdrew and lowered me to standing.

"Come on," he ordered, linking our fingers together and hastily stuffing his cock back into his pants. "Let's get out of here."

I took a couple of steps, following, before I shook my head and pulled my hand free. "What about—" I gestured to the unconscious man. I hoped he was just unconscious.

Carter shrugged one shoulder and grabbed my hand again. "He deserved it."

This time pure shock saw me comply when he tugged me out of the alleyway and back toward our hotel, but by the time we reached the lobby I was practically sick with guilt.

"Carter," I started to say, jogging a few paces to catch up from where I was trailing behind. "We—oh, what are you doing?" He had his phone in hand—the one not grasping my fingers like a vise—and was texting.

He glanced up from his phone, meeting my eyes as we paused in front of the hotel elevators. Rather than dropping my hand, he used the one holding his phone to press the call button. "I'm ordering an ambulance to check on your mugger," he murmured, "though I'm sure he will be fine, I didn't hit him *that* hard."

I screwed up my face, remembering how much blood there had been. "Um...okay. I guess."

The elevator arrived and we stepped inside, Carter scanning his keycard and pressing our floor while I closed my eyes a moment. My head was *thumping* and dimly I remembered being hit before the guy tried dragging me into the alleyway. Before Carter saved me.

A deep shiver ran through me and I dislodged my hand from Carter's so I could wrap my arms around myself. That man hadn't wanted my purse, and if it wasn't for Carter I dreaded to think about how it would have ended.

Carter turned toward me, taking one quick look at my posture before scowling and wrapping me in his tight embrace. An unexpected sob ripped from my chest as I leaned into him, my arms snaking around his broad frame and holding on for dear life. The hug wasn't sexual, it was *safe*.

"I've got you, Spark," he murmured into my hair, his face buried in the crook of my neck.

I closed my eyes, hot tears squeezing from between my lashes and running silently down my cheeks. Carter Bassington was a goddamn tornado, but right now I was safe in the eye of the storm.

At least for right now, there was nowhere else I'd rather be.

## Chapter Twenty-Three

The rest of the evening was a blur. Carter took me back to his room and directed me to shower while he called for room service. When I got out, clean and wrapped up in a hotel robe, he gently held an icepack on my cheek while growling at me to eat the food that'd arrived.

More than a little bit, I wanted to kiss him again. I wanted him to fuck me until I passed out from sheer exhaustion, but instead he just…held me. It was unexpected, but not unwelcome.

In the morning, I woke up before him. He slept soundly with his body curled around mine and one hand grasping my bare breast where the robe had fallen open in the night. I lay there for some time, deciding whether to lean into his touch…whether he'd be into waking up with my lips wrapped around his cock. But ultimately my own fear of rejection and guilt over everything that'd happened saw me slide out of his bed and scurry to my own room without waking him.

"Holy crap, Ashley," I whispered to myself as the door to my room clicked shut behind me. Somehow through all the madness I hadn't lost my access key because it'd been in my coat pocket rather than my purse. My phone and wallet were probably still in the alleyway, though, which took me into a whole new line of worry.

"Fuck!" I whispered, pacing my room. My phone and wallet were in the alleyway beside the scene of a very violent assault. Surely the police would be here soon to question me?

My stomach churned and I raced to the bathroom just in case the anxiety decided to make me vomit. Thankfully, I had a pretty strong gut and instead I just splashed my face with cold water then cringed to see the bruise shadowing my cheek.

It didn't hurt too much, though. Probably could be covered with makeup. The ache between my thighs was a different matter, though I was the only one who knew about that.

My face in the reflection turned pink just thinking about how I'd let Carter fuck me against the brick wall of the alleyway. What had I been thinking?

Clearly, not a lot. Just that I was insanely attracted to him, and emotions were at an all-time high. Yeah. That was it. Adrenaline was a hell of an aphrodisiac, and we hadn't been thinking clearly, either one of us. I'd almost bet that in the light of a new day, Carter would be back to his aloof, bad attitude once more and pretend nothing happened.

With a small sigh of disappointment, I left the bathroom and hunted through my small suitcase for a fresh outfit. According to our itinerary, we had a private tour of the catacombs booked for this morning. Part of me was anxious to see how Carter would behave but part of me was already resigned to the fact I'd be touring alone again.

It was only when I sat on the edge of my bed to put on shoes that I realized…Carter's room faced the other side of the hotel with no view of the Eiffel Tower. And his room had been noticeably smaller. Had he done that deliberately?

Surely not.

I dismissed the thought as the hotel maybe mixing up our keys and headed down to the lobby to get coffee and a croissant before the tour guide arrived.

A silly little spark of hope stayed alight as I sat in the coffee shop, sipping my café au lait and nibbling on the most buttery delicious pain au chocolat...watching the door and hoping Carter might show up. But eventually I had to mentally scold myself for being desperate and brush the crumbs off my dress.

Carrying the weight of disappointment, I charged my bill to the room and made my way into the main lobby to meet my guide. It was the same gentleman from the day before, and he greeted me with a warm smile while gesturing for me to accompany him outside.

I murmured a polite thank you as he held the car door open, and I slid inside.

The thump of the door closing made me flinch with its finality. Carter wasn't coming.

I'd been a fucking *idiot* to let things go so far last night. He'd been nothing but rude since we landed in Paris, and there I was practically *begging* for his dick in a dirty alleyway. Talk about leaning into the slander. Nate would have a fucking field day if he found out.

A burst of regret coated my tongue with bitterness as I thought about Heath. What would Heath say?

I desperately wanted to text him...to maybe try and explain myself and blame it all on the adrenaline before Carter could brag to his friends...but I didn't have my phone, so could do nothing.

The door popped open again, making me gasp in fright and cut my melancholy thoughts short.

"Sorry I'm late," Carter said, flashing me a totally disarming smile. "Shift over, Spark."

Stunned, I did as I was told, making space for him to climb into the car and pull the door shut behind himself. He buckled his seat belt, told our driver we were good to go, then turned to me with narrowed eyes.

"You snuck out," he accused. "I almost overslept this tour."

I stared back at him with confusion. "I just figured...um...you weren't coming."

A flash of a sly grin touched his lips, but quickly disappeared again as he handed me something. "Here, I figured you'd want this back."

I gaped at the purse he'd put in my hand. It was the one I'd lost in the alleyway. "You—" I cut myself off, opening it to check that my phone, cash, ID—it was all still inside. "How?"

He shrugged. "It's a mystery."

I blinked twice. "It's a mystery?"

He nodded. "I'm very mysterious."

Words failed me. He was *confusing*, that was for fucking sure. Still, I had my phone and ID back, which must mean I wouldn't be questioned by Parisian police about the assault of a mugger.

"Thank you," I said softly. "Is the guy…?"

"Fine," he replied, a little frosty. "No lasting harm done."

I breathed a sigh of relief, my shoulders sagging. "Thank fuck. I was so scared he'd died or something."

"So…are you looking forward to seeing the catacombs?" he asked, changing the subject entirely, as he picked up my hand from where I'd rested it between our seats.

Tongue-tied, I watched him link our fingers together and the spark of stupid hope within me burst into a fire of delight.

"Um, yeah," I finally replied, remembering that he'd asked a question.

His smug smile told me that he knew exactly what kind of effect his touch was having, but it didn't stop him. So much for him pretending nothing had happened between us. He was officially throwing me for a whole damn loop.

It was only a short drive to get to the entrance for the catacombs and for the first part of our private tour Carter *mostly* behaved himself. He held my hand, our fingers intertwined, but he was polite and curious about the information our tour guide presented.

When the guide's back was turned, though, he didn't miss an

opportunity to brush against me, cop a quick feel or brush a kiss over my skin, to the point I was flushed and flustered barely half an hour into the tour.

"Stop it," I whispered eventually, when he'd very casually tweaked my hard nipple and I'd accidentally moaned out loud.

His grin made me roll my eyes and I whacked him with the back of my hand. "Cut it out," I murmured. "Or I'll drag you into one of these alcoves to make good on all that teasing."

Carter's brows shot up in surprise. "Would you?" He glanced around, gesturing to all the skulls and bones of long dead humans. "Down here?"

I licked my lips, my thighs tightening with anticipation. "Would *you?*"

He stared at me a moment, then cleared his throat. "Pierre? You can go."

Our guide—who had wandered some distance away from us—circled back with a puzzled expression. "Sir?"

"You can go," Carter repeated, handing him a wad of Euros. "We will find our own way out."

The guide looked like he wanted to argue, but glanced down at the cash in his hand and nodded slowly. "Very well, sir, please ensure you follow the markings." He indicated what he meant, then gave me a polite nod and walked away.

My lips parted in shock. "Um...is he leaving us down here?"

"What were you saying about the alcoves, Spark?" His gaze was dark and hungry in the dim light. My breath caught.

I wet my lips, suddenly nervous. "Ah...I feel like they have security cameras down here? What if—"

Carter tilted his head, giving me a teasing smile as he took a few steps backward into one of the little alcoves in question. "We'd have to be quick, I imagine another tour group isn't far behind us... Unless, of course, you're scared?"

I glanced to the side, locking eyes with a skull. Fuck. I was kind of scared, but not of the ghosts and skeletons…I was scared of Carter himself and what this was all doing to me.

"It's okay, we can just head back to the hotel," he suggested, letting me off the hook. "I wouldn't mind getting you—*oof!*"

"Shut up," I ordered, shoving him against the alcove wall and gripping the back of his neck, "and kiss me."

He didn't need to be coaxed or convinced, crushing his lips to mine in a desperate frenzy. Maybe I wasn't the only one who'd been turning into a flustered mess with all the casual touches, because the speed that he had my panties around my ankles was shocking.

"Are you going to be quiet this time?" he asked in a dark whisper as I kicked my panties off my feet and he spun me around to face the wall.

I found a smooth section to brace my hands on as he lifted my skirt and spread my cheeks. My only response to his question was a low, barely muted moan as he lined up with my pussy from behind and pushed in just the tip.

"Spark…" he groaned, kissing my throat. "You're going to be my undoing. I need more."

He slipped in a little deeper and I gasped. "Carter…*please.*"

"Fuck," he exclaimed, then slammed the rest of the way in.

A scream tried to escape my throat, but I swallowed it back, turning my face to bite my own wrist and muffle the noise. But holy shit it wasn't easy. Carter thrust hard and fast, fucking me with a feverish need and his hand snaked around under my dress to find my clit.

I quaked under his touch, my eyes rolling shut as he played me like a violin. His thumb and index finger pinched my clit savagely, giving me no respite as he fucked me against the skull-lined wall. It was absolutely no surprise when my orgasm detonated barely a minute later and I nearly lost my balance as my legs trembled.

He held me tight, his thick cock buried deep as I convulsed, and he whispered curses as he joined me in release. It was *fast* but so fucking good it blew my damn mind.

"Shhh," he murmured in my ear as I gasped for breath, my vision swimming with stars. "Another tour is about to find us."

"Fuck," I groaned, pouting as he withdrew from my soaking cunt. "Can we go straight back to the hotel?"

"God yes," he enthused, grabbing my face in a bruising grip and kissing the breath out of me. "Come on." He grabbed my hand and started jogging down the seemingly endless corridor. He didn't give me any time to find my panties, and it wasn't until we were climbing into the back of a taxi that I noticed…thanks to the slick spill of his cum coating my thighs.

I groaned, biting my lip with embarrassment. "Carter…my underwear."

His gaze heated like an inferno. "Shit…now I know you're not wearing any, we'll be lucky to make it back to the room."

I couldn't help smiling like a loved-up idiot. He was disheveled himself, shirt half untucked and lips flushed. Sexy as *hell* and I'd already forgotten all the reasons why it was a bad idea to become involved with him.

True to prediction, we didn't make it to the room…but it was me who initiated by hitting the elevator *Stop* button and pouncing on him. I couldn't get enough, even though the little voice of reason in the back of my mind warned that it was an *awful* idea. That I was setting myself up for a world of pain when we got back to Nevaeh University.

I told that voice to shut the fuck up.

## Chapter Twenty-Four

The rest of that day and night in Paris wasn't entirely spent in bed. There were also a few sessions in the shower, over the arm of the sofa, and one heartbreakingly perfect fuck against the window as the Eiffel Tower twinkled at midnight.

Our flight home the next morning consisted of us both sleeping like the dead...until Carter woke me just before landing so we could join the Mile High Club.

And then on the drive back to Nevaeh, he closed the privacy screen and ate my pussy like he had something to prove. Like he wanted to make thoroughly sure I wouldn't be running back into Heath's arms when we arrived.

When the car pulled up outside my dorm, he took his time kissing me in the backseat, stealing the breath from my lungs and the sense from my brain. He murmured something about needing to get home to sort some "things" out, and I didn't even bat an eyelid.

Carly had been waiting for us to get back and threw herself at me when the car—and Carter—drove away.

"You're back!" she exclaimed, hugging me tight, "I need to know all about it. Tell me everything. Oh my god, you smell like sex." She gave a dramatic gasp, pressing her hands to her mouth.

I winced, shushing her. "Just…let's get up to my room. I should get changed."

"And shower," she added with a heavily judgmental glare. "I hope you used protection."

Another wince. We definitely did not.

Stupid? Yes. Hot as hell? Also yes. Who knew I had a kink for fucking bareback? And exhibitionism, apparently, seeing as some of the best sex with Carter had been the quickies when we were *undoubtedly* seen by strangers.

With a sigh, she tucked her arm through mine and walked with me up to our rooms on the third floor, chatting about some drama that happened in her last class.

"So is Carter the reason I haven't heard from you since Saturday?" she asked once I returned from the shower wrapped up in a bathrobe with a towel on my hair.

I dodged her intense stare and tried not to blush. "Um…sort of. I lost my phone on Saturday night."

"Oh damn, that sucks," she lamented, sitting cross-legged on my bed.

"Yeah," I agreed, tugging the towel from my hair to dry it. "I got it back, thank goodness, but uh…things happened and I haven't had a chance to charge it."

Her lips pursed. "*Things* happened, hmm?"

"Yup. Things. So, um, what'd I miss here?" I busied myself hunting my phone out of my overnight bag and plugging it into the charger. I was exhausted. Between the whirlwind two-night trip to Paris and time zone changes and…extracurricular activities…I felt like I could happily sleep for a month.

Carly was filling me in on some gossip but my head was buzzing and I hadn't been concentrating at *all*.

"…talking about where you guys placed your ducks to win…"

she said as I forced myself to pay attention. "Nate was so confident he'd won—like he always does—that he had the whole Paris trip booked for him and Paige."

I grimaced. "Yay, another reason for him to hate me."

Carly wrinkled her nose. "Sorry. I should have warned you to let him win."

"No, don't be silly. I never would have *let* him win, even if it was in my best interest. Besides, he and Paige are probably over."

She quirked a brow. "Uh…that's news. What happened?"

I hesitated, realizing I was treading thin ice with her own history with Nate. "She's cheating on him."

Her jaw dropped. "You're fucking kidding. With who? How'd you find out? Was this a pillow talk thing with Carter? Oh damn, does Heath know?"

"About Nate and Paige? Probably."

She gave an exasperated growl. "About you and Carter, Ash, keep up!"

I groaned and scrubbed my hands over my face. "No. Unless Carter says something…I don't totally know where we stand on all that."

"You didn't talk about it before getting back?"

My face heated. "We were, uh, occupied."

She snorted a laugh and hopped up off my bed. "Okay well, I say this as your friend because I don't want to see you hurt…Carter isn't a relationship kind of guy. Set your expectations low, for your own sake." Carly grabbed me in a quick hug. "You're clearly half asleep. Let's catch up before class tomorrow?"

Thank fuck. I locked my door after her—not that it seemed to stop Nate from breaking in—and crashed out in my bed. Her question about Heath kept tugging on my mind, though.

Grabbing my phone off the nightstand, I powered it up and searched for my chat thread with Heath. No new messages. The last one was when I'd replied and asked when he was free to chat, before leaving for Paris with Carter.

An uncomfortable feeling of dread curled through my belly. Was that a coincidence? My paranoid mind immediately jumped to conclusions, wondering if it'd been Carter's plan all along to sleep with me in Paris...that he'd discussed it with Heath before we left. Fucking hell, what if it was all a joke?

I shook my head, raking fingers through my hair.

"Don't be stupid, Ashley," I whispered to myself. There was *no way* he could have orchestrated that incident with the mugging and how the adrenaline affected me afterward. Right?

So why could I suddenly not stop thinking about Abigail's diary? All the horrible things she accused the DBs of in those pages...I desperately wanted to read it again.

Unable to shake the anxiety, I typed out a message to Heath, letting him know I was back.

I stared at the screen for several moments, waiting, then it updated with *read* and the text bubble popped up to show Heath typing.

My heart lodged firmly in my throat as I waited for him to reply, holding my breath. We'd been *fake* dating...but it still felt a little bit like I'd cheated. It wasn't an enjoyable feeling, that was for sure.

HEATHCLIFF:

> You're back! How was Paris?

I bit my lip, analyzing his message and then over-analyzing it in search of tone. Was he being snarky? Like *how was Paris, you whore?* Or did he mean it as a bored pleasantry like *how was Paris? I genuinely don't care.*

Or...fucking hell.

Maybe he just wanted to know how Paris was?

So...should I tell him? No. No, not like this.

Riddled with indecision, I typed out my reply.

ASHLEY:
> It was okay. Have you been?

He responded quickly, like he was waiting for my message. That was a good thing…right?

HEATHCLIFF:
> I have, it's a beautiful city. What are you doing tonight?

A heavy breath gusted out of me. He seemed…normal?

ASHLEY:
> Sleeping. I'm wrecked.

I bit my lip again, taking a chance with my next message.

ASHLEY:
> Coffee before class in the morning?

Because I really wanted to tell him about me and Carter in person. Yeah I definitely still had a bit of a crush on Heath too, but more importantly I wanted to keep him as a friend, if that's what we could call what we were.

HEATHCLIFF:
> Dancing Goats at 8? It's a date.

He undoubtedly meant it platonically, but I still didn't love the twist of guilt and anxiety that knotted up my stomach. Then again, would I change anything given the chance? Did I regret sleeping with Carter? Not in a million years.

Sleep wasn't hard to find once I turned out my light and put my phone back on charge. I didn't dream, and didn't stir even once, and when my alarm went off I hit snooze three times before forcing myself out of bed.

"Damn girl," Carly greeted me when I answered my door to her knocking. "You look...is that a bruise?"

I groaned and touched a hand to my cheek. "Yeah."

Her brows shot up in alarm. "Do I need to kill Carter? It's against society rules but I'll do it."

I grinned, unable to help myself because she was dead serious. "You're off the hook for homicide today, babe. Carter actually saved me when I got mugged in Paris."

Her lips parted in shock. "Oh. Really? Carter did that?"

I nodded, my cheeks warming at the memory of everything that happened *after*. "Come in while I cover this up with concealer. Heath is meeting us for coffee in ten."

She playfully teased me about my so-called love triangle while I dabbed concealer all over the bruise on my cheek. It'd darkened up enough that even a double layer of makeup couldn't hide it entirely, but it was better.

Carly wrinkled her nose at the finished effect, but shrugged and looped her bag over her shoulder. "Let's go. We don't want Heathcliff thinking you've stood him up, do we now?"

I sighed, tucking my arm through hers as we walked. "Hey, you said something last week about you being related? Heath never mentioned any siblings, though..."

"We're cousins," she explained. "Not super close, either. But the family money started with our grandfather, Atticus Briggs. You know, Atticus Records?"

"*Ohhhh*, I see." They were one of the biggest record labels *ever*, so the wealth of both Heath and Carly made sense. "So you encouraging me and Heath is a purely biased opinion then?"

She laughed. "Yes. Mostly. But also Carter is a scary motherfucker with a short fuse and history of broken hearts. I just don't want you to be the next in his long line of collateral damage."

That was a sobering thought and I mulled it over a few moments while we walked across the campus lawn. "I don't think that's…Ugh, I don't know. Am I a total airhead if I say it felt different with him? Like I felt like I had peeled back the mask for a day."

Carly gave a thoughtful hum. "I hope so. Hey, how'd you go with our Early Modern Europe assignment? Did you get it done?"

"I did, thank fuck, on the flight over to Paris. The whole…duck challenge sort of derailed my plans to study for Language Acquisition and Literacy Development though, so I need to buckle down tonight. Library session?"

"You got it," she agreed. "I can give you a copy of my notes from yesterday's class too."

I murmured my thanks, but up ahead I'd spotted a familiar face that made my heart race. *Shit. Why was Carter here with Heath?*

"Ash!" Heath called out, noticing us. "Good morning, sunshine."

I gave him a tight smile as he approached, but my gaze kept darting to Carter who stared back at me with a dark, unreadable look in his eyes. What was he thinking? Had he told Heath already? Were we a thing now?

"Hey, you," I replied, accepting his warm hug. "How was your weekend?"

"Boring as batshit compared to a whirlwind tour of Paris. Did you have fun? I know your company was fairly unpleasant, but Carter said he was on his best behavior, right?" He tossed that question over his shoulder to the man who'd so recently had his tongue inside my pussy.

Carter just nodded. "Mm-hmm. I had better shit to do rather than play tourist. Ashley had the guide all to herself."

It wasn't entirely untrue, at least for the first day...but the harsh tone he used made me feel an inch tall and my stomach dropped.

"Probably a good thing," Heath shot back, smirking as he looped an arm around my shoulders. "I was a little worried you might have tried to seduce my girl in the city of love and then we'd have a fight on our hands."

He said it jokingly, but my skin turned to ice. My eyes locked with Carter's just waiting for some kind of reaction. Some kind of *acknowledgment* of what we'd done.

What I didn't expect—even though I should have—was the cold laugh that he huffed out. "You know me better than that, Heathcliff. I don't generally entertain overpriced whores, and she's definitely not my type." His sneer in my direction cut me like a dozen knives. "No offense."

"Dude, not cool," Heath sighed, shaking his head.

Carter just shrugged. "True, though. I've gotta run. Catch you later, bro." He nodded to Heath, then walked away without even glancing my way again. I stared after him, shocked to my core, but his lazy swagger didn't falter as he disappeared into the morning student crowd.

"Ash, are you okay?" Carly asked softly, touching my arm and making me realize I was still staring.

I wet my lips, trying to control my emotions but it was a losing battle. My stomach clenched and rolled, and my palms started to sweat.

"Yeah. Totally fine," I lied. "Just need to run to the bathroom real quick. Grab my coffee? I'll be right back."

Heath called out after me, but I was already bolting for the Dancing Goats restroom.

I felt *so stupid.*

## Chapter Twenty-Five

There was no hiding the fact that I'd been crying when I returned from the bathroom to get my coffee. Worse still, when I'd tried to clean up my face I'd smudged the concealer off my bruised cheek, and it'd taken both Carly and I *physically* holding Heath to stop him running after Carter to kill him.

He hadn't been willing to back down until I'd insisted that Carter hadn't hurt me. At least not like that. The state of my heart was a private matter that I definitely wasn't interested in discussing.

By the time I finished explaining what'd happened at dinner in Paris—with Carter being a massive asshole and me stupidly walking out on my own—and the subsequent mugger attack, we were all late for class.

I promised to explain the rest later—with no intention of ever doing so, when the rest involved me and Carter fucking like horny cats for twenty-four hours straight—and ran to my early Humanities class.

The professor gave me a hard glare when I tried to quietly sneak in and slid into my seat. Embarrassed, I kept my head down and forced myself to focus as much as I could under the circumstances.

My next class of the day was with Carly, thank fuck, but also with

Jade and I really *really* didn't want to risk a run-in with her. Not after the cuts Carter had left on my confidence.

Trouble was, Jade apparently wanted nothing more than a run-in with *me*. The moment she walked into the lecture hall, she searched me out then deliberately sat her happy ass down behind Carly and me.

"Go away, Jade," I muttered, giving her a glare over my shoulder. "I'm too tired for your crap."

She smirked back at me. "You don't want to hear all about my weekend with your boyfriend?"

I inhaled, ready to put her in her place, but the professor chose that moment to start the class and announce a practice quiz. Total silence was required, which saved me and Carly both from enduring an hour of Jade's bullshit.

Thankfully, I breezed through the quiz and handed my paper in while Jade was still frowning at her test like it'd personally offended her. I wasn't hanging around for her to toss out silly high school insults and taunts, so I texted Carly that I would meet her at lunch.

I texted Heath next, letting him know where I was going, and he immediately called back.

"You're going to the campus cafeteria?" he asked when I answered the call.

"Uh-huh," I confirmed. What had Jade meant about her *weekend* with Heath? Her "date" with him was only Friday night...wasn't it?

"I'm done for the day so I was heading home. Come with me? I'll cook way better food than the cafeteria can serve."

I slowed my pace, considering his offer. I wasn't the biggest fan of cafeteria food and I wouldn't hate hanging out with him *off campus* for once. But then again...

"No one else is home," he added when I said nothing. "It'd just be us. Carter is in classes and workshops until late tonight, and I haven't seen Nate or Royce in days."

Maybe Nate had believed me after all?

"Okay, sure," I agreed. "If you're sure Carter isn't there..."

"I'm sure," he promised. "Meet me in the parking lot behind Essex Hall. I'll drive."

I was only a minute or so away from there, so ended the call and changed my direction to meet Heath.

He beat me there, which was good since I had no clue what kind of car he drove. Nate had abducted me in a F250 Shelby and Royce gave me a lift home in his Bugatti, while I'd only ever taken chauffeur cars with Carter but with Heath I wasn't sure what to expect.

It sure as fuck wasn't what I found him standing beside.

"I definitely wouldn't have picked you as a bike guy," I admitted, approaching with a grin.

He smiled back at me, stroking a hand over the leather seat of his Ducati Streetfighter. "No? What were you expecting then?"

I pursed my lips, tapping my chin thoughtfully. "I don't really know...maybe a Tesla?"

He gave a dramatic gasp. "Ouch. You wound me, Ash."

I laughed. "Yeah right. So, uh, we're taking this? My car is over on the dorm lot if you want me to drive."

"Are you scared?" Heath quirked a brow, tilting his head with curiosity.

I licked my lips, eyeing the bike, then turning my gaze back to him. Damn it, that flutter of attraction was still alive and well even after everything Carter just put me through.

"I'm not...*not* scared," I admitted. Then I bit my lip as another question crowded my brain, desperate to be asked. "Why did you leave me on read all weekend?"

Surprise flickered across his face, then quickly faded into a sheepish guilt. "That was a dick move, I'm sorry."

I frowned. "It was, but why did you do it?"

His gaze skated away, and he rubbed a hand over the back of his neck. "Um...would you believe me if I said I lost my phone?"

I shook my head. "Nope, you're a horrible liar and you texted me back just fine last night." And it would be way too coincidental if he also lost then found his phone the same weekend I did.

Heath puffed a sigh. "Yeah, fair call. Um...okay fuck. I found out that you and Carter won the duck challenge and I, uh, I got jealous. Everything I tried to say was coming out all wrong and I didn't want you to *know* I was salty about it so I just...left you on read."

"Jealous that we won?" *Because you wanted to go to Paris with Jade?* "Or..."

Heath rolled his eyes. "Or. I was jealous of *Carter*, Ash. Because he had just been handed this absolutely perfect, romantic adventure to go on *with you* and I fucking knew he wouldn't let the opportunity slip through his fingers. And he didn't, did he?" It was an accusation, because although I'd explained the mugging over coffee that morning, I'd omitted the part where Carter had thoroughly seduced me.

My face heated and I bit my lip. I couldn't lie, so I just gave a small nod and dropped my gaze away from his. Fuck, now my eyes were heating with tears and I was feeling like an even bigger idiot than I had this morning when Carter rejected me.

"Hey, Ash baby, I'm sorry," he crooned, stepping forward to cup my face in his hands. "I wasn't—" he cut off with a sigh as he lifted my face and saw my eyes swimming with unshed tears. How could he not, one more blink and they'd spill.

As fast as that thought formed, it happened. Heath frowned, his thumb swiping the fresh tear from my bruised cheek as he gazed into my eyes.

"I'm sorry. I wasn't trying to make you feel bad. I just wish I had warned you or...I don't know. Maybe if I'd been a little more honest last week, then things could have played out differently." He gave me a sad smile, and I tried to choke back the nearly overwhelming emotions suddenly assaulting my mind.

"Honest about what?" I whispered. "I already knew Carter was a massive asshole, but that didn't stop me being a fucking moron and falling for his bullshit."

Heath gave a lopsided smile. "True. But maybe if I'd told you how I felt then it might have been *us* in Paris instead. Did you seriously place a duck on old man Lintan's bare ass?"

I laughed, sniffing back my tears as he released my face. "Um, yeah. What do you mean, though, about how you felt?"

He ran a hand through his dark hair, messing it up in the sexiest kind of way. It reminded me of how disheveled he'd been after his massage, when he'd tried to pay me for a happy ending.

"I wanted to tell you that our fake relationship wasn't working out," he finally said, his voice a low murmur and his gaze lowered. "That I didn't think we should fake date anymore."

I took a step backward, stunned. "Oh. Um…sure, yeah, I guess that makes sense after all—"

"Because I can't *fake* date someone that I want to *actually* date," he cut me off. "And I legitimately can't get you out of my head, Ashley. Pretending I'm kissing you for appearances isn't enough and to be frank, it's fucking with my head."

My lips parted to respond, but no words came out. I was speechless. And confused. Where did we stand *now*, knowing I'd fucked his best friend this weekend?

"So, um…" That was all I managed to get out before I fumbled my words again and pursed my lips.

"Ash?" Heath said in a soft voice, his palm raising to my cheek once more. "Can I please kiss you?"

Shock saw me blinking like a damn owl. "What about—"

"I fucking hate that he hurt you, but it doesn't change how I feel about you," he told me, his hazel gaze so intense it was like he could see right into my soul. "So, can I?"

My heart was officially hammering so hard in my chest I worried I might suffer a cardiac event. My palms were slick with sweat, and my skin tingled…so I nodded.

A puff of relief escaped him as he leaned in, his lips meeting mine softly and slowly. I trembled slightly as I leaned into his touch, reciprocating his kiss with nervousness. It wasn't our first time kissing, not by a long shot. But this was different. This didn't have the baggage of selling a fake relationship or setting up a transaction to damn my reputation. This was a kiss purely because we *wanted* it.

Heath gave a small groan as I parted my lips, his hold on my face slipping into my hair and tightening as his tongue delved inside my mouth. The world around us blurred into nothingness as I lost myself in his kiss.

Lost myself in denial for the stinging heartache Carter had left me with.

That infuriatingly logical part of my brain whispered that maybe I was just using Heath for a rebound, knowing perfectly well that Carter would be furious. But I didn't care.

"Incredible," he groaned, reluctantly backing off some moments later. "Just like that first kiss…"

I grinned, remembering exactly what he meant. When I'd kissed him in my massage room, after he'd given me a six-grand tip.

"Come on, let's get out of here." He grabbed the black helmet from his bike's handlebars and placed it on my head.

"What about you?" I protested as he adjusted the chinstrap. He only had one helmet, as far as I could see.

Heath shot me a sexy wink. "I'll be fine." He swung his leg over the bike and gave me a teasing smirk. "Hop on, babe, I'll drive slow."

I groaned, but awkwardly climbed onto the bike behind him nonetheless. It was totally foreign to me, and I thought for sure I would tip us both over, but he just grabbed my hands and placed them tighter around his body.

"Hold on, okay?"

That was all the warning I got before he kicked the engine over and the bike roared to life between our legs. Holy hell.

It took me half the drive to feel comfortable enough to release my white-knuckled grip on Heath's shirt, but by the time we arrived at his apartment complex I was seriously enjoying myself. My legs shook when I hopped off, but I couldn't stop smiling.

"That was amazing!" I exclaimed when Heath helped me out of the helmet. "How have I never been on a motorcycle before? Ugh, I've been missing out!"

He laughed, seemingly enjoying my enthusiasm, then grabbed my chin in his long fingers. "*You're* amazing," he murmured, then kissed me again.

I could definitely get used to *not so fake* dating Heathcliff Briggs. Even if I did know, deep down, it was an awful idea. But we could enjoy the moment for now and discuss the more serious aspect later, surely.

"I'm sure you already know," he said, linking our hands as we waited for the elevator, "Max bought this apartment for us when we started at Nevaeh."

I hummed. "Right. Because Nate is too good to be in a dorm with the peasants."

Heath grinned, shaking his head. "Cute, but there aren't any peasants in Nevaeh. No, he actually got us the apartment because…" he trailed off, rubbing the back of his neck like he'd just reconsidered what he was going to say. "Because one of us was going through some stuff. It was just safer if we had our own space."

That was intriguingly cryptic, but I had to assume it was about one of the other boys. That Heath had realized it wasn't his place to share his friend's secrets, so I wouldn't push for more info.

"Oh shit," he said as the elevator dinged on his floor and we stepped out. "I totally forgot. You're not allergic to dogs, are you?"

I frowned as he led the way down the hall. "Uh…no, I'm not. You have a dog?"

Heath sighed, stopping at a door marked with an *Essex* nameplate rather than a number. He used his keys to unlock it. "I don't, but Carter does. It's the source of major fights with Nate right now, but he's a stubborn fuck and refuses to take the mangy mutt back to the pound."

My mouth went dry.

"Come on in," Heath coaxed, opening the door. "*That* is the dog. Lady."

Sure enough, there she was, curled up on what could only be described as a doggy throne of the plushest fabric beside the leather sofa. It was the flea-ridden mutt Jade had left in my room.

# Chapter Twenty-Six

Heath hadn't been exaggerating when he said his cooking was better than cafeteria food. He made us chicken and basil pesto penne with fresh asparagus and zucchini, topped with freshly grated parmesan and poured us both a big glass of Riesling to accompany the meal.

It was quite possibly the best pasta of my life, and I insisted on doing the dishes when we were done, already having mentally blown off my afternoon classes. I made a promise to myself that I'd catch up from tomorrow and not skip any more lectures, but for right now I couldn't seem to make myself leave.

Doing the dishes, though, somehow turned into a make out session with my bum parked on the counter and Heath's hands gripping my thighs like a lifeline.

"Well shit, I didn't expect to find *this* in the middle of a school day," Royce drawled, the door slamming behind him as I scrambled out of Heath's embrace. "I thought you were in Rome with Bass, Squirrel."

"Paris," I corrected, swiping a hand over my puffy lips, "and we got back last night. How's Paige?"

Royce's eyes narrowed. "I think you've mixed me up with your stepbrother."

I glared back at him, unflinching. "Have I? Hmm, how silly of me."

He held my gaze, giving a small shake of his head. "So I guess there's no hard feelings between you two about the whole Jade situation, then?"

That was twice I've had the feeling more went on than just the duck challenge. It was on the tip of my tongue to ask, but that'd be playing into Royce's game…whatever the fuck that was. It'd sobered me up from the lust-drunk haze I'd fallen into, though, so I grabbed my bag from where I'd left it and slung it over my shoulder.

"I think that's my cue to leave," I told them with a tight smile. "Thanks for lunch, Heath."

Heath scowled at Royce, then grabbed his motorcycle keys. "I'll drive you," he offered.

"Thanks," I said with a shake of my head, "but I'd rather take a cab."

I exited the apartment before it could turn into a whole thing, and heard Heath cursing out Royce as I stabbed the elevator call button. It was right there, having just delivered Royce, so by the time Heath came running after me the doors were already closing.

"Ash, please let me—" he tried to say, but the doors slid shut and I did nothing to stop it.

My spirits sank faster than the elevator car and by the time I reached the street, I was back in that uncomfortable funk of anxiety and disappointment as I'd existed in all morning.

What the fuck had I been thinking, falling into Heath like that? Was I really so naive?

Apparently yes.

With a stroke of luck, I hailed a taxi and slid inside right as the sky opened up and rain began pouring. How utterly fitting for the way my mood had just plummeted.

Fucking Jade. Then again, it wasn't entirely her fault. Heath was the one who'd invited her to the gala and if he was supposedly so into me as more than a fake-girlfriend, why hadn't he invited me? That way we actually could have had a chance to do Paris together.

Also...why the hell had Carter kept the dog? He'd been taking care of her too. She was clean and brushed, and all the fleas were gone. Not to mention the abundance of plush dog beds and toys in their apartment. Heath had mentioned that Carter took her for walks twice a day, and set her up with a synthetic grass toileting area on the balcony. It was a lot, especially for a stray that I sent to the apartment as a joke.

My phone pinged in my bag several times during the short trip back to campus, but I ignored it. I already knew it'd be Heath apologizing for Royce when in actual fact he needed to explain what the hell was going on with Jade.

I'd already missed one of my afternoon lectures, so rather than race to my second, I headed for the library instead. At least I could get some course reading done in silence.

Rather than my usual study table—where Heath often met me—I ventured up to the mezzanine level and located a cozy little study nook buried between Late Baroque Composers and early medieval poetry. No way would anyone come looking for me there.

I settled in and pulled out my laptop from my bag, then glanced at my phone. Sure enough, there were several new messages from Heath, but I swiped them off my screen and opened the message thread from an unsaved number.

Part of me assumed it was Carter. We hadn't exchanged numbers somehow, but maybe he was apologizing for being such a colossal *fuckwit*.

It quickly became apparent that was *not* the case.

UNKNOWN:

> Don't trust anyone. Paris was all part of their plan.—AM

My mouth went dry and I read the message several times as though I thought the words would change before my eyes. Heart racing, I typed a reply.

ASHLEY:
who is this?

I sat there for several minutes, just staring at the phone in my hand and waiting for a reply yet when it finally came through, I nearly jumped out of my skin.

UNKNOWN:
They're playing with you. Don't be an idiot and believe the DB's lies. Get out while you still can.—AM

Scared and confused, I started to reply that I wasn't in the mood for cryptic games, but the unknown number sent a follow-up message. This time it was a link to a news article on a French website.

I pulled the website up on my laptop so I could run it through translate and read it with an open mouth.

*...badly beaten corpse of an unidentified man found stuffed into a dumpster...*

It had to be a coincidence. Carter said that guy was *fine*.

*...inquiries are ongoing but with no solid leads. The victim has not been formally identified, but an anonymous tip to this news channel claims it's the body of wanted serial rapist Antoine Boucher.*

Frantic, I scanned the article that my computer had badly translated, desperate for some kind of connection to confirm what the unknown number was implying. There was no conclusive time of death, though, and the body had been found at a location miles from where I was attacked.

It was just a coincidence.

Inhaling deeply, I tried to control the tremor in my hands as I reached for my phone once more.

ASHLEY:
Who is this?

There was no use trying to plead innocent to what they'd implied. There was *no* connection to Carter and me, but they were telling me that they knew what'd happened. Right? They were using a totally unconnected murder in Paris—and there must have been plenty to choose from—just to prove they knew what'd happened.

But only Carter and I knew. Did he tell someone?

Before any reply came through, my phone was abruptly snatched from my hand and I startled so hard I almost fell off my chair.

"Who are you texting, Layne?" Nate asked, blatantly reading the message thread then frowning. "Who the fuck is this?"

"Give it back!" I snarled, reaching for it but he just leaned out of my reach, still scowling at my phone.

Under his breath, he started muttering and it took me a hot second to work out he was reading the news article in French.

"What the fuck is this about, Layne? What does this dead guy have to do with the society?" His tone was accusing now, and I stood up to try and grab my phone back.

Once again, he held it out of my reach. The stubborn look on his face made it abundantly clear he wasn't letting it go without an answer.

"I don't know, okay? You can clearly see that by the fact I replied with *who is this* twice," I snapped. "Now can I have my phone back?"

His eyes narrowed with suspicion. "You want me to believe some *random stranger* texts you out of the blue with an ominous warning and then an article about a dead guy in Paris—where you just were—and you have no idea what the connection is? Bullshit. What happened in Paris, Layne?"

Gritting my teeth, I refrained from trying to jump to reach my phone like a little kid. Nate was nearly a foot taller than me and had extended his arm way out of reach.

"What happened in Paris?" I was *so damn tempted* to tell him I'd fucked Carter just to piss him off. But that, I now realized, was simply playing into the *Ashley is a whore* ideology he was subscribing to. "None of your fucking business, Essex. Maybe if you were so desperate to go to Paris you should have tried harder in the duck challenge."

Irritation flickered across his face and his jaw tightened. "That's how you want to play it? Fine. I won't tell you who is sending these messages."

*Wait, what?*

"You know who it is?"

He shook his head, his whiskey brown eyes softening ever so slightly. "No. But I could find out in about three minutes if you wanted to know."

I did want to know. Really fucking badly, because I was thoroughly freaked out about who could have witnessed what happened that night. Or who Carter might have told. He didn't strike me as the kind of guy to share potentially damning information like that though.

Then again, what the fuck did I know about him really? That he has a big dick and knows how to make me orgasm in under a minute? That wasn't exactly a glowing character reference.

"Please can you tell me who is texting?" I asked, attempting to school my tone into some semblance of polite.

"I *can*," he confirmed, nodding.

Anger burned through my chest and I gritted my teeth. "*Will you*, please, tell me who is texting?"

He pursed his lips, acting like he was thinking about my request while I became increasingly irate.

I sighed heavily. "Fine. What do you want in exchange? You and I both know I can't afford to pay anything."

He arched a brow. "Oh? Turning tricks doesn't pay what it used to, hmm? Well, I think we can come up with another arrangement." His gaze shifted from my face, quickly dipping to my chest where I'd failed to re-button my blouse properly after making out with Heath.

Disgusted, I took a step backward. "Ew. No. I'm not that desperate to know who it is."

Nate sneered back at me. "As if, Layne. I'd rather stick my dick in a nest of fire ants. Just fail the next society challenge."

I folded my arms under my breasts and could have sworn I caught him checking out my cleavage again. It was quick, though, I couldn't be sure. "That's it? Promise to fail the next duck challenge—or whatever other dumb shit you do—and you'll trace this phone number? That sounds too easy."

"Like I said, it's a three-minute hack at best." He lowered his arm but didn't offer the phone back. "Deal?"

I rolled my eyes. "Fine. Deal." Because I knew no one else with the skills to hack *anything* and his offer seemed harmless.

Nate dipped his head. "Great. You don't mind if I use this, do you?" Without waiting for my answer, he slid into my seat and pulled my laptop closer.

I bit back the need to curse him out, and settled for anxiously drumming my fingernails on the bookshelf beside me while he typed in what could only be called a foreign language. All zeros and ones and symbols and commands...it briefly occurred to me that he could be installing viruses on my laptop just to be an asshole, but it was also too late to stop him if that were the case.

"Huh," he eventually said out loud. "That's weird."

"What's weird?" I demanded. "Who is it?"

Instead of answering me, he grabbed my phone once more from

the desktop where he'd placed it and handed it to me. "Call the number."

I blinked a couple times. "Sorry?"

"Call the number back," he instructed.

I let out a frustrated sigh. "Okay, hacker genius, this nullifies our agreement. I could have—"

"Just do it, Ashley," he snapped, seeming on edge for some reason.

And he called me *Ashley*. Nate *never* used my first name.

Unnerved, I unlocked my screen and pulled up the message thread. Then I pressed *call*.

"Speaker," Nate ordered, his intense gaze on the phone not on me.

I pressed the speaker icon right as the call failed to connect.

*"The number you have dialed is no longer in service. Please try again."*

"I don't get it," I admitted. "They just canceled the phone number right after sending me those messages?"

Nate looked genuinely concerned, gesturing for me to hand him the phone. I did, because now I was even more freaked out than before.

He typed out a message quickly, just a simple *hello?*

It sent and delivered.

"What the fuck?" I asked, confused as to how messages were delivered if the number wasn't in service. "Nate...what's going on?"

He licked his lips, his complexion somewhat ashen. "I wish I knew. Um...the number belonged to someone who went to school here, but the contract was canceled two years ago. When she died. This doesn't make any sense."

My blood chilled. The messages were all signed AM as in..."Abigail Monstera?"

Nate's brows shot up. "Yeah. How did you know?"

It was a good fucking question.

# Chapter Twenty-Seven

As helpful as Nate had been, I still didn't trust him as far as I could throw him, so there was no way in hell I'd go telling him all about Abigail's diary in my room. His confusion about how I knew her name sort of confirmed he hadn't been the one to take it, as well. Unless he was a hell of an actor but he seemed to hate me too much to fake anything resembling that vulnerability.

I brushed him off with a weak explanation about campus rumors, but he'd still seemed haunted as he left me in the library.

My focus was totally shot, so a half hour later I gave up trying to study and packed my things up. Heath had tried texting again, and I replied as I walked out of the library.

ASHLEY:
> I think I need to know what else happened with Jade. Not the gala…what happened while I was in Paris?

His reply came quickly and sliced me deep.

HEATHCLIFF:

> you mean while you were in Carter's bed?

My jaw dropped and I stopped dead in my tracks, staring at my phone in shock. He wasn't wrong, but at the same time it stung.

ASHLEY:

> Wow. Really? Forget it, today was a huge mistake.

HEATHCLIFF:

> Fuck. I didn't mean that. Can we meet and talk in person?

I raked my fingers through my hair, anxious regret swirling through me like fucking food poisoning. I knew better than to trust these guys—*any* of these guys—and yet I kept falling for their bullshit. What was wrong with me?

Biting my lip, I stared at my phone, debating what to reply. Agree and talk it out like adults? Or tell him to go to hell because my feelings were hurt?

Before I could make a decision, someone grabbed me from behind and tried to hook a bag over my head...*again*. I ducked my head just in time to dodge the maneuver, fighting back against the person who'd grabbed me.

"Let me go!" I shouted, panicking. "Help! Someone help me!" I was on the path outside the campus library and it was still daylight. Someone must surely be around to see I was being assaulted.

Thrashing, I kicked out at the much larger attacker but it was no use. There were two of them, and the second came back around to bag my head once more. But not before I got a good look at them...

Or rather, at their masks.

"I don't want to play your stupid games!" I yelled, trying really fucking hard not to hyperventilate when the bag tightened around my neck, holding it secure. "I quit! Let me go, I don't want to be in your stupid society!"

Neither one of the masked assailants said a word, just strong-arming me into submission as they zip tied my wrists and started hauling me along the path. My vaguely messed up sense of direction guessed they were taking me toward the parking lot, not the dorms, and my anxiety kicked into a higher gear.

What did they always say about not letting kidnappers take you to a second location?

This was the society, though. The masks and robes were a dead giveaway. So maybe this was just another stupid trick, like the whole jumping off Cat's Peak thing had been? That gave me a small measure of reassurance, knowing it was all just smoke and mirrors.

Hell, this might even be Nate again. He'd just asked me to fail the next challenge so did that mean he knew a challenge was upcoming? Like right now, and he was involved?

"Listen," I tried in a calmer tone, attempting to keep up and not fall, but also having absolutely no vision whatsoever. "I really, really don't want to play these games. I didn't want to be in the Devil's Backbone Society to start with so if you could just...pretend like you didn't find me and I'll submit a written resignation to whatever committee runs this show? That would be great."

No reply. They just kept marching me forward and the distinctive roll of a van door alerted me to the fact we were at the parking lot already. Shit, that was quick.

"Come on, guys," I tried again. "This is too far. Let me go and I'll—"

The one at my back shoved me hard and I tumbled forward, hitting the metal floor of the van. Fuck.

"This is insane!" I exclaimed, groaning a little with pain. Not having my hands free to break my fall meant I'd taken the hit on my hip and shoulder, but thankfully avoided hitting my face. "You're literally abducting me in broad daylight. The school has cameras, there's evidence! I could report you to—"

My threats cut off with a sharp sting in my arm. I sucked a sharp inhale, confused for only a moment before the realization dawned. Chemical taste hit my tongue at the same time as my head started spinning…they'd fucking drugged me.

As I slipped into unconsciousness, familiarity sparked in my foggy mind. Abigail had written about a similar experience. In her version, she'd been dumped in the forest and left to find her way back to campus with no food, no map, nothing.

Apparently, that's what I was in for, but at least I had the hints Abigail had left in her journal. She'd gone into *detail* recording her ordeal…I just needed to remember what she had written.

When the drugs eventually wore off, the first thing I noticed was how cold I was. Shivers wracked through my whole body before I could even make my eyelids open. When I finally peeled my gritty lids apart, dread pooled in my guts.

I was right.

The DB dickheads had dumped me in the middle of a forest somewhere and it was pitch-black night. How long had I been drugged? How far had they taken me? I had no clue. It hadn't even been dusk when they took me, though, and based on how high the moon was now…it'd been a while.

Another shiver chased through me and I sat up, rubbing my bare arms.

*Wait. Why are my arms bare?*

I'd been wearing a sweater and jeans when they'd taken me but not anymore. Nope, somewhere along the way I'd been stripped of my clothing all the way down to my black lace bra and panties. Hugging my arms to myself, I looked around in the clearing where I'd been dumped, hoping they'd left my clothes somewhere nearby.

Nothing.

Instead, I found a scrap of paper nailed to a tree with one word scrawled across it.

WHORE.

Well. That definitely suggested Nate had a hand in this whole mess, seeing as he was the only one really pushing that tired old narrative. Was he trying to kill me, though? It wasn't winter yet but it was definitely too cold to be running around in underwear at night.

"Fail the challenge, huh?" I muttered aloud, rubbing my arms for warmth. "Fuck *that*. I bet the only way to fail this is to not make it back, and I'm not fucking dying out here."

Not interested in hanging around and freezing to death, I peered around for some kind of location clue. Had they dumped me in the same place Abigail had been taken? That would be ideal, because then I could refer back to her description. If I could remember it, of course.

"What was the first thing she saw?" I asked myself aloud, pacing around the clearing while I wracked my brain. Trouble was, the drugs had left me fuzzy and a little disoriented. Not to mention the way my head was pounding with a chemical headache.

*...when I woke up I thought a monster with a dozen eyes was standing over me, about to eat me alive. When nothing happened, I realized the truth. It was just a tree. A really creepy old tree with branches like arms and a twisted bark pattern that emulated eyes...*

The diary passage came back to me right as I laid my hand on a tree with what seemed like a dozen eyes. Hope surged and I grinned. They'd brought me to the same place, and Abigail had left me all the clues I needed to get home.

"Fail the challenge? Eat a dick, Nate."

I set off, following the somewhat hazy memory of Abigail's notes to find the next significant marker she'd mentioned. Still, even knowing I had the map in my mind didn't help how cold I was, or the fact that I was barefoot in a dark forest.

By the time I found the stream Abigail had described, my teeth were chattering and my feet throbbed from the dozens of sharp sticks I'd stepped on. Paranoid about infection, I sat down on a rock and dipped my feet into the icy stream to wash some of the dirt out.

Pain lanced through both feet, and I sobbed as I hugged myself. Fucking Nate. He'd taken it way too far this time, and I was sick of keeping my mouth shut. The minute I got back, I was going to Max with everything he'd been putting me through. Enough was enough.

I took a little time to rest there at the stream, letting the cold water numb my feet and then drinking a little. Was it safe to drink? No clue. But expiring due to dehydration sounded pretty shit, so I had to take the risk.

Eventually, I forced myself to keep going. I needed to, just to stay warm. For a little while I tried to jog to raise my core temperature but when I tripped over a log and smacked my cheek on a rock I had to admit defeat and stick with a slower pace. This time with an even worse headache and blood dripping from a cut on my face.

By the time the sun began rising, I started to wonder if I'd gone the wrong way or missed a turn or…something? But it was pretty simple to follow the line of the creek, surely I hadn't fucked it up that badly?

At a loss for what to do, and quickly losing confidence, I continued my achingly slow pace along the path of the creek, and *finally* spotted the collapsed bridge Abigail had written about.

It was such a relief to see that I burst out in tears, running the last short distance to get there. Frantic and sobbing, I searched for the bag of supplies Abigail had described. In her version, she'd found an old hiking pack with sleeping bag, water, first aid and dehydrated foods.

Either things had changed, or her find was just a lucky coincidence that had nothing to do with the challenge because no such treasure waited for me. The tears came harder when I had to admit to myself that I was shit out of luck. The only thing I found to even hint at what she'd described was an old flannel shirt snagged on one of the broken bridge supports.

It was torn and filthy, but it was better than nothing. My hands shook as I struggled to free it from the rotten wood, then I grimaced as I threaded my arms into the sleeves.

The garment smelled atrocious, but it offered a small measure of warmth so it was officially my most prized possession. I huddled into it, grateful for how big the previous owner must have been as it hung well past my bum when standing. Curled up into a little ball, I could get my whole body inside, so I decided to take a rest like that and hope my body would warm up with the rising sun.

I just had to pray there were no hungry bears lurking this area... though I'd still take my chances with a bear over Nate right now. Exhausted, I fell deeply asleep with little effort at all.

# Chapter Twenty-Eight

"I need to say it again, Ashley, you should be going to the hospital. You could have hypothermia and that cut on your cheek looks awful." Professor Reynard had already made her opinion crystal clear, but I had been firm in my request when she picked me up on the side of the road.

I shook my head, huddling into the scratchy blanket I was wrapped in. "I'll see the campus doctor," I mumbled for the tenth time. "I'm fine."

Somehow, I felt like I needed to see this cursed challenge all the way through. If I let Professor Reynard take me to the hospital before returning to campus, would I fail? I had no clue. I only knew what Abigail had done, and since her notes had helped me find my way out of the forest, I trusted her.

The elegant fifty-something woman sighed heavily but turned into the Nevaeh University. She'd found me stumbling along the side of the road some fifteen miles away, in the early hours of the morning. It'd been almost twenty-four hours since I reached the broken bridge but I was alive. Sort of.

"At least let me escort you to the clinic?" She was well-meaning, and incredibly kind, but she—like all the campus faculty—probably had no clue about the shit going on under their noses.

I licked my chapped lips. "No. Thank you."

She sighed again, slowing to stop in front of my dorm building. "Ashley, I'm not buying your story about getting lost after a party. If someone hurt you, then—"

"Thank you," I cut her off in a clipped voice. "I appreciate the ride. But I'll be fine after a hot shower."

Before she could protest further, I climbed out of her Mercedes and left her blanket on the seat. Gritting my teeth against the aching pain in my feet, I forced myself to put one foot after another as I headed for my dorm.

Carly pushed open the lobby door, heading out of the building with her phone pressed to her ear but when she saw me she stopped dead in her tracks.

"Ashley?" she gasped, dropping her phone as her eyes widened. "Oh my god, you're back!"

I nodded, in too much pain to make words come out my mouth. When she rushed forward to hug me, I flinched away.

"Holy shit," she breathed, face full of concern as she took a better look at me. "Holy *shit*. Babe, what happened to you? Where have you been? Everyone has been going out of their minds—"

"Layne?" A familiar voice barked through the air, making me flinch.

I stiffened, starting to turn around but Carly cursed.

"Not now, Nate!" she yelled, "Just...*fuck off*!"

Even as wrecked and hurt as I was, I could recognize how much it took for Carly to speak to Nate like that. I put a weak hand up, trying to convey that I was fine and she didn't need to fight my battles for me.

All too quickly Nate was in my face, grabbing my arm aggressively like he was going to shake me. I lashed out, though, swinging my fist to hit him in the jaw.

It connected, but it was weaker than a wet kitten swatting a fly. The only reason it had any effect at all was simply for shock factor.

Nate dropped my arm, stepping back with a bewildered look on his handsome face.

"Layne, what the fu—"

"Fuck you," I spat, anger the only thing keeping me on my feet. "Fail the challenge? Kiss my ass. If you wanted me dead, you should have done it yourself."

I tried to hit him again, but he caught my wrist. I stumbled, off balance, and my strength failed. I tumbled, totally unable to catch myself from falling, but Nate caught me.

"Ashley!" Carly yelped as Nate scooped me up in his arms. "Nate, put her down!"

"Carly, shut up!" he snapped, holding me tighter and striding away from my dorm.

I was too weak to fight back. I'd made my point, I'd completed the challenge, and the whole fucking society could rot in hell for all I cared.

Carly rushed to catch up, grabbing Nate's arm to try and stop him even as my head spun and my vision spotted. I couldn't have stood on my own two feet now even if I wanted to. I was done.

"Stop! Nate, where are you taking her? What did you do?" My friend was genuinely panicked and ready to go to war for me. Fuck I loved her.

"Nothing!" he roared.

I scoffed. "Liar."

"Nathaniel Essex, I swear to fucking god I will *scream* if you don't put her the fuck down and step away. She thinks you had something to do with this? You're not taking her anywhere. Or so help me—"

Nate wasn't listening, not remotely taking her seriously as he continued striding toward the parking lot with me held in his arms like a sack of rice. For all I was fighting back, I may as well have been.

"Nate!" Carly screeched.

"I'm taking her to the fucking hospital, Carly," he snapped with cold fury. "If you're concerned, come with us."

The last thing I heard before slipping into unconsciousness was the beep of his truck unlocking. Then somehow it morphed into the beep of a heart rate monitor as I drifted back into waking.

Confused and scared, I blinked my eyes to clear the grit and looked around. I was in a hospital room, a private one with an enormous vase of flowers by the window and a huge leather armchair in the corner. An armchair within which Carly slept peacefully with her red-blond hair a total mess and her clothes crinkled to hell.

How the fuck did I get there? How long had it been? The last thing I remembered was flagging down a car and finding one of the university professors driving...

No, that wasn't right. She dropped me back and I saw Carly and...*Nate*.

That fucker.

All the anxiety and fear rolled through me from the last...however fucking long I was in the forest. Chills chased across my skin and I gingerly pulled the hospital blanket up higher. I was wearing a gown under the sheets, but it was softer than the standard scratchy crap most doctors used.

Surprisingly, I wasn't dying of thirst anymore. There had been a moment before Professor Reynard picked me up that I genuinely considered drinking from a muddy puddle. I'd been so thirsty, but I was okay now.

Following my own train of thought, I glanced down to my hand where a thick cannula and IV line had been taped down. That line was attached to a half empty bag beside the bed, which solved the mystery. I'd been rehydrated while I slept, I guess.

"Ash?" Carly asked in a quiet voice, stirring in her uncomfortable position. "Are you awake?"

"I think so?" I replied, my voice husky. "Unless this is all part of a weird head injury dream." Which was definitely a possibility seeing as I wasn't in any pain and that seemed...odd.

Carly gave a slightly unhinged laugh, unfolding from the armchair and approaching my bed. "Girl, this would be a fucked-up kind of dream because you are a *mess*. I need to let your doctor know that you're awake. Is that okay?"

I hesitated, nervously looking around the room without even realizing what I was doing.

"It's just me," she said softly, sinking her butt into the seat beside my bed. "I wouldn't let anyone else in here until you could give consent, I even stationed security in the hall to make sure no one snuck in while I was peeing."

Surprise ripped through me and my eyes widened and my lips curved in a smile. "You're my hero. Thank you. Security was probably not necessary, but I appreciate you nonetheless."

She wrinkled her nose, squinting. "You're joking, right? I nearly ended up in a fistfight with Nate while you were in the ER."

My jaw dropped. "What? Why?"

"Because the arrogant fuck was telling the nurse he was your brother and legally responsible or some bullshit like that. I politely informed him to go fuck himself and that he wasn't any more your *family* than a pregnant porcupine was." Carly grinned, clearly proud of herself. "Besides, since you were unconscious and not carrying any ID or money, I signed all your admission paperwork and put you under my insurance."

I gave a startled sound, lifting my hospital bracelet to read the name. "Tracy Briggs. Uh, how does your sister feel about me stealing her identity?"

Carly shrugged. "She'd be cool with it." Her little sister was studying abroad, but from what Carly had told me she seemed like a nice kid. "Besides, Nate made a big enough stink that everyone knows that's not actually *you* but it was nothing a generous donation to the hospital couldn't fix."

I smiled, reaching out to squeeze her hand. "Thank you. I'm lucky to have you, Carly." Then an unpleasant thought struck me and I winced. "Uh, assuming you had no idea about what just happened to me? If you knew and didn't warn me—"

"No! Fuck no!" she vehemently denied. "I have to assume it was something society-related from what you said to Nate but I swear on my own life, I knew *nothing*. And honestly, I don't think he did, either. When I tell you everyone was losing their damn minds with worry, I mean *everyone*. Nate included."

I didn't believe that for a second, he was probably just putting on a good show. For what? I had no clue. I was too foggy to argue, though.

"I should call your doctor," Carly said when I didn't comment. "If you're okay for me to do that?"

I nodded, resting my head back against the pillow. "Yeah. Probably a good idea. Thank you, girl, you're the best."

She shook her head. "Stop it, you're making me blush. You'd do the same for me."

Before I could make her uncomfortable with my gratitude, she hopped up and slipped out of the room. I caught a glimpse of a heavyset security guard standing right there, guarding the door, and I let out a long sigh. Carly wasn't fucking around, and I loved her for it.

I closed my eyes while I waited, but within a few minutes she was back with a distinguished male doctor. He was calmly professional as he checked me over, chatting in a comforting manner all the while. There were a few questions about what had happened to me, but purely from a medical care point of view. I told him everything, not caring about keeping secrets.

When he was done, he hung my chart back on its hook and gave me a serious look. "I think you should speak with the police about what happened to you, Ashley." He'd been using my real name the whole time, and Carly hadn't blinked twice. I figured she'd told him. "Kidnapping, assault, drugging…these are serious offenses and if you know who is responsible then they need to be held accountable. You could have died. You do realize that?"

I nodded. "I do. I think that's what they hoped would happen."

His lips pinched and he gave a sigh. "It's up to you. I'm keeping you another night for observation and fluids, though. Are you hungry? I'll send one of the nurses in with food shortly."

The doctor left, and Carly just stared at me with tears in her eyes, horrified. "Babe…that's…"

"Fucked-up? I'm well aware." I sighed, then shivered. "Can I be a pain in the ass and see if they can get me another blanket? I'm stupidly cold for some reason."

"Um, maybe because you spent nearly two days walking around the woods in your underwear in late October?" she replied, incredulous. "But yes. Be right back."

True to her word, she was back within a matter of minutes carrying a stack of extra blankets and an assortment of chocolate bars.

"I grabbed these from the vending machine, but the nurses are planning on bringing you real food as well," she said, depositing the stash onto my bedside unit and unfolding the blankets onto my bed.

A pissed off sort of scowl pulled her expression tight, though, and I squinted at her suspiciously.

"What happened?" I asked. "You look…you know. Stabby."

She took her time getting my blankets spread out, avoiding eye contact all the while, then sighed. "Heath wants to see you. He made me promise to ask."

I frowned. "No."

"Oh thank god," she exclaimed with a rush of relief. "Because I already told him to go sit on a cactus and spin, so I really didn't want to have to apologize if you were happy to see him."

That made me chuckle. "You're good. I don't want to see any of them. Nate set this whole thing up, I'm sure of it, but there's no way he acted alone. *Don't trust them.* That was the message I got right before it happened, and it's time I started listening."

Carly nodded soberly. "Got it. Help yourself to snacks, I'll go tell him not to hold his breath."

I did as I was told, grabbing a Special Dark from the pile and damn near inhaling it while she was gone from the room. It was all quiet for a while, until the door opened again and I heard her yell a parting remark.

"Not my problem, Heathcliff, take it up with Nate. This is *his* fault." Then she slammed the door once more. "Done. Now…are you going back to sleep or are we hanging out?"

I snuggled deeper into my blankets, my head still like cotton wool from whatever medication they had me on. "Hanging out," I mumbled. "Sleepy hanging out."

Carly just nodded and started dragging the wide armchair over from the corner. "That, we can do." She got the chair to where she wanted, right beside my bed, and got comfy. "Let's see what movies we've got to choose from." She flicked on the overhead TV using the remote, and started searching, but I just smiled and patted her leg.

"I'm glad you're here, friend," I said quietly.

She patted my hand back. "I'm glad you're here too, friend. Let's never scare each other like that again, okay?"

I nodded. "Deal."

It was an agreement I intended to keep.

# Chapter Twenty-Nine

Sometimes all a girl needed was a hug from her mom. Sometimes, that tight embrace could make all her problems melt away and the anxiety lift. Sometimes…it fixed everything.

But sometimes the problems were too big for a hug to fix, so her embrace served to offer support and remind a girl she wasn't in it alone.

"Ashley, baby, why didn't you call me sooner?" my mom asked as she hugged me close, stroking my hair. "You could have died. Your doctor said—"

"I know," I mumbled into her shoulder as tears flowed from my eyes.

Mom didn't push the issue, always being one for the whole *don't cry over spilled milk* way of thinking. What was done, was done, and hindsight was useless now. She sighed, continuing to hold me while I cried.

Eventually, my tears dried up and I released her. "Sorry, I just—"

"Hush. We don't apologize for needing support, darling." She smoothed my hair back with her fingernails, stroking my bruised cheek gently. "Gosh, you poor thing. What can I get for you? Coffee, or something stronger?"

I gave a sobbing laugh, wiping my eyes on my sleeve. We'd not long arrived at Max's house after Mom picked me up from Prosper Private. She'd apparently given Heath a thorough dressing-down when she'd seen him in the waiting room—for no real reason other than the fact he was there and looking guilty—then hugged Carly so hard my friend burst out crying too.

Mom had that way with people. She made them feel safe enough to let their walls down and release their tightly held emotions.

"Um, coffee is fine," I replied, "seeing as it's not even midday."

Mom shrugged. "Okay, no need for that. I'm just being hospitable." But she'd also been teasing so I wouldn't take her up on it. She left me curled up on the leather sofa while she went to ask Max's housekeeper for coffee and cake.

I'd not spent a lot of time in Max's home, but I could see Mom's influence on the decor. Little things here and there, making the place warmer and more inviting. Most noticeable was the addition of framed photographs, displaying their wedding and honeymoon... and little kid photos of both me and Nate, along with several old pics of the four boys together. They'd been friends a long time.

"Okay. So, I think I need to hear everything from the beginning," Mom announced, returning to the living room and planting her hands on her hips.

I nodded. "I think so too. But I think Max also needs to hear what's been going on." It made me feel like shit even thinking about tattling to Nate's dad about his bullshit...but things had gone too far.

Mom's brows lifted. "Oh. I see."

I grimaced. "Yeah." A shiver rolled through me and I rubbed my arms.

Mom frowned and grabbed a sweatshirt off the back of the sofa. "Here, put this on. It's Max's but he won't mind."

"Thanks," I murmured, accepting the garment and pulling it on. It was a cashmere knit pullover and smelled of fresh laundry detergent.

"I'll go get him. You wait here." Mom left the living room and I snuggled into the sofa deeper. I had taken a dose of painkillers before leaving the hospital and it was still firmly in effect, which was nice. My doctor had warned me that everything would hurt when it started to wear off, though.

Max's housekeeper, Susan, carried a tray in a few minutes later with coffee and cake loaded up.

"Here you go, honey," she murmured, handing me one of the coffee mugs directly before setting everything else out on the coffee table. "How are you feeling?"

I smiled. "I'm okay. Thank you."

Her hard stare told me I didn't look *okay* by any means, but I was well aware. The bruise from Paris on my left cheek was fading but my right side was a mess. I'd needed a stitch in my cheek from where I'd split my face on the rock and the bruising covered a good third of my face. Not to mention the dozens of scrapes on the rest of me. My feet were bandaged, but with luck they'd heal up quickly.

"You don't hesitate to call for me if you need anything else," she told me, and I nodded my agreement.

Mom returned with Max a moment later, but to my dismay they weren't alone.

"Nope," I snapped, sitting up straighter. "Not him. Get the fuck out."

Nate's eyes narrowed in a scowl. "I live here, Layne, get over it."

*Liar.* He lived with his friends near Nevaeh, but I guess he would always technically have a room in Max's house as well.

Max shot a troubled look between the two of us and sighed. "Carina, maybe it's better if Nate gave Ash some space?"

Mom had her lips pursed, though, a stubborn tilt to her head. "No, I think whatever Ash has to say includes Nate. Isn't that right?" Her glance between us was accusing and I choked back my fury at seeing him.

Nate said nothing, just folding his arms and staring at me with his dark eyes. Unreadable as always.

I wet my lips, then jerked a nod. Fuck him, I refused to be intimidated. "Yes. It does."

Mom's soft smile was encouraging and proud. She wanted me to face my problems, and it was about damn time I did.

She and Max sat down and Nate leaned his back against the doorframe like he was preparing to flee. It was better he stayed for this, so there could be no misunderstandings.

"Go ahead, Ashley," Max coaxed gently.

I drew a deep breath, searching for the words to explain what'd happened. I needed to start at the beginning and tell them about how Nate keyed my car. About how he sent Heath to proposition me and paint me as a prostitute. But instead, my anger and hurt skipped ahead to focus on the part I was *most* irate about.

"Nate tried to kill me," I blurted out.

Shock and outrage morphed his expression and he jerked out of his relaxed pose. "What the *fuck*? I did not! Why the hell—"

"Ah ah ah," Mom cut him off, holding her hand up. "That's enough, Nathaniel, it's Ashley's time to speak and we are going to listen."

His eyes pinched as he shifted his gaze to my mom, somewhat bewildered. "But Carina, she's lying. I never—"

"Nathaniel. I understand that you have some big feelings about this right now, and that what Ashley is saying might hurt your heart." She spoke to him like a toddler and I nearly laughed. He was so shocked he didn't even talk back. "You can hold on to those big feelings until she's finished, or you can whisper them into your hand to hold for later. But right now, Ashley is talking. Got it, got it?"

I cracked a smile, I couldn't help it. My mom just sarcastically gentle parented Nate like he was a three-year old, and it was fucking hilarious.

"Um," I tried to remember where I'd been, but amusement was

shaking up my anger and a glance to Nate's furious, red face nearly sent me into a rage.

"Ignore him, Ash," Max suggested. "Tell us what happened, please."

I wet my lips, shifting my gaze to my mom instead so I could block Nate out. "Nate and his friends are part of a secret society, it's called The Devil's Backbone." Neither Mom or Max flinched. Instead, they just shared a quick look, and I frowned. "You know about it?"

Max gave a small nod. "We're not unaware. Carry on."

I blinked my confusion, gently combing my fingers through my hair as I processed that information. "Um, okay. Well they're the ones who abducted me from campus on Tuesday. They tied me up, drugged me, stripped me, and dumped me in the middle of the fucking forest. I bet they never thought I'd make it out alive, though." This last part was directed right to Nate with a victorious sneer, and he glowered back at me with arms folded across his chest.

Mom and Max were quiet for a moment, then Mom reached out to hold my hand. "Honey, from what I understand of the Devil's Backbone that's not the sort of thing they do. Now, I'm not saying you're wrong, I believe you believe it was them. But can you help us understand why?"

My jaw dropped in a touch of outrage. "Okay. Sure. Let's see... there's the fact that Nate specifically told me to *fail the next challenge* a whole fifteen minutes before I was attacked."

"I didn't mean—" he started to protest, but Mom hushed him with her hand in the air once more.

"Then there was the note nailed to a tree beside where I woke up, reading *whore*," I continued, "which is Nate's favorite insult for me, since he seems to think I'm a working girl."

Mom and Max both whipped their heads around to stare at Nate, and he had the grace to look sheepish as he stuffed his hands in his pockets. He didn't try to defend himself, though, so maybe gentle parenting worked.

"Oh, and maybe that it's not the first time he'd abducted me? Or are we pretending like you didn't break into my dorm room in the middle of the night and drag me up to Cat's Peak?" I glared daggers in his direction and he blinked back in shock. Did he *really* think I was keeping his shit secret after he tried to kill me? The gloves were off.

"Nathaniel," Max scolded, horrified.

He wet his lips, giving his dad a tight smile. "It's not how it sounds. It was a harmless prank."

"Uh-huh, sure," I said sarcastically. "That's why Royce needed to patch up my injuries afterwards? So harmless. Oh, and while we're on the evidence stack, I literally *saw* my attackers before they put that fucking hood over my head. So no amount of smooth-talking is convincing me this wasn't part of your dumb society shit."

Nate straightened up, alarmed. "You saw them? Why didn't you—"

"They were in those robes and masks that you all wear," I snapped back. "Which I think you already know."

Max gave a long exhale, scrubbing a hand over his face. "Okay. Thank you for telling us, Ashley. Is there anything else we need to know?"

I hesitated. Should I tell them about Abigail's diary? How her notes were the only thing that helped me survive? I bit my tongue and shook my head. I'd keep that to myself, for now—if Nate really didn't know about her diary, I didn't want him finding out from me.

"No, that's the important stuff," I said quietly.

Nate shook his head. "No it's not. Tell them about the text messages."

Shock made me double take. "Excuse me?" Why the fuck would he be volunteering that information? It made no sense, and it sure as hell didn't make things better for him and his friends.

Nate pulled out his phone and crossed the room to hand it to me. It wasn't *his* phone, it was mine.

"Where...where did you get this?"

His jaw tightened. "I found it outside the library. I went back to find you and instead I found your broken laptop and your handbag scattered all over the path. You've got a new message from Abigail."

My mouth went dry and I looked down at my phone.

"Who's Abigail?" Mom asked, looking between the two of us for answers.

I frowned, staring at the *one new message* icon but not brave enough to open it just yet. "You found my stuff?" I asked in a weak voice, focusing on the wrong part.

"Nate was the one who reported you missing," Max said softly. "He's been working with the police to find you and to actually investigate."

It didn't make sense. "But you knew where I was. Why waste the police time when you—"

"Because I *didn't*," he growled. "I had nothing to do with this, Ashley. When I said to fail the next challenge, I was thinking about ducks...not *dying*."

I shook my head slowly. "I don't believe you."

"Clearly," he muttered, dropping to sit in one of the chairs opposite where I was curled up on the sofa. "But when have I ever lied to you?"

My mouth opened to point out dozens of lies he'd told, but as soon as they popped into my head I realized the distinction. Telling lies *about* me wasn't the same as lying *to* me. He'd always owned his shitty behavior, hadn't he?

"Honey, who is Abigail? What are these messages Nate's talking about?" Mom squeezed my hand, bringing me back to focus.

I sniffed, shaking off the weird moment between Nate and I, and turning my attention back to my phone. Before I could talk myself out of it, I opened the message.

UNKNOWN:

> It's started now. You'll be dead soon, just like me.—AM

"Ashley is getting threatening text messages from a dead girl," Nate explained, clearly deciding that if I was spilling his secrets, he'd spill mine.

Max and Mom looked suitably alarmed by this information, and I sighed. "They're not threatening," I corrected. "They're warnings. I think. Abigail was in the society too, and had all these awful things happen to her. She's just trying to warn me before I also end up dead."

"But...she's dead?" Mom asked, clearly confused. "How can she be contacting you?"

I grimaced. It was a great question.

"That's what I want to know too," Nate replied. Smug fuck. Look who was acting the concerned brother all of a sudden. He needed to win an Oscar for the way he performed in front of our parents.

Max huffed an annoyed sound. "Okay, so someone is pulling a sick joke pretending to be a ghost. I'll have one of my people look into this." He reached out his hand, and I passed over my phone without protest. "For right now, though, I want to sort out this ugliness between the two of you."

I swallowed back a groan. I really didn't want to play happy families with Nate, and I was sure he felt the same.

"Sounds good to me," Nate said, startling me. "I've got nowhere else to be."

"You're such a prick," I hissed. "No one is buying this act."

"Okay, Ashley, that's enough," Mom scolded. "You're both acting like children."

My cheeks heated and I sulked a little. "He started it."

Susan, the housekeeper, appeared in the doorway and knocked

lightly to get attention. "So sorry to interrupt. The boys are here. Would you like them to come in or…?"

Mom sighed, then gave Max a long look. Something passed between the two of them like they shared a telepathic connection and Max gave a small shrug. "I'd like them to come in if it's okay with you, Ashley? Either they can help resolve this animosity, or they're involved which also requires addressing."

I flinched, unable to hide my reaction to that. Yeah, he could say that.

"Sure," I grudgingly agreed. "May as well rip the Band-Aid off all at once, I guess." Although it was going to hurt a whole shitload more than a Band-Aid if I discovered Heath was part of the abduction.

…or Carter for that matter. Then again, if "Abigail" was to be believed, Carter had already killed once, so maybe he was capable.

This was an awful idea, but it was out of my control. I just had to trust that I was safe here with Mom and Max, regardless of how this all turned out.

## Chapter Thirty

When Susan said the boys were here, she meant *all* of them...which surprised me. Or maybe, I justified in my mind, they were just here to see Nate and got swept up in our family therapy session unintentionally. Regardless, it quickly became hard to breathe under the intense stares from all four boys.

Royce just seemed bored and somewhat curious, Heath and Carter were *intense* and I avoided eye contact with them both, but Nate was unreadable as ever. Still playing nice guy for our parents, I guess.

"Okay, so clearly something unpleasant is going on with you all," Max started. "Ashley made some pretty serious allegations about DB pranks going wrong and is quite convinced that Nate set up her kidnapping with the intention of her dying in that forest."

"And by all accounts, it's a miracle she didn't," my mom added, her brow pinched.

Max nodded his agreement. "And I know the four of you well enough to know that if Nate was involved, you all were. So...what do you have to say for yourselves?"

The boys were all silent for a moment with some degree of shock on their expressions—except for Nate, who just looked irritated.

It was Royce who spoke first. "You think we tried to kill you, Squirrel? For real?"

I wet my lips, forcing myself to back myself. "Yes. I do. This wasn't a silly prank for initiation, Royce, look at my face." I gestured to where my cheek had been stitched, and the bruising around it. "I just spent two days in the hospital being treated for dehydration and hypothermia, not to mention the fact I can barely walk thanks to hiking *barefoot* through a forest."

He stared back at me with laser-like intensity. "Not disputing the nearly died part, Ash. Just that you think we would do that to you."

I pursed my lips, flicking my gaze to Nate. "Yeah well, can you really blame me?"

Royce blew out a long breath. "Fuck."

"Language," Mom scolded, and Royce shot her a sheepish smile.

"Sorry, Carina. I meant *fork*."

Heath leaned forward, catching my peripheral attention even as I refused to make eye contact. "Ashley...you think *I* had something to do with this?"

*No.* But then again... "I don't know what to think, Heath," I admitted in a small voice. "The evidence points to Nate, and considering everything else I would be an absolute fool to trust any of you." Against my better judgment, my eyes flicked to Carter as I said that, and saw his flinch as my words hit home.

"I see," Heath murmured, giving a sad nod.

I hated that I wanted to immediately take those words back and tell him that *he* was the exception. But it wouldn't be true. Just because I fell for his charm for a few hours didn't change the bullshit with Jade or the fact he lied about us sleeping together.

"What would you think if roles were reversed?" I asked softly. "If I'd done and said everything the four of you have?"

"Doesn't it seem a little convenient?" Max asked, and I startled a little. I'd forgotten he and Mom were sitting here, listening to everything. Thank fuck no one had outright addressed the tension in the room.

Carter spoke for the first time since walking into the room. "How so?"

Max gave me a small apologetic smile. "Sorry to jump in, honey. This might sound like I'm biased and I assure you that's not my intent. But doesn't the evidence seem *too* convenient for Nate to be involved? The note, the DB masks, the messages...couldn't it be someone trying to sow distrust and isolate you from the very people who could protect you?"

My lips parted but no words formed. Because no, that hadn't occurred to me. I was thoroughly convinced Nate was behind everything.

"You think someone is imitating DBs, Max?" Heath asked, thoughtful.

Max shrugged. "It's a possibility, isn't it?" The question was directed at me, but I was still at a loss for words. Was it?

"How, though?" Royce asked, clearly pondering the notion. "They'd need to know about Nate's, um, *very incorrect* opinion of Ashley to leave that note."

Nate shot him a sharp glare. "Very incorrect? Did you forget—"

"Stop it," Heath snapped. "That never happened. I *lied*."

Well, *shit*. I could have been knocked over with a feather if I weren't safely seated.

Nate's expression of shock and confusion was nearly worth it, though. He started to draw a breath to speak, but Carter cleared his throat.

"I think that's a conversation for another time," he interjected, giving a not so subtle nod toward my mom sitting right there listening intently.

She grinned, waving a hand. "Oh, don't mind us, sweetheart, you just pretend like we aren't here. Max, hon, do we have any popcorn?"

I rolled my eyes, amusement tugging at my lips. "Yeah...that's not relevant right now. What would even be the point of framing Nate, though? If I died out there...why would it matter who *I* thought was responsible?"

"But you didn't," Nate pointed out. "Why?"

I scowled, anger rising in my chest. "Sorry to disappoint, Essex. I guess I'm just a cockroach."

He rolled his eyes. "Not what I meant, Layne. By all accounts, it's a *miracle* that you made it out. So *how did you?* You're not local, you've never been in those woods, you have no hiking or survival experience whatsoever...so, how did you get out alive?"

A chill raced down my spine as the answer slapped me in the face. The diary was the reason I made it out alive...but I no longer *had* the diary. Which meant someone else did. Maybe someone who was responsible for Abigail's death?

My head swirled and I reached a shaking hand for my coffee to try and refocus my rapidly building anxiety. It wobbled so badly in my hand that I sloshed it on myself, though.

"Shit," I whispered, putting the mug back down and picking the wet fabric away from my chest to see the coffee stain on the cashmere knit. "Sorry, Max."

He flapped a hand to indicate he didn't care, and I peeled the coffee-soaked sweater off with a mental note to handwash it for him later. No sooner had I taken it off than a replacement hoodie smacked me in the face.

"Ow, what—" I complained, grabbing the offending clothing.

Nate just sighed. "Just put it on, drama queen. You look cold."

I wanted to tell him to go fuck himself, but I was already shivering again and his hoodie was warm...fuck it. I put it on, but I *didn't* say thank you.

Mom broke the incredibly tense silence—within which Heath stared at Nate like he wanted to gut him with a fork—by handing me a slice of cake on a plate. "You need some sugar."

"Thanks, Mom," I replied, accepting the cake and little fork she offered.

"Okay," Max redirected. "So...I'm not sure what you just thought of, Ash, but is it fair to say you're not *quite* so sure Nate is the one trying to kill you?"

I ate a bite of delicious cake—banana with cream cheese frosting—and licked my lips as I offered the tiniest of nods. Because as much as I hated to admit it, there was now doubt in my mind.

Max accepted that admission, though, with a nod of his own. "Good enough. For what it's worth, I've known these boys their whole lives and been legal guardian for these three misfits since they were twelve. I like to think I'm a decent judge of character, and to put it straight, whoever dropped you in the woods is straight-up evil. That's not these boys, and it's not my son." He said it gently, not defensive just...factually sincere. "Now, that's not to say they're faultless. Whatever else has been going on needs to stop, Nate, immediately."

Max's tone hardened dramatically with that and Nate hung his head as he nodded silent agreement.

"I mean it. All four of you. I don't know what the hell caused this tension with you all and Ashley, but it reeks of childish bullying and I won't stand for it. Do you hear me?"

They all murmured a chorus of *yes, sir* and I stared in wonder. Max had more than just authority over them...he had their respect. That much was evident in the shamed slouch to their shoulders and downcast gazes. A bunch of children being scolded by their favorite adult.

That reaction, more than anything that'd been said, created more doubt in my mind about who'd been responsible for my kidnapping. It didn't make sense, but my chest ached with uncertainty nonetheless.

"Ashley, I do feel strongly that someone is trying to drive a wedge between you all—as if these boys weren't doing enough of that already—and that is very concerning." Max frowned, clearly thinking something over. "Maybe you could consider transferring to a different school?"

That suggestion rocked me and I sat up straighter. "No."

Mom seemed bewildered. "No? Honey, why not? Someone tried to kill you and—"

"And you told me never to back down to bullies." Another pointed glare in Nate's direction. "Besides, I hardly think scholarships are transferable."

Max and Mom did another one of those psychic looks and I knew what was coming before they even said it.

"We could—" Max started.

"Absolutely not," I cut him off firmly. As if I needed Max offering to pay my postgrad tuition and housing right there in front of the boys who'd been accusing me of prostituting myself. "Not even remotely an option. I'll stay at Nevaeh and simply quit the dumb secret society so I should be of no further interest to…whoever it is pulling strings."

Mom bit her lip, giving Max a worried look. "Is that possible?"

Max sighed, shaking his head. "I don't know. But given the circumstances…Nate, I trust you can sort that out?"

My archnemesis jerked a nod.

"If I might," Royce spoke up, "offer another suggestion? Perhaps it would be safer for Ashley if she isn't alone so much? That way, for one thing, she can't be grabbed like she was, and for another she'll know for a fact that we aren't responsible because she can keep an eye on us personally. Keep your friends close and enemies closer and all that."

I wrinkled my nose, attempting to process his idea. "You want me to stay in your apartment?"

Royce shrugged. "Why not? I'm sure we can make space."

A very unladylike snort escaped me, even as my insides flushed warm with the idea of sharing a bed with Heath…or Carter…or both. Shit.

"No," I managed to choke out.

Royce seemed undeterred. "Okay, well I'm sure we can work something else out."

Max and Mom were already nodding their heads, and I knew he'd won them. Royce did sort of have a good point, though. If they were responsible for keeping me safe...then none of them could hurt me. Right? So even if Nate *did* orchestrate the kidnapping, he wouldn't be able to do anything more without stitching up his friends.

With a tired sigh, I mumbled a half-hearted agreement, then placed my barely touched cake down on the coffee table beside my mug. "I'm actually not feeling so great," I told my mom, turning up the sad panda eyes. "Is it okay if I lie down for a bit?"

"Of course!" she gushed, hopping up from her seat and extending her hands for me to grip onto as I gingerly stood. My feet were cut and bruised so much that even through the painkillers, it hurt to put weight on them.

The boys just stared. Fucking *stared* like I'd just whipped my pants off and started pushing a baby out right there on the sofa.

Heath was the first to snap out of it, thank fuck. He sprung up and smoothly took over for Mom, looping his arm around my waist and supporting me as I gritted my teeth and hobbled out of the room.

We were halfway up the stairs before he spoke to me.

"Do you think we could talk alone?" he asked softly, watching my steps like an eagle as I laboriously climbed the stairs.

I shook my head. "Not now," I replied, slightly out of breath. "I just really, really need sleep. And time."

He nodded. "Got it. Sleep and time."

He didn't push the issue, just silently helped me get to the guest room Mom had told me was mine the first time I visited, and pulled back the blankets for me to climb inside.

"Can I get you anything?" he offered once I was comfortably horizontal. "Water? Medicine? Pajamas?"

I smiled, my eyelids already heavy. "No. But thank you. Um, for what it's worth...I never thought you were in on it. I'm annoyed about other things, but I don't think you want me dead." *Unlike your friends.*

Heath said nothing to that, just sat on the floor beside my bed and stroked his fingers through my hair until I drifted to sleep.

## Chapter Thirty-One

Mom and Max insisted I stay with them a few more days while my body healed from the ordeal I'd been through. I didn't argue, either, since my inability to walk easily had me in a foul mood and I didn't want to be in a position where I needed to run for my life just yet.

To my surprise, although the other boys all returned to school, Nate stayed. I found him in the kitchen on my second morning, half asleep and making coffee…wearing nothing but a pair of loose pajama pants. His toffee-colored hair was all messed up like he'd been running his hands through it and—

"I'm not making you coffee, if that's what you're waiting for," he informed me, making me snap out of my little daze.

I'd been staring. At *Nate*. Was I concussed? Maybe.

"Why not? A real man would," I clapped back, fighting the blush creeping into my cheeks as I grabbed a coffee mug out and parked it beside the machine. Daring him.

He glowered, but after pouring his own cup he moved the pot to mine and filled it. "Black, like your soul."

I scoffed, taking my mug back. "If that's not the pot talking to the kettle…" I grabbed out some cream and caramel syrup, tweaking the bitter coffee to suit my sweet tooth while Nate stared in horrified fascination.

It was harder than it should have been to *not* look at his body. But fucking hell it was right there in all its washboard glory.

"Why are you still here?" I asked, finding a distraction. "Didn't your friends go back to school yesterday?"

He hummed a sound of affirmation as he sipped his black coffee, leaning against the counter like he had nowhere better to be. "It's quieter here, and I need to focus on my coursework for a few days. Carter has a dog in our apartment…"

I grinned, loving that Nate sounded very anti-canine. "I'm aware."

He glared daggers. "Yeah well, it's constantly whimpering and begging for belly scratches which is counterproductive when I'm trying to work on my PhD thesis."

Confused, I tilted my head. "Your PhD thesis? I thought you were in a master's program, but…you're working toward a doctorate?" Actually, now that I said it out loud, I vaguely remembered he'd told me that before. I just either didn't pay attention or didn't believe him at the time.

He met my gaze with a flat stare. "What, like it's hard?" His lips curved up in a slight grin and he started to leave the kitchen then paused. "I guess you can keep the hoodie…seeing as you seem to like it so much."

Then he was gone, and my face burned with mortification realizing I was wearing *his* hoodie again. It was insanely comfy and it'd been right there beside my bed when I woke up so I'd just put it on… but in my defense I had thought he was gone. Damn it.

Then something else occurred to me, and it was possibly one of the most shocking things I'd realized in a long time.

Nathaniel Essex had just quoted *Legally Blonde* to me.

"What the *fuck?*" I whispered aloud, then took a gulp of my coffee. Maybe I was still half asleep and imagining things? Yeah. That.

After that weird encounter with Nate, it seemed like he was everywhere. I couldn't go anywhere in the house without running into him and it was driving me up the fucking wall. For a guy supposedly working on his thesis he sure didn't spend much time at a desk.

Four days after being discharged from hospital my feet were healed enough that I gave my thanks to Mom and Max, and relocated back to my dorm on campus.

"You're back!" Carly squealed with excitement when Max's driver dropped me off in front of the dorm. I'd texted her on my way and she'd been waiting for me to arrive, the adorable human. "I missed you."

I laughed, accepting her hug. "You could have visited," I argued. "It's not *that* far from here." In fact it was only an hour drive on the opposite side of Lake Prosper.

"Mmm yeah not while Nate was there, thanks," she replied with a short laugh.

I grimaced. "Yeah, good point. Sorry that's…uncomfy."

She shrugged. "It is what it is, and honestly with the beauty of hindsight I can see that I dodged a big old bullet with him. I don't have the patience for his diva mood swings."

I chuckled at that description, but for some reason all my mind could conjure up was the memory of him relaxed and casually sipping his coffee…shirtless…with that little smile on his lips.

"Well, anyway, I'm back and I officially want nothing more to do with DBs so there's absolutely no need for our paths to cross with Nate or any of his friends again." I made the declaration firm, convincing myself as much as I was her.

Carly gave me a skeptical squint as we rode the elevator up to our floor. "Uh-huh. Except for the fact you have a massive crush on my cousin and you spent a romantic weekend in Paris getting dicked down by his sexy British hothead friend, and then there's Royce…"

I wrinkled my nose, stepping out when the doors slid open. "What about Royce?"

"Uh…" Carly gave me a puzzled look, then shifted her gaze to my door.

A pool of dread filled up in my belly and I shoved my door open to find the blond philanderer himself unpacking a bag into my dresser. "Hey roomie!" He grinned his shithead grin and grabbed me in a hug. "This will be fun. How do you feel about bunk beds?"

"Absolutely not. Royce, what the hell? Get out of my room!" I shoved him off me—quickly noting that he'd been quite gentle in his hug—and pointed a shaking finger to the open door.

He shook his head. "Nope. You're stuck with me for at least the next five nights. I thought you'd be grateful."

I spluttered, tripping over my words as I tried to make a dozen thoughts connect. "Grateful?" I finally managed to squeak. "For *what*?"

Royce sat his ass up on my bed, then scooted back against my pillows to get comfortable and I noted his feet were bare. His shoes were neatly placed by the door. That was…oddly polite and far too intimate.

"Well, it was going to be Carter playing babysitter but then he said something to Heath, and it turned into a, uh, physical altercation which resulted in a stalemate and so…here I am. The compromise. You're *welcome*." He patted the bed beside him. "Come sit, let's work out schedules."

Frustrated, I turned to Carly for help. She just spread her hands helplessly. "Sorry, girl. He said you knew…and honestly I'm not mad about Operation Protect Ashley."

"Mmm that name is a work in progress," Royce added. "But technically you *did* know. We discussed it the other day. Sort of."

Another strangled noise escaped me in lieu of words.

Carly checked her invisible watch dramatically. "Oh, is that the time? I need to go…umm…wash my hair. See ya!" And disappeared.

"Traitor!" I yelled after her, even as her door shut quickly across the hall. I sighed and turned my attention back to Royce. "Seriously, get out."

His smile was more sly this time. "No can do, Squirrel. Shut the door and come chat with me." He patted the bed beside him again and a ripple of uncertainty chased through me.

I wet my lips, folding my arms over my chest. "No thank you. I'd like you to leave, Royce. My room isn't big enough for the both of us."

He drew a breath, smoothly sliding off my bed and leaning past me to shove my door shut. "Nonsense. I don't take up much space."

Frustrated, I clenched my jaw as I glared up at him. Damn these guys for all being so much taller than me, it was really hard to achieve *threatening* when I had to crane my neck for eye contact.

"Royce...I don't need—"

"Hush, Squirrel. I'll spell it out for you. Either you accept my generous offer to play roomie, or I can ask Nate to do it. But either way, you *will* have a buddy attached to your hip twenty-four seven until we can find whoever is trying to frame us for trying to kill you. Clear?" His smile was cold, and the implication was clear. He wouldn't be moved on this.

"Why Nate?" I argued, refusing to give up so easily. "Why not Heath?"

His eyes sparkled with amusement. "How curious you didn't suggest Carter. Methinks something happened in Geneva between the two of you."

"Paris," I corrected, and he just smiled wider. Shithead.

"Same thing. And the answer is that Heath and Carter are clearly not thinking with their *brains* when it comes to you, otherwise they wouldn't have come to blows over this little arrangement. So...what's it going to be, little Squirrel? Me or Nate?"

Bloody hell. He really wasn't going to back down on this issue and I had a strong feeling that no matter how hard I complained, no one would forcefully make him leave. Royce, for all his sly teasing, had a darkness to him that I definitely didn't want to encounter head-on. I couldn't blame others for steering clear.

Jaw clenched tight, I sighed. "Fine. But you're sleeping on the floor and if you snore, I'll smother you with a pillow. Clear?"

His lips tilted in a lopsided grin. "Deal. Now, let's compare schedules so we both don't skip too many classes. After all, failing out of Nevaeh University would be a hell of an embarrassment for our families."

Frustrated, I pushed him aside and glanced around at all my things he'd been rearranging. He'd cleared out one of my drawers and made it his own…pushy prick. "I have a lot of coursework to catch up on and no laptop so I hope you like hanging out in the library."

"Ew. Let's just go buy you a new one," he countered. "You need it for taking notes and turning in assignments anyway."

I rolled my eyes. "I'm well-aware. But that means…" I trailed off, not wanting to explain that buying a new laptop would dip heavily into my savings. Which meant I needed to get a job to replace that money. But Royce wasn't wrong about needing to get one sooner rather than later.

"I need to get a job," I said with a sigh.

His brows lifted with surprise. "I'm assuming you intend to be stubborn about this and not let me simply buy you a new computer?" I nodded and he stuffed his hands into his pockets. "Very well. What kind of job would you like?"

"Ideally working at a day spa. I'm fully qualified as a massage therapist and it pays a hell of a lot better than coffee shops. Even without inappropriate propositions from entitled rich boys." I gave him a pointed look, and he just shrugged…totally unapologetic. "Max mentioned there's a spa at Prosper Country Club. Maybe I'll try there?"

Royce nodded thoughtfully. "Yes, that's a good option. Shall we go now?"

I hesitated, then realized I had nothing else to do for the day—aside from catching up on studying which would go smoother *with* a computer—so nodded. "Fuck it, may as well. Uh…let me just see if I can get some makeup to cover up the worst of my face first."

"Maybe a change of clothing…if I might suggest?" Royce gave my attire a long look and I screwed my eyes shut with regret. Stupid Nate and his stupid cozy hoodie.

"Yep." I agreed, quickly pulling the offending garment off and tossing it aside. "That."

Royce made himself comfortable reclining on my bed and scrolling his phone while I sat at my little study desk to fix my face. Ultimately, there was fuck all I could do where the gash in my cheek had been stitched but I managed to cover the bulk of the bruising with a thick layer of foundation and concealer.

When I was ready, Royce hopped up and put his shoes on. "My car or yours?" he asked, holding the door open for me to exit ahead of him. He followed me out into the hall and locked my door with *his own key*…what the fuck?

"Um, mine," I replied, scowling at the key in his hand.

He grinned, pocketing the key and ignoring my glare. "Awesome. Can I drive?"

"Fuck no," I scoffed. "Not in your wildest dreams, Royce D'Arenberg."

He shrugged and tossed me one of his utterly disarming smiles. "We'll see."

## Chapter Thirty-Two

Royce basically handed me the job at Prosper Country Club. Apparently he knew the general manager and just introduced me to him as the newest massage therapist. As embarrassed and flustered as that made me, I wasn't going to look the gift horse in the mouth. As he pointed out, I was more than qualified and experienced, and the general manager had seemed happy to hand over the contract.

I justified it to myself that it was just good timing. The manager mentioned they'd been short-staffed for a while, so there were more than enough hours available.

With that done—I wouldn't start work for another two weeks to be sure my injuries were healed—Royce and I swung past the electronics store to grab my new laptop then headed for the campus library.

"What are we studying?" he asked as I got settled in and powered up my new computer.

I raised a brow. "I don't know about you, but I'm reading notes from all the lectures I missed this past week. What *are* you studying, anyway?"

"You don't already know everything there is to know about me?" Royce pressed a hand to his chest in mock hurt. "Wounded, truly."

"Uh-huh, sure you are."

"I'm a doctoral candidate in social psychology. Wanna know what the other guys are studying?" He asked it as a loaded question, and I tried to pretend I didn't notice his tone.

"I already know Heath is studying for his master's of fine arts, and Nate's doing a PhD for…something. Doctorate of being a giant pain in my ass at the moment." I muttered it under my breath, but Royce chuckled anyway.

He was across the table from me, in Heath's usual spot, and rocking on his chair in a way that was begging for him to fall over. "No interest in Carter's studies? Interesting…or was that discussed during your weekend in Berlin?"

I huffed a frustrated sigh. "Paris. Hey, what does Paige think about you sleeping in my room? I already have enough drama from Jade, I really don't need Paige sending feral animals into my room too."

Royce's teasing humor evaporated and his eyes narrowed. "I don't know what you *think* is going on there, but Paige is Nate's girlfriend."

"*Right*. Of course. Silly me. Nate's girlfriend that you happen to be fucking…like at the gala." I met his eyes, unflinching.

He stared back at me for a moment, like he was weighing my level of threat. Then he gave a small shrug. "It was a momentary lapse of judgment, never to be repeated. Nate doesn't need to know."

I snorted a laugh, shaking my head. "I already told him."

The legs on Royce's chair slammed back down with a bang. "When?"

I glanced up from the setup screen on my laptop. "Like…the morning after the gala when he broke into my room."

"He…what? Why would he do that?" Royce was genuinely confused and more than a little panicked. Good. He deserved to sweat for fucking his friend's girlfriend.

"Because he overheard Carter and I talking during the duck

challenge, about Paige being a cheater. Carter obviously wasn't man enough to tell him the truth so I did." I peered at him critically. "You weren't exactly subtle. But if it makes you feel better, he didn't believe me."

The relief gusting out of Royce was visible in the sag of his tense shoulders. "He didn't? Okay. Good. That's…hmm."

I tapped my fingernails on the table, waiting for my computer to complete its system update. "Doesn't seem like a great friend move, if you ask me." Not that I was one to talk, given my Carter-Heath situation, but I wasn't claiming to be innocent.

"Good thing I wasn't asking," he snapped back, then sighed and ran a hand over the back of his neck. "Like I said, it was a stupid spur-of-the-moment thing. Happened once and won't happen again."

That seemed contradictory to what Carter had said…but maybe he was just reading too much into whatever flirtation had happened prior to the gala. "None of my business," I muttered.

Royce didn't say anything more on the matter and I let it drop as my laptop finished its set up and I went to work installing the programs I needed and linking my cloud drives with all my study notes saved.

We worked in silence for a while until a cupcake and iced coffee appeared beside me.

"Do you want this? They gave me the wrong order again," Heath said, standing beside the table with an endearing smile.

Royce gave a dramatic groan. "That was *so cheesy*. Are you for real? Does that shit work on you, Squirrel?"

I huffed a frustrated sound. "Royce…can you fuck off for five minutes? Please?" It was high time Heath and I had a chat and I didn't need entitled gallery commentary.

Royce smirked, glancing between the two of us. "Five minutes, huh? That's sad, Squirrel, he can do better than that. Make him work for it."

"Royce!" Heath exclaimed, "Seriously, bro. Fuck off."

The blond smartass raised his hands defensively, rising from his seat. "Okay, chill. No need to get all snippy. I'll go for a walk, but Heath—"

"I know," he cut his friend off. "I'm not an idiot."

"Debatable," Royce replied with a grin, but then did thankfully wander off into the stacks to leave us alone.

Heath sighed and slid into his usual seat, the one Royce had just vacated. For a moment, he just sat and held eye contact with me, seemingly comfortable in silence.

"I heard you and Carter had an altercation," I said softly, breaking the silence reluctantly.

He nodded thoughtfully. "Yes...Royce is a hopeless gossiper. Any embarrassing stories you might want about us, he'll be happy to share."

I smiled and slid my laptop aside so I could give him my full attention. "Thank you for my coffee and cupcake, Heathcliff."

His answering smile was warm. "Any time, Ash. How are you feeling?" His gaze shifted to my cheek and his eyes pinched. "You did a good try covering the bruises up."

I sighed, propping my chin on my hand, one of the few places on my face that didn't hurt. "Thanks. I had to make myself presentable to get a job."

"You got a job? Where?"

A grin creased my face and my cheeks warmed with fond memories. "At the Prosper Country Club...as a masseuse."

His whole face lit up at that. "Can I book an appointment? My shoulder is killing me and you know exactly how to loosen it up."

I rolled my eyes, trying really hard not to think about what'd happened after I loosened up his shoulder. Or how good he'd looked naked and covered in oil. Fucking hell.

"You don't need an appointment, Heath, you could just ask. I didn't know it was hurting you." I got out of my seat and circled around behind where he sat. "This one?" I laid my hand on his left shoulder, squeezing gently.

His answer with a small groan and I smiled to myself, starting to massage his neck and shoulder on that side. Sitting up, clothed, no oils...it wasn't ideal but I could offer some small measure of relief.

"How'd you hurt this?" I asked, unsure if he'd already told me and I'd forgotten.

"Tennis," he replied with a grunt as I got my thumb into the deep knot.

I hummed a sound in response and dug deeper into his rock-hard muscles. It'd be hurting him now, but he'd feel the relief when I was done. Besides, Heath was a big tough guy, he could take it.

"So..." I prompted, feeling like he had things to say and not wanting Royce to come back and ruin the moment.

Heath sighed. "So I wanted to explain the Jade thing. Why I asked her to the gala is the easy part. She's devious and wanted to win, and I *thought* you wanted nothing to do with the society. After the incident with initiation, the elders council told us it was your choice whether you were in or out...I thought you'd made your preference crystal clear."

I processed that as I massaged his shoulder. "That's fair...I guess. Carter didn't really give me much choice, though."

"That's sort of his style," Heath muttered with an underscore of anger. "Taking things he wants without asking."

I bit my lip, thinking of all the things Carter wanted—and took—while we were in Paris. Not that I'd been saying no.

"Anyway, the *other* Jade thing was what Royce alluded to that day at our apartment. That one is just...look, it doesn't sound good but I assure you that absolutely nothing happened. After you and Carter left for Paris, we'd all gone out drinking at one of the bars in town and everyone overindulged. When I woke up Sunday morning, Jade was in my bed."

That stopped me cold. Of all the things I could have imagined...I wasn't sure I'd been expecting that. "She was in your bed?"

"Yeah," he confirmed. "Naked."

"Oh. I see."

"Ouch...Um..." He tried to shift out of my grip, and I startled at how I was digging my nails into his shoulder a whole lot harder than needed.

I quickly released my violent grip, scolding myself mentally. "I'm assuming there's a perfectly reasonable explanation?"

"Yeah, she's insane," he replied with a huff. "I know nothing happened, I went to sleep alone and no amount of alcohol would make me fuck her, but she was trying her luck."

I wet my lips, thinking of an appropriate response. Did I believe him that nothing had happened, and that he hadn't encouraged her? Yes. Because I also knew Jade, and as far as she was concerned Heath and I had been dating.

"And that's all?" I asked after a few moments of silence.

Heath twisted in his seat, looking up at me. "That's all, Ashley. Total transparency." His arm snaked around my waist and he pulled me around the chair to sit in his lap. "I really, really didn't want you to think—"

"I don't. I just...you guys don't have the most trustworthy track records." I pursed my lips, holding his gaze as I rested my arms around his neck. "I'm also not really in a position to judge after Paris."

Heath shrugged slightly. "Well, that was my fault for not doing this again sooner."

"Doing what?"

"This." He cupped a hand to the base of my skull, pulling me in to kiss my mouth deeply. I gasped, my lips parting as he kissed me harder and all the noise faded into the distance. Why was I mad at him again?

A fake cough interrupted us some moments later, and I would have fallen out of Heath's lap if he hadn't been holding me so tight.

"Well, well, well," Royce crooned, leaning against the bookshelves beside our table. "I am *shocked* at you, Ashley Layne. This is a library. A place of *learning* and here you are—"

"Fuck off, Royce," Heath growled, leaning back in to kiss my neck.

Royce was clearly enjoying himself, though, mischief written all over his face. "No can do. Hey Ash, weren't you asking me earlier if I'd swap sleepover duty with Carter?"

Dick. "No, I wasn't. You're lucky I respect books so much, or I'd throw one at your head right now."

He just chuckled and took my seat at the table. Then the shit took my cupcake. Oh…now we were at war.

"Did you tell her about your weird dream, bro?" he asked Heath, who stiffened somewhat under my hands.

Heath shook his head. "Not yet." He shifted his attention to me. "I've been having weird dreams about being in the forest."

I cocked my head, not understanding. "Like I was?"

He nodded. "Since you told us what happened…I dunno, like my subconscious wanted me to insert myself into your shoes."

"Ah," I said, smiling. "Because I told you to imagine the roles were reversed. Your subconscious must have grabbed onto that and played it out literally within your dream."

He sighed, giving a weak smile. "That's what dickhead over there said too. You know he's studying to be a psychologist, right? Fancies himself our personal shrink."

"Or maybe it's just that I'm smarter than you," Royce added. "Speaking of psychology, though, don't you have Human Development now?"

Heath checked his watch, then cursed. "Yeah. I better go. Can we meet up tonight?"

"No, I'm busy hanging out with Squirrel," Royce answered, despite the question having been directed at me. "But I think Carter will be home. Maybe you two should hit the gym and burn off some testosterone while me and Ash paint each other's nails."

Heath gave a frustrated sigh, then kissed me quickly before lifting me off his lap. "I better go. I'll call you."

He grabbed his bag and took off at a jog out of the library and I turned my attention to Royce, who stared at me expectantly.

"What?" I snapped.

He grinned. "Nothing."

Yep, I was definitely going to smother him in his sleep, smug fuck.

# Chapter Thirty-Three

We were a solid two hours into our road trip when I finally had enough of Royce's never-ending requests to drive, and caved. It was kind of worth it to see the grin on his face when I tossed him the keys after filling up the car with gas.

"Really?" he asked, beaming. "You're not just fucking with me?"

I rolled my eyes and climbed into the passenger seat which he'd been occupying since we left campus. "I don't know why you want to drive my car so badly. Your Mercedes-Benz Vision AVTR is worth four times as much and has a shitload more gadgets going on. Like those seat warmers. I wouldn't mind some of those." I mumbled the complaint as I cranked up the heating and turned all the vents in my direction.

I was constantly cold these days. It'd been ten days since I returned to campus, eighteen days since my hike through the woods, and I still couldn't get warm. Royce thought it was in my head, and I thought he should shut the fuck up.

"Because yours is a real car," he replied, turning on the ignition and stroking the steering wheel in a disturbingly sexy way. Royce… was fucking with my head. He'd caught me checking him out a couple of days ago when he came back from the shower in just a towel and now was making my life *hell*.

He smirked at me, catching me staring at his hands. "She purrs so nicely when her engine gets revved," he told me with the thinnest of veils over his innuendo and I groaned.

"You're insufferable," I growled. "Just drive. The sooner we get to this dumb getaway the sooner we can leave, right?"

He pulled out of the gas station and flicked my indicator to rejoin the main road. He smiled gleefully at the mechanical click of my indicators and I shook my head. Rich boy had never driven a car more than two years old before.

We were—after days of back-and-forth arguments—on our way to a Devil's Backbone Society fete. It was a countryside weekend getaway where several chapters of the society from different universities got together and...partied, I guess? The guys had assured me there were no challenges and the only games were friendly entertainment ones. There *should* be no danger and as I was attending as a plus-one—not a society member—I would be essentially left alone.

I hadn't been able to focus much on looking into Abigail more. After reaching the ends of what the easily accessible internet could provide, it seemed like I'd need a hacker or a PI to help get more info there. I wasn't completely convinced, especially with the idea that I'd be ignored at the event. But failing that, Nate argued, I was still safer there with the four of them than at Nevaeh alone.

That was the only part we agreed on. And I didn't hate having Royce as my constant shadow, so it would be weird without him for a whole weekend.

After ten or fifteen minutes, I relaxed with confidence that he actually knew how to drive my stick shift vintage and wasn't going to grind the gearbox. We'd fallen into a really easy rhythm these past ten days. Dare I say, we'd become friends?

"So...now that I know you want to fuck me, I guess I'll have to challenge Heath to a duel," he announced sometime later, making me choke on the sip of soda I'd just taken.

I spluttered while he grinned and smacked him with the back of my hand. "I do *not* want to fuck you. And no one is challenging anyone to a duel in my name, you fucking dork."

He hummed thoughtfully. "Did you know that a dork is actually a whale's penis? So I think that's a compliment. Thanks, Squirrel, I do have an above-average dick but I'm a little uncomfortable to hear you've been looking. Creep."

My face heated, and once again I cursed my quickness in blushing. "That's blatantly made up, Royce. And I haven't looked so couldn't comment."

He shot me a sly look. "Sure you haven't…just like Carter hasn't been trying to swap out for sleepover duty every day this week."

If I wasn't already blushing, I'd be doing it now. Royce had been spinning the narrative that Carter desperately wanted to get me alone but I wasn't buying it. Royce just liked shit stirring. If Carter really wanted to talk, he'd call. Or he'd approach me in person. Neither of which he'd done.

Heath, on the other hand, had been doing everything possible to spend time with me and didn't seem to give two shits that Royce was around when he kissed me.

"How about some music?" I suggested in the least subtle conversation change in history.

Royce scoffed a laugh but didn't press the issue as I turned on the radio and browsed through the channels. My car didn't have Bluetooth or smart anything, so it was radio or nothing.

In total, the drive took seven hours, and I let Royce keep his position as driver for the remainder of the trip while I napped on and off. Long car rides sucked, but the alternative had been to take a private jet with Nate, Heath, and Carter…as well as Paige and Jade. No fucking thank you. Carly—the traitor—had left a day earlier to visit her gran on the way and was meeting us there.

"Fucking hell," I murmured as we drove up the long oak tree-lined driveway. "This looks like a castle."

Royce nodded. "Close. I believe the architect was heavily inspired by the Palace of Versailles."

I grimaced, eyeing the opulence with distaste. "Here's hoping no one loses their head. How many people are at this thing?" Because there were *a lot* of luxury cars parked on the perfectly manicured lawns.

"Uh…for the day's events I believe it's roughly two hundred. Not everyone is staying on site, though. Just us—twenty from Nevaeh—and two other chapters. So like sixtyish total."

I wrinkled my nose, unbuckling my seatbelt. "There's that many rooms? This place is enormous."

Royce gave a laugh, turning my car off and sliding out of his seat. "Yeah. It really is. Let's go find where we're staying, roomie." He pocketed my keys and draped an arm over my shoulders.

I had to bite my cheek to keep from glancing up at him, already painfully aware how good he looked. The last thing I needed was to see the golden sunlight lighting up his blond hair like he was some kind of religious figure.

"Hi Royce!" a woman called out from somewhere nearby, but he didn't react. Instead he just led me up the marble steps to the front door and opened the impressive wooden door.

"After you, my lady," he teased, gesturing for me to enter the replica palace.

On a huge pinboard displayed in the foyer we located our room assignment—yes, we were still sharing—and took the fancy key from the hook.

"This reminds me of that key you've got," I told Royce as we ascended the huge grand staircase in search of our room. He had a pretty antique style key on his keyring that I'd admired a few days ago when he'd left them lying on my desk.

He glanced at the key in my hand and nodded. "Sort of. Except mine is *functional*." Because his wasn't a key, it was a bottle opener. Typical guy.

Our room was lovely, if a little small. Royce told me that he'd get someone to grab our bags out of the car later if I wanted to go meet up with Carly, and I agreed enthusiastically.

We found my friend in the Great Room, playing poker with a bunch of guys I'd never met. She looked like she was winning too, judging off the pile of sparkly rocks on the table in front of her.

"You're here!" she exclaimed, leaping up to hug me quickly. "Sorry boys, I'm out. Good game, though." She quickly scooped her pile of gems into a velvet pouch and hurried us out of the room once more.

"Carly Briggs, were you card sharking?" Royce asked in a scolding tone. The two of them had developed a cute sort of friendship since he'd moved into my room, and I quietly loved it.

Carly smirked. "Maybe. Not my fault those dumb shits from Zenith were too blinded by the power of cleavage to see me pocketing cards."

Royce just laughed, grabbing her bag and peering inside. "Holy shit, good score. Nice." He offered her a high five and she smacked it hard.

I was confused, though. "Why the stones and not playing chips?"

They both shrugged. "Immediate value versus symbolic value. No one trusts the house to pay out fairly." He pulled out a handful of Carly's stones to show me as we approached the bar in the atrium. "Buy-in is a lesser value stone like these. Peridot, citrine…crap like that. Then instead of increasing by dollar amounts it just, you know, makes sense. Aquamarine, sapphire, emerald, ruby, then diamonds. You get the idea."

My eyes bugged out. "They're *real*? I thought they were…actually, forget it. Of course they're real. You guys are fucking nuts."

Carly and Royce both grinned like twins. They'd bonded over their privileged upbringings and shit I could never relate to. Like the struggle of having to choose between spending Christmas in Aspen or Zermatt. Poor darlings.

Royce ordered drinks for us all—spicy margaritas—but then paused before handing me one.

"I don't know if I should let you drink, Squirrel. Are you going to start hitting on me if you have a few cocktails? I don't want to make things weird..." He winced dramatically and I resisted the urge to toss the damn drink in his face.

Carly snort laughed so hard I worried she would choke on her drink. She was more than amused by Royce's antics, and I rolled my eyes.

"You guys suck," I muttered, grabbing the drink from Royce's hand and glancing around the atrium. "Where's Heath? He would never be so mean."

"Nonsense, you just haven't seen that side of him," Royce corrected with a laugh, taking a long sip of his own drink. "Mmm, that's good. Spicy. Wet." He licked the salt rim seductively and I walked away. As funny as he was...it was also doing silly things to my hormones and I really badly did not need to start mistaking his jokes for actual flirtation.

There were people milling around throughout the whole place, so it was no great shock when I bumped into someone just a minute later. Annoyingly, though, it sloshed half my drink down my front.

"Oh come on," I complained just a moment before a strong hand grabbed my arm and jerked me to the side, out of the atrium and into one of the internal halls. Shock saw me drop my drink entirely, but then I quickly realized who was to blame. "Carter. What are—"

"We need to talk," he snapped, basically dragging me along as he strode across the hall and jerked open a door. "In here, quick." He ushered me inside and I immediately found us shut in a linen closet.

"What the fuck are you doing?" I snapped, trying—and failing—to open the door again. He just blocked it with his body and unless I was ready to start screaming, I was trapped. Then again, given the general attitudes of the guests I doubted anyone would come to investigate even if I did scream.

He folded his arms, parking his shoulders on the door. "Spark. Please." The vulnerability and longing in his voice struck me like a knife.

I stiffened, rage filling my chest. "Don't you dare take that tone with me, Bassington."

He sucked a long breath, nodding slightly. "Fair enough. But we need to talk and Royce has been utterly insufferable with blocking access to anything even remotely private with you so—"

"So what? Your phone doesn't work? You don't want to say what you need to say in front of him? Save the bullshit, Carter, I'm not buying. You had your fun in Paris. You won. What more do you want from me?"

A frustrated sound escaped him just a split second before he grabbed me, whirling us around so my back was now against the door and his hand pinned my hips. His other was on my throat, his favorite place, but it was a gentle touch. "What more do I want, Ashley? Where do I even start? I can't get you out of my head, I want—"

The door opened abruptly and I tumbled out into Royce's arms.

"Hey roomie, what's going on here?" he asked, steadying me with a firm hold on my waist. "No leaving my line of sight, remember? Safety in numbers."

Carter's expression was a tortured twist of frustration, anger, and longing. "Royce, please. Just give us a minute."

"She doesn't want a minute with you, Carter," Carly snapped, glaring absolute venom at the achingly handsome man gripping the linen closet doorframe. "And I don't fucking blame her. What was it you said, again? You *don't entertain overpriced whores.*"

He flinched, but I refused to let myself feel bad for him. Instead, I turned my gaze away and brushed a hand down my shirt. "I think I need to change. Let's go." Very deliberately, I took Royce's hand in mine and turned my back on Carter.

He'd had every part of me in Paris. For just a day and a half, I would have given him the whole world. But not anymore. I owed him nothing.

## Chapter Thirty-Four

The first night of the retreat, Royce complained so much about the floor—it was hardwood rather than carpet—that I let him share the bed with me. Then he instantly made me regret it by joking around that I needed to keep my hands to myself and building a pillow wall between us.

At the time—in the dead of the night—I had been less than impressed with his teasing and kicked all the pillows off the bed. In the morning, when I woke up to find myself snuggled up against him and my leg literally draped over his body, I had to admit maybe the pillow wall wasn't a bad idea.

By some small miracle, though, I managed to extract myself from what was a very compromising position—that Royce would honestly *never let me forget*—without waking him. Which really was a stroke of luck because he usually woke up way earlier than me.

I tiptoed out of the room to shower and dress, and came back to find him scrolling his phone in bed like he didn't have a care in the world.

"Good morning, Squirrel," he greeted me with a lopsided smile. "How'd you sleep? I didn't take up too much space, now did I?"

I rolled my eyes, mainly to avoid meeting his gaze and blushing.

"Um, nope, totally fine. Barely even knew you were there." *Liar.* "So what are we doing today?"

"I was just checking the schedule," he replied, patting the bed for me to join him. "Looks like breakfast and brunch runs through until eleven, then it's Jurassic Croquet on the south lawn."

I perched on the mattress, peering at the event schedule on his phone without sitting too close. "What the fuck is Jurassic Croquet?"

Royce put his phone down and grinned up at me from the pillow. "You'll see. Are you sure you don't want to sleep in a little longer? We could cuddle."

I stiffened, then second-guessed myself. He wasn't referring to how I'd slept...I didn't think. He was literally just making a suggestion, and not a serious one at that.

"Tempting offer," I replied sarcastically despite the truth to my statement, "but I already texted Carly to meet for breakfast. You can sleep, though. I'm sure no one will try kidnapping me again here with all these people around."

He scoffed, climbing out of the big bed. "Yeah right. Have you forgotten Carter's little stunt last night? All he did was prove how *easy* it would be to snatch you away." He tugged his T-shirt over his head, revealing his washboard abs and that deep V line above his boxers as he hunted through his bag for a clean shirt.

"Why *are* you so dedicated to protecting me, Royce?" I asked with genuine curiosity. "Just a few weeks ago, I was little more than gum on your shoe."

He shrugged, pulling on a new T-shirt. What a shame. "It's not all about *you*, my dear. Someone tried to frame Nate for kidnapping and attempted murder. I intend to see that doesn't happen again, while he investigates who might have really done it."

I nodded slowly. "I see. So...it's not about my safety at all. It's about saving Nate's reputation?"

Royce grinned. "Exactly. But if it makes you feel better, I think you're pretty hot and I like hanging out with you." He winked, then pulled on his jeans. "Come on, let's go find Carly then."

I wasn't really sure how to feel about that, so I said nothing and followed him down the grand staircase in search of the dining room. There were a lot less people floating around, which wasn't a huge shock considering how hard some people partied the night before.

Within the dining room, a huge buffet was laid out like they were catering a royal feast. Every single possible breakfast food had been provided, and then some. Royce chatted casually with some guy he introduced as Chad while filling his plate, but I didn't pay attention. I was all tangled up in my head about Royce's motivation for becoming my full-time shadow.

Was I an idiot for thinking he cared about *me*?

Yes. Probably. That seemed to be the running theme with these guys.

"Good morning, gorgeous," Carly greeted me with a side hug. "How are you this beautiful morning? How did you two sleep?"

Royce shot her a suspicious look over his shoulder. "You seem... cheery. Did you get laid last night, Carly Briggs?"

Her smug smile said it all. "A lady doesn't kiss and tell, Roycey."

He snickered. "Good thing you're not a lady then, huh? So who was he?"

"None of your business," she replied, zipping her invisible lips shut.

Royce took that as his invitation to start guessing every single person Carly had interacted with before we'd gone to bed, and I carried my plate over to one of the vacant tables to eat.

A waitress came by to take coffee orders, and conversation shifted to the Jurassic Croquet.

Heath joined our table when I was almost finished eating and greeted me with a borderline inappropriate for public kind of kiss. It was easy to lose myself in his kisses...even if things hadn't progressed any further. Yet.

"So...are you guys dating now?" Carly asked across the table when Heath pulled me into his lap. I liked it there, he held me so tight and warm.

Royce scoffed. "Surely not. Otherwise Carter wouldn't be dragging Squirrel into dark closets during parties. That'd be *asking* for trouble."

Heath stiffened with tension. "Carter did what?"

"Royce," I snapped, "You are *such* a shit stirrer."

"Okay, um, so are you playing croquet today, Heath?" Carly asked quickly, making a weak attempt at changing the subject. "I heard Jenkins vomited so hard he had to go to the hospital last night, so Nevaeh will be down a team member."

Heath shook his head, adjusting his hold on my waist so his thumb stroked my hip. "No, not this time. Nate will be, though."

"Ugh. Hate him, but love that for our team. We should make sure we get good seats, Ash." Carly stuffed the last of her breakfast pastry in her mouth and washed it down with coffee. Apparently she meant *right now*.

Heath and Royce accompanied us as Carly looped her arm through mine and led the way outside to the South Lawn where the croquet game would take place. It was cold outside, though, and thanks to my new permanent state of frozen I found my teeth chattering in no time.

"Give me your room key?" Heath asked Royce. "I'll grab Ashley a coat."

Royce handed it over without complaint, then nodded approvingly as his friend disappeared back inside. "Points to Heathcliff. But points will be deducted if he returns without a hoodie for me too."

"Over here!" Carly called out, waving us across to some grandstands set up beside the lawn. I wanted to comment that this seemed odd for croquet but then again, I'd never been to a croquet game so what did I have to compare against?

Heath returned with my coat—and nothing for Royce—and

the seats around us steadily filled up with more spectators until the game was officially announced. I didn't pay a whole lot of attention to the formalities and over-the-top dramatics, but the moment the game itself started...I was confused.

"What are they...those aren't standard croquet hammers are they?" Because although I'd never physically attended a game, I was fairly sure the stick was meant to be a uniform shape. These were not.

"Mallet," Heath corrected. "And no, that's why it's called Jurassic Croquet. To play, you need to provide your own Jurassic period mallet."

That really didn't clear things up at all, until someone knocked their ball through a hoop close to us, and I got a better look. Then gasped.

"No. You're kidding, right? They're not *seriously* using—"

"Dinosaur bones?" Carter finished my sentence, sliding into the gap between Carly and I...leaving me sandwiched between him and Heath. Not the worst place to be, had Carter not shown his true colors after Paris. "They are, actually. It's an old DB tradition, so much so that legacy families have taken to collecting bones simply so their children can play this game."

My jaw dropped. "But why? That's so...excessive."

Carter shrugged, slouching back in his seat and propping his elbows on the tier behind. "That's kind of the DB's whole premise. Bored rich kids doing obscenely excessive things simply because they can."

Heath scoffed a bitter sound. "Don't act like you're above it all, Bass. I seem to remember a certain society fete where you—"

"Ancient history, Heathcliff," Carter snapped, cutting off whatever his friend was about to say.

I folded my arms, sitting rigidly between the two of them. Suddenly the croquet match was way less enjoyable. The fact that I didn't understand the rules, half the players seemed drunk from the night before, and the uncomfortable knowledge that they were potentially damaging and destroying *actual dinosaur bones* definitely didn't help matters.

Nevaeh's team won, apparently, and the guys climbed over the grandstand seats to congratulate Nate with hearty slaps on the back and whoops of excitement. Carly just gave me a knowing look and shook her head.

"You get used to it," she offered weakly, and I wrinkled my nose.

"I'd rather not, to be honest. What's next?"

Unsurprisingly the rest of the day consisted of much of the same. Typical rich people sports, with an over-the-top excessive twist to them. Polo? Not on horses, don't be ridiculous. No, the players for that burst out of the stables riding emus.

Target shooting involved destroying what were probably once priceless paintings, and of all things a gladiator *race* with miniature ponies and the competitors all dressed up like insane Romans.

That night, I built the pillow wall without explanation, but somehow when I woke the next morning I was back in Royce's arms once more. Thankfully, like the day before, he was still asleep and I could extract myself and rebuild the wall before he noticed.

I justified it to myself by deciding I must have been cold and sought out his warmth while I slept.

The morning followed a similar pattern of stupidly expensive, wasteful amusements, then the afternoon and evening was meant to be a casino party. Carly had helped me choose a black dress from my less than inspiring closet before we came away, but I stuck out like a sore thumb dressed in the finest Tarjay had to offer amongst a sea of couture.

"You look beautiful, Squirrel," Royce murmured in my ear as I fidgeted and tried to ignore the stares of other women. "They're just jealous because clearly you didn't need a Portia Levigne dress to snag a date with a fucking catch like me."

I laughed, despite my nerves. "You're so full of yourself," I muttered. "No wonder you don't have a girlfriend."

He just shot me one of those arrogant smiles. "Nah, it's because I'm just waiting for you to admit you're falling in love and drop Heathcliff like a sack of bricks."

"Uh-huh, because you'd never seduce a girl with a boyfriend. Oh. Wait." I snapped my fingers, smirking, and his eyes narrowed.

"Low blow. Foul on the play. Rude. What are you drinking?" He guided me over to the bar with a hand on the small of my back, and I asked the bartender for a glass of champagne. I didn't really intend to drink much, but it was nice to have in my hand for something to do.

We spotted Carly at the poker tables and made our way over, watching her clean up with another heavy pouch full of diamonds before she called it quits.

"I need to pee," she announced, taking a quick sip from my glass before lowering her voice. "And dispose of the extra cards."

I chuckled, somewhat impressed that she was such a cheat. "I'll come too."

Royce started to follow, but Carly poked him in the chest. "We don't need you shadowing *that* hard, friend. Chill a minute."

"I can't let Ashley out—"

"I know, I know," Carly snapped. "We are literally going to pee, though, and nothing has happened all weekend, right?"

Royce ran a hand through his hair, torn with indecision. "Carly…"

"Roycey…" she replied, mimicking his tone. "This isn't up to you."

She had a good point. "I'll be right back," I assured Royce. "Go blow Carly's hard-earned gemstones on roulette." Before he could argue, I tugged on my friend's hand, and we hurried out of the room in search of a bathroom.

"Sorry if I was being pushy," she said once we were out of the noise. "I just got the feeling you needed five minutes without Royce breathing down your neck. But also I wanted to ask *what is going on with Carter?*"

I groaned, rubbing the bridge of my nose. "Your guess is as good as mine. Oh, in here." I indicated a bathroom that I'd found earlier in the day, not far off the main atrium. It was just a single cubicle, more of a powder room, so I let Carly go first and thought nothing of it.

Like she'd said, nothing bad had happened all weekend. For that matter, nothing bad had really happened since my kidnapping nearly three weeks earlier. So in fairness, my guard was down.

That was probably why I didn't see the sharply-dressed sleazebag with floppy yellow-blond hair sidling up to me until he quite literally grabbed my ass in both hands. And squeezed.

# Chapter Thirty-Five

"Hey, hot stuff," the guy said, his breath so full of whisky it stung my eyes. "We haven't met, I'm Bartholomew Criterion. Like the financial institution. You've heard of us, I bet."

I had, but no way was I stroking his ego when he was physically assaulting me. I shoved against his chest, trying to extract myself from his hands on my ass. It was fairly fruitless, though, as he seemed to take it as encouragement to grind his flaccid cock against my hip.

"I'm not interested," I snapped, "take your hands off me. Now."

He laughed, not taking me seriously in the least. "You're cute. And this pussy must be dripping narcotics or something to lock down D'Arenberg so tight. He owns this fucking palace and he's slumming it with you in the guest rooms? Must be worth it." He leaned in closer, like he was trying to kiss me and I ducked.

"Seriously. Get the fuck away from me!" I was scared now, but I knew Carly would be out any second now so that helped me keep my head. No need to scream when it could be handled more diplomatically, right?

Flashes of Paris crossed my mind, and I shuddered. Had Carter really killed that guy? What would he do to Bartholomew if I screamed? Assuming he cared…

The drunk guy just laughed like I was playing games, pinning me to the wall. "I heard you like getting passed around. Everyone's talking about how you're spreading these legs for everyone in the Nevaeh chapter. Why don't you show me what's got everyone so worked up, huh?"

"Fuck off!" I shouted, shoving as hard as possible. My panic spiked dramatically when he barely moved a couple of inches. Drunk or not, he was stronger, bigger and heavier…and he had his mind set on getting what he wanted.

Carly chose that moment to exit the restroom and did a double take. "Whoa, Bart, you need to take your hands off my friend immediately."

Bartholomew shifted his slightly unfocused gaze to my friend and sneered. "Oh yeah? Are you going to make me, Carly?"

Her brows rose like she was shocked at his actual audacity. "No," she admitted, folding her arms with a small smile playing at her lips. "But he will."

I saw the fist coming just milliseconds before it connected with the side of Bart's head. He released me so abruptly I nearly tumbled with him if not for Carly grabbing my arm and jerking me into the doorway with her.

Shocked, I watched Bartholomew Criterion of the financial Criterion Group get his manners corrected in the form of an ass-kicking. But the violence wasn't the shocking part…it was who was dealing it out.

Not Carter…but *Nate*.

"Stop!" I finally managed to shout, wrenching free of Carly's grip to intervene. "That's enough. Nate, *stop*!"

He spun to glare at me, breathing heavily, then glanced back at Bart who was moaning in pain and attempting to crawl away on hands and knees. Nate's eyes narrowed and he used his foot to send Bart sprawling once more.

"Nate! Enough!" I shouted, grabbing his arm to pull him away.

His venomous glare shifted back to me, and for a long moment we just locked eyes. No words exchanged. Then he turned to Carly with a furious twist to his lips.

"Where the fuck were you?" he spat.

Carly turned white as a sheet. "I was—"

"This isn't her fault," I snapped, tugging his arm again to draw the ire *away* from my friend.

He swung that inferno fury my way. "No. It's yours. Maybe think about how it looks when you're sharing a room with Royce and sucking face with Heath during the day, I'm shocked this didn't happen sooner."

I dropped his arm, taking a step back in shock. "Victim-blaming is a bad look, Essex."

He shrugged. "Act like a cheap slut, don't be surprised when people treat you accordingly." Fists clenching and unclenching at his sides, he stalked away from us without another word. His shoulders remained rigid and his stride clipped with barely restrained violence just bursting to get out.

For a moment, neither Carly nor I said anything. Then she took my hand in hers and gave me a tug in the direction Nate had just gone. "Come on," she said softly. "Let's go find Royce."

I was too shaken up from the whole incident to even make a joke about Royce giving us grief. Talk about proving his point that I couldn't be out of his sight for five minutes. Then again, this wasn't the same as when *someone* in the society kidnapped me. That had been a deliberate, planned out challenge. Bart was just a drunk sleazebag who'd been raised so entitled he didn't comprehend consent.

They weren't the same thing, but Royce wouldn't care.

We found him at the roulette tables with Heath and Carter both. Nate was nowhere to be seen.

Carter saw me first, rising halfway out of his seat in alarm, which told me I wasn't hiding my shock very well. Hell, I probably looked like I'd just seen a ghost with how drained I felt.

For a moment, I thought he would come to me and hold me like he'd done in the elevator after I was mugged. How he wrapped me up in his arms and whispered that I was safe. But he checked himself and lowered himself back into his seat as Royce and Heath turned my way.

"What happened?" Heath asked, alarmed. *He* leapt up and gathered me up in his arms, offering his strength and causing tears to prick at my eyes. Against my better judgment, I glanced over Heath's shoulder to where Carter sat. He stared back at me, but after a tense moment turned his gaze back to the roulette table. Dismissed.

That cut deeper than I'd have liked, considering I was literally wrapped up in Heath's embrace.

Carly quickly recounted what had happened, and Royce ordered us a round of drinks. The waitress brought them over quickly...much quicker than expected given how many people were in attendance and needing service. Which only made me remember what Bart had said while breathing all over me. Royce *owned* this palace-replica? Surely not. I must have misheard, or Bart was too drunk to make sense.

Still, I made a mental note to ask Royce later.

"Do you want to go somewhere else?" Heath asked softly as Carly finished explaining everything. "We don't have to stay at this thing."

"Let's go swimming," Royce suggested, totally off-the-cuff.

Heath scowled. "I meant just me and Ashley..."

"And he meant his bedroom," Carly added with a smirk. "Roycey, why you gotta cockblock your friends so hard?"

She had a good question. Royce just smirked his mischief smile. "Isn't it obvious? I desperately want Ashley to fall in love with *me* so letting Heath get his dick wet is totally counterproductive to my evil plans. Keep up, Carly babe, it's a long game."

I rolled my eyes at his heavy sarcasm. "Remind me why I haven't smothered you with a pillow yet?"

His grin spread wider. "Because the plan is working."

"I'm up for swimming," Carter announced, inserting himself into our conversation suddenly. "Let's go."

Royce shrugged and pushed out of his seat. "You heard the man. Drink those first, though." He gestured to the shots of tequila sitting between Carly and me. "It'll help settle the shock."

With logic like that, I wasn't going to argue. Carly picked up her shot glass and clinked it against mine. "Cheers, girl."

I sighed, and nodded, then tossed the shot back. It burned down my throat and I coughed, but the resulting warmth wasn't unwelcome. In fact, it was quite nice. I accepted the chaser of soda that Heath offered me, anyway.

"Swimming in this weather doesn't sound particularly appealing," I admitted as the five of us left the casino party. The guys all seemed to know exactly where they were going, which didn't surprise me at all. This was apparently a yearly trip for the Devil's Backbone Society.

Heath had his arm around my waist as we walked, and I happily leaned into his side. "You'll see," he told me, dropping a kiss on my hair. "But if you'd rather privacy..."

Did I want to go back to Heath's room and *finally* take things further than kissing? God yes. So badly, yes. But the hard look Carter tossed over his shoulder right at that moment made me hesitate.

Then Nate's words echoed back through my head. *Act like a cheap slut and people treat you accordingly.* He was an asshole of the highest degree, but maybe he had a point.

"It's cool, I'm happy to hang out. Just don't expect me to swim because I really don't want to catch frostbite."

Carly laughed at that and shook her head. Which made sense when a few minutes later Royce pushed open the double doors to the *indoor and heated* pool room. There were already a few other people in there, sitting on the edge with drinks in hand, but it was still a shitload quieter than the casino hall.

"Uh, did I miss the memo about wearing a swimsuit under my

dress?" I asked as Carter pulled open a huge double door fridge and pulled out an armful of bottles.

Royce just laughed and started stripping out of his suit, tossing the garments onto one of the lounger beds. "Swimsuits are just glorified underwear, Squirrel. You *are* wearing underwear…aren't you?"

His curious stare as he stripped right down to his boxers made me blush way too fucking hard. Only Heath's hand on my waist brought me back to earth and I forced a weak laugh. "Of course I am, pervert."

Royce shrugged. "That's a pity." Then he whooped and cannonballed into the pool, sending a huge splash all over us.

Carter handed Heath a beer, then placed a pair of champagne flutes down on the small drink table beside the lounger while he opened a bottle for Carly and I. Kind of sweet, I guessed?

"You coming in?" Heath asked, already unbuttoning his shirt.

I shook my head, sitting down on the side of a lounger. "Uh, I'm good here. You go for it, though."

Another heavy splash sent a wave of water over us again and I grinned to see Carly in the pool and trying to drown Royce. What a queen.

Heath arched a brow, untucking his shirt from his pants in a downright seductive way. I wet my lips, watching as he unbuckled his pants. "You sure?"

I glanced from him to the pool where Royce was splashing Carly in the face, like she was his annoying little sister. Cute as hell, but given how mixed up my hormones had been from waking up in Royce's arms…I really didn't need to be basically naked in the pool with him *and* Heath right now.

"Yep. I'll hang out here." I assured him, then nearly choked on my own breath when he stripped out of his pants and shoes. He knew it too, shooting me a smirk before doing a run up bomb into the water right on top of Royce.

Carter offered me a glass of champagne, silently sitting on the lounger I was perched on the edge of. I took it without a word and sipped the bubbly wine nervously. Had I just made the wrong choice? I'd assumed Carter would be joining the other boys in the pool, not lurking on the edge with me.

"Spark..." he said softly, his fingertip trailing down the line of my thigh ever so softly. The motion was so subtle that *no one* else could have seen it, but my breath caught nonetheless.

I shook my head, shifting so my back was to him. "Don't."

"I can't help it," he muttered in response. "This is torture."

Irritation flared up and I quickly downed my entire glass of champagne. "You know what? I changed my mind." I stood up, turning to glare at him while I unzipped my cheap black dress and let it fall to the floor. It left me wearing just a sheer lace bra and panty set, and Carter visibly stopped breathing as he stared. "How's that for torture?"

He swallowed hard, his deep blue eyes dripping regret but he said nothing. I shook my head and extended my middle finger before turning and diving into the pool.

"Ashley's here!" Carly called out in glee, swimming over to me. "What did Carter say?" She asked it quietly as she approached, keeping her voice low as the steam from the pool created an illusion of privacy around us.

I swiped water from my face, trying to remember if I used waterproof mascara or not. Carly's makeup was halfway down her face, but she still managed to look beautiful. "Nothing. I just didn't want to miss the fun. Wait, where's Royc—"

My question cut off with a squeak as the prankster himself launched me out of the water. I flopped like a whale, so very graceful, and tried to hold my laughter while underwater so I wouldn't drown.

Another impact rocked the water around us while I swam beneath the surface to escape Royce's antics, and I popped back up to find myself face to face with Nate.

Where the hell had he just come from? Then again, these were *his* friends, so it stood to reason he might want to hang out with them...

Frowning, I watched a swirl of red wash from his hands as he ducked back below the surface. Was that blood?

Heath glided over and scooped me up in his arms, instantly allowing my mind to totally dismiss Nate. My legs wrapped around Heath's waist as he held me in the warm water, and he gave a small groan of frustration.

I smiled, looping my arms around his neck. "Maybe I do need to come check out your room tonight," I whispered, brushing a teasing kiss across his lips. Fuck Nate and his slut-shaming, I was doing nothing wrong with Heath.

"Shit," he murmured, returning my light kiss with one of his own. His hands slid lower to hold my ass and he gave a moan when he realized I wore a thong. "Now I won't be able to get out of the water without everyone seeing what you do to me."

I chuckled, then kissed him properly. His hand moved to my head, fingers tangling in my wet hair as he claimed my mouth with a desperate hunger that nearly made me forget where we were.

"No fucking in the pool," Royce announced, splashing us both. "It's bad for the chemical balance."

Heath groaned and cursed, but *did* turn down the heat between us a few notches. Mainly, I suspected, because he too remembered we had spectators.

Sure enough, when I swiveled in his arms, more than one set of eyes were on us. The surprising part, though, was how it stoked the fire within me rather than extinguishing it. Especially the way Carter stared.

We all swam and drank for a while longer and shockingly Nate was not as insufferable as he often was. He didn't apologize for the shit he'd said earlier, and I didn't expect him to. But I *did* overhear him expressing some kind of remorse to Carly over how things had gone down between them the year before.

It was right as we were all heading to our rooms, wrapped in towels and more than a little drunk, and Carly was so shocked that

I heard her agreeing to let sleeping dogs lie. She *did* add that he needed to get Paige and Jade under control and I was proud of her for standing her ground on that.

Nate didn't agree outright, but he also didn't *disagree*. He just nodded thoughtfully and headed off in the direction of his own room. Or maybe Paige's? I hadn't seen her at all this weekend, but she must be somewhere in the enormous mansion.

"Are you coming to my room?" Heath asked in a sexy whisper as he kissed my neck. We'd been stealing more sneaky kisses since Royce splashed us, and it had me insanely turned on. So much that I could have happily orgasmed just from the way his fingers intertwined with mine while we walked the halls.

I nodded, incapable of words that weren't going to make me sound like a bitch in heat.

We were almost at my and Royce's room, though, so I paused to unlock the door for Royce. He was still arguing that I shouldn't sleep in Heath's room for *safety*, but the argument was weak enough we were both ignoring him.

"Let me just grab some dry clothes," I murmured, pushing open the door. The moment it opened, a smell hit my nose and I reeled back. It wasn't overpowering but it was…different. Our room usually smelled distinctively *Royce* thanks to his unique cologne but right now the room smelled *bad*.

"What the fuck?" Royce said, clearly smelling the same thing. He flicked the lights on, and immediately swiveled to step in front of me, trying to block the view of the room. He was too slow, though. I'd already seen the very dead, very bloody decapitated corpse stretched out across the bed.

The eyes of the detached head stared right at me, right *through* me from where it sat on the nightstand, and I recognized the victim.

Bart. Sleazy Bart. Dead and naked in my bed.

## Chapter Thirty-Six

After Bart's corpse was found in my bed, the whole retreat was shut down. Everyone was sent home early, and I found myself driving the seven hours back to Nevaeh with very different company in the car. Royce and Nate stayed at the mansion, speaking with the authorities—particularly after they caught wind of Nate punching Bart only hours earlier—but I'd refused to hang around to wait for my shadow. Instead, I ended up with Carly and Heath joining me for the drive…and at the last minute, Carter jumped in the back seat.

We all barely spoke the entire drive home, and I flat-out refused to share the driving with anyone else. When we arrived back into Prosper, though, I was faced with the dilemma of not having Royce in my room.

"Drop Carly off," Heath told me when I voiced my concern. "You can come stay with us tonight."

My head was hazy and I was so damn tired I could barely see straight, so I agreed without complaint. It wasn't until I parked underneath Heath's apartment building that I realized the error of my ways.

I should have suggested that Heath stay at my dorm instead, because I had only just clicked on the fact that Heath lived *with*

Carter. And Nate...who I strongly suspected was the one who killed Bart. I said as much when we found the body—to Nate's outrage—but apparently he had a solid alibi. Before he'd joined us in the pool, dozens of people had witnessed him and Paige engaging in a blow out break-up after he'd caught her kissing some random guy in the casino room.

I couldn't forget the swirl of blood that had washed off his knuckles in the pool, though.

"Everything okay?" Heath asked as I hesitated, not getting out of the car. Carter was already grabbing our bags out of the trunk, and we were here now...

I sighed. "Yeah. Yeah, just...tired."

He nodded his understanding as I climbed out of my car and locked it. "Understandable," he murmured. "Thanks for driving, though. I really didn't want to wait until Nate was done to take the plane."

I yawned, rubbing my eyes. It was well past midnight, and my tequila hangover had kicked in halfway through the drive. The three of us were silent in the elevator up to their apartment, then once inside Heath showed me directly to his room. I resisted the urge to glance back at Carter, no matter how badly I wanted to see his reaction. I was too damn tired to care.

Heath sorted me out with one of his T-shirts and a pair of boxers to sleep in, then offered up his private bathroom so I could shower. That, in itself, justified the decision to stay with him rather than in my dorm. The last thing I wanted to do was shower in the communal washrooms.

I took my sweet time, washing my hair with his shampoo and loving that I came out smelling like Heath, then dressed in his clothes. Sure, I had my own bag with me, but this was better.

When I emerged from the bathroom in a cloud of steam, I found him stretched out on his huge bed with just a pair of loose shorts on.

"Ashley Layne," he said with a teasing voice, "you're staring."

I smiled, unapologetic. "Do you blame me?" I tossed aside the towel I'd been using to dry my hair and crawled onto the bed beside him. Then hooked a leg over and straddled his lap.

His hands raised to rest on my hips, his thumbs stroking my waist beneath the oversized T-shirt. "You look good in my shirt, but I bet you'd look better out of it…"

I laughed, because it was such a cheesy line and we were both half dead. There was no delusion that either of us had the energy for sex, no matter how much we wanted it. "You look as tired as I feel, Heathcliff."

He grimaced as I climbed off of him—retreating from temptation—and lay on my side to face him. "I haven't been sleeping well," he admitted. "It's all starting to catch up a bit."

I reached out to stroke his messed-up hair as he settled on his side as well. "Academic stress or life stress?" Both of which were totally relatable.

He gave a small shrug. "I'm not sure. It just feels like every time I manage to fall asleep I'm plagued by awful nightmares and wake up more tired than I was before sleeping. I haven't been keeping up so well in my human development class though, so I wonder if that's it. Stress fucks with my head something wicked."

Concern for him rippled through my bones as I gently swiped my thumb over the dark shadow beneath his eye. "Maybe," I agreed. "It wouldn't surprise me. With all the society drama, I'm shocked that anyone actually graduates from Nevaeh. God knows I'm barely keeping up on my coursework right now."

Heath gave a sleepy blink. "We need more study dates. Preferably without so many clothes."

"Or Royce," I added with a smile.

He just chuckled, his eyes already closed. "I dunno, I reckon he'd jump at the chance."

I wet my lips but said nothing. Royce was…confusing. Heath was joking, I was pretty sure. Royce wasn't into me as anything more than a curious entertainment even if I didn't hate the mental image that conjured. But Heath seemed to be almost asleep so I didn't want to keep talking if he had a chance of resting. I stayed quiet, stroking his hair lightly until his breathing evened out, then I carefully reached over to turn out the light.

Sleeping beside Heath was incredibly comfortable. I snuggled into his warmth, and he draped his arm around me, holding me close even though he was already asleep. It took no effort at all to drift off.

What I didn't anticipate was how intense his nightmares really were. He woke me with a fright as he jerked, shouting something incomprehensible. For a moment in my own sleep-dazed state, I thought someone was attacking us but it became quickly apparent that he was stuck in a nightmare.

"Are you okay?" Carter asked from the doorway, making me gasp. "He didn't hurt you?"

I drew a deep breath, trying to control my racing pulse as I sat up. "No. Just startled me, that's all." Heath thrashed a little, moaning something about...blood? "Does this happen a lot?"

"Lately, yes. Every night. Sometimes a lot more violent. Sometimes with sleepwalking." He gave no emotion to his words, just stating facts.

I shivered, wanting to help Heath but not knowing how. "Is this why Royce wouldn't swap sleepover shifts with Heath?"

"Part of the reason, yes," Carter confirmed. "If you can wake him up, he should go back to sleep fine. The nightmares only seem to happen once a night."

I stared down at Heath, his features hard to make out in the thin light of dawn. We'd barely been asleep for a couple of hours. The way his body jerked and the panicked tone of his mumbles...whatever he was dreaming must be terrifying.

"Do you want me to do it?" Carter offered. "You can go sleep in Royce's bed if you'd prefer."

I inhaled sharply. "Not offering your own?"

"Would you accept?" His question was pointless, he already knew the answer.

"I'll be fine," I replied after a heavy pause. "You can go back to sleep, I'll look after him."

Carter gave a heavy sigh. "If you need me…"

"I won't." I turned my face away, waiting until I heard the door click shut before reaching over to turn Heath's bedside light on. He didn't react to the light, but his brow was deeply furrowed and his jaw clenched so hard I could hear his teeth grinding.

Everything I'd heard was *not* to wake sleepwalkers, but Carter seemed like he knew what he was talking about?

Cautious, I gave Heath's shoulder a little shake. "Heath, hey, wake up you're having a bad dream." Another jerk and mutter about trees this time, but he didn't wake. I tried again, shaking him harder. "Heath. Wake up. You're—"

His eyes popped open as he gasped, unfocused gaze locking on me with a glassiness hinting at unshed tears. "Ashley?"

"Yeah, it's me. You were dreaming and—*oof*." The intensity of the hug he grabbed me in knocked the air clean out of my lungs, but I wasn't complaining. He was fucking *shaking* as he held me tight, his face buried in my neck.

"You're okay," he was murmuring over and over. "You're okay. You're here. It was just a dream. Fuck, what is *wrong with me?*"

"Hey, stop it," I scolded gently as I hugged him back, stroking his spine. "There's nothing wrong with you. It's just a shitty way your brain is working through some stuff. Happens to everyone."

His heart was pounding so hard I could feel it against me, so I just lay there and let him hold me until his breathing slowed back to normal.

Eventually, his grip relaxed slightly. "I'm sorry," he whispered. "I didn't hurt you, did I?"

Carter had asked the same thing. "Is that something you're worried about doing?" That would definitely explain Royce's insistence at remaining my only sleepover buddy.

He exhaled heavily, his breath ruffling my hair as he adjusted our position. "Yeah. One of the first nights with these intense nightmares, I was sleepwalking and punched Nate."

I laughed, despite the situation. "Well, I think that's less about your nightmares and more about Nate desperately needing to be punched."

Heath chuckled slightly, then shifted so we could lie facing each other once again. Just like we had before falling asleep. "Nate…look, the way he's behaved with you is unforgivable and I'm not going to make excuses for him. But he's actually a good person, deep down."

"Really, *really* deep?" I asked skeptically. "Why does he hate me so much?"

"It's not you. Not really. I think…I mean, I can't speak for him but from what I know it's more about Max and your mom, and what them getting together meant for *his* mom. Nate was always so confident his parents would get back together after their split, but then all of a sudden Carina moved in…"

I scowled. "So he decided to take out his resentment on me?"

Heath offered a sleepy lopsided smile. "He started with your mom a few years ago, but have you met her? The woman is a fucking saint. No matter how cruel he was, she'd just smile and tell him that big feelings were always so tough to work through or some shit. It drives him *insane* but at the same time made him realize she wasn't going anywhere." He yawned, rubbing his eyes. "Anyway. The wedding getting moved up on the timeline made him go a bit…you know."

"Psychotic?" I offered, and Heath grinned. "I won't pretend that makes any sense, but I can appreciate that the Nate you know is a very different person than the one I do."

"Yes," he murmured. "That."

I stroked my finger down the side of his face, loving how his lashes fluttered and he leaned into my touch. "I can handle Nate. But if it turns out he was the one who orchestrated my kidnapping—"

"He didn't," Heath said firmly, eyes snapping open again.

I shrugged. "Okay. But if it turns out he *did*..."

"Then I'll kill him myself," he replied without even a hint of joking. "Whoever did that to you is pure evil, Ashley, they deserve everything karma can dish out. But that's not Nate."

I didn't respond, instead just buried my fingers in his hair and kissed him. Because I believed that *he* believed Nate...but I wasn't so sure.

"Go back to sleep," I whispered against his lips.

He gave a contented sound, looping his arm over my waist to pull me close, his legs intertwining mine. "You'll stay? Even after my nightmare?"

"Of course I will," I replied, kissing his throat. "There's nowhere I'd rather be."

And I meant it. Cuddled up in Heath's embrace was fast becoming my favorite place in the world. Except...it seemed odd not to have Royce nearby. I'd grown quite fond of his constant company. I hoped he was okay.

# Chapter Thirty-Seven

Carter had been right about Heath sleeping well after waking from his nightmare. So well that neither of us woke until well after midday and then decided to stay in bed a little longer. As tired as we'd been when we got back, it felt totally new to be alone with him…in bed… with no one to interrupt. I wasn't going to pass up that opportunity for anything.

"Ash…" he groaned as I palmed his hard dick through his boxers. "Fuck, I could get used to waking up like this."

We'd woken up snuggling, which turned to kissing, which was now—hopefully—turning into a whole lot more. I wanted him to fuck me so badly it almost hurt, so yeah, I was taking matters into my own hands. Literally.

His hips rocked, the front of his boxers already damp from pre-cum as I teased him through the thin fabric. I'd seen him naked and hard just once before, and at the time I'd been *trying* not to look. The memory did not disappoint, now that I had my hands on him.

"Holy hell, Ashley," he breathed, flipping our positions so that I landed flat on my back with him poised between my legs. It was a shame about all the clothing between us, otherwise we'd be in the perfect position to hit a home run. "You are…" he trailed off, dipping his head to kiss me deeply. "Incredible."

I cupped his face, pulling him back to my mouth so I could kiss him while his hand slipped under the waistband of the shorts I was wearing. Fucking hell, I was so worked up I was sure I might climax simply from the touch of his hand inside my panties, but then his fingers slipped lower and—

"Good morning, roomie! Did you miss me?" Royce burst into the room with what had to be the worst timing in the history of bad timing. He raised a brow when he saw the position we were in, but didn't *leave*. "I'm not interrupting anything, am I?"

"Yes," Heath snapped. "Get out."

His hand was still inside my pants, and I gave an unintentional squirm, which somehow resulted in Heath's finger finding my clit. Entirely without meaning to, I whimpered.

Both Heath and Royce stared at me, and my face heated.

"Royce…" I said, trying and failing not to sound breathless. "Please…fuck off."

He just continued staring for a moment, like he'd forgotten what he was doing there in Heath's doorway. Then he blinked twice and seemed to snap out of it. "No can do, sorry, Squirrel. We have a situation, Heathcliff. Put your dick away and get dressed."

Heath groaned, resting his head on my chest and *devastatingly* removing his hand from my shorts. "Can it wait just a few minutes?"

Royce shook his head. "Nope. It's urgent. Come on, Briggs, pull it together. Ashley's a big girl, I bet she can finish herself off in no time without you. Right, Squirrel?"

I glared daggers at him as Heath reluctantly climbed out of bed. "I hate you."

His answering grin was way too damn smug. "Sure you do, roomie. But you might want to tag along on this little trip. Unless, of course, you're happy hanging out here with Carter? All alone… lots of time to shoot the breeze, maybe discuss travel? I'm guessing you and Heath already had the whole *non-monogamous* chat and everyone's on the same page?"

Fuck that chat, no matter how important it was. I was already up and out of bed, grabbing my jeans and a clean sweater from my bag. "I'll be ready in two minutes," I announced, ducking into the bathroom and closing the door firmly. Once I'd peed and dressed, Heath was fully clothed and waiting for me in the living room with Royce and Carter.

Avoiding Carter's intense stare, I tugged my shoes on and followed Royce and Heath out of the apartment. To my surprise, Carter tagged along which made for yet another uncomfortable elevator ride when he stood far too close for comfort.

"This better be important," Heath grumbled, yawning.

Royce shrugged. "Decide for yourself." The elevator dinged open at the garage level in the basement and he led the way out. My car was parked in one of the guest spaces and a few places down I spotted Royce's Bugatti beside Heath's Ducati. It wasn't until we drew closer that we spotted the situation Royce was alerting us to. Or... the *shit*-uation.

"Oh wow," Carter exclaimed with a cough. "Is that—"

"Shit?" Royce finished, "Yes. And a lot of it."

Heath's Ducati was coated in dark, putrid smears and the *smell* was enough to knock out an elephant. I gagged a little and pulled my sweater up to cover my nose and mouth.

"That's...fucking hell," Carter commented, summing up exactly what I was thinking.

Heath just stood there in shock, staring at his vandalized bike in horror. In addition to the smeared shit all over the vehicle, there was a perfectly formed turd right there on the seat. A log that looked suspiciously *human* too.

Eventually he gusted a sigh and rubbed his temple. "Yeah. Right. Let's check CCTV I guess."

Carter already had his phone out. "I'll call one of my guys and get this cleaned up."

"Thanks, man," Heath murmured, his expression drawn and pale. He weakly gestured for us to head back to the elevator and none of us protested... The whole garage smelled awful now that we were paying attention.

As we reentered their apartment, my phone buzzed in my pocket.

"I'll call building security about the cameras," Heath said with a tired sigh. "Royce...any chance you want to be my favorite friend and get us coffee?"

Royce scoffed. "After you left me and Nate to deal with Bart last night? You're dreaming."

The image of all that blood and Bart's lifeless eyes popped into my head and I shivered, hugging myself. I had been blocking it out for the whole drive back, but now there was no avoiding it. A guy was *murdered* in my bed. That had to be personal, there was no two ways about it.

"I'll get it," Carter announced, disappearing out of the apartment without waiting for anyone to respond.

The door slammed after him, and Royce arched a brow at me. "If he returns with coffee for you and not me...you owe me a hundred bucks."

"What? No way!" I protested, shaking my head.

Royce shrugged. "Fine. I'll take a blow job instead."

My mouth parted in panicked shock, speechless because I wouldn't *hate* that even though he was just messing around. Luckily Heath heard him and smacked him around the back of the head as he walked past with his phone to his ear.

"Ow! Heath don't act like you wouldn't get off on watching," Royce teased, doubling down on his offer.

My face was beet red, I was sure of it, so I crossed to the balcony where Lady—Carter's dog—was sleeping in the sunlight. Behind me, I heard Heath scolding Royce, and Royce laughing. Shithead just loved to watch me squirm.

"Hey Lady," I murmured, sinking to my knees on her artificial grass so I could pet her. "Remember me? You destroyed my bedroom."

The dog just groaned and showed me her belly for scratches. The feral mutt had turned into a pampered princess *real* quick. Spoiled little shit. I smiled as I obliged in belly scratches and she lolled her tongue out of her mouth in the picture of relaxation.

Royce and Heath seemed to be arguing about something inside, so I ignored them and got comfy with Lady in the sun. Sometime later, the balcony door slid open and Carter joined me with my favorite coffee in hand.

"I figured you could use this," he said quietly, handing it over.

Stunned, I uttered a *thank you* then glanced through the glass to find Royce miming a blow job…which made me blush again. Fucking hell. Nate had apparently arrived home too, so he shot a bewildered look between Royce and I, then turned to Heath with his hands spread in confusion.

"I don't want to talk with you, Carter," I said softly, avoiding looking up at him. "But can you tell me why you kept the dog?"

He crouched down and scratched Lady's belly, making her leg jiggle. "I can…if you'll hear my explanation for everything else."

I clicked my tongue, rising to my feet. I was still *so angry* when I thought about how he treated me after Paris. "An explanation isn't an apology, Bassington. I'm not interested in excuses. Not after…" I swallowed the rest of that sentence, shaking my head. "Too little too late."

He groaned, running his hand over his face. "Spark, wait. Just—"

I was already gone, stepping back inside and closing the sliding door behind me to cut off what he wanted to say. It'd been three fucking weeks. If he wanted to *explain* anything, he'd had plenty of time to do it. Hell, he could have *explained* things before we got back from Paris and I might have understood.

"You okay?" Heath asked, glancing up from his laptop.

I gave a tight nod, sitting down on the sofa beside him to sip my coffee. My phone buzzed again in my pocket and I remembered that I hadn't checked the last message. It was probably Carly, though, asking what'd happened with Heath.

Putting my drink down, I pulled out my phone. Then froze.

"What is it?" Nate asked. My eyes flicked up from my phone to find him staring at me intently. "It's her, isn't it?"

I swallowed hard, then nodded.

"Show me." It wasn't a request; it was an order. I complied without hesitation, handing the phone over to him and flinching when our fingers touched.

Nate frowned at me, then turned his attention to the screen to read the two messages from the dead girl.

UNKNOWN:

> Go back to campus, you're not safe.

UNKNOWN:

> Bart was an accident. You were the intended target. Don't lose your head, Ashley, go back to campus.

I hadn't had a message from the mysterious out of service number since returning from the woods, but apparently she wasn't done with me. Not yet…and probably not until I was dead.

Holy shit. Bart was meant to be me? Someone intended to murder me at the retreat. It made no sense. Why was he there in the first place? Why was he naked?

Who the fuck was doing this?

"Hey, Layne," Nate said sharply, snapping his fingers in front of my face. "You're freaking out. Stop doing that."

"Wow," Heath muttered from beside me, heavy on sarcasm. "Best advice ever, Nate. Good work." He rubbed circles on my back, attempting to soothe me. I could hear my short, sharp breaths but couldn't seem to get a grip.

"She's going to hyperventilate," someone said, but my head was already swirling and I closed my eyes. All I could think about was the cold of the forest, the pain in my feet as I walked endlessly, and the bone deep *fear* that I wouldn't make it out. It was all right back on the surface like it had been as I experienced it.

Someone's firm hands pushed my head down between my knees as I sat on the edge of the couch. Strong fingers gripped my hair, holding me in that position while my breathing started to slow and deepen.

"…grab her stuff…" I dimly heard Royce saying. "I'll drive her car back to school."

"You better not," Heath replied. "Ash doesn't let anyone drive her car. She can leave it here and pick it up another day."

"It's fine," I croaked, drawing a deep, shuddering breath as the hand in my hair loosened. I sat back up slowly to find it'd been Nate who'd helped. "Royce can drive my car. I'll…"

"We'll work it out," Heath assured me as I trailed off. "I promise, Ash, we won't let *anything* happen to you again. You're not alone, okay? You've got us."

I wet my lips, a million questions swirling through my head. I had him, of that I was confident. I had Royce, the best shadow a girl could ever want. But Carter? *Nate…?* I wasn't so sure. But the desire to believe Heath meant all of them was an uncomfortable ache within my chest, if only to stop second guessing everyone's intentions. For my own sanity.

Carter met my questioning gaze, and I froze, unable to look away. His eyes swirled with so many emotions it was impossible to read, but somehow I got the point. He agreed with Heath. Our sex life aside, he would protect me.

Even if it meant killing.

## Chapter Thirty-Eight

After returning to campus everything went quiet. No more creepy messages from a dead girl, no more random acts of violence or destruction...at least for the rest of the week. Everyone was just acting like the weekend getaway—and Bart's death—hadn't happened. Except for Royce, who pitched a well-planned argument *via PowerPoint presentation* about why it was a good idea that he share my bed rather than sleep on the floor.

Honestly, I couldn't even deny him because he'd put a lot of work into his slides. Thankfully, he seemed to be sleeping heavier because each morning when I woke up back in his arms once more, I was able to slither out and rebuild the pillow wall without waking him.

Small mercies. I dreaded to think the teasing he'd dish out if he realized I was cuddling up to him in my sleep.

After the shit incident and the following messages from Abigail, Heath and I had sat down for a more serious discussion. Both our courseloads were getting more intense and with the amount of distractions going on, we were falling behind. Not to mention his nightmares...

As much as I wanted to be there and help him work through it,

I could see how badly they were playing on his mind. He assured me that he'd speak about it with his therapist, and I was both surprised and impressed that he *had* one.

Even though we agreed to slow things down, it didn't stop us stealing kisses whenever we saw each other throughout the week. Sex was...currently off the table, though. Much to the disappointment of my libido. Mental health seemed more important.

A week after we returned to campus, Heath seemed to feel he was making progress with his therapist. He'd met me for breakfast and coffee before leaving for his session, and I'd sat in on Royce's Psychopharmacology lecture thanks to our new schedule. He sat in on mine—and actually seemed to enjoy them—and I sat in on his. Surprisingly I found his Ethical Social Responsibilities really interesting, and it was taught by Professor Reynard, who'd rescued me when I emerged from the forest.

The first class I sat in on with Royce, she'd delayed the lesson to ask me how I was doing which was very sweet.

We'd just left that class and Royce was chatting with a classmate as we wandered down the hall in the general direction of the cafeteria. We had an hour to kill before my class and I had my head down, texting Carly as we walked. Which was entirely my excuse for not seeing Carter until he grabbed my hand.

"Hey, what—" I started to protest as he linked our fingers together.

"Royce, I'm taking over," he announced, jerking me into an empty classroom and slamming the door so fast I wondered if Royce even noticed what'd happened.

He had, though. My shadow was always paying attention.

"Carter! Not cool, bro. Come on, we discussed this. Ashley doesn't *want* to talk and you need to respect that." Royce pounded on the door, but Carter had already locked it.

"No, I don't!" he shouted back. "Just fuck off before you go drawing attention. I'll deliver her to her class."

I rolled my eyes, folding my arms. "I'm not a dog that you have shared custody over."

"Squirrel," Royce called out with an edge of panic. "Say the word, roomie, I'll break this door down."

Carter glared at me, his back against the door. He was practically *daring* me to scream for help. Dick. "She's *fine*, Royce," he snapped.

"Squirrel?" Royce asked again, needing to hear it from me.

I sighed, throwing my hands in the air. "I'm fine, Royce. If I don't show up at class, make sure you search the campus dumpsters for my body."

Carter's eyes widened, and it was a sick sort of confirmation. Or maybe I was reading too much into it and he just thought I was being dramatic.

Royce didn't respond for a moment, and I thought maybe he'd already gone. But then a thump sounded like he'd just hit the door. "Bass, do *not* fuck this up." With that cryptic statement, he must have walked away because silence hung thick in the empty classroom for several long moments.

"Well?" I prompted, growing edgy waiting for him to say something. "You went to a lot of effort and Royce is probably going to punch you later. So say what you need to say."

His jaw tensed as he stared back at me, refusing to be hurried. Confident bastard.

"You're acting like a child," he said, and my jaw dropped.

"Excuse the fuck out of me?" I exclaimed in a strangled voice. "Exactly where do you find the audacity, Bassington? Is that a bonus that comes with your black Amex or something?"

He shrugged one shoulder. "Facts remain facts, Spark. I've been trying to talk to you alone for weeks, to explain things and *apologize* but you've been making it fucking impossible. So yeah, I had to go to more extreme lengths because it's eating me up inside."

"Because I don't *owe you anything!*" I shouted, anger exploding out of me. "I don't owe you my time, or the opportunity to explain.

Don't you fucking get it? I trusted you! I believed every fucking thing you told me in Paris. Do you have *any* concept how badly you hurt me when we got back?"

His shoulders sagged and he nodded. "Yeah. I do. Because that was my intent, because I thought it would just be *easier* if you hated me and I was so fucking wrong, Spark. I just…" He broke off with a frustrated sound, scrubbing his hands over his face. "I know I'm way past the point of apology, but can I please explain? If nothing else, I want you to understand this whole fucked-up mess is not personal."

A shocked laugh bubbled out of me. "Are you fucking serious? Carter, you—"

"I know. I *know* what I said and how it seems. Please. Will you just please let me fill in the blanks?" He pushed off the door and closed the distance between us, reaching out to touch my face.

Before his hand could connect, I stepped backward, out of reach. He followed.

"Spark…"

I shook my head. "Don't fucking play that game, Carter. Your cute nicknames have no power here."

His lips curled up slightly as I took another step back and my butt hit the desk at the front of the black box style classroom. "I don't think that's true…you love when I call you Spark. Like when—"

"You're off topic," I quickly interrupted before he could start sexy-talking and making me remember all the incredible sex we'd had in Paris, and how he used to moan my nickname as he came.

He nodded, his gaze dropping away from mine even as his hand lightly rested on my waist. I didn't push it away. He drew a breath, like he was about to say something, then sighed as the words failed him.

I just waited. He wanted this talk so fucking badly he was willing to force me into privacy…I wouldn't give him another opportunity.

"My family are Devil's Backbone legacies," he finally said softly, his thumb stroking my waist. I'd worn a cute little woolen skirt with a knitted sweater and thigh-high socks, and Royce told me I looked *smoking hot* when I dressed. Right now I was wishing I'd worn steel armor or at very least jeans. Somehow my sweater had risen up in a way that allowed Carter's thumb to stroke my skin beneath and it was *distracting*.

I swallowed, trying to ignore his touch as I leaned my butt on the desk behind me. "Okay...I figured most are."

He nodded slightly. "My mother is still quite involved with things. She's not on the elders council but she has her fingers in a lot of pies. Anyway, she was informed of our win and subsequent prize trip while we were already on the plane heading over, and she was...not happy."

I clicked my tongue, remembering the dramatic shift in his attitude after I woke up. How he'd been fun and engaging and then abruptly cold and distant. "Because I'm not a society legacy?" I guessed.

He sighed. "Even if you were, she'd still have the same reaction. It's...stupid, and so complicated, and honestly there's a lot I'm embarrassed to admit. But she warned me to keep my distance so that's what I tried to do."

"Until I got mugged and you saved me," I said softly, remembering that night in vivid detail. It was crystal clear in my mind, right down to the smell of the blood on his hands when he covered my eyes and told me *just don't look*.

I shivered, hugging my arms around myself.

Carter shifted ever so subtly closer, his index finger stroking a lock of hair out of my face. "Yeah. Until I lost control..."

Did he mean he lost control in beating that guy half to death? Or in fucking me against the alleyway wall?

"So what changed when we got back?" I asked, glossing over the rest of the trip. How he hadn't cared who saw us fucking in the catacombs, or that our tour guide knew what we were doing, or the hotel staff that must have seen us in the elevator.

He swiped a hand over his face, looking pained. "The guy in Paris...I didn't call an ambulance. I called a guy who's worked for my family for basically my whole life. He fixes things. I asked him to make the problem disappear and he did."

My mouth went dry. "That guy was dead, wasn't he?" His small nod made my whole stomach drop out of my body. "Holy shit."

"I'm sorry," he whispered. "I shouldn't have lied but I didn't want his death on your conscience."

"So why are you telling me now?" I whispered, panicked and distraught. Tears burned in the backs of my eyes and all I could think of was *how did Abigail know?*

Carter cupped my cheek, his thumb swiping a tear that escaped. "Because that's why I said the things I said when we got back. I was so...fucking hell, Spark, I *am* so obsessed with you I just wanted to make it work. But the guy I called to *fix* my mess reports to my mother. When we got back, she made her threats clear."

My head was spinning. His mother was willing to hold this threat over him? What kind of sick parent could do that? "Why?"

That was what I needed to know. Why the fuck did his mother care who he was sleeping with?

His lips pursed for a moment, and I could tell he was searching for the right words. Finally he sighed. "She has plans for my future, involving the daughter of one of her business associates."

My lips parted in shock. "She's...marrying you off? What is this, the eighteen hundreds? You're an adult, Carter."

He shook his head. "It's not that simple."

I scowled, horrified at his mom. "Who is the girl? If you tell me it's Jade, I'm fucking done."

A short laugh shook out of him and his lips curved deliciously. "It's not. I've actually never met her, to be honest. And usually my mother doesn't care what I do so long as it stays casual. But with you...it was different, and I think she got scared."

Was that a compliment? It was hard to know for sure.

I blew out a long breath, shaking my head. "So you were a fucking prick to me because your mommy said she doesn't like my pedigree?"

He winced. "Essentially. Yes. But the point I wanted to make was that I hate myself for saying that shit and I'm spending every minute of every day wishing I could go back to Paris."

My stomach bottomed out and my brain stuttered.

That...wasn't what I'd expected. I didn't really know what I'd expected but it wasn't the heartfelt honesty I was getting.

"Okay. Thanks for telling me, I guess."

*Dammit, now I have flutters in my belly.*

He frowned. "That's it?"

I shrugged. "That's it."

His deep blue eyes locked on mine for a long, tense moment, then he tilted his head thoughtfully. "Can I kiss you?"

The laugh I barked was horribly unladylike. "Not a chance in hell."

His eyes narrowed. "You're blushing, Spark."

"I absolutely am not. Now, if you're done with your confession, I need to go find Royce." I pushed off the desk and brushed past Carter, aiming for the door but he caught my hand as I passed.

One swift tug and I was back in his arms like it was the most natural thing in the entire world. My common sense fritzed out and I turned to putty as he held me, his lips brushing over the sensitive part of my neck just below my ear.

"Please," he whispered in that sexy, husky voice of his. "Give me something to cling to as I suffer in silence while you fall in love with Heath."

Fuck. He was breaking my heart all over again. "Damn it, Carter, you can't keep—"

His mouth met mine, swallowing my protests with a kiss hotter than the surface of the sun. Whatever I'd been about to say, it was totally gone from my brain. Just *poof*, disappeared. Carter had that effect on me and god damn if he didn't know how to kiss. The man must be part incubus, because my whole body lit up from his caresses.

Fuck it. He owed me this. A proper farewell. I kissed him back, throwing my arms around his neck and loving the way he lifted me off the ground to clear the gap between our heights. Then my ass was back on the desk where I'd been perched just a moment ago and his hands were on my thighs…

"Carter…" I gasped as he hooked his fingers under the elastic of my panties and started to drag them down. "You asked if you could *kiss* me."

He tossed my panties aside, sinking to his knees between my spread legs. "I didn't specify where."

Oh. *Oh shit*. Okay. He licked a long, teasing line down my cunt and I squirmed, collapsing back onto the desk. Carter ate pussy like it was his fucking job, and I wasn't going to stop him now that we'd come this far. Instead, I hooked my legs over his shoulders and threaded my fingers into his short hair, spurring him on.

"Oh my god," I gasped as he tugged my clit with his teeth, nearly making me lose my mind. "Carter this isn't *fair*."

"I know," he admitted, kissing my inner thigh lovingly. "But it's all I've been thinking about since the last time I tasted this sweet cunt."

My back arched as he pushed two fingers into my core, his tongue lapping at my clit furiously. Whimpers and moans rolled out of me unfettered as he pushed me to the edge of climax then shoved me right off the cliff. I desperately tried to clamp my lips shut, muffling my own screams as my thighs clamped his head.

He didn't pull away, even though he had to be suffocating, until my legs relaxed, and I released my grip on his hair. Even then, he kissed my inner thighs and seemed reluctant to let me go.

"Carter," I gasped, breathless and dizzy.

He hummed his response, ever so slowly rising from his knees but keeping his hands on my body all the while.

"Fuck," I whispered. "This is the stupidest thing I've done in a long time, but..." He arched an eyebrow in question, and I tossed caution to the wind. I sat up and grabbed the front of his jeans, pulling him closer. "I need you to fuck me properly."

Surprise saw him freeze a moment, but when I popped open his fly and palmed his hard dick, he snapped out of it.

"Shit, Spark," he hissed as I stroked his length. "I don't deserve this."

I didn't reply, because he was right. He didn't. But I did, so I reached up to grab his face, pulling him lower to kiss me as he lined up and thrust inside. I moaned into his kisses as he started to move, his hips rocking as his cock filled me to the point of slight discomfort.

He only fucked me like that for a few moments before pulling out, whispering a curse, and flipping me over with strong grip on my waist. I gave a startled squeak, which quickly morphed into a gasp as he thrust back in, fully seating himself in me from behind. The edges of the desk bit into my thighs as he pounded my cunt hard and fast, my eyes practically rolling into my head with how incredible it felt.

"Carter!" I cried out as another orgasm started to build within me. "I'm so close."

He slowed, but seemed to strike deeper than ever as his hand circled my throat. I moaned pathetically at the familiar hand placement, arching my back as he leaned down to bite my earlobe. Such a weirdly specific trigger, but it worked for me and Carter damn well knew it.

My climax was blinding, rocking through me so hard I would have ended up on the floor if not for how strong he held me. He whispered something as I rode the intense waves of pleasure, but I couldn't make out the words. Just the intent, which I now knew was utterly meaningless.

He came a moment later, hissing my nickname as his cock jerked and pulsed, pumping his hot load into my still spasming core.

For the longest time, neither of us moved, the room filled with the harsh, gasps of our jagged breathing, but we remained locked together on the desktop until eventually Carter withdrew with a heavy sigh.

"Spark, I don't think I can—" he started to say as I flipped my skirt down and turned to face him.

Then a distant scream cut through the class and we both straightened up in alarm.

"What was that?" I asked, as if he knew any more than I did.

He shrugged, quickly fixing his clothes and handing my panties back to me, which I pulled into place even as I started toward the door. Carter paused with his hand on the door, glancing back and running his gaze over me from head to toe.

I assumed he was checking I was decent before jerking the door open, but as we raced into the corridor—joining other students hurrying toward the main lawn—I wondered if he wasn't taking a mental snapshot…since that would *never* happen again.

## Chapter Thirty-Nine

Another scream came from outside and students all rushed through the halls to see what was going on. A guy bumped into me in his haste, and I stumbled, falling to the ground. I hissed in pain as the hardwood floor met my knees, but Carter was right there offering his hand to help me up.

I took it, letting him pull me to my feet, but once we started moving, he didn't let go. It was curious and distracting and I didn't try to pull away.

"Someone's tied to the flagpole," someone nearby said, just as we reached the doors.

Carter shot me a worried look, and I quickened my pace as we burst outside and followed the gathering crowd. Moments later we were pushing our way through the throng of shocked and generally curious onlookers gathered around the flagpole because sure enough, there was a guy tied totally naked to the pole way too damn high to get down easily.

It was him that was screaming.

Royce and Nate were close to the pole, and when we started toward them Carter dropped my hand. It was such a small thing, but it seized my heart in a vise instantly.

"What's going on?" Carter asked.

Royce glanced between the two of us, his gaze flickering back and forth until he sighed and reached out a hand to me. It stunned me enough that I took it, letting him reel me into a hug.

He'd seen that shit had gone down between us and made the choice to comfort me, rather than punch Carter. Best shadow ever. I wrapped my arms around his waist holding on tight.

"I'm okay," I mumbled, dimly hearing Nate and Carter talking behind us.

Royce gave an irritated sound. "You're not."

Okay, fine. I wasn't okay. But there was no way in hell I'd let Carter see me cry, so I sniffed back the looming tears and swallowed the emotion clogging my throat.

"Fake it 'til you make it, right?" I whispered, releasing my squeeze on Royce's body. "How are we getting this guy down?"

He gave me a troubled frown, then let me go…sort of. He kept his arm around my shoulders, hugging me to his side as if to send a message to Carter. That he was on team Ashley.

"Janitor is on his way with a ladder," Nate informed us, folding his arms across his chest and scowling up at the hollering guy. "But how the fuck did this happen in the middle of the day? No one saw anything? It doesn't make sense."

Ice-cold familiarity trickled down my spine. "It's not the first time, though, is it?"

Nate swung his scowl my way. "What do you mean?"

I wet my lips, uncomfortable with his full attention. "I mean, Abigail mentioned something very similar to this happening when she was a student here. Except it was at nighttime so sort of easier to get away with that, than this."

His eyes narrowed. "Abigail mentioned this…*when?*"

Oh fuck, they still didn't know. I hadn't told anyone, not even after the forest. "In her diary," I said quietly. "She kept a record of everything that happened while she was at school here. That's how I know she was murdered by the society."

Three sets of shocked eyes locked on me and I squirmed. Maybe I should have mentioned the diary sooner, but in my defense none of them had really endeared themselves as totally trustworthy... except maybe Heath.

"Where's Heath?" I asked, changing the subject as the janitor arrived with a ladder and started setting it up.

Nate shook his head. "Don't try and gloss over that little revelation, Layne, *what fucking diary?*"

"He's still at therapy," Royce answered. "Apparently it started late so it will likely run late too."

"What diary?" Nate repeated, taking a step closer as if he could intimidate me with his size. He could. But I wasn't letting on. "Is this the diary you accused me of stealing from your room the first week of school?"

I nodded and he threw his hands in the air.

"I'm not sure I understand, Spark," Carter said, and I bit back the desire to shut down his nickname once more. "You have a diary that details our society doing...awful things? And you never told us?"

I licked my lips again, nervous. "I don't have it anymore. It went missing the first morning Nate broke into my room, so I figured..."

"You figured I stole it," Nate replied. "Why?"

I inhaled deeply. "Because if it wasn't you, then it means someone else was in my room while I slept. And as much as I dislike you, I prefer to think it was you rather than some unknown other threat."

That admission seemed to slap him in the face, and he reeled back somewhat, horrified confusion etched all over his handsome face.

"I think we should discuss this in private," Royce suggested, giving a pointed look at the dozens of random students around us, all within earshot. "Let's deal with this first—" he pointed to the sobbing guy being cut down by the elderly janitor "—then Ash can tell us about this diary when we don't have an audience."

He had a good point. Just as many spectators were watching *us* as were watching the flagpole rescue.

Carter nudged Nate with his elbow. "Royce is right. One thing at a time." He shot me a dark, longing look and I looked away. I was a fucking idiot for letting him back into my panties.

The guy on the pole was finally free, being awkwardly carried down the ladder by the janitor so Carter hurried over to assist, taking the pale, naked, sobbing dude in his arms like he would a scared kitten.

Nate jerked a sharp nod and followed as Carter carried the guy away from the crowd, likely heading for the campus clinic. Royce and I trailed behind, and the janitor just muttered under his breath about stupid hazing pranks.

"Ash!" Carly called out as we passed into the admin building where the clinic was located. "What's going on?" She jogged to catch up, gesturing to where Carter and Nate just disappeared with the flagpole guy.

"Hazing prank, apparently," Royce replied with skepticism. "Ashley thinks it's the society, though."

I tried to ignore the accusation in his tone, hurrying down the hall to the clinic. They already had flagpole guy sitting on one of the cots with a big silver hypothermia blanket wrapped around his shoulders. Carter and Nate both stood over him with their arms folded and the most intimidating glares on their faces, which stopped me in my tracks.

"What happened?" I asked, sensing a shift. They weren't worried, confused, or concerned…they were *furious*.

"This sniveling prick," Nate said, jerking his chin to the shivering guy. "Said Heath was involved in getting him up there."

"He was!" the guy insisted. "I saw him!"

"Bullshit," Carter spat.

Carly moved closer, touching my elbow. "That's not possible," she said quietly. "I just saw Heath leaving Dr. Fox's office looking like hell. He said he'd been in like a two-hour session and was wrecked."

I nodded my agreement. "Carly's right. Sorry, uh, what's your name?"

"Morrison," the guy supplied. "Morrison Butler."

"Right, sorry. But like Carly just pointed out, Heath has been with Dr. Fox all morning. I don't think you were hanging up there for more than two hours with no one noticing...?" I posed it as a question because shit, crazier things had happened.

Morrison shook his head, frowning. "I don't...I don't think so. It's confusing, I don't know how I got there. I went to sleep in my bed and woke up *there*."

"So how are you accusing Heath of being involved?" Nate demanded.

Morrison seemed frustrated. "Because I saw him! When I woke up and realized where I was, he was standing there on the lawn staring up at me. Then when I screamed, he took off running."

It didn't make any sense. "You saw him?" I repeated. "His face?"

Morrison hesitated, frowning. "No, of course not his face, he wore one of those creepy fucking Society masks and robes." Silence rang out through the clinic and Morrison seemed to realize what he was saying. "It was Heath. I *know* it. He has a pretty distinctive build, and, um, I could see his forearms."

"*Right*," Nate drawled, his posture relaxing. "You recognized his build—under a black robe—and his...forearms?"

Morrison's face flamed red and his gaze darted around the room. "You're making this sound bad, but I know it was him. I'm not...it was *Heath Briggs*, I'm sure of it."

"Butler, I don't think I need to say this," Carter said in a quietly serious voice, "but you're making a very serious accusation of a senior society member...and your evidence is *forearms*. Which you saw at a distance, while in a state of panic. Would you like the opportunity to rescind your statement before this goes further?"

Oh. So Morrison Butler was in the society too. That made sense.

Morrison was clearly panicking now, sweat dripping down his

brow as he looked between all the guys as if searching for an ally. "But…"

"Think carefully, Butler," Nate suggested. "Are you sure enough that you want to go down that path? Considering we know he's been with Dr. Fox all morning and can easily be verified with the doc directly?"

Morrison swallowed, seeming to shrink down inside his silver blanket. "Maybe I was mistaken."

A small collective sigh ran through us all.

"Is there anything else you can tell us?" Royce offered. "Any idea how they got you up there, or why no one saw anything? Surely this was a two-man task at minimum."

Morrison shook his head, miserable. "No. I screamed as soon as I saw where I was and then everyone came running out of the buildings."

Royce nodded. "Okay well, if you think of anything, please let us know." He glanced over his shoulder to the front of the clinic. "Nurse Tracy is here. We'll leave you to get checked over."

We all filed out, ignoring the puzzled look of the clinic nurse as she headed inside with a clipboard in hand. Nate paused to speak with her, but the rest of us continued on out of the building.

I started toward my dorm, but Nate caught up with us a moment later and grabbed my upper arm in a bruising grip. "We need to talk," he snapped, redirecting me away from my dorm.

"Ow, Nate! Let me go!" I snapped, jerking in his grip. He wasn't letting go, though, practically dragging me as he strode purposefully toward the student parking lot.

Carter overtook us and stopped Nate with a hand on his chest. "Let her go, Nate," he ordered. "Ashley knows we need to talk; you don't have to hurt her."

Nate stared at Carter a moment as if in shock, then dropped his grip on my arm. "Fine. Layne? Get in the damn truck." He jerked a finger at his truck parked some fifty yards away. "We'll talk at the apartment."

I was two seconds away from digging my heels in and refusing to go...but then I'd end up with all four of them crammed into my tiny dorm room and even the idea of that was uncomfortable. So I gritted my teeth and continued across the parking lot reluctantly.

I'd much rather have driven myself, but with how tense everyone was I decided it wasn't worth the fight. I just climbed into the backseat of Nate's truck and relaxed when Royce slid in beside me and Carly hopped in the other side.

"Carly," Nate snapped when he climbed into the driver seat and saw her in the back. "This doesn't involve you."

She scoffed. "Like hell it doesn't. I'm in the society too, and Ash is *my* friend. If anything, it involves me more than you. So either shut up and drive, or Ash and I can deal with this ourselves."

"Hey," Royce protested, and Carly rolled her eyes.

"I mean, me, Ash, and Roycey can deal with this ourselves." She patted Royce on the head. "Sorry, twin."

He smirked, because I'd called them twins a few days ago when their personalities aligned a little too much and they were now running with it.

Nate just grumbled something under his breath about infuriating women and turned on his ignition. It was only a five-minute drive to their building from campus, so I needed to get my story straight.

But I was so torn...total honesty? Or play my cards close?

It felt like a lose-lose situation, but if Abigail's diary was to be trusted, then the worst was yet to come. Maybe telling the guys everything, letting them help, would be the difference between me and Abigail. Maybe they would be the reason I survived.

Or it could all go up in flames.

That was the risk I had to take.

# Chapter Forty

Heath was already home when we arrived, lying on the couch and absentmindedly stroking Lady's fur as she snored beside him. He glanced up when we all piled through the front door and raised a brow in question.

"Bro," Royce grimaced. "You look like shit."

He wasn't wrong. The ever-present dark circles under his eyes seemed deeper and his eyes were bloodshot. Still drop dead handsome, no question about it, but I was worried for his health.

"Thanks a lot," he groaned. "Dr. Fox was brutal today. I feel like I've been run over. What was happening on campus? Everyone was buzzing about something when I got out of my session."

"You didn't hang around to find out?" Carly asked, her eyes narrowed with suspicion. Heath gave her a puzzled look even as I elbowed her. "What? It's just a question."

"I thought you're the one who saw Heath leaving Dr. Fox's office?" Carter pointed out, and she just shrugged.

"Yeah, I did. But I would have had to have been curious enough to hang around. I wasn't."

"Guys…" Heath said, sitting up and wincing. "What the fuck is going on?"

A freaking potato could tell he had a headache, so I left the guys to explain the flagpole incident while I went in search of painkillers. I found some beside Heath's bed and brought them back with a glass of water.

"Thanks, babe," he murmured, taking them gratefully. "So Butler tried to accuse me based on…nothing? He just doesn't like me?"

"Sounds like he likes you a little too much, if you ask me," Nate commented, already sitting in one of the armchairs like it was his throne. "His insistence that he knows Heath's *build* and forearms kind of came off obsessive, don't you think?"

Carly snorted. "I totally got the same vibe."

"Well even so, I don't like the accusation," Heath admitted, running a hand over his face. He reached for his phone on the table and dialed someone on speakerphone.

Confused, I glanced at Nate who sighed and shook his head. "We don't suspect you, bro, you don't need to—"

Heath held up his finger as the call connected with a man who answered with a professional, "Hello, Heath?"

"Hey, Dr. Fox," Heath replied. "You probably already heard, there was a hazing incident on campus today. The victim has accused me of being responsible."

The man on the phone gave a small grunt. "Impossible. You were here in my office all morning."

Heath nodded, like he was relieved to have a credible alibi. "Thanks, Doc. I just wanted to make sure the air was cleared."

"Not a problem, Heath. I have no problem confirming this if anyone else requires my statement."

Heath chuckled and ended the call, tossing his phone back on the table.

"We didn't actually think you'd done it," Royce muttered, a little sullen.

Carly shrugged. "Doesn't hurt to verify, though. But now *that* is cleared up…who the hell did do it? Are we believing that this is someone in the DBs that you four don't know about?"

Three sets of eyes swiveled my way, and I tensed in my awkward position on the arm of the sofa Heath was on. I swallowed hard under their scrutiny and swiped my sweaty palms on my skirt.

"So, okay, the diary."

"What diary?" Heath asked, still catching up.

Royce huffed a disgruntled sound. "At least she's been keeping it a secret from *all* of us and not just *some*." He scowled my way and guilt twisted my insides. I did trust Royce…didn't I?

Nate quickly gave Heath and Carly the vague details I'd let slip beneath the flagpole while I nervously hopped up and went to get myself some water. When I returned to the living area, I sat down on the edge of the sofa.

"Okay, so…basically I found Abigail Monstera's diary the first week I was here. It was hidden in a false panel in my room, I guess she used to live in the same room? She was on the same scholarship as me and her diary started with her basically saying that if anyone found it, then she must be dead."

"Which she is," Nate confirmed. "Two years ago, drowned in Lake Placid during spring break."

I frowned. "Spring?"

He nodded. "Yes. That was why no one found her body for so long, because the campus was empty for the break. Her corpse was so bloated, wrinkled, and unrecognizable, they needed to use dental records to identify."

Blinking, I searched my memory of her diary and of the articles I'd found online about her death. The newspaper had been worse than vague so that didn't surprise me. It had focused mostly on her life since her death was ruled suicide. But…

"Her diary ended somewhere in winter," I said aloud. "Just before Christmas, I think? I just…I assumed that was when she died?" But now that I said it out loud, it didn't make sense. The lake would be frozen over so unless she fell through the ice, she couldn't have drowned.

No one else spoke, clearly waiting for me to explain with a fraction more context so I closed my eyes and tried to make sense of where to start.

"Abigail kept a diary of everything that happened to her, because she was convinced the Devil's Backbone was murdering people and covering it up. She tried to speak up and asked to leave the society and they threatened her. Scared her badly enough that she started writing it all down as evidence."

Someone made a scoff of disbelief, and I opened my eyes to see it was Royce. "Sorry, Squirrel, but that's...not right. No one gets threatened when they want to leave the DBS."

I shrugged. "Have you ever tried to leave?"

That made him pause. "No, I haven't. But you have."

Nate shifted in his seat, drawing my attention, and something about the way he inspected his cuffs made me suspicious. My eyes narrowed. "Nate? I have left the Society without being threatened...haven't I?"

He wouldn't meet my eyes, and my stomach bottomed out.

"Nate?" Heath prompted. "You said it was taken care of."

"I'm working on it," he muttered, swinging his gaze up to scowl at me. "This isn't about that. You were telling us about this smoking gun of a diary you've been hiding from everyone."

My jaw dropped in shock, processing what he was implying. "Nate, you can't—"

"The diary, Layne. Tell us about the diary. You said that the flagpole incident has happened before? When?" Nate was refusing to let me change the subject, and I glowered death back at him.

Still, I needed to finish explaining so we could finally be on the same page. "Yes. Abigail wrote about it happening to someone else in her initiate group, but it was done overnight and when they found the girl in the morning, she had frostbite so bad her little toe needed amputation? Or...something like that."

"So it must have been later in the year," Heath murmured thoughtfully. "It's cold now, and being naked outside wouldn't be good, but I don't think it's frostbite weather."

I shrugged. "I don't know for sure. When I first read the diary, I thought maybe it was just made up. An exercise in fiction or something. It wasn't until I started doing some research and the details matched up that I believed her record."

Nate looked angry and confused. Mostly angry, but probably because he was confused. "I don't remember that happening, do any of you guys?"

The other boys and Carly all shook their heads, and it only just struck me that they would have known Abigail. They were all already at Nevaeh when Abigail was at school, when she was writing that diary. Surely they had seen the things she wrote about? Or... had been involved?

A chill ran through me and I hugged my arms around myself.

"Why didn't you tell us about the diary, Ash?" Heath asked gently.

At the same time, Carter sat forward with intensity. "Is that how you made it out of the forest? Did Abigail go through the same thing?"

I chose to answer Carter, because Heath's question was a whole lot harder. "Yeah. She had survived it and left as many details of the path she took as possible. I probably backtracked a dozen times, trying to remember what order things were in, but eventually..."

"Fucking hell," Heath breathed, scrubbing a hand through his already mussed up hair.

"What about the other shit?" Nate pressed. "Did she write about anything else that's been happening? Bart?"

I swallowed hard, then nodded. "Sort of. Nothing so specific but she wrote about a gala event where they had challenges, and when someone failed, they were beaten half to death."

Carly gasped, pressing her hand to her mouth. "Martin."

Carter blinked his confusion. "Those DBs we saw in robes that night…there was no reason for them to be there. I assumed it was just some of the grads playing pranks on first-timers."

Nate was pissed right the hell off now, surging to his feet. "So all along, you've known what's going to happen next. You could have warned any of us and you thought, nah I'll just see how it all goes? What the fuck, Ashley? You could have died in that forest and you just figured it'd be *fun* to see if the diary entries were accurate?"

My lips parted in shock at his aggression. "You think I enjoyed that?! Why in the fuck would I think it would happen to me? Or to anyone for that matter? It could have all just been coincidence or… or…I don't know!"

"Bullshit," Nate spat. "I bet you—"

"Okay, that's enough!" Heath barked. "Ash, where's the dairy now? Can we read it?"

I shook my head, glaring daggers up at Nate. "It went missing out of my room the weekend of the lake party."

"She thought I stole it," Nate elaborated. "Which I did not."

"Then where'd it go?" Heath asked, clearly frustrated that it was taking so long to get all the relevant information.

I shrugged. "I have no idea. If Nate didn't take it, then…maybe I lost it?" At this point I had to question everything, including myself. Also, it was a more comfortable idea than the alternative.

Nate scoffed. "Yeah right. As if you wouldn't have turned your room upside down before accusing me."

"So, someone else took it," Heath concluded. "From your room, Ash, probably while you were sleeping. And this hasn't scared the fuck out of you? You didn't think you wanted to share this information with anyone else? What if that person returned and—"

He cut himself off, visibly biting back the rest of his words and closing his eyes for a moment.

I said nothing. He was one hundred percent right, and I had very little justification for keeping the diary to myself other than the one obvious fact.

"You didn't trust us," Carter said, seeming to read my mind. "Which is fair, given how things were at the time."

"But not since then. You could have told us at any point since then," Royce argued, a deep scowl on his brow. "You still don't trust us."

I couldn't tell him he was wrong, no matter how much it hurt to see how disappointed he was in that realization. Part of me really still *didn't* trust them. Any of them. So I just hung my head and twisted my fingers, unable to find the words to make it all better without lying.

"You're a fucking idiot, Layne," Nate spat. "You've got some of the most loyal, determined, and *well-connected* men standing right here in this room ready to blow up their perfect lives to keep you safe and you *still* have trust issues? Pull your head out of your ass."

I gaped at his cutting words. "Excuse me?"

His left eye twitched in fury. "What happens next, Ashley? Hmm? What should we be preparing for *next*? Another beheading in your bed? More kidnapping and relocation? What's it going to be?" His tone had shifted from frustrated to outright aggressive and it made me shrink back slightly.

Royce rose to his feet, putting a hand out. "Nate, that's enough. You've made your point."

Nate was too far gone in his anger, turning on Royce. "Of fucking course you're leaping to her defense! You need to stop falling for other guys' girlfriends, Royce, the pussy isn't worth losing your friends over."

Royce paled, glancing at me in irritation. "Nate, man, I'm sorry. Paige just—"

"Paige?" Nate exclaimed, horrified. "I was talking about Ashley and Heath. You fucked *Paige?*"

Royce reeled back, panic etched all over his face. "I thought you knew! Ash said you knew!"

"He did know," I snapped, folding my arms. "He just chose not to believe me."

Nate's head looked like it was about to explode and a quick glance at Carly said she was watching the whole show so intently I bet she hadn't blinked even once. Karma's a bitch and all that.

"Come on, man," Carter stepped in, trying to smooth things out. "Royce wasn't exactly the only guy Paige cheated with."

Nate gaped at him. "You too?"

Carter scoffed. "Not a chance in hell. No freaking way. I wouldn't risk that for all the tea in China."

"No," Royce sneered. "You'll just drag Ash into a classroom against her will for a quick fuck then crush her heart all over again when you've blown your load."

"*What?!*" Both Nate and Heath exploded at the same time, spinning on Carter in outrage. My face flamed and panic tears burned at the backs of my eyes. This whole thing was such a mess and I was hurting *everyone* around me.

Trembling, I slowly stood up and moved closer to the exit. "This is all my fault," I said quietly. "I'm so sorry. I never meant—"

"Damn fucking right it's your fault!" Nate barked. "None of this would have happened if you never started school here. All you do is *ruin lives*, Layne. Just like your mom."

That was the final straw for me. I turned on my heel and left the apartment, speed walking to the elevator and stabbing the call button repeatedly. Thankfully the car was right there and opened immediately, but there was still a tense, breathless moment waiting for the doors to shut before any of the guys could stop me.

But they didn't even try. At the last moment, Carly slipped into the elevator. Just in time to wrap me in her arms as my tears started falling.

She said nothing, though, and I didn't blame her. Royce's statement that I still didn't trust them included her too, and there was no way she'd missed it.

I was a trainwreck. No wonder none of my friendships ever lasted. Carly deserved better, and that knowledge only made me cry harder.

## Chapter Forty-One

To my surprise, Carly didn't drop me like a hot rock after our Uber brought us back to campus. She just looped her arm through mine as we walked up the stairs to our floor, then told me she was getting changed into her pj's—despite it barely being midday—and coming to my room for movies.

We got cozy together in my bed, watching chick flicks on my laptop and *not* talking about the messy scene at the guys' apartment. It was nice, but eventually I had to fess up and apologize for not trusting her with the diary information.

Incredibly, she just shrugged. "I get it," she told me. "But I hope you know I've got your back, no matter what."

That, obviously, just turned me into a puddle of emotion again and she changed the subject by asking me about what happened with Carter. Reluctantly, I told her. Then she cracked up laughing so hard tears came out of her eyes and she couldn't get words out.

"I don't...I don't know what's funny," I admitted, grinning at her antics.

She flapped a hand at me but was still laughing too hard to form words. Weirdo. Her cackles were contagious though, and I found myself chuckling just because she was so delirious.

"I'm so confused," I admitted between giggles.

She finally sobered up enough to dab her eyes and draw a breath. "Sorry," she said between easing laughs, "Sorry, it wasn't even that funny. I just started thinking about Nate's *face* when he realized all three of his friends are besotted with you. He looked like he was going to shit his pants." More giggles.

I rolled my eyes, still grinning. "It's not like *that*. Carter will probably go back to pretending I don't exist and Royce is just a giant shit stirrer."

"Uh-huh," she snickered. "Sure. Holy shit, is that the time? No wonder I'm starved."

"You go eat. I'm not in the mood to leave my bed for at least another year." I snuggled down deeper into the blankets.

"Oh my god, drama. I'll order in so you don't have to leave your nest. Hey, where's Royce's bed gone?" She peered over the edge of my bed, looking at the patch of floor that Royce had set up as his camp bed for the better part of two weeks.

My face flamed. I *also* hadn't told her about my new sleeping arrangement with Royce. "Um, it's just in the closet." Technically true. That was where the spare bedding had been stored when he graduated to sharing my queen size bed.

Carly didn't question that response and went about ordering us dinner on her delivery app. It actually ended up being a really enjoyable night, despite the lingering pit of nausea in my stomach over how I left things with the guys.

She offered to stay the night with me, but I insisted she sleep in her own bed. No one had so much as knocked on my door the whole time Royce was babysitting, they weren't going to suddenly break in now.

Reluctantly, she agreed, but made me lock my door after her and then tested it from the other side before wishing me sweet dreams.

All of a sudden, I was alone for the first time in a month. Alone, and so fucking sad. I crawled into my bed and curled up on the side

Royce had claimed as his own, hugging a pillow to my chest. I really fucked things up today.

I must have fallen asleep like that because the next thing I knew I was jerking awake as my door opened and someone slipped inside. The light from the hallway lit up my intruder for just long enough to ease my fear.

"Royce," I said on a heavy exhale, sinking back into my bed.

He locked the door again, then opened the closet to pull out his bedding. "Go back to sleep, Ash," he murmured, and my heart sank.

Ash. Not Squirrel.

He slept on the floor that night, and the subsequent nights. We barely spoke, but he still followed our schedule as it was before the big argument. Just without the fun, and the joking. The air between us at all times of day was positively icy which wasn't helped by the fact that I went out of my way to ensure I didn't run into *any* of the other guys. Taking extra shifts at the country club helped and gave me a breather from Royce.

Heath's texts and calls went unanswered—my guilt over destroying their friendships was too intense to choke down—and Carter didn't try. I wanted to pretend that didn't hurt, but it did.

Nate was probably *thrilled*.

The day before Thanksgiving break—we had a whole week off, which should have been nice—I found myself hiding out in a shower cubicle with Carly just to get a break from the oppressive *silence* in my room. She was leaving in a few hours to travel to her grandparents' mansion in Vermont...with Heath. They had a whole big family get-together that Carly seemed to be dreading.

"Are you sure you won't go home?" she asked for the dozenth time as I sipped my takeaway coffee, sitting on the little bench seat within the shower stall. "Your mom must miss you."

I nodded. "I'm sure. She already told me that Max and Nate have plans to watch the football game so I'd rather not put myself under the same roof as him. I'll be fine here. With everyone gone, I might actually get ahead on my coursework."

She sighed, tugging out her hair tie and re-doing her ponytail. "Fine, I guess. I'm kind of jealous. Will Royce stay too?"

I grimaced. "I don't know. Surely he has family he needs to see? I certainly haven't asked him to stay."

"Okay, but considering how he's kept up the protection detail even when he's *pissed* sort of indicates he won't leave you here for ten days alone." Carly was just full of logic today. I didn't like it.

Changing the subject, I asked her what was happening with the guy she'd been *casually talking with* lately. He was *not* a DB which was interesting, since she said her family would strongly disapprove. I suspected that was part of the appeal.

Smiling like crazy she told me about the filthy text messages they'd been exchanging and showed me the pictures she'd taken for him. Tasteful nudes, she called them.

"Wait so you *still* haven't met up?" I gaped at her in shock.

She shrugged. "You'd have heard about it if we did. But…I kind of like the anticipation. I like the conversation. It's nice."

Just as I was about to *awwww* at her, the cubicle curtain jerked open, and Nate glared at us both.

"Excuse me!" I exclaimed. "We're showering! How rude."

"Hilarious. Carly, don't you have a plane to catch?" He folded his arms, glaring down at us both sitting on the shower bench seat.

My friend glanced at her watch then cursed. "Good save, Essex. Uh…if I leave right now will Ashley make it out of this cubicle alive or…"

Nate rolled his eyes. "Carly…"

"Dead serious question," she replied with a shrug.

He exhaled heavily like we were the most insufferable people on earth. "Yes, Layne will live to see another day. Now please go, Heath's waiting out front for you."

Carly grabbed me in a hug, muttering to me that if Nate got

out of line I can always kick him in the balls. I laughed and bid her safe travels before she left me alone with a very irritated Nathaniel Essex…inside a shower cubicle.

"Do you want to explain what you two were doing in here?" he asked after some moments. "And don't tell me *showering*. Royce was worried you might have drowned because you've been *showering* so long."

I shrugged. "I don't owe you answers. What do you want?"

He puffed his cheeks out, running a hand over his hair with frustration. "You need to come home for Thanksgiving."

My brows hiked. "Home? Where *exactly* is that?" Max's house wasn't my home, and I knew my mom had her house listed for sale and vacant. So…technically for me, home was right here at the dorm.

His teeth gritted. "You know what I mean. Carina expects you there for the holidays."

"No she doesn't, I already told her I was staying at school. Besides, since when do you give a fuck what my mom thinks? Last I checked, you hold her with the same lack of respect as you do me."

His left eye twitched which told me he was *really* pissed off but trying to keep it in check. How fun.

"All right, fine. You need to come home *with me* for Thanksgiving so that Royce isn't stuck here babysitting you the entire break. He needs to go home, his dad is going to be there for the holiday and he hasn't seen him in nearly three years. It's important for *Royce* so can you please put our issues aside and think of him for once?"

I swallowed the harsh truth of those words like a bitter pill, pulling my knees up to hug them to my chest. "I never asked him to stay. He should go."

Another long-suffering sigh. "He won't though."

"So just lie to him. Or I will, if you're too pussy to do it." I stood up, intending to go out there and tell Royce whatever he needed to hear, so he'd leave for the holidays.

Nate blocked me with his arm across the front of the cubicle. "We aren't doing that," he snapped. "What's it going to take, Layne? Hmm? What's your price?"

Confused, I frowned up at him and regretted my bare foot status. He was too damn tall, especially in the close confines we were currently in. "My price? To spend a ten-day break with an insufferable bully like you?"

"Yes," he hissed. "And pretend we don't hate each other. What's it going to cost? A new car? Your Firebird must be about to fall to pieces by now."

A laugh of disbelief bubbled out of me. "You're not serious. For starters, that car is a goddamn classic, and you not recognizing that fact only speaks to your lack of character. And for another—and I know this one will be *really* hard for your immature pea-sized brain to process—I'm *not for sale*. I wasn't then, and I'm not now. Not everything in life can be bought, Essex."

He pursed his lips, nodding slowly. "I see. So, you're still holding a grudge for Royce keying your car?"

My jaw dropped. "Royce did it? That *motherfucker!*"

"Irrelevant right now, isn't it? He did what I asked him to do, so I'm the only one to blame." He dropped his arm and moved further into the cubicle, leaning his back on the tiled wall and stuffing his hands in his pockets. "I'm sorry. Is that what you wanted to hear? I'm sorry that we keyed your precious vintage car, and that we set you up to seem like a money-hungry whore. Happy?"

I scowled, facing him in outrage. "Are you joking? That's the best apology you can muster up? You must really not care if I do this Thanksgiving trip."

He threw his hands up. "I said I'm sorry, what more do you want from me? You want me on my knees? Here." He dropped to his knees right there in the shower, putting his hands together. "Please, Ashley, will you come home and make *both* our parents happy?"

Fucking hell, talk about a low blow. Throwing a guilt trip in with his apology was just the kind of dirty tactic I should have expected from him. "It's not enough," I stated. "If I come home with you, then I want you to do this apology all over *with more sincerity* and I want you to apologize to my mom. In front of Max. With *feeling*."

His lips parted and his eyes widened with confusion. "Apologize for what?" I flattened my glare and a small, guilty smirk touched his lips. "Okay, fine. Deal. Anything else? Money? Jewelry?"

I shook my head. "Nope. Just human emotion and a display of remorse. You can handle that, can't you?" I was skeptical whether he actually could, but I couldn't be the reason Royce missed out on seeing his dad.

Nate extended his middle finger in response. He was still on his knees in the middle of the shower cubicle though, so I simply reached over and turned on the tap.

"Fuck! Layne!" he roared, cold water dousing him.

I laughed, ducking back out of the shower before he could retaliate, my evil chortle echoing through the bathroom in a way that cheered me right up. So much for my nice quiet break alone at school...though I didn't hate the idea of seeing Mom and Max.

Nate, without realizing, had actually done me a favor. Hell must be chilly today.

## Chapter Forty-Two

Nate and I didn't speak for the drive to Max's house, not one word. Then when we arrived, he turned on his fake friend act so thoroughly it creeped me right the fuck out. For the first few days, I just straight-up avoided him. He followed through on our agreement to apologize to Mom, so I couldn't complain.

By the day of Thanksgiving, the mood had shifted somehow. The night before, Mom had baked four different kinds of pie, along with some other surprising treats. Baking wasn't Mom's strong suit, but I had to admit, the pies smelled *amazing*. Mom and Max were sickeningly in love as they prepared our Thanksgiving meal together with music playing. They'd been up before dawn, and there'd been breakfast waiting when I came down. While Mom and Max were having such a good time, I tried to stay out of the way of their kisses and PDA. Which explained how I found myself helping Nate set the table.

"What time does the game start?" I asked as he folded the linen napkins into swans for each place on the oversized table. Why he decided on swans, no clue. Where he learned how to do it, also no clue. Kind of fascinating to watch? Undecided.

"Not until three," he murmured, frowning at the swan he was

working on. Its neck kept drooping and he was growing visibly frustrated with it. "That's why we're eating dinner so early. Dad didn't want Carina to feel rushed. It's like…a big deal to her that we're both here."

He shot me a quick look, and I pursed my lips. "I'm aware." Mom had said as much when we arrived—and every day since. It meant a lot for her to think Nate and I were getting along.

"I wasn't taking a dig," he said with a short sigh, giving up on his napkin swan and shaking it out to start again. "I just meant maybe it wouldn't kill us to visit for dinner more often. For our parents."

There was an odd tone to his voice, but when I looked over his focus was entirely on the napkin he was folding. Maybe I imagined it?

"Yeah, I guess," I murmured. I really did love spending time with Mom and I'd have to be an idiot to not see how worried she was after my last stay…when I accused Nate of trying to kill me.

The doorbell rang as Nate finished his swan—with an erect neck this time—and I arched a brow his way. "Are you expecting anyone else?" I asked. As far as I was aware, it was just the four of us for dinner. Dad couldn't get leave from his job, Mom's parents lived in Florida, and Max's parents were both deceased.

Nate shook his head. "Nope. Dad would have mentioned if we needed more place settings. Maybe it's…" he trailed off as voices from the foyer trickled through to us. "That sounds like—"

"Surprise!" Carly yelled, bursting into the dining room. "I bet you missed me."

She totally brushed past Nate, launching a hug on me and I laughed as I hugged her back. Heath followed her into the room somewhat less excited and exchanged a bro-hug with Nate.

"Carly and Heath are joining us for dinner," Mom announced from the doorway, "can you set some extra places?"

"Got it," Nate replied, crossing to the cabinet at the side of the room where place settings were all held.

Meanwhile Carly had released me from her hug and Heath held

out a hand...not forcing me to embrace him but making it crystal clear that it'd be welcomed. My breath catching, I took his hand and let him reel me in.

His arms closed around me and I was *home*. My cheek pressed to his chest, my eyes closed, I melted.

"I missed you," he murmured, kissing the top of my head.

I drew a deep breath, inhaling his uniquely *Heath* scent. "I'm sorry. I hate that I caused so much tension between you all. Nate's a dick, but the rest of you don't need me fucking up your lifelong friendships."

"Hey!" Nate protested, and I ignored him.

Heath loosened his hold enough that he could cup my face in his palm and tip my head back, meeting my eyes. "This isn't on you, Ash. Friends fight, especially friends who've basically lived as brothers for more than ten years. It'd take a lot more than one argument to split us all up."

It was on the tip of my tongue to point out the tension with *us* was also about me and Carter, but I swallowed it back. We could dissect that mess later, in private, if he wanted.

"Heathcliff," Max called from the kitchen, "come help me with drinks for everyone!"

"Yes, sir! Coming!" Heath replied, then dropped a quick, sweet kiss on my lips. "Can we please be good again? It's torture being ignored by you."

My answer was to grab the back of his neck and kiss him back, albeit less sweet and quick than he'd kissed me.

"Heathcliff!" Max called out again, and I released him with a laugh.

"Okay, go." I told him. "But for the record, I'm glad you're here."

He disappeared back out of the dining room, and I watched him go, then realized I was staring and cleared my throat. Nate's eyes locked on me were the first thing I saw when I looked away from the door and I frowned back at him.

"What?" I asked.

He shook his head. "Nothing." He shifted his gaze to Carly. "So what happened at the Briggs family reunion? Atticus can't be pleased that you two have dipped out."

She shrugged. "I don't think he'd be shocked. You should have seen the arguments going down between Dad and Uncle Nash." Then to me she added, "That's Heath's Dad. They—and their younger brother, Zeth—have a really unhealthy rivalry going on. It's a whole thing. The only reason we lasted as long as we did is because Uncle Zeth didn't even show up."

Nate grimaced, shaking his head. "Is Heath all right? Nash can be a bit..."

Carly gave him a pointed look. "Why do you think we're here?"

I looked back and forth between them, attempting to fill in the blanks. "His dad is abusive?" The wince Carly gave confirmed my guess, and my stomach dropped. "I didn't know. That's awful."

Nate nodded vaguely, twisting up another swan. "That's why Max took over as his guardian when we were eleven. He basically lived with us already, it was an easy transition when his parents moved to Hong Kong."

I knew I loved Max, but that fact made me love him even more. My heart ached for Heath, but I got the feeling Royce and Carter weren't in much better situations. Hadn't Max mentioned being guardian for all four boys during high school?

"Um, have you heard from the other guys?" I asked Nate nervously.

He quirked a brow at me, seemingly startled by my question. "No...but that's not unusual."

I nodded, accepting his answer because guys were generally pretty awful at discussing *feelings*...not that I was a lot better. But still, when we finished setting the table and headed through to the living room, I pulled out my phone.

Things were worse than awkward between us, but my gut said I needed to check in.

I kept it brief, sending the same thing to both Royce and Carter both.

ASHLEY:

> Happy Thanksgiving <3

As soon as I sent it, a flood of anxiety filled me. Carter would obviously ignore me, and now that I'd sent it I realized he wasn't even celebrating Thanksgiving. He was in Europe somewhere with his mother...probably planning his arranged marriage.

"You okay?" Heath asked, handing me a cocktail from the tray he'd carried into the living room.

I gave him a tight smile as I accepted the drink. "Fine. Are you?" I gave him a closer look as he sat on the sofa beside me, noticing a slight redness to his cheekbone.

His answering smile was sad, and he dropped a kiss on my shoulder. "I am now."

My phone buzzed in my hand and my heart leapt into my throat. Royce must have replied. Biting my lip, I unlocked the screen and did a double take when I saw the message was from Carter.

CARTER:

> Spark?

It occurred to me, I'd never text him before so he likely didn't have my number. Still...it got him to reply.

Heath glanced over at my phone and I stiffened. We hadn't discussed the Carter thing, and I didn't want him getting the wrong impression.

"I just sent them both a Happy Thanksgiving message," I said quietly, feeling like I needed to explain. "Just in case...um..."

"In case their holiday is going similar to mine?" he guessed, snuggling me into his side. "Probably a good idea." He kissed my neck, just under my ear and I sighed with relief.

Deciding not to reply to Carter—because I had nothing to say—I checked my message thread with Royce. We had a lot more text history thanks to his roommate position, but my latest message sat on *read*.

At least he'd seen it? That was something, even if he wasn't going to reply.

My phone buzzed again, but not from Royce.

CARTER:
> Has Nate been playing nice? He promised to be on his best behavior.

I bit back a smile, reading the message in my head with Carter's voice. I could just imagine how that conversation with Nate had gone...then I found myself questioning why the fuck Carter cared.

Again, I refrained from responding. He made his position abundantly clear, despite the incredible sex. He wasn't going to risk his mother's wrath by pursuing things with me and frankly, I didn't blame him. Not when there was a murder involved. Not when he was in that position *because of me* in the first place.

Carly carried the conversation, telling us about some argument her family had been engaged in before she and Heath left, and I tried my best to pay attention when my head was miles away. Would Royce reply eventually? What was Carter doing? I was glad to have Heath and Carly here, even if the circumstances sucked.

Heath's phone dinged a few minutes later and he shifted to pull it out of his pocket. Sliding the screen open, he draped his arm back around my shoulders, making no effort to hide the message as it displayed.

CARTER:

> Are you at Max's? With Ash?

Heath gave me a quick glance before typing his reply.

HEATHCLIFF:

> Yeah, how'd you know?

CARTER:

> Your bike is in the driveway, dickhead, that's how. Open the door.

Heath barked a laugh out loud. "Carter's here."

Nate grinned—an actual honest-to-god *genuine* grin—and rose to his feet. "I knew he'd show up sooner or later. Dad! Carter's joining us!"

Max's laugh echoed from the kitchen. "Told you. Carina owes me fifty bucks."

Confused, I looked to Heath for an explanation. He just shrugged. "Carter's mom is an insufferable bitch," he said matter of fact.

"Heathcliff," my mom scolded, having just come in carrying a tray of snacks.

Heath just shrugged. "It's true, though. She has exactly zero time for him too. He never lasts the entire holiday break before snapping and flying home."

He got up from the couch as Carter entered the room like a dark prince returning from court. Fuck he was gorgeous. The heated glance he sent my way as he bro-hugged Heath nearly set me on fire too. Was I seriously getting turned on by the two of them embracing? Yes, apparently.

The moment I mentally acknowledged that fact, my imagination inserted myself between them in that hug. Naked. *Shit.*

Biting my cheek, I prayed my blush wasn't obvious and gave Carter a small smile in greeting.

"Aw, come on Spark, that's all I get?" he asked in mock outrage. "It's Thanksgiving!" He extended his hand and I flicked a quick glance to Heath. He was smiling, though, his expression more relaxed and content than I'd seen in *months*, so I sighed and let Carter pull me up from the sofa to hug.

The breath knocked right out of me as I sank into his embrace, and painful emotion thickened in my throat. This wasn't fair. He'd apologized for hurting me the first time, then did it all over again.

"I'm so sorry, Spark," he whispered directly against my ear, his words only for me and no one else. Had he read my mind, or were my thoughts that obvious? "Please forgive me, I can't let you go."

What the fuck did *that* mean?

I was saved from having to reply by Max and Mom joining us. Carter released me with a brush of a kiss on my cheek, then turned to greet Max with exuberance. Now the overabundance of food made a lot more sense. Max had known the boys might show up and wanted to be prepared.

"Anyone heard from Royce?" Mom asked, glancing between the guys.

They all shook their heads. "The Colonel had a five-day break, so he was hoping to spend some time with him," Nate said. "I'm sure we'll hear from him once Mike goes back to base."

Max and the others all seemed to understand, and I wondered if that was why Royce had left my message on read. He was just busy spending time with his dad…The Colonel.

Everyone seemed in a great mood as Carly dragged out some board games and Mom ducked back and forth from the kitchen while the food finished cooking. We all played Monopoly until things got heated with our banker—Nate—being accused of embezzlement by Max.

I tried to enjoy myself too, but I kept checking my phone, hoping Royce would reply. Even a thumbs-up would do. Just…something. I didn't know if we were okay, but I desperately wanted to know if he was at the very least.

We all helped to bring the food out to the dining table—now set for seven—and Mom poured champagne for all of us. Max started carving the turkey as Carly chatted with Heath about the teams playing later. Carly loved the competition way more than me. Carter tossed flirtatious grins across the table at me, seeming to make a sport of making me blush.

Then the doorbell rang.

Without even realizing what I was doing, I dashed out to answer it and nearly cried when I found Royce standing there. His shoulders were slumped and his eyes red-rimmed and puffy. The smell of whiskey on his rumpled shirt was intense, but I didn't hesitate when he stepped forward and grabbed me in a hug so tight it nearly cracked my ribs.

"Can I sleep with you tonight, roomie?" he mumbled into my hair, lifting me off the ground with the intensity of his hug. "I don't like being alone."

My heart cracked right the fuck open. "I don't like being alone, either."

A deep shudder ran through him, and I just hugged him back. Someone breathed a disappointed curse behind us, but I knew no one else was surprised to see Royce show up.

As awful as I felt for the guys that their plans didn't play out, I was overwhelmingly glad Max had created such a safe space for them all to come home to. And that my mom was a part of that warmth now. She chose well, even if I did feel for my dad in all of this—who did he have?

I was also glad for me 'cause they were all here with me too.

## Chapter Forty-Three

Nate did me a huge favor in dragging me home for the holidays. Somehow, those last few days with all the guys there—and my bestie—made me almost forget all the horrible shit going on at school with the Devil's Backbone Society. No creepy messages arrived from Abigail, no naked beheaded men turned up in my bed, it was just *fun*.

Royce claimed the other half of my bed as though our weeklong ice out never happened and reasoned that it was saving me the uncomfortable decision of choosing between Heath and Carter. He wasn't wrong, either. Both seemed totally at ease with the fact that I was attracted to *both* of them, and although they respected the fact we were in my mom's home—and therefore fucking all over the house was out of the question—it didn't stop them shamelessly flirting. Much to Nate's disgust.

Once Royce had sobered up somewhat on Thanksgiving, he'd told us that his father—The Colonel—had simply not turned up. No call or text to let his only son know he wouldn't be home…just never showed. While my first instinct was to check if something had happened, Max quickly assured me that this was not the first time. Nor would it be the last.

Carter refused to talk about whatever happened with his mother, but whatever *had* happened, it'd drastically changed things between us. I wasn't sure how to feel about that.

The best part about our few days all staying at Max's house? Heath seemed to be sleeping better. The dark circles under his eyes lightened and he just seemed to breathe easier, without the weight of his own mind smothering him constantly.

All that changed when we returned to school, though.

Thanks to my recently increased workload at the country club—which I'd volunteered for while avoiding the guys—I didn't have any time for my study dates with Heath, or really to do anything that wasn't work, sleep, or attend class. If not for Royce literally sharing my bed, I wouldn't have seen any of my friends at all.

When I got back to the dorm after work a week after returning from break, I was surprised to find Nate waiting for me in my room. My *locked* room.

*Again.*

"Do you have your own key too?" I asked, folding my arms as I glared at him. We'd found some semblance of a truce during our stay at Max's but the moment we returned, he shed his nice guy act like a seal skin. The mood swings gave me whiplash and I had zero patience for him.

Nate just gave me another of those long-suffering sighs. "Of course I do. You just worked that out? How the fuck did you earn a scholarship again?"

"Nate…fuck off. I just worked ten hours straight—" thanks to a colleague calling in sick at the last minute "—and I'm wrecked. Your petty bullying crap needs to take a break until I can sleep."

His jaw tightened. "Yeah well, that's sort of what this is about. Where's Royce?"

"I told him to go home when my shift kept getting extended," I replied with a shrug. "No sense in him waiting around for hours on end. I took an Uber home, so he could take a break from Ashley duty." Which, technically, was not what I'd agreed to when I told him to go home. I was supposed to call him to pick me up when I finished, since he had my car.

Nate shrugged it off. "Whatever. I need you to talk to Heath."

Worry sparked in my gut. "Why, what's happened?"

"Nothing, yet, but…I'm concerned. We all are. He hasn't slept more than an hour here and there all week, he's like a zombie. Can you…just…I don't know. Can you *try* talking with him or maybe convince him to sleep?"

Guilt damn near choked me. I hadn't seen him in days, thanks to my workload, but I'd been texting. I guess it was easy for him to put on a happy face over text message. "Yeah, of course. Where is he now?"

Nate exhaled with so much relief it only increased my stress. It had to be bad if he was asking *me* to help. "Library, I think. He lost his shit at me earlier when I suggested he take sleeping pills and took off on his bike. He's been crazy stressed about his Human Development assignment though, so I think he went to the library."

I nodded, dropping my bag and crossing to my closet to grab some fresh clothes. I was still in my spa uniform, and I reeked of aromatherapy oils despite how many times I'd washed my hands. "I'll find him," I said, not bothering to turn away as I yanked my uniform shirt off. I was wearing a bra, and Nate had seen me in less at the pool so now wasn't the time for false modesty.

"Jesus, Layne," Nate muttered, scrubbing a hand over his face.

I arched a brow as I tugged a clean knit sweater on. "What?"

He shook his head and sighed, looking pained. "Nothing. Just let me know if you find him at the library? I'll head home and see if he's there."

"Yeah, for sure." I tugged my loose black trousers off and grabbed my jeans, ignoring the disgusted twist of Nate's lips as I did so. "Has he seen Dr. Fox since we got back?" I sat on the edge of my bed to pull on some warm boots since it was frosty outside.

Nate nodded. "Twice. I don't think it's helping, though. If anything, he's worse than ever this week. Like his mind is punishing him for being so happy last week. I don't know, I'm just fucking worried. Keep me updated?"

I grabbed my coat and keys and gestured for him to leave the room ahead of me. "Of course. Tell Royce to take the night off, I'll see if I can get Heath to sleep here."

"If he has nightmares—" he started to warn, and I flapped my hand dismissively.

"I know, I know, wake him up and he should sleep better afterwards."

"No," he growled, grabbing my arm to get my attention as I stabbed the elevator call button. "He sometimes lashes out. If he thinks you're some monster in his dream, he could hurt you."

I blinked, confused. "I'll skip past the obvious question of why the fuck you'd care and go straight to my answer of *I'm a big girl, I'll be fine*."

He huffed an irritated sound as we got onto the elevator. It was a quick ride to the ground floor and once outside I started in the direction of the library. Nate stopped me with that infuriating grab on my upper arm, though.

"What?" I snapped, spinning to glare at him.

His left eye twitched. "Just *be careful*, you reckless shithead. If you need us to help—"

"I'll be fine."

I jerked my arm free of his grip and pulled my coat closed against the cold as I hauled ass across the lawn. It was just the quickest way to the library from my dorm, even if a shiver of fear ran down my spine on the way. Sunday evening was *quiet* on campus, but I hadn't fully appreciated how quiet when Royce was always with me.

To my intense relief, I made it into the library without any zombies leaping out of the bushes, but when I passed through the main entry, it hit me that my hands were shaking. Not just from the cold, either, but from badly suppressed terror about being snatched by robed, masked weirdos again.

I said a polite hello to the students working on the desk, then took the stairs two at a time to get to my usual study spot where Heath and I always met.

At first, I thought the table was empty and disappointment chilled me. Then I heard ragged breathing and looked again.

"Heath!" I exclaimed, rushing over to where he sat in the corner, his knees up to his chest and his arms wrapped around them. "Hey, it's me. What are you doing?"

His study notes and books were scattered on the floor all around him, but they looked more like he'd given up and tossed them, rather than any sort of strategic order.

"Ashley," he exclaimed, jerking his head up from his knees. "Shit. Um. What…what are you doing here? Where's Royce?" He looked past me, expecting to see my shadow lurking.

I stifled my gasp to see how he'd deteriorated in the past week. Those dark circles were back with a vengeance and his eyes were so bloodshot it hurt to look at him.

"Heath, why didn't you call me sooner?" I asked with a heavy exhale of regret and guilt. Hands trembling, I started packing up his notes while he watched with confusion.

He shook his head, swiping a hand over his face. "Um, I'm okay. I was just really tired so thought maybe I'd sit on the floor. I'm okay, though, really. How was work?"

Absolutely nothing about him said he was *okay* other than his words and even those came out husky and weak. A wave of anger rolled through me that Nate hadn't called me sooner. Or Carter, for that matter.

"Work was long," I replied, stuffing all his books and notes into his bag and slinging it over my shoulder, "and I'm tired. You seem tired too. Will you stay in my room tonight?"

Heath blanched. "Where's Royce?"

I smiled, offering him my hand and pulling him to his feet. "He got sick of me not laughing at his jokes and went home. In my defense, they just weren't funny."

He frowned, seeming a bit dazed. "He left you alone? That wasn't the agreement."

I shrugged. "Yeah, but I'd rather spend time with you, anyway. Is that okay?"

"Of course," he said, draping his arm around me as I looped mine around his waist. "I won't sleep, but I can keep you company until he gets over his tantrum."

I bit my lip, holding back my worries. "That'd be great. So, tell me about what you were studying."

That kept him talking—or mumbling—the whole walk back to my dorm, so he didn't question the odd change of schedule with Royce any further. Once inside my room, I slipped out of my jeans and into some comfy pajama pants, quietly noting that Heath hadn't even noticed that I'd taken my clothes off. It was concerning.

"Hey, I just got some new herbal massage oil in the mail," I said, lying my ass off, "can I try it out on your shoulder?"

He nodded, half asleep, and took his shirt off before blinking at me with a frown. "Didn't you just get off work? Your hands must be exhausted."

"Nah, they're fine. Lie down for me, honey." I found a bottle of oil with chamomile, lavender, and neroli to promote restful sleep.

"Mmm, did you just call me honey?" he asked, stretching out on my bed face down.

I swatted his butt lightly. "Take your jeans off too."

He arched an amused look my way. "Yes, ma'am. If you just wanted to get me naked you could have said so."

I grinned back at him. "I won't object. And yes, I called you *honey*. Because you're as sweet as, and your name starts with H so…I dunno. I'm not great with nicknames."

He wiggled out of his jeans, tossing them aside before getting comfortable once more. "I like it," he mumbled with his cheek in my pillow. "If we're using alliteration, what does that make Nate?"

I thought for only a moment. "Neanderthal, obviously."

He chuckled. "Harsh."

"He called me *Reckless Shithead* earlier so I'm being nice by comparison." I squeezed out some oil into my hands and warmed it up before starting on Heath's gorgeous back. "How's that pressure?" I asked, slipping into work mode far too easily.

His answer was a long moan, and I smiled.

"That smells like lavender," he murmured after a few minutes. "I don't... It's not a good idea for me to fall asleep here, Ash."

I bit my lip, trying not to let him know how concerned I was for him. "How come? We've slept in the same bed before. It was nice."

He sighed, his muscles relaxing under my hands. "The nightmares are worse. I'm..." He paused, swallowing. "I'm scared of my own mind right now."

Fuck. That admission gutted me. I felt awful for not seeing it sooner.

"Have you spoken with Dr. Fox?" I asked gently, still massaging him without pause. If he could relax enough, he would sleep. I was sure of it.

"Mmm," he mumbled. "He said it's just stress."

That made me frown. Just stress? No freaking way. Heath just confessed he was scared of his own mind but his therapist said it was *just stress?*

"You need a new therapist," I said out loud.

He just hummed his response, his breathing already deepening. Good. He needed to sleep so badly it hurt me just looking at him. And if he woke with a nightmare, then I'd simply reassure him that he was safe and hopefully coax him into an actually restful sleep.

I continued to massage his tight muscles even after I was sure he'd passed out, because goddamn he was tense. His body needed it, even if he wasn't awake to enjoy the sensation.

He'd needed me this week and I hadn't been there. I was here now and I wasn't going anywhere. One night's sleep wouldn't fix it nor would one massage, but it was a start.

## Chapter Forty-Four

Despite all my best efforts to stay awake and watch over Heath, I failed. He was just so tempting to cuddle with and he'd reached for me in his sleep, pulling me into his embrace. The next thing I knew, I woke up to him thrashing and shouting *no* over and over.

"...I don't want to do it..." he moaned, flinching like he was scared of something, his arms flailing.

"Heath," I said aloud, scooching up to my knees and grabbing his waving arm. "Hey, Heath, wake up."

"...I don't want to hurt her! Stop! Don't! Why can't I stop?" His words came out on a distraught sob, tears slicking his cheeks even as his eyes screwed tight.

Worry flooded my chest and I shifted my grip to his shoulder. "Heath, wake up! It's a dream."

He wasn't responding to me, though, his head trapped in whatever dark loop had been haunting his nights, and his next thrash saw his legs kicking out. Scared he'd fall out of my bed, I swung my leg over his hips, sitting on top of him as I cupped his face with my hands.

"Heath, honey, come back to me. You're just dreaming. You're safe here with me." I slapped him lightly, wanting to wake him but not *hurt* him.

To my intense relief, it worked. His thrashing eased, and the tense furrow in his brow smoothed out. For a moment I thought he'd just slipped into restful sleep, but then his dark lashes fluttered open and his unfocused gaze darted around my dimly lit room. I'd left my study lamp on, facing the wall, just in case this happened and he needed to see where he was.

"Ash?" he croaked, finally focusing on me. "Are you—what's happening? Am I in your bed?"

I smiled, the fear draining out of me and leaving me a little shaky in its wake. "Yeah, you are. I found you in the library, remember?"

He shook his head, frowning. "Not really. I mean…sort of? It feels like a dream." Then he seemed to realize I was straddling him while wearing just panties and a T-shirt. His hands cupped my hips and a small grin touched his lips. "Actually *this* feels like a dream."

A small laugh bubbled out of me as I leaned down to kiss him lightly. "I was scared you'd fall out. Sitting on you seemed like a safe option."

He groaned, guiding my hips lower until my core ground against his *very* hard cock. "I'm okay with that decision. Sound logic, right there. If this was how I woke up every night, maybe I'd be all right with the nightmares."

My amusement quickly morphed into a gasp as his hips bucked, promising so damn much. And we'd been cock-blocked by Royce for *so long* would it really be bad to take things further?

Ugh. Damn it, that wasn't the plan.

"Heath," I moaned, then, contradictory to what I'd been about to say, I planted my lips against his again for a much less gentle kiss. His hands shifted from my hips to slide beneath my T-shirt, feathering over my ribcage in a way that made me squirm with need.

He kissed me back deeply, swallowing my unvoiced protests as effectively as if they hadn't existed in the first place.

What were we meant to be doing again?

Oh, right. Sleeping.

"Shit, Heath, I was supposed to help you sleep," I confessed with regret. "Not *sleep* with you. You're exhausted and—"

"And I *always* sleep better when I've, um..." he seemed to realize what he was saying and trailed off, thinking of another line of reasoning.

I laughed, kissing his scruffy jaw. "When you've blown your load, honey? Is that what you were going to say?"

He gave a pained grunt. "That doesn't sound sexy. Um, what I *meant* to say...was...uh I'm not likely to fall asleep until I know *you* aren't frustrated and tense."

"Oh, I see," I said with a chuckle. Then all of a sudden, my shirt was whipped up over my head as if by magic and tossed aside. "Smooth move, Heathcliff."

He grinned, all traces of exhaustion gone from his expression despite how the dark circles remained. "Thanks, I've been thinking about that one for a while." Then he cupped my bare breasts in his hands and I moaned a shitload louder than I intended to.

"I should have kicked Royce out weeks ago," I gasped as he tweaked my nipples, playing with them in a way that made my whole body tremble. "Fuck, Heath...I'm supposed to be taking care of you, not taking advantage..."

His hand slipped into my hair, dragging my face back to kiss. "If you *really* wanted to take care of me..." He said it teasingly, as a joke. Silly man should know me better than that.

My kisses moved from his lips to his jaw, then his throat...chest...abs...

"Ash..." he moaned. "I was kidding."

"Were you, though?" I challenged, looking up at him with an arched brow. "Heathcliff...I really, *really* want to suck your dick. Is that okay with you?"

His jaw dropped. Then he nodded quickly, like words were failing him.

I grinned back then slithered down the bed to peel his boxers off. He gasped as I palmed his hard length, tugging his boxers down just far enough that they were out of the way.

"Ash," he groaned as I pumped my hand slowly, taking in his size with wide eyes.

"Shh," I hushed with a small chuckle. "Let me play."

He groaned, his fingers threading into my hair as I licked his tip. He jerked in my hand and I smiled, loving the effect I could have on his body. Wetting my lips, I circled my tongue around his thick tip and kissed it lovingly.

Another moan from him rewarded me, and his fingers flexed in my hair like he wanted to rush me and barely held off. Was Heath maybe the kind of guy who got rough in bed? I had a small inkling that maybe all the polite respectful Heathcliff Briggs flew out the window once clothes came off.

Still, I didn't have the patience to make him wait any more and took him further into my mouth. My lips closed around him, sucking lightly and delighting with the way his hips jerked up from the bed. Perfection.

He gasped as I gripped his base with my fist, pumping that extra length as I slid my lips further down, taking more and more until he was firmly lodged against the back of my throat.

"Fuck," he exclaimed as I swallowed, my throat contracting around him. "Holy shit, Ash." Those fingers flexed in my hair again, and I would have smiled if my mouth weren't so full. I bobbed up and down on him for a few moments while he squirmed and panted, then something snapped his control.

His hand on my head clenched, his fingers twisting the roots of my hair as his hips bucked, slamming his cock deeper into my throat. I gagged, and he thrust deeper.

"Fuck, shit, Ash, I can't—" he stammered, and I gripped his thighs with encouragement. Showing him I was okay with getting my throat *fucked*. Because that was what was happening. I wasn't sucking his cock, he was fucking my mouth. Seriously unexpected, but in no way unwelcome.

The thick vein in the underside of his dick pulsed against my tongue, and I thought for sure he was about to blow. Instead, he pulled out of my mouth with a rough gasp.

"Ash, shit, I'm sorry," he panted, his fingers releasing my hair.

I shook my head, licking my slick, puffy lips. "I'm not. But why'd you stop?"

His eyes wide, he stared down at me...then his mouth ticked up in a sly grin. "Because I don't wanna come down your throat, babe."

"Oh?" I asked, smiling as I planted my hands either side of his chest, bringing us face to face. "Well in the interest of better sleep... where would you like to do it?"

He dragged his lower lip through his teeth, eyes heavy as he stroked his hands up my sides. Then flipped us over so my back hit the mattress. "I don't have a condom," he muttered as he tugged my panties down. "But I *badly* want to come inside this sweet pussy..."

A small, very brief question crossed my mind as to whether Carter had told him we never used protection. But that seemed like a douchebag thing to do, given how Heath and I were practically dating.

"Do it," I agreed, breathless. I could have told him that I had an IUD for birth control and that we would just have to *trust* that neither of us had any communicable diseases but...heat of the moment and all that. Heath didn't need convincing, either, notching his tip between my pussy lips and thrusting in with one deep motion.

I cried out, my body tensing in shock at the *sizable* intrusion, but I was more than ready for it, practically dripping with arousal already.

Heath's breath shuddered as he paused, fully seated. "Ash, holy crap, I wanted to—"

"It's fine," I assured him with a small laugh. "You were already so close."

With that permission, he rocked his hips only a couple of times, slamming into me with a gasping grunt while his cock jerked and pulsed, unleashing his hot seed within me.

I cupped his face, bringing his lips to mine to kiss him even as he panted for breath. He kissed me back, then shook his head with a groan.

"That…wasn't my plan," he muttered. Then he withdrew and shimmied down the bed to hook my legs over his shoulders.

I gasped, peering down at him with disbelief. "Heath, you can't—you literally just—"

"I know," he replied, spreading my folds with his fingers as he got a close-up view of the mess he'd just left. "Fuck me, that's so hot."

Then he slipped his tongue right on in there.

Shock saw me squeak, but at the same time…holy hell. Yes.

He went to work with his mouth, licking every fucking millimeter of me, cleaning things up with nothing more than his tongue until I was a shaking, whimpering mess. Then he sucked my clit and pushed two fingers inside my cunt to finish me off. Somewhere in the midst of my *bone-shakingly intense* climax, I begged for more and he added a third finger. It stretched me in a noticeable way, but the sensation only drove me into a longer, more out-of-worldly orgasm that quite literally left me seeing stars.

Everything turned blurry for a few moments as my body trembled with aftershocks, and Heath repositioned us until I was comfortably spooned against him in the most incredible afterglow.

"Mmm I don't know about you," I murmured, my voice thick, "but I'll sleep well now."

He chuckled, kissing the back of my neck. "Definitely."

It took some time for both our breathing and heart rates to return to normal but neither of us were in a hurry to go anywhere. It was a blissful sort of comfort, being naked in Heath's embrace.

At some stage, we both must have fallen asleep. I remembered being warm and secure, totally at peace in my slumber, but then some time just before dawn—the sun was *just* starting to peek over the horizon—Heath sat up with a jerk, waking me.

"Heath?" I mumbled, rubbing my eyes with the back of my hand. "What are you doing?"

He didn't respond, just got out of bed silently and pulled on his pants and shirt. I yawned, snuggling back into the warm patch of bedding he'd left. He probably needed to pee, and since it was a shared restroom it made sense to dress.

My eyes closed again, and I must have drifted back to sleep. But then I woke up again with worry tripping through me. The sky was still dark but my phone said half an hour had passed, and Heath wasn't back.

# Chapter Forty-Five

Panicked, I raced down to the bathroom without even pausing to dress. Heath was nowhere to be seen, though, the entire washroom dark and empty. Running back to my room I dragged on some clothes, stuffed my feet into boots and tossed my coat on.

My sleep foggy mind wasn't working *fast* enough, and I fumbled my phone as I ran for the elevator. It came up from the ground floor which made me think Heath had gone outside. Maybe it was a coincidence, there were *loads* of other people in the building who were using the same elevator but…it was a gut feeling.

My first thought was to call Heath, but the faint ding coming from my room said he'd left his phone behind. Shit.

Royce's number rang out, going to voicemail and I canceled the call. Carter next, with the same result. Finally I tried Nate.

"*You've reached Nathaniel Essex, please leave your—*" I ended the call with a growl of frustration.

Of course they wouldn't answer, though. It was four-thirty in the morning, they'd all be asleep. But then where in the *hell* had Heath gone? He was barefoot, I'd seen his sneakers beside my bed as I got dressed, and it was bitterly cold outside.

The elevator seemed to take a year to reach the lobby, then I burst outside so fast I nearly tripped over my own feet.

"Heath?" I called out into the darkness, hoping somehow that he hadn't gone far. Was he sleepwalking?

The cold bit into my skin with determination and I pulled my coat around myself, shivering. If he was sleepwalking, he could be anywhere. But what if he wasn't? What if he was just…fuck, I had no clue. But my gut said that someone was messing with his head, maybe forcing him to do something against his will?

If that were the case, then I'd bet my car the Devil's Backbone was behind it.

With absolutely no better ideas, I started hurrying across the silent, empty campus toward the drama department. That was my only lead, and if I didn't find him there…Maybe the library? Or check if he'd turned up at his apartment?

Nate would kill me. The one time he asked me for help, and I'd fucked up.

"Heath?" I called out as I walked, hoping beyond all hope he would respond. All I got back was the echo of my own voice, and it churned the anxiety even harder.

Shivering, I yanked on the main doors for the drama department and my heart almost leapt out of my chest when I realized they were unlocked. That was a good sign, surely? That had to mean I was in the right place?

"Heath?" I called again as I stepped inside the dark building with more than a little trepidation. Fucking hell, this was how bitches died in horror movies. Was I going to be one of them? Yes. For Heath…yes. "Heathcliff, are you in here? Honey, it's cold. Let's go back to bed…" I tried to push calm and casual into my voice, but even I could hear the tremble of fear.

My footsteps echoed ominously as I advanced down the dark corridor, heading for the dressing room where Royce had patched up my scrapes back at the start of this whole mess. That was my only lead because I had no idea where the mysterious clubhouse was actually located. I'd never made it that far.

Lights were on inside the dressing room, but it was empty.

"Heath?" I tried again, just in case…what? In case, what, he was hiding under the table? Come *on*, Ashley.

Wetting my lips, I glanced around and tried to work out what the hell to do next. Had he been here in the drama building? Or was this all a coincidence?

Choking down the undeniable feeling of hopelessness, I exited the building once more and closed the doors behind me. What now? Maybe the library, since he'd been in a bit of a daze when I'd found him there. He might have returned for some reason?

Shit, I didn't know. Nothing made sense right now.

I pulled out my phone and tried Nate again. If anyone was going to wake up and help…it was surely him. He was the one who'd come to me with concerns so maybe he'd be waiting on my call. Frustratingly, though, it rang out to voicemail again.

The cold seemed to have intensified while I was inside because my breath came in dragon puffs as I stomped my way through the campus to reach the library. It only took me a few minutes, but somehow I got my hopes up that I'd find Heath there all dazed and confused. So when I approached the doors and found them firmly locked, my heart dropped out my ass.

"Fuck!" I exclaimed. Then tried dialing Nate again. Maybe if I was annoying enough, he'd wake up and take my call.

Voicemail again.

Redial.

This time as it rang out, I thought I heard a phone ringing somewhere nearby.

"Nate?" I called out into the half-light of pre-dawn. I don't know why the fuck he would be out here at this time, but…I dialed his number again but this time kept the phone away from my ear so I could listen.

There it was again. The happy tune of a mobile phone ringtone.

I hurried in the vague direction the sound was coming from, around the side of the library building and then skidded to a stop when the sound cut off. Searching all around, I saw no one. Absolutely no one.

Another redial, but this time...no ringtone echoed back at me. Had I imagined it?

I started across the lawn, wandering with no real purpose and no clue where to look next, until I was ready to give up. I needed to go to the guys' apartment and wake them up. Four sets of eyes had to be better than one, and maybe if we were lucky, Heath had just sleepwalked home.

With a defeated sigh, I turned to head for my car. Then I gasped and stopped in my tracks. There in the distance, lit up by the glow of dawn, three robed figures slowly walked across the lawn carrying... something heavy?

I wanted to call out and see if Heath was one of the robed idiots, but flashes of Abigail's diary filled my brain. Images of Bart's decapitated head in my bed. That was enough to keep my mouth shut, but I still moved closer nonetheless.

For several minutes, I followed silently. None of them seemed to notice me trailing behind, and the closer I got the clearer the picture. All of them wore the black robes and masks from the Devil's Backbone ceremonies, and they each carried two gas cans.

Alarm spiked through me when I made that realization. Were they going to set fire to something? I had to intervene...didn't I?

Or...would I end up getting hurt? It might not even be Heath; it could just be a coincidence. Fucking hell, how many coincidences in one night were too many? Then I spotted his feet. His bare feet beneath the robe.

"Heath!" I called out loudly, no longer caring how stupid I was being.

He didn't react. None of them did.

I hurried closer, calling his name again, but still got no reaction. Doubts crowded my mind but I ignored them as I approached the three creepy figures and grabbed the barefoot one's arm.

"Heath, what are you doing?" I demanded, giving his arm a little shake in case this was a sleepwalking thing.

No response.

"What the fuck?" I exclaimed out loud. "Hey! Heath!"

He just kept walking, as though I didn't exist. All of them did. Like fucking *zombies*.

Panicked and downright scared, I hurried to keep up, circling in front of him and reaching for his mask. I needed to see him to be *sure*.

"Heath!" I shouted, tossing his mask aside with some relief that it was, indeed, Heathcliff Briggs. I'd found him, thank *fuck*, I'd found him! "Hey, honey, wake up. You're sleepwalking." *I think?* Although it was unlike any sleepwalking I could have imagined. His eyes were wide open and fixated beyond me.

Where were they going?

I glanced over my shoulder, puzzled, then spotted the old science hall. Was that where they were going? Maybe…maybe there was a truck broken down on the far side that needed fuel? Or maybe one of the applied science classes needed a shitload of gas for an experiment and, um, and they'd asked the DBs to deliver it? Fuck, I didn't know.

Heath didn't see me there, didn't stop when I tugged on his arm, all I could do was watch in horror as the three robed zombies disappeared inside the science building. I didn't follow, because I was just downright terrified. I knew where he was, so now I just needed to…

The fumes of the fuel reached my nose, and dread pooled.

I sucked a breath, preparing to run in there and drag Heath out by whatever means necessary, but before I could take a step, someone grabbed me.

A scream escaped my throat, and I thrashed, kicking and hitting, flooded with adrenaline and pure desperation but my captor simply swept me up off the ground and held me tight as he ran *away* from the doomed building.

It took me a moment, but then—

"Nate?" I gasped, somehow recognizing his scent. It was the same as the hoodie that I'd worn far too often without washing it. "Wait, stop! Put me down! Heath—"

"I know," he grunted, his grip so tight it was hurting as he literally *ran* across the lawn. "You can't stop them, and you can't get caught up with what they're doing. It's not safe."

My head spun. "What do you mean? Nate, we can't just—"

"We can!" he barked, his voice edged with genuine *fear*. "We fucking can, Ashley, and we will. What the hell do you think it'd do to him if you got hurt again? Do you want that on his conscience? I can tell you right fucking now, I don't."

That shut me up. At least until Nate burst through the lobby door of my building and pressed the elevator button with his foot. He didn't set me down on my own feet until we were inside the elevator with the doors closed. Presumably so I couldn't go running back into danger.

"I don't understand," I said in a small voice, hugging my arms around myself as he paced the small space anxiously.

He nodded. "I know."

That was it. The elevator reached my floor, and he grabbed my hand, all but dragging me along the hall and opening my door with his own key. I wasn't even mad about it, because my fingers were too cold to hunt my own keys from my pocket.

"Get in," he ordered, and I silently complied.

Nate stepped in after me and closed the door firmly, locking it. Then, only then, did he exhale heavily and sink to the floor with his back against the door.

Only then, did I realize...he too wore the black robe of the Devil's Backbone Society.

# Chapter Forty-Six

> Where there's smoke, there's fire. Dear Reader, trust your gut...everyone lies. Even those closest to you. I would know.

"Nate," I said in a shaking voice, "what are you wearing?"

His head snapped up from where he'd rested it on his knees, like he'd totally forgotten I was there and I'd startled him with my question. The similarity to how I'd found Heath in the library was frightening, and now that I paid attention...Nate also looked pretty rough. Not his usual aesthetic at all.

"What?" he asked, blinking like he was trying to clear his head.

"What are you wearing?" I repeated, gesturing to his robe. "Was this some insane DB prank that I interrupted?"

He looked down at his clothing, then frantically shrugged the robe off and balled it up like it was made of spiders. He tossed it away from himself, panting and wide-eyed. Something bad was going on, and my whole body trembled with fear.

"Nate," I said again, trying to hold his attention. "What just happened out there? Heath—"

"No," he said firmly, shaking his head. "No. It's...it's not a DB prank. I...I don't know what it is." There was so much uncertainty in his voice it rocked me. I'd *never* heard Nate unsure of himself and yet here he was sitting on my floor, confused and scared.

Wetting my lips, I sank to my knees on the floor. "Hey, Nate... look at me for a moment."

His darting gaze shifted up from the floor and locked on mine. That usually mysterious whiskey brown gaze of his was totally changed. It was enough for me to push aside my fear that he was involved in something dangerous, and I shuffled forward until I could grab his hands.

"Hey. Just focus on me for a moment, okay? Something weird is going on. What do you know? What's going on out there?" I wanted to look out my window, to try and see Heath in the distance even though I knew it wasn't possible...but right now Nate needed grounding.

He gave a small headshake, confusion etched all over his face. "I don't know," he whispered. "I swear...I have no clue."

I swallowed hard, trying another tact and desperately attempting to remain calm. "Okay, how about we start with last night. You asked me to find Heath, remember? You were here and left when I went to the library?"

He nodded, a small frown appearing over his brow. "Yeah. I went home and waited for you to call and tell me whether you'd found him...but you never did. I was worried, so I came over and you guys were fast asleep."

That made me jerk. "You broke in again?"

Nate scowled. "I wouldn't have needed to if you'd just texted me to say Heath was fine."

Fair. But still...

"Okay, creep. What happened after that?"

He sighed, running a hand through his hair. His other hand still grasped mine like a lifeline. "I didn't want to wake him when he was *finally* sleeping so I went home and went to bed. Then...that's where it gets weird. I woke up because my phone kept ringing, like on and on. But I wasn't in my bed. I was out on the Nevaeh south lawn in full DB costume and...I don't have *any* memory of getting there. Or why."

I licked my lips. "That was me, trying to call you."

He gave a small nod. "I know. I was so confused then saw all your missed calls, then saw the others in their robes and..." he trailed off, blowing out a long breath. "It was really obvious they weren't conscious, or not responsive at any rate. I turned my phone to silent and started running for help and then I heard you."

"And you grabbed me before I could follow Heath," I said quietly. "What if he gets hurt? He was sleepwalking."

Nate shook his head. "I don't think so. That was different."

"Nate! *What if Heath gets hurt?*" I repeated the important part.

"What if *you* got hurt?" he countered. "I don't think you fully appreciate what that'd do to him...to any of them."

That pulled me out of my spiraling panic. "What?"

Nate arched a brow. "Carter and Royce...They were there too. Did you not notice?"

My lips parted but no words came out. I'd assumed it was just some random DBs with Heath, it hadn't crossed my mind that it was them.

"I don't know what they—we—were doing, but it doesn't take a rocket scientist to put the pieces together," Nate continued. "I don't fucking know why or how but I know that they weren't snapping out of it and I did *not* need one of them hitting you."

That was when I noticed the blooming redness on his cheek and eyebrow. Someone had punched him *really* recently. Fucking hell.

"Nate, we need to stop them," I pleaded. "We need to wake them up or get them out or...something! We need to do *something*!"

He shook his head. "I am doing something. I'm keeping *you* safe!"

Exasperated, I dropped his hand and scrambled to my feet. Maybe I could see something—

"Is that smoke?" I asked, sniffing the air.

Nate climbed to his feet as well, a scowl etched across his face as he joined me at the window. "Shit," he breathed. There in the distance, the unmistakable glow of fire. A big one.

With him away from the door, I flicked the lock open and raced out into the corridor, pressing the elevator call button before he could even make it out my door.

"Ashley! Dammit!" he shouted, running to catch up and sliding inside just a moment before the doors shut, then turned his fury my way. "What the fuck do you think you can do now? Last I checked, you're not a fucking firefighter, nor do you have a water tanker stashed in the parking lot!"

"I don't know!" I shouted back. "Maybe nothing! I *don't know*. But I will literally crawl out of my own skin with anxiety if I just sit in my room, waiting. Wouldn't you?"

He stared at me, speechless. Then threw his hands in the air as the elevator reached the ground floor. "Fine. But for the love of *fuck*, Layne, stay with me." To punctuate that point, he grabbed my hand in his as we started running across the lawn once more.

The building was well ablaze when we got there, the flames so high it was astounding. Nate put in a call to emergency services, and I frantically searched the shadows for any sign of the arsons.

"Drama building?" I suggested when Nate ended his call.

His response was just to take off running in that direction with my hand still clamped in his, dragging me behind him as my much shorter legs tried to keep up.

The dressing room was empty, but the smell of smoke was so intense it made us both cough. They'd been there, but not anymore.

"Where now?" Nate asked, scrubbing a frustrated hand over his face and hair. "Fuck!" He lashed out, kicking over the chair and just looking so fucking defeated.

I could relate.

"Let's go to your apartment," I said, quietly reaching for his hand again since that seemed to ground him. Like it reminded him we were in this together. "If...I don't know. I just think we check there. Maybe they went home if they thought they were sleepwalking? Or they woke up here, confused, and went home?"

He nodded thoughtfully. "Yeah. Yeah, that's a good idea. Okay, let's go." He kept hold of my hand as we jogged across campus to the parking lot where my car was parked. Thankfully, I had my keys in my pocket so in just six minutes we were pulling into the underground parking lot beneath Nate's apartment.

He paced the elevator again, like a stressed-out lion, and I hugged my arms around myself, dreading what we might find. Or not find. If the guys weren't here...were they still inside the burning building?

My mind rejected the idea as utterly abhorrent, but...what if they didn't get out? What if they all burned to death in there, never having snapped out of the trance? Bile burned in my throat at the thought of it, and I all but climbed Nate's back as he unlocked his front door and swung it open.

"Whoa, calm down," Royce groaned from the kitchen, squinting at us. "Where's the fire?"

Relief smacked me so hard I nearly keeled over, and Nate seemed similarly speechless.

"Y-you're okay," I finally stammered, crossing to the kitchen island where he stood in a towel, fresh from the shower. I glanced to Nate, confused as all hell. Had he been wrong? Was Royce never there?

Royce grunted, not seeming to notice our weird behavior. "Okay is a stretch. Probably a good thing you ditched me for Briggs last night, Squirrel. My head is *killing* me. I might be coming down with something."

Another long look from Nate, who closed the front door and approached more cautiously. "Have you seen Heath this morning?"

Royce frowned, glancing between the two of us. "No, why would I? I thought he and Ash were finally consummating the relationship. Wait, why are *you two* together?"

I wet my lips, shaking my head. "Not important."

Royce's brow lifted. "Agree to disagree."

Before he could push the issue further, Carter sleepily walked into the kitchen, rubbing his eyes. Then he saw me and smiled a lazy smile.

"Spark's here," he observed out loud, changing his course to greet me with a huge hug.

I hugged him back, inhaling deeply then coughing. He smelled of smoke. And gasoline.

"Carter, why do you—" I started to ask, then a thump came from Heath's bedroom, interrupting me.

Nate's brows shot up. "Carter, man, did Heath come back here last night?"

The gorgeous, half-asleep smokestack shook his head. "Don't think so."

Urgency gnawed at my gut, though, and I slipped out of his eye-watering scent cloud. "I'm going to check his bedroom. Maybe he slipped in when you two were, um, asleep…or something."

Backing away, I waited until Carter turned away before gesturing to Nate to smell him. Then I softly knocked on Heath's door before twisting the knob.

"Heath, honey?" I called out, "Are you here?"

The door swung open, and a scream ripped from my throat. My hands gripped the doorframe, holding me upright where I otherwise would have collapsed in horror.

The thump we'd heard was the chair falling.

My beautiful, troubled boy was there in the middle of the

room, a makeshift noose around his neck as he hung from the ceiling fan.

TO BE CONTINUED...<br>
*Watch Your Back*<br>
Devils Backbone #2

**DISCOVER MORE TATE JAMES
WITH THE FIRST BOOK
IN THE MADISON KATE SERIES**

# CHAPTER 1

*I shouldn't be here.*

If my father knew...

But I would take those risks to witness this fight. This *fighter*.

Music boomed from the speaker beside me, and the crowd got louder. More frenzied and impatient. Adrenaline pulsed through my veins, pushing my own excitement to such a level that I could barely stay still. I started bouncing lightly on the balls of my feet just to keep from screaming or fainting or something.

A grin curled my lips, and I nodded my head to the familiar tune. "Clichéd choice but could have been worse," I muttered under my breath. "Bodies" by Drowning Pool continued to rage, and I pushed up on my toes, trying to catch a glimpse of one of the reasons we'd skipped out on our shitty Halloween party.

"MK, I don't get it," my best friend, Bree, whined from beside me. Her hands covered her ears, and her delicate face was screwed up like she was in physical pain. "Why are we even here? This is so far from our side of town, it's scary. Like, legit scary. Can we *go* already?"

"What?" I exclaimed, frowning at her and thinking I'd surely just heard her wrong. "We can't leave now; the fight hasn't even started yet!" I needed to yell for her to hear me, and she cringed again. She had reason to. In a crowd dominated mostly by men—big men—Bree and I stood zero chance of even seeing the octagon, let alone the fighters. Or if I was honest, one fighter in particular. So we'd climbed up onto one of the massive industrial generators to get a better view.

The one we'd picked just happened to also have a speaker sitting on it, and the volume of the music was just this side of deafening.

"Babe, we've been here for over an hour," Bree complained. "I'm tired and sober, my feet hurt, and I'm sweating like a bitch. Can we *please* go?" She tried to glare at me, but the whole effect was ruined by the fact that she still had a cat nose and whiskers drawn on her face—not to mention a fluffy tail strapped to her ass.

Not that I could judge. My costume was "sexy witch," but at least I'd been able to ditch my pointed hat. Now I was just wearing a skanky, black lace minidress and patent leather stiletto boots.

It was after midnight on October 31, and we were *supposed* to be at our friend Veronica's annual Halloween party. Yet Bree and I had decided that sneaking out of the party to attend a highly illegal mixed martial arts fight night would be a better idea. Even better still, it was being held in the big top of a long-abandoned amusement park called The Laughing Clown.

Like that wasn't an infinitely better way to spend the night than being hit on by a boy with a Rolex and then spending all of three minutes with him in the backseat of his Bentley.

Yeah, Veronica's parties all sort of ended the same way, and I, for one, was over it.

"Bree, I didn't force you to come with me," I replied, annoyed at her badgering. "You *wanted* to come. Remember?"

Her mouth dropped open in indignation. "Uh, yeah, so you wouldn't get robbed or murdered or something trying to hitchhike your way over the divide! MK, I saved your perky ass, and you know it."

I rolled my eyes at her dramatics. "I was going to Uber, not hitchhike. And West Shadow Grove is not exactly the seventh circle of hell."

Her eyes rounded as she looked out over the crowd gathered to watch the fights. "It may as well be. You know how many people get killed in West Shadow Grove *every day?*"

I narrowed my eyes and called her factual bluff. "I don't, actually. How many?"

"I don't know either," she admitted, "but it's a lot." She nodded at me like that made her statement more convincing, and I laughed.

Whatever else she'd planned to say to convince me to leave was drowned out by the fight commentator. My attention left Bree in a flash, and I strained to see the octagon. Even standing on the generator box for height, we were still far enough away that the view was shitty.

My excitement piqued, bubbling through me like champagne as I twisted my sweaty hands in the stretchy fabric of my dress. The commentator was listing his stats now.

Six foot four, two hundred and two pounds, twenty-three wins, zero draws, zero losses.

*Zero losses. This guy was freaking born for MMA.*

It wasn't an official fight—quite the opposite. So they didn't elaborate any more than that. There was no mention of his age, his hometown, his training gym…nothing. Not even his name. Only…

"Please give it up for"—the commentator gave a dramatic pause, whipping the crowd into a frenzy—"the mysterious, the undefeated, The Archer!" He bellowed the fighter's nickname, and the crowd freaking lost it. Myself included.

"Paranoid" by I Prevail poured from the speaker beside us, and by the time the tall, hooded figure had made his way through the crowd with his team tight around him, my throat was dry and scratchy from yelling. Even from this distance, I trembled with anticipation and randomly pictured what it'd be like to climb him like a tree. Except naked.

"I'm going to guess this is why we came?" Bree asked in a dry voice, wrinkling her nose and making her kitty whiskers twitch. Her costume wasn't as absurd as it could be, since most members of the crowd were in some form of Halloween costume. Even the fighters tonight wore full face masks, and the commentator was dressed as the Grim Reaper.

"You know it is," I shot back, not taking my gaze from the octagon for even a second. I hardly dared blink for fear of missing something.

One of his support team—a guy only a fraction shorter with a similar fighter's physique and a ball cap pulled low over his face—took the robe from his shoulders, and my breath caught in my throat. His back was to us, but every hard surface was decorated with ink. We were too far away to see details, but I knew—from my borderline obsessive stalking—that the biggest tattoo on his back was of a geometric stag shot with arrows. It was how he'd gotten his nickname. The stag represented his star sign: Sagittarius, the Archer.

"Ho-ly shit," Bree gasped, and I knew without looking at her she had suddenly discovered a love for MMA.

"They say he's being scouted for the UFC," I babbled to her, "except they said he has to stop all underground cage matches, and apparently he told them to shove it."

Bree made a sound of acknowledgment, but knowing her, she didn't even know what the UFC was, let alone understand what an incredible achievement that was for a young fighter.

"Shh," I said, even though she hadn't spoken. "It's starting."

In the makeshift octagon, the Archer and his opponent—both wearing nothing but shorts and a plain mask—tapped gloves, and the fight was officially on.

# About the Author

Tate James is a *USA Today* bestselling author of contemporary romance and romantic suspense, with occasional forays into fantasy, paranormal romance, and urban fantasy. She was born and raised in Aotearoa (New Zealand) but now lives in Australia with her husband and their adorable crotchfruit.

She is a lover of books, booze, cats, and coffee, and is most definitely not a morning person. Tate is a bit too sarcastic, swears far too much for polite society, and definitely tells too many dirty jokes.

Website: tatejamesauthor.com
Facebook: tatejamesauthor
Instagram: @tatejamesauthor
TikTok: @tatejamesauthor
Pinterest: @tatejamesauthor
Mailing list: eepurl.com/dfFR5v